D1452468

LEMISTRY

A Celebration of the Work of
Stanisław Lem

Edited by
Ra Page & Magda Raczyńska

First published in Great Britain in 2011 by Comma Press
www.commapress.co.uk
Copyright © remains with the authors and translators 2011
This collection copyright © Comma Press
All rights reserved.

'Invasion From Aldebaran' & 'Darkness and Mildew' by Stanislaw Lem were first
published as 'Inwazja z Aldebarana' & 'Ciemność i pleśń' in *Inwazja z Aldebarana*,
1959. 'The Lilo' first appeared as 'Materac' in *Zagadka* [The Enigma], 1996.
Reprinted by kind permission of the Estate of Stanisław Lem.

Artwork © Stanislaw Lem, reprinted by permission of the Estate of Stanisław Lem.

'The Apocrypha of Lem' by Jacek Dukaj was first published by Agora Press, Poland,
2008; reprinted by permission of the author and the publisher.

'The Melancholy' was originally commissioned by Jeremy Osborne at Sweet Talk
Productions for broadcast on Radio 4 as part of the *Why, Robot?* series. It was first
transmitted on 18th May 2010. It subsequently appeared in *Interzone*
magazine #229, Jul–Aug 2010. Thanks to the editor there, Andrew Cox.

This book was originally developed as a concept by Louis Savy (of SciFi London)
and Magda Raczyńska (of the Polish Cultural Institute in London), with later
support from Ian Whates of NewCon Press. The contributions by Jacek Dukaj,
Adam Roberts, Piotr Szulkin, Ian Watson, Wojciech Orliński, and Andy Sawyer were
all originally commissioned and edited by Raczyńska, Savy and Whates. The
contemporary Polish texts were edited by Magdalena Petrynska.

The right of the authors and translators to be identified has been asserted in
accordance with the Copyright Designs and Patents Act 1988.

A CIP catalogue record of this book is available from the British Library.

ISBN-13 978 1905583324

The publisher gratefully acknowledges assistance from Arts Council England, North
West, as well as the Polish Book Institute in Krakow for its support towards the
translation of Lem's stories (www.polishbookinstitute.pl).
This book has been co-commissioned by Comma Press and the Polish Cultural
Institute in London.

Set in Bembo 11/13 by David Eckersall.
Printed and bound in England by MPG Biddles.

Contents

APOCRYPHA

Introduction

When Philip K. Dick wrote a letter to the FBI in 1974 denouncing the Polish writer Stanislaw Lem as a communist agent, he didn't stop at saying he was a mere Party stooge:

'Lem is probably a composite committee rather than an individual, since he writes in several styles and sometimes reads foreign, to him, languages and sometimes does not.'

Typically, even in the depths of paranoia, Dick was being insightful. There are several Stanisław Lems. Firstly, there's the one that art-house film lovers will recognize: the sombre, meditative Lem, haunted by the unknowable 'other' of alien intelligence and convinced of the limitations of Man's capacity to understand – that is to say, the *Solaris* Lem. Next, there is the Visionary Inventor Lem, the writer who in 1964 predicted the advent of virtual reality (in his essays *Summa Technologiae*), or who in 1961 first described what we now recognise as an eBook (*Return from the Stars*), not to mention whose story 'The Seventh Sally' inspired the *Sims* computer game. Then there is the Lem whose work is regularly but subtly appropriated by mainstream SF cinema – we can see clear nods to him in the blue pill/red pill moment in *The Matrix* and, as the new translations in this collection show, it doesn't stop there. And, of course, there's the Comedic Lem – that impish genius behind the robot comedies of *The Cyberiad* and *Pirx the Pilot*, whose influence we can trace through writers like Douglas Adams, Rob Grant and Doug Naylor. Indeed because much of Lem's short fiction has been translated into English by a single person – the brilliant

Michael Kandel – it is perhaps this latter, comic version of Lem that remains predominant, at least in terms of what is available to English speaking audiences.

But the Lems don't stop there. Commissioning a celebration of this writer's work is not just an exercise in measuring the extent of his influence (one contributor confessed: 'Everything I've ever written has been influenced by Lem'). It is also a voyage into the sheer variety of Lems still 'out there', insufficiently recognised for reasons of translation or simple genre-phobia. In putting together this book, it was important for us to use it as an opportunity to explore some of these 'other' Lems. The three stories we've plucked, from the volumes of work that remain untranslated, hopefully offer a decent cross-section of these 'other' Lems, and provide a good introduction to his work for the unfamiliar reader.

In 'Darkness and Mildew' (1959), we encounter the entirely terrestrial Near Future Lem, with its particular vision of organic, evolutionary science (this is a Lem we've only glimpsed before in stories like 'Doctor Diagoras' and 'The Sanatorium of Dr Vliperdius'). In 'The Lilo' (1996) we meet the metaphysically nervous, Cartesian Lem, with his worries about the increasingly blurred lines between the real and the unreal. Thirdly in 'Invasion from Aldebaran' (1959) we meet the Linguistic Acrobatic Lem, a writer in love with poetry, nonsense speak and wordplay (put to subversive, political ends, of course).

These latter iterations of Lem are also reflected in the contemporary contributions to this book. The evolutionary technologies Lem described so brilliantly are here given over entirely to the scientists to chew on: nanotechnologist Dr Sarah Davies, robotics engineer Professor Hod Lipson, and computer pioneer Professor Steve Furber all demonstrate quite how 'on the money' Lem was. Likewise, Lem's existential concerns are revisited in Wojciech Orliński's Las Vegas-set virtual reality story, 'Stanlemian', while his high-wire wordplay and Borgesian trickery form the basis of two new 'reviews of nonexistent books' by Frank Cotttrell Boyce and Jacek Dukaj, as well as other texts playing games with us here.

The relationship with Philip K. Dick is illuminating in other ways. These two writers, more than any others of their era, used the short story as a thought experiment to test the boundaries of the 'verifiably real' in a rapidly changing technological landscape. But where Dick applied his concerns to a broader societal canvas – government institutions, faceless corporations – Lem posed the question at an individual level. Lem had a genuine affection for machines, not an *unheimlich* revulsion, or socially conservative fear, but a fondness. Michael Kandel's introduction to *Mortal Engines* describes how in his youth Lem would feel sorry for discarded radio components and bits of machinery, and would often take them home with him. He viewed mechanisms paternally, and it is with this fatherly affection that he sets his 'artificial progeny' free, to roam the world independently, with his blessing. Indeed it is this affection for machines that positioned Lem well ahead of the curve when it came to the problem of artificial intelligence (see Hod Lipson's essay).

Coupled with this affection was a kind of existential stoicism that is unique to Lem (or unique to the aforementioned 'Committee of Lems'). He viewed the blurring of reality and virtual reality calmly and with a degree of humility, in some cases even mischief. He suggested ways of keeping tabs on reality: in *The Futurological Congress* it is through the countersomniac drug 'up'n'at'm'; in Orliński's story here it's christened the 'Lemian'; and in the newly translated opening story, it's the tiny detail of the colours of a striped lilo hanging outside a shop. Indeed one can't help feeling it can be traced, subconsciously or otherwise, all the way to the spinning top in Chris Nolan's film *Inception*. For Lem, there are ways of navigating through this chaotic new world: devices for keeping your bearings, compasses.

Part of Lem's stoicism was also a realisation that, just as you can never fully understand another human being, you cannot and should not try to understand another type of intelligence. This 'unknowable-ness' would have struck panic into the hearts of early SF pioneers – as Andy Sawyer writes, key editors like Hugo Gernsback and John W. Campbell sported an almost Victorian sense of conquering the unknown: it was *there* to be understood. But for Lem, adopting an external, behaviourist approach to intelligence, or, to put it very differently, taking intelligence on trust, is a fundamentally liberating process. It is a starting point, not an end. Rather as Alan Turing's 1936 demonstration of the *limits* of logic and computation gave birth to the concept of the computer (the 'Turing Machine'), so Lem's acceptance of the limits of our ability to *understand* those machines ushers forth a way in which we can live together with them. Calmly.

Along with 'knowable-ness', we also have to loosen our grip on 'identity'. As early as 1957 Lem was picking at a question that would occupy him for much of his career: how can someone remain the same person when all the cells and atoms that make them up are entirely replaced every few years? (See Toby Litt's 'Melancholy' for a re-wiring of the same conundrum). In *Dialogs,* Lem rephrases the question: if a person were to die and a perfect, artificially constructed duplicate of that person's body and brain were switched on immediately afterwards, would that duplicate be the same person? Jacek Dukaj's 'The Apocrypha of Lem' rewords the question one more time: if we were to rebuild an artificial Lem and set it running with all the same conditions and stimuli that the real Lem was subject to, would that entity *be* Lem? Indeed if there were different ways of 'setting' those conditions and stimuli, *which one* would be Lem?

This anthology is a non-robotised version of just such an experiment. It plays a posthumous Lego game of artistic influence, piecing together Project Lem one disciple at a time. It is our hope that, in among these dedications, you, the reader, can make out an impression of the original, like a ghostly face reflected in rippling water.

The Committee, we'd like to think, is still in session.

RP & MR

ORIGINALS

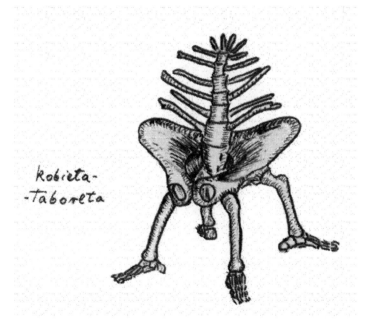

kobieta-
-taboreta

The Lilo

Stanisław Lem

Translated from the Polish by Antonia Lloyd-Jones

I

'My dear doctor,' I said, 'you are not just my personal physician, but a family friend. The problem I'm going to confide in you is not a medical one at all, of course, but I find myself in a situation where I can no longer trust anyone – apart from you.'

Dr Gordon, a psychiatrist, puffed on his pipe and regarded me with an expression that seemed to imply he was holding back a forbearing smile. Perhaps he thinks the same thing is happening to me as happened to my father, the thought flashed through my mind, but either way I had to go on talking.

'What's more, you are obliged,' I added a little more dryly, 'by doctor-patient confidentiality, like the Seal of the Confessional. So the fact of the matter is – are you listening carefully? – they're already onto me. They've "got a fix" on me, as they say on television and in the press. I'm not one hundred percent sure, but...'

'Just a moment,' said Gordon. He methodically shook all the ash out of his pipe into a silver ashtray decorated with three little cherubs. 'First of all, tell me about this "getting a fix" on you. I guess you're talking about a personal threat – you mean they want to kidnap you, right?'

'Naturally. There have already been so many similar

cases. Here I have Monday's *New York Times*. They describe in detail how "kidnapping into virtual reality" occurs, and what happened to Bill Harkner. I actually used to know him – we were at the same college. You've read this, haven't you?'

'I just glanced at it. After all, as you know, it's not my specialty. The evil use people make of modern technology is already so widespread and diverse that no single person can serve as an expert on every matter. But please go on. You can be sure,' he said, smiling faintly, 'that whatever you say in my consulting room is for my ears only...'

'Well, anyway, you know it was purely by accident that Bill's kidnapping didn't end in his death?'

'Yes, I do. Of course. The electricity supply in the district where they were keeping him in the attic simply stopped working, and he woke up, that is, he realised who he really was and what was just an illusion conjured up by phantomatisation. So you think they've got designs on you as well? On what grounds?'

I wasn't entirely sure if Gordon was taking my concerns seriously enough. Maybe he would have preferred me only to succumb to the delusions common to his area of expertise? But either way I'd already gone too far, I had to keep talking.

'It's like this,' I said. 'Only five years ago the whole story of investments in "virtual technology" or "virtual reality" seemed unimportant to me. I thought it was just a fad, like the yo-yo used to be, and I didn't want to buy into "Visionary Machines", although my brokers were urging me to go in with at least a twenty-percent shareholding. But I didn't believe them. Whereas I did immediately imagine that just as computer crime had started to happen, "virtuality crime" was sure to come along too. And I was right, but perhaps you can understand that a man of my position in society, held in high regard and so on, is hardly going to get involved in something that's ideal prey for journalists and thriller writers?'

'You don't have to tell me all that,' said Gordon. His pipe

had gone out, and he was poking about in it, which I found rather objectionable, because I expected him to focus greater attention on my words. After all, I was not just the average man, not just any old patient of his: he had always respected me well enough for his quarterly bills to reach a record high.

'All right,' I continued. 'In any case, I was correct enough in my expectations that ever since the quality of virtual reality has caught up with the quality of the real world, ever since it has been increasingly difficult to tell phantomatic illusions apart from ordinary reality, the whole business has taken on a nasty look... and gathered momentum.'

'Yes, I know.' After some effort Gordon had managed to get his pipe going again. 'I know. These so-called kidnappings have become systematic, thanks to the appearance of an evident motive. All the "virtual" kidnappers have to do is to "disconnect" a man and all his senses from the world and "connect" him to a computer that simulates the world. But really, my dear fellow, you should take the entire matter either to some good lawyers – you have no lack of those – or to some phantomatic engineers. Psychiatry doesn't have much to offer here...'

'It's strange what you're saying,' I replied, 'because the whole trick is in HOW the person who thinks he's been shut away in an electronic illusion is to convince himself what's REALLY happening to him – whether he's awake, or whether he's in some sort of electronic straitjacket...'

'You know what?' His pipe had sizzled and gone out again. 'Maybe we should stop pussyfooting around the issue and get to the real point? WHO has designs on you? WHY do you think they want to perform what we call sensory deprivation and restitution under the influence of a simulation programme? Where do your fear and suspicions come from?'

'From the fact that just like me, Bill was a shareholder

in IBV Machines, and our accounts were pretty similar, what's more, each of us has been and is surrounded by persons, let's just say "persons who may be counting on a legacy"...'

'Do you suspect someone in the family?'

'Doctor, you are a medical man, not a lawyer. If I had more precisely justified suspicions, I would consult a private detective via one of my security people. I do not suspect anyone in particular, and I would rather not talk about it. The point is simply that no one is entirely sure how they kidnapped Bill, or in what circumstances; that they did stick some sort of cap with electrodes on his head; that they put him in the corner of an attic; and that he lay there for two weeks, not really eating anything, although he thought he was swilling away at the best restaurants, surrounded by some sort of odalisques or nymphs. He always did have a weakness for girls of lighter morals and heavier mass, but that's not what I wanted to say. When the current went off, he managed to get out, but he'd lost something like fifty-five pounds and could hardly crawl to the phone. Who was behind it he doesn't know, or he *says* he doesn't know, but I can guess. It was all about what's called *vacuum iuris*. My lawyers explained it to me. If there's no law, there's no crime. He would have died of starvation up there, and some time later his corpse would have been found, but of course all the evidence of the "kidnapping" would have been removed, so it would have looked as if he'd gone mad, let's say, and starved himself to death, and then the heirs' lawyers would have gone into battle. That's how it's done these days: that's what they write about it.'

'I get it. And so you suspect one of your relatives or people who've got legacies in your will of similar designs, and you want...'

'I'm sorry, doctor. I never did, and I don't now intend to talk to you about any inheritance or about what might happen to my millions. I merely wish you to enlighten me professionally as to HOW one can distinguish falsified reality from genuine reality. That's all. If you will permit me, I shall deal with the rest of it elsewhere.'

'You know what? You're upset. No, please don't interrupt me. For now, I stress: FOR NOW you are in a state of genuine reality, and what I can tell you about methods for differentiating it is marginal to my medical specialty. A programmer could probably tell you more and do it better...'

'But no programmer is obliged to keep absolutely quiet about what I confide in YOU. Public knowledge of my fears alone could undermine my credit. So dammit, doctor, are you going to edify me or not?'

'As far as it is in my powers.' His pipe had gone out again and I felt like tearing it from his hand and throwing it out of the window. '"Getting a fix on" someone, as you called it, relies, as we know, on filming, photographing, sound-recording and so on the environment familiar to the candidate as meticulously as possible. Then the context of the programme is made out of it. Apart from that, of course they must get to know the candidate's most intimate, private life; apparently, they sometimes hold "dress rehearsals" involving stuntmen. The more precisely they succeed in recording EVERYTHING that constitutes the environment of the person in question, their family, their friends and so on, the greater the chance that the kidnap victim will let himself be caught on their hook and won't be able to tell illusion from reality.'

'But I know that. You can read that in any newspaper. Why are you telling me this?'

'In order to explain that this sort of imitation of a familiar environment is practically unfeasible. Impossible. You only have to have some old letters in your safe or a photograph from the distant past that you remember well, and if suddenly you can't find anything, the suspicion that you've been kidnapped will become highly legitimate. At that point you can't turn to anyone for help or advice... you know why not?'

'I've read about it. Because if I'm shut away in an

illusion the person I ask for help will ALSO be a product of that illusion and will try to convince me I am in reality.'

'That's it. That's just it, and this is the most perfect technologically manufactured method of producing solipsism in history, what Bishop Berkeley...'

'Spare me the bishops, doctor. Then what do you do? Come on, tell me.'

'To make differentiation as difficult as they possibly can, as a rule the programmers transfer the kidnap victim into an environment that is entirely alien to him. Let's say, for example, a courier accosts him on his doorstep with a telegram, or he gets a call from an alleged friend telling him to make his way immediately to such and such a place – he does what he's told, and his ability to discriminate gets lost in real reality. People close to him are also "eliminated" somehow. His wife has suddenly had to go away, the butler has been carted off in an ambulance because he's had a heart attack, and so on.'

'Aha. You mean sudden changes in everyday life will be a warning portent?'

'Apparently so, but these are not fully reliable portents: the whole thing will be designed according to the programmers' ingenuity.'

'So what the hell do you do then?'

'You should do what the programmers would never be capable of inventing: they call it "breaking the programme". Then a total void appears before the phantomatised person, as proof that he is NOT in reality.'

'How can I know what some gangster of a programmer is incapable of devising?'

'There's no panacea for it. At that point there is a PLAY situation: you play with the machine, that is the computer, to which your brain is connected, and you have to determine on your own – entirely on your own, by yourself – what is still possible and what is not.'

'Meaning that if I were to see a flying saucer landing

with little green men...?'

'Oh, my dear fellow, they will never go for such primitive things. Reality has to be reliably imitated. I can't tell you any more than that, I can only give general advice: while you're sleeping, having a bath, or at your morning ablutions, you must be exceptionally wary. But you have your own bodyguards, don't you?'

'Yes, I do. Thank you, doctor. I won't say I was expecting any miracles from you, but you have disappointed me a bit. I'll come and see you again next Friday...'

II

The armoured Ferrari in which I drove home moved as if it didn't weigh three tons at all. I was pleased with this purchase. My people drove ahead of me and behind me. It occurred to me, without the least satisfaction, that my way of life was making me more and more like a Mafia boss. More and more artillery – less and less trust. It would have been good to go off to some isolated place very far away, but then I'd have to book tickets and hotels – hell knows where some bugging device might be lurking. Dr Gordon was certainly right to say one should stay in the middle of one's familiar environment – that would still be the safest bet.

There was a tailback. We stopped, and the air conditioning did what it could, but it was starting to get a bit smelly in the car. Bulletproof glass – well, that was something. Lately the tailor had been trying to talk me into a bulletproof vest, but it weighed almost six pounds, and anyway, they say nowadays they shoot either below the belt or at the head. Soon we'll be going about in steel or titanium helmets, I thought. The lights changed and the Ferrari jumped forwards as softly as a cat. I was sitting on my own in the back seat, separated from the driver by a glass screen. I had a bad taste in my mouth following the conversation with Gordon, goodness knows why. I ran a hand over my head – high time to get my hair cut. I can't bear those men's pigtails. But how was I to do it in a way that didn't involve the risk of them 'getting a fix' on me? It occurred to me that despite the authenticity of the story about Bill, the psychiatrist hadn't taken my suspicions entirely seriously. That's what a psychiatrist is for – I thought, trying to silence this suspicion. Can you live like this for long, in a protective cocoon? Shouldn't you get in touch with some really serious authority? How to PREVENT a kidnapping – that's the point, not how to recognise whether it has ALREADY happened... We drove up to the gate, which opened automatically, and I could already hear the dogs barking. The dogs won't deceive me, they won't betray me or cheat me, I thought, as Peter opened the car door for me.

III

I had Rossini, my barber, ordered for ten o'clock. Just before breakfast the butler came up to tell me that Rossini had been taken to hospital, because he had collapsed, but was sending his assistant to see me. Indeed, shortly after nine a young man with dark hair appeared, a typical Italian, but just to hand me a neatly sealed packet. Inside I found a letter from Rossini wrapped in polystyrene packing chips: in his grandiloquent style he informed me that he could not vouch for his 'cousin', so he was advising me to go and see his brother-in-law on the very edge of Manhattan. Opposite the barber's shop there is a sporting goods store; this brother-in-law of his could not come to me, because he had no one to leave in charge of the shop. Just in case I had a call put through to the hospital for Rossini to confirm the authenticity of the letter. He did: so the secretary told me. I considered the situation. If I start to suspect everyone, eventually I'll end up at Dr Gordon's in a locked ward. So I instructed my bodyguards to go off to the wretched barber's shop and report to me from there whether the air was clean. It was. I drove there, and had to walk a short way. Indeed, on the other side of the little alley there was a store with various oars, bathing trunks and lilos hanging in the window. One of them had red-and-blue stripes. It was pleasantly cool inside Cocconi's barber's shop, and apart from him, there wasn't a living soul. I told him to wash and cut my hair, and once he got down to work I glanced out of the window again. One of my people was standing right by the door. I don't like having my hair washed, but I lay there calmly, wrapped in fragrant cloths like a baby as the barber combed my hair and then pulled a hairnet over my head.

'Please take it off.'

'The haircut will hold its shape better...' he objected feebly.

'Take it off this instant.'

He took it off, and dried my hair, which really did look blown around, but it didn't matter. As I went outside, I looked across at the sporting goods store and was surprised to see that now there was a green-and-white striped lilo hanging in the window. I beckoned over one of my security people.

'Oh, yes,' he said, 'they changed the display while you were at the barber's.'

What was there to add? The Ferrari moved off again, and having touched my head a few times, I convinced myself my hair was cut short and was still a tiny bit damp. But something was making my heart or my stomach ache. I ordered the chauffeur to drive across the other bridge, where there were always dreadful tailbacks. The bodyguards were behind me. There was no reason, but somehow I felt debilitated. High time to go and see Gordon, I thought, because even without all this phantomatic threat I was going to get some sort of neurotic disorder. We spent half an hour pushing our way across that wretched bridge, and once we were getting near my house, the air was suddenly shaken by a powerful explosion. Just around the corner the police stopped us. There had been a bomb, and naturally, it had been planted outside my residence. My suspicions began to increase. I went as close as the people from the fire brigade would let me, stood beside a policeman, and examined the façade, which was surrounded by smoking rubble; an entire floor had been reduced to small pieces of masonry and glass, blown into the depths of the mansion, from which smoke was also emerging. Now I was wondering what I should do in order to convince myself that this was genuine reality. I remembered some photographs of girls hidden in a safe upstairs, especially of that Lily, which I had never shown to anyone. I was sure of that. I could remember the combination, but how was I to get upstairs? I would have to organise an entire campaign with the purpose of extracting the strongbox: a crane, people, I could already see the blasted safe dangling in the grip of some steel cables, as the rest of the semi-demolished wall came tumbling straight down on top of it, and the whole lot fell amid clouds of dust into the pitch-dark cellars.

Then I did something designed to be in keeping with Dr Gordon's instructions. I had them take me to that sporting goods store opposite the barber's, where I went inside and demanded an inflatable lilo with red-and-blue stripes.

'We haven't got that one any more,' piped up a small sales assistant with the bald pate of a skinhead. 'There's a similar red-and-green one, Sir... this is it.'

'But I want the one that was hanging in your window an hour ago.'

'We sold that one. We can order you one the same, we can get it today...'

I left the shop without another word. I looked in on the barber – he bowed to me. I was at a total loss now. I examined my own hands; I couldn't go home, so I had them take me to the Ritz, where I rented a suite. First I called my wife in Florida, then Dr Gordon. I didn't tell my wife anything – I had no desire to talk to her about the losses she had suffered as a result of the house being wrecked; I had more urgent business with Gordon, but my call was picked up by an answering machine.

So I sat on a couch with a hideous bee pattern at the Ritz, drank some disgusting tonic water and considered deep down what to do. The reception desk had already notified me three times about reporters greedy for an interview, but I said I had too much to think about right now, and told two of my security people to stand outside my door. I took a very careful look at them first, but I couldn't spot anything. Frankly, I had never examined my bodyguards' faces before, and now it came back with a vengeance. They were just the same as earlier, or not. In any case, either way they swapped shifts every six hours. If I had started questioning them (about what?), at most I'd have provided extra, strategically crucial information for the computer programmer who had taken control of my brain – IF it had really come to that. What I disliked the most was the nasty scene at the barber's, that moment when he had pulled the net over my hair: I hadn't seen it. Couldn't that have been the electrodes? A sort of typical phantomatising cap? Perhaps, I thought, I'm lying in a stinky old chest in an attic and I can't see a method of gaining certainty that I am at the hotel FOR REAL. What should I do? What should I do?

I considered the following scenarios in turn:

1.) I'll summon all my lawyers, my insurance broker, stockbroker, cashier, secretary and so on to the hotel for dinner, and scrutinize them properly. However, if they had 'got a precise fix' on me and my environment, they wouldn't be my people, just phantoms produced by a computer;

2.) I can summon the chamber maid (the one who brought me the tonic, and then something else as well – she wasn't at all bad-looking) and rape her; however, if she has nothing against that sort of thing and doesn't scream her head off, I won't find out anything about the phantomatisation – at best I'll get into a mess I haven't the least desire for right now;

3.) I can pretend I've had a fit of madness: but that is the silliest option, because they'll cart me off to a mental hospital;

4.) I can murder someone, but if I am in genuine reality, that won't do me much good;

5.) I must do something unexpected and totally unpredictable.

Having decided on number five, I took the elevator down to the ground floor and entered the hotel kitchen. Very profitably, for there were all sorts of knives, like butcher's ones, neatly hanging on the wall, but for starters I grabbed the handle of a vast cauldron full of soup and splashed the entire contents over two kitchen porters in white 'turbans' who stared at me in a stupor. However, as I had got away with this stunt of mine, at least in the immediate term, I picked up a large fork and started randomly throwing about slices of beef that were frying in skillets; by now several people dressed in white were running towards me. That's not enough, I said to myself, can't a millionaire spill soup and fling a few chops about on a pure whim? I'm behaving like the ultimate idiot – but there's no helping it, I must gain certainty...

With a knife in my hand I ran out of the kitchen, down a few corridors and reached the lobby. There were several young women standing in front of the reception desk, so I tore the skirt off one of them – however, she was wearing completely ordinary pink panties – then I tried pulling another's one's hair and just imagine, it came off in my hand, because she was wearing a wig. Hearing shouts and squeals behind me, and seeing that I had to keep going, and that I should exercise no measure of restraint in this lethal grappling with the COMPUTER, I swung the knife at the receptionist. I got him all right.

IV

Now I'm sitting in a cell charged with murder, while my lawyers are trying to get an expert opinion from a psychiatrist to explain that I was acting in a state of insanity. If it doesn't go well, I might even get the electric chair.

But can I be sure?

It all depends on whether someone really did buy that blue-and-red lilo just as the barber was cutting my hair, or whether that lilo disappeared because the gangsters' programmer wasn't precise enough. Either way I'm in the dark; I tried hanging myself, but the sheet tore.

But did it really?

Darkness and Mildew

Stanisław Lem

Translated from the Polish by Antonia Lloyd-Jones

I

'Is THAT THE last one?' said the man in the mac.

With the point of his shoe, he tipped some crumbs of earth down into the bottom of the pit, where acetylene flames were roaring beneath leaning figures with gigantic, shapeless heads. Nottinsen turned away to wipe his teary eyes.

'Dammit, I've mislaid my dark glasses. The last one? I hope so. I can hardly stay upright. What about you?'

The man in the shiny mac, which had fine drops of water trickling down it, put his hands in his pockets.

'I'm used to it. Don't look,' he added, seeing that Nottinsen was glancing into the depths of the pit again. The earth was steaming and hissing under the acetylene torches.

'Just to be sure at least,' muttered Nottinsen, and squinted. 'If it's like this here, can you imagine what must have happened over there?' He nodded across the highway, where slender wisps of steam were rising from the turned-down edges of a crater, burning with a violet light from the gleam of invisible rays.

'He can't have been alive by then,' said the man in the mac. One after the other, he turned each pocket inside out and shook the water from them. Fine rain was still falling.

'He didn't have time to take fright, and he can't have felt a thing.'

'Take fright?' said Nottinsen. He tried to look into the sky, but immediately pulled his head into his collar to keep off the rain. 'Him? You didn't know him. Well, of course you didn't,' he realised. 'He'd been working on it for four years – it could have happened at any moment in those four years.'

'So why did they let him do it?' said the man in the damp mac, glowering at Nottinsen.

'Because they didn't believe he'd succeed,' said Nottinsen grimly.

Blue flames that stung the eyes were still licking the bottom of the pit.

'Really?' said the other man. 'I... kept a bit of an eye on it while it was being built,' he said, glancing towards the faintly smoking crater a few hundred yards away. 'It must have cost a pretty penny...'

'Thirty million,' admitted Nottinsen, shifting from foot to foot. He could feel his shoes getting soaked through. 'What of it? They'd have given him three hundred or three thousand million if they'd been sure...'

'It had something to do with atoms, right?' said the man in the waterproof mac.

'How do you know?'

'I heard about it. Anyway, I saw the column of smoke.'

'From the explosion?'

'And why did they have to build it so far off, anyway?'

'That was his wish,' replied Nottinsen. 'That was why he had been working on his own – for the past four months, since he managed to...' He looked at the other man, and lowering his head, he added: 'It was meant to be worse than atoms. Worse than atoms!' he repeated.

'What could be worse than the end of the world?'

'You can drop a single A-bomb and then stop,' said Nottinsen. 'But one *Whisteria* – just one would be enough! No one would have been able to stop it! Hello down there,' he shouted, leaning over the pit. 'Not so fast! Don't be in a hurry! Don't move aside the flames! Every inch has to be properly annealed.'

'That's none of my concern,' said the other man. 'But if that's the case, how will a bit of fire help?'

'Do you know what it was meant to be?' asked Nottinsen slowly.

'I'm no expert on it. Aldershot said I was to help you, using local forces, that they were... that he was working on some sort of atomic bacteria. Something like that.'

'Atomic bacteria?' Nottinsen started to laugh, but immediately stopped. He cleared his throat and said: '*Whisteria Cosmolytica*, that's what he called it. A micro-organism that destroys matter and gains vital energy from the process.'

'Where did he get it from?'

'A derivative of controlled mutations. In other words he started with existing bacteria and gradually subjected them to the effect of increasing doses of radiation. Until he reached *Whisteria*. It exists in two states – as a spore, as harmless as flour. You could sprinkle the streets with it. But if it were animated and started to multiply, that would be the end.'

'Yes. Aldershot told me,' said the other man.

'Told you what?'

'That it was meant to multiply and consume everything – stone walls, people, steel.'

'That's right.'

'And that then it couldn't be stopped.'

'Yes.'

'What's the use of a weapon like that?'

'That's why it couldn't have been applied just yet. Whister was working on how to stop the process, how to make it reversible. Do you see?'

The man looked first at Nottinsen, then at their surroundings – rows of concentric craters with banks of earth around them, getting smaller into the distance and veiled by the first hint of twilight, from which here and there the steam was still trailing – and gave no reply.

'Let's hope none of it has survived,' said Nottinsen. 'I

don't suppose he did something so crazy without being sure he could reverse it...' he said to himself, without looking at his companion.

'Was there a lot of it?' said the other man.

'A lot of spores? It depends how you look at it. They were in six test tubes, in a fireproof safe.'

'Up there, in that office of his on the second floor?' asked the man.

'Yes. There's a crater there now that's big enough for two houses,' said Nottinsen and shuddered. He looked down at the flickering flames and added: 'Apart from the pits we'll have to burn the entire area, everything within a radius of five kilometres. Aldershot's coming tomorrow morning. He has promised to mobilise the army – our people can't deal with it on their own.'

'What does it need to – get started?' the man asked. Nottinsen gazed at him for a while, as if he didn't understand.

'To make it active? Darkness. There was a light on in the safe and there were special accumulator batteries in case of a break in the current – eighteen bulbs, each with a separate circuit, each independent of the others.'

'Darkness, and nothing else?'

'Darkness, and a kind of mildew. The presence of mildew was also needed. It provided some sort of organic catalyst. Whister did not state it precisely in his report to the sub-committee – he had the documents and everything downstairs in his room.'

'He clearly wasn't expecting it,' said the man.

'Maybe it's exactly what he was expecting,' muttered Nottinsen indistinctly.

'Do you think the lights went out? But where did the mildew come from?' said the man.

'Not at all!'

Nottinsen stared at him wide-eyed.

'It wasn't them. It... it... they multiply in a totally nonexplosive way. Quietly. I assume he was doing something involving the big paratron in the basement – it was about finding a way of stopping their development and to have it ready in case of...'

'War?'

'Yes.'

'And what was he doing in there?'

'We don't know. It was something to do with anti-matter. Because *Whisteria* destroys matter. The synthesis of anti-protons – the production of a force-containing membrane – fission – that's what its life cycle is like.'

For a while they gazed in silence at the men working below them.

The flames at the bottom of the pit were going out one by one. In the grey-blue twilight people were climbing up, pulling supple coils of cables after them – they were enormous, in asbestos masks with rain trickling down them.

'Let's go,' said Nottinsen. 'Are your people on the highway?'

'Yes. You can rest easy. No one will get through.'

The rain was getting finer; at times it seemed nothing more than condensed mist was settling on their clothes and faces.

They walked across a field, passing the shattered, scorched and twisted fragments of trees that were lying in the tall grass.

'It came all the way here,' said the man walking beside Nottinsen as he turned and looked behind him. But all they could see was grey, ever more rapidly darkening mist.

'This time tomorrow it'll all be behind us,' said Nottinsen.

By now they were close to the highway.

'So... could the wind carry it further?'

Nottinsen looked at him.

'I don't think so,' he said. 'Most likely the very pressure of the explosion must have ground them to dust. What's lying here,' he said, glancing at the field, 'are the remains of the trees that were standing three hundred yards away from the building. There's nothing left of the walls, the apparatus, or even the foundations. Not a crumb. We've sifted it all through nets – you were there at the time.'

'Yes,' said the man in the mac, without looking at him.

'So you see. We are doing what we're doing just in case, to have complete certainty.'

'It was meant to be a weapon, then?' said the other man. 'What was it called? What did you say?'

'*Whisteria cosmolytica*,' said Nottinsen, trying in vain to make his sopping wet collar stand up. He was feeling colder and colder. 'But in the department it had a cryptonym, they like cryptonyms of the kind, you know – "Darkness and Mildew".'

II

In the room it was cold. Raindrops were streaming down the windowpanes. The blanket had slipped on one side, a nail had come loose, and beyond the garden a bit of the muddy road was visible, and some air bubbles floating on the puddles. What time was it? He made an estimate based on the greyness of the sky, the shadows in the corners of the room and the weight on his mind. He did a lot of coughing. He listened to his joints creaking as he pulled on his trousers. He fished out a pot and a teabag from among the papers on his desk and made some tea; there was a teaspoon lying under the window. He slurped noisily; the hot liquid was bitter and pale. As he was looking for the sugar, among the books he found the soap-encrusted shaving brush which had gone missing three days ago. Or was it four? He examined his chin with a thumb – the stubble was still scratchy, like a brush, and hadn't softened yet.

A pile of newspapers, underwear and books teetered dangerously, until with a loose rustle it tumbled over the edge of the desk and disappeared, raising a small cloud of dust that made his nose itch. He sneezed slowly, at intervals, letting the invigorating power of the sneezes fill him. When had he last moved his desk aside? A ghastly job. Maybe he'd better go out? It was pouring.

He shuffled over to the desk, took hold of the edge that was against the wall, and gave it a tug.

It shuddered, and sent up a cloud of dust.

Then he pushed with all his might, just worried in case he felt his heart react. 'If it makes a noise I'll give it a rest,' he decided. It should be all right. He stopped worrying about all the things that had fallen behind the desk – now it was just a trial of strength, a test of his health. I'm still pretty robust, he considered with satisfaction, as he watched the dark crack between the desk and the wall grow wider. Something that was wedged in there slipped and then rolled with a crash onto the floor.

Perhaps it was the other teaspoon, or maybe not – a comb, more likely? he wondered. But a comb wouldn't have made such a metallic sound. Perhaps it was the sugar tongs?

The darkness between the cracked plaster and the black border of the desk was already yawning the width of a hand. He knew from experience that now it would be hardest, because the desk leg was just about to get stuck in a big gap in the floor. It happened. The leg clicked into place. For a few moments he wrestled with the dead weight.

An axe, an axe for this piece of junk! he thought, with joy diluted by rising rage that made him feel younger. He went on struggling, though he knew it was futile. The desk would have to be set rocking, then tipped and lifted, because the leg nearest the wall was shorter and came off. Better it didn't fall off, cautioned the voice of reason – then he'd have to shove books underneath it, straighten the nails by the sweat of his brow and bang the leg in with a hammer. But he already felt too much loathing for the stubborn great lump, which he'd been feeding on bits of paper for all these years.

'You brute!' The words burst out of him with a groan,

and he could no longer keep his efforts regular. Sweating, with the smell of dust and perspiration in his nostrils, he tensed his back, exerted himself, and started rocking the inert weight; as usual at moments like this he got the fine feeling that his inflamed rage alone would be enough to raise and push aside the big black piece of junk without the slightest effort!

The leg jumped out of the rut and bashed into his fingers. He stifled a painful groan, as spite was added to his anger, then leaned his back against the wall and pushed with his hands and knees. The black gap grew, and he could have squeezed in there now, but he furiously went on pushing. Then the first ray of light hit the great graveyard emerging behind the desk, which came to a standstill with an agonising screech.

He slid onto a pile of overturned volumes which had flown down onto the floor at some point during the struggle. He sat on them for a while, as the sweat cooled on his brow. There was something he meant to remind himself about – oh yes, that his heart hadn't made a noise. That was good.

The cave he had carved out in the thick darkness behind the desk was invisible apart from its entrance, in which lay some soft dust kittens, as light as down. Dust kittens – that's what the mouse-grey bundles were called, little balls of cobweb-like dirt that gather under old cupboards and multiply in the entrails of sofas, felted, mossy, and suffused with particles of dirt.

He was in no hurry to investigate the contents of the forced-open nook. What might be in there? He felt pleased, though he couldn't remember why he had shifted the desk. The dirty underwear and newspapers were now lying in the middle of the room – he must have sent them flying over there with an unconscious kick while he was pushing the desk aside. From his sitting position he moved onto all fours and slowly put his head into the semi-darkness. Once he had blocked out the rest of the light and could no longer see anything, he breathed dust into his nostrils and sneezed again, but angrily this time.

He retreated, spent ages blowing his nose, and decided to move the desk further back than ever before. He felt along its back wall, which creaked in warning, steeled himself, leaned forward and pushed, and the desk moved far more easily than expected, almost into the middle of the room, overturning a bedside table. The teapot fell over and the tea spilled out. He gave it a kick.

He went back inside the opened treasure trove. The slightest movement sent up copious clouds of dust from the barely visible parquet blocks, on which there were some vague shapes lying about. He fetched a lamp, put it down on the sink to one side, plugged it in and turned around. The wall that had been obscured by the desk was entirely covered with strands of cobwebs, dark twists of them, as thick as rope in places. He rolled up a yellowed newspaper and started using it to pull out everything he could find and gather into a single heap; he worked away, holding his breath, bent low amid clouds of dust, and found a curtain ring, a hook, a piece of a belt, a buckle, a crumpled but unused piece of writing paper, a box of matches, and a partly melted stick of sealing wax. All that was left was the corner between the skirting boards, right against the wall, covered with a sort of greyish horsehair or felted remains; with the tip of his slipper he nervously reached in there and got a fright that was almost a thrill – something small and springy bounced off his big toe, which was sticking out of a hole in his slipper. He started to search for it, but couldn't find anything.

'I imagined it,' he thought.

He pulled a chair up to the desk, not the one with a leg missing – he preferred not to touch it – but the other one, which had a bowl sitting on it. He knocked it off, and it clattered clamorously; he smiled, sat down and started inspecting the things he had found behind the desk.

He carefully blew off the grey film of dust. The brass curtain ring shone like gold, and he tried to put it on his finger – too big. He brought the rusty, bent hook close to his nose. With a clump of limestone mortar stuck to its sharp end, it had the distinctive quality of an object that has been through a lot – its top flattened, great passion had clearly been vented on it in the past, and the marks from blows had frayed tiny slivers of metal off its sides, now eaten away by rust and crumbling at a firmer than usual touch. The pointed end, lumpily blunted, had clearly come up against hard opposition in the wall – ripped from its hole root and all, it reminded him of a tooth; he caringly touched the lonely stump protruding from the gum, as if to express sympathy for the hook.

He threw the rest of the things he had found into a drawer and twisted the lampshade.

Leaning across the desk he looked down, at the floor – in the yellowish lamplight the hideous shagginess of the wall showed black, and sleepily floating, sparkling, broken gossamer threads were drifting from the desk boards. In the middle, a used, dust-coated envelope lay on the parquet, stamp and address side up; there was something resting underneath it, raising its edge – something small. Like a nut.

Hardly had he thought: a mouse – than revulsion seized him by the throat. He held his breath and without looking, started to haul up a bronze paperweight, heavy as iron. His heart stood still in anticipation that he wouldn't be quick enough, and that any second now a horrible grey streak of frightful fleeing object would scuttle out from under the envelope. But nothing happened – the envelope went on lying there, slightly raised, with the lamp illuminating it, and the cobwebs just went on quivering with their own, steady life. He leaned even further, and lying flat on the desk by now, dropped the paperweight with force; it hit the envelope with a soft thwack, as if pressing something springy to the ground, then swayed and dully plopped onto the floor in a cloud of grey dust.

At that point a sort of frenzy of disgust and despair came over him – wildly, recklessly, he began to knock everything within reach onto the envelope: some fat volumes of German history, dictionaries, a silver-plated tobacco box – until beneath the languidly floating gossamer threads a chaotic pile arose, at the bottom of which, amid the echo of falling objects, in some mysterious way he could still sense an invincible, live, self-defending elasticity.

In a paroxysm of alarm (he felt instinctively that if he didn't kill *it* there would be revenge), groaning with exertion, he heaved up a wide, cast-iron ash-pan; he nudged a pile of books aside with his foot, and with a superhuman effort he hurled the ash-pan at the bulging edge of the envelope.

Just then something casually bopped him on the feet; he felt the same live, warm touch as before. His throat bursting with a panic-stricken shriek, he rushed blindly towards the door.

In the hall it was much brighter than in the room. He held onto the handle tightly, struggling to stop his head spinning. He aimed his gaze at the half-open door. He was gathering his strength to go back into the flat, when a black dot appeared.

He didn't notice it until the moment he stepped on it. It was smaller than a pin head, and looked like a seed, a speck of dust or soot, raised by an idle puff of wind just above the floor. His foot did not touch the floorboards. It slipped, or rather rolled, as if it had hit an invisible, bouncy little ball that immediately slid aside. Losing his balance, he did a desperate dance and crashed into the door, banging his elbow painfully. He picked himself up, sobbing with agitation.

'It's nothing, old man, it's nothing,' he muttered as he got up off his knees. He hissed as he tried to move his leg – it was intact. Now he was standing by the threshold, casting desperate looks at the surrounding area. All of a sudden, just above the floor, against the background of the open door into the garden, where the rain was murmuring steadily, he spotted the black dot. It was quivering gently in a corner between the sill of the exit door and a gap in the floorboards, slowly coming to a standstill. He leaned over it further and further, until he was almost bent double. He stared and stared at the black dot, which close up seemed to be slightly elongated.

A tiny spider on such thin legs that I can't see them, he concluded. The thought of the creature's thread-like legs filled him with sickening uncertainty. He stood very still, with a handkerchief extracted from his pocket. He folded it to make a trap, and then withdrew his hand indecisively. Finally he lowered a loosely dangling end of the handkerchief, and brought it close to the teeny black spider. It'll take fright and run away, he thought. Then I'll have peace.

But the black dot did not make off. The end of the handkerchief wasn't touching it, but had sagged a finger's width above it, as if it had run into an imperceptible obstacle. He jabbed helplessly at the air with the crumpling, curling corner of the handkerchief until, growing audacious (he found his own resourcefulness breath-taking), he pulled a key out of his pocket and prodded the black dot with it.

His hand could feel the same thing as before, springy resistance, as the key buckled in his fingers, and the black dot sprang up just in front of his face and started dancing fretfully, making diminishing vertical leaps, lower and lower until it came to a stop again in the corner between the doorsill and the floor. It happened so quickly he hadn't the time to be really shocked.

Slowly, squinting, as if in front of a frying pan full of bacon spitting on the fire, he unfolded the handkerchief and covered the black dot with it. It dropped gently and bulged, as if there were a ping-pong ball lying underneath it. He picked up the corners, artfully brought them together, and tucked them all in at once – the spherical shape was trapped. He touched it, first with the end of the key, then with his finger.

Indeed it was elastic, and bounced under pressure, but the harder he pressed it, the more distinctly its resistance grew. It was light – the handkerchief did not weigh more than when empty, or at least he couldn't feel that it did. His legs had gone numb, so he straightened up, leaned his other, free hand against the wall and hobbled into the room.

His heart was beating fast as he placed the knotted handkerchief under the lamp, on the desktop, now cleared of clutter. He switched on the light and looked for his glasses; after some thought, sparing no effort, in only the second drawer he found a magnifying glass with a lens as big as a saucer in a rusty black ring with a wooden handle. He pulled up a chair, shoving the fat, randomly scattered open books out of the way, and started carefully unknotting the handkerchief. Once again he broke off his activity, got up, and in the clutter under the window he found a glass dome for preserving cheese, cracked on one side, but intact. He placed it over the handkerchief, leaving just the corners sticking out, and pulled on them, until it slowly unfolded, covered in stains and damp patches.

He couldn't see a thing. He brought his head closer and closer, until his nose touched the cold glass of the dome, and the unexpected contact made him shudder.

The black dot only appeared under the magnifying glass. Once enlarged, it looked like a tiny grain of corn. It had a lighter, greyish bulge at one end and two green spots so tiny that they were hardly even visible through the magnifying glass at the other. He wasn't sure if it was the refracting light that was giving them this shade, or the thick glass dome. By tugging gently at two corners, he managed to extract the entire handkerchief from under the dome. It took about a minute. Then an idea occurred to him. He slid the dome across the desktop until the glass rim stuck out over the edge of it; then on a long thin wire he introduced a match he had prepared in advance, after striking it against the box at the last moment.

For a while it looked as if the match would go out; then, when it flared up more intensely, he couldn't move it in the right direction, but finally he managed to do that too. The small yellowish flame came close to the black dot, which hung an inch above the desktop, and suddenly fluttered restlessly; pushed in a tiny bit further, it seemed to wrap itself around an invisible bulge. It stayed like that for a while, shot a final, bluish spark and went out – only the charred matchstick went on glowing for a while.

He relaxed, shoved the glass dome back underneath the lampshade and spent a long time staring motionlessly at the black dot, which was very faintly moving under the glass dome.

'An invisible sphere,' he muttered, 'an invisible sphere...'

He was almost happy, but he didn't even know it. The next hour was occupied with placing a saucer filled with ink underneath the dome. An entire system of matchsticks and wires proved essential in order to position the subject under examination within the saucer. The surface of the ink sagged almost imperceptibly in one spot, just where the lower part of the sphere ought to be coming in contact with it. Nothing else happened. His attempts to coat it in ink came to nothing.

At noon he felt a gnawing pain in his stomach, so he ate the rest of the porridge and some crumbly biscuits out of a cloth bag, washed down with some tea. On returning to his desk, in the first instant he couldn't find the black dot, and felt violent fear. Forgetting caution, he raised the dome and feverishly felt the surface of the desk with his hands spread wide like a blind man. At once the spherical shape calmly rolled into his fingers. He clenched his hand and sat there, full of gratitude, reassured, muttering to himself. The invisible sphere was heating up his hand. He could feel warmth emanating from it, and started toying with it ever more riskily, rolling it, weightless, from one hand to the other, until his gaze caught on something shining in the dust under the stove, where some rubbish had spilled out of the overturned bin. It was a small crumpled-up sheet of tinfoil from a chocolate. Instantly he set about wrapping the sphere in the foil. This went far more easily than expected. He just left two small holes at opposite ends, made with a pin, so that by inspecting it under the light, he could examine the presence of the tiny black prisoner inside.

When he finally had to leave the house to buy something to eat, he trapped the sphere under the dome, and to be extra certain he pressed it down some more and surrounded it with books on all sides.

From then on the days went by splendidly. Now and then he tried some experiments with the sphere, but for the most part he lay in bed, reading his favourite passages in old books. He curled up under the blanket, gathering the warmth as best he could, only stretching out a hand to turn the page. Absorbed in vivid descriptions of the deaths of Amundsen's companions amid the ice, or in Nobile's grim confidences about cases of cannibalism after the crash of his polar expedition airship, he occasionally cast an eye upon the dome, where the sphere glowed gently beneath the glass; once in a while it altered its position slightly, shifting gently from one wall to the other, as if something invisible had pushed it.

He didn't feel like going shopping or cooking dinners, so he ate biscuits, and if he had a little wood, he baked potatoes in the ash pan. In the evenings he plunged the sphere under water or tried to prick it with something sharp – he nicked a razorblade on it, without any visible result – and it went on for such a long time that his composure was starting to deteriorate. He was contemplating a major event: he thought of dragging an old vice upstairs from the cellar, in order to grip the sphere and crush it right down to the little black dot in the middle, but this involved such a lot of bother (God knows how long he would have to rummage in old scrap metal and junk, on top of which he wasn't sure he could shift the vice, which he had carried down there three years ago), that the idea never got further than the planning stage.

On one occasion, he heated the sphere for a long time on the fire, with the result that he burned right through the bottom of a perfectly good saucepan. The tinfoil had gone dark and smouldered, but the sphere itself had not suffered any harm. He was starting to grow impatient, and he was having thoughts about taking strong measures, because he was feeling ever more certain that the sphere was indestructible; this resistance was beefing up his satisfaction, when one day he noticed something he really should have spotted much earlier on.

The tinfoil (a new piece, because the old one had been ripped to tatters in the course of various experiments) had torn in several places at once, and the inside was showing through the gaps. The sphere was growing! As soon as it dawned on him he started to shake all over. He took it under the magnifying glass, spent a long time examining it uncovered, inspected it under a double lens which he dug out of the bottom desk drawer, and was finally sure he hadn't been mistaken.

Not only was the sphere growing, it was also changing shape. It was no longer completely round – two gentle bulges had appeared on it, like poles at either end, and the black dot had lengthened out, so that now it was visible to the naked eye. Behind its tiny notched head, by the pair of greenish spots, a faintly glowing line had appeared, which was gradually breaking loose with a movement harder to perceive than the motion of an hour hand on a clock, but by the morning he could be sure the phenomenon was progressing beyond all doubt. The sphere was now elongated like an egg with two equally fat ends. The black dot at the centre had distinctly swollen.

The next night he was woken by a brief but tremendous noise, as if a massive plate of glass had suddenly cracked in a big frost. It was still ringing in his ears as he leapt up and ran to the desk barefoot. The light dazzled him – he stood with a hand in front of his eyes, desperately waiting until he could see again. The glass dome was intact. Nothing about it appeared to have changed. He tried to look for the longitudinal black thread, but couldn't find it. When he discovered it, he went numb because it had contracted so much. In terror he lifted the dome, and something rolled up against the back of his hand. Leaning low, he brought his face close to the empty desktop, until at last he could see.

There were two of them, heated, as if lately removed from boiling water. In each one a tiny little nucleus stood out – a matt black dot. An inexplicable state of bliss, sheer emotion came over him. He was trembling, not with cold but with excitement. He put them on the palm of his hand, warm as hatchlings, and breathed on them gently to avoid blowing them, almost weightless, onto the floor. Then he wrapped each one carefully in tinfoil and put them under the dome. He stood over them for a long time, earnestly desiring to discover what else he could do for them, until he went back to bed with his heart racing, feeling a little resentful of his own helplessness, but calm and almost moved to tears.

'My tiny ones,' he muttered, as he sank into blissful, nourishing sleep.

A month later the spheres no longer fitted under the dome. After the next few he had lost count – he couldn't keep track of them anymore. Barely had the black nucleus taken on the usual dimensions than the sphere began to swell at the opposite poles. Only once did he manage to be watching at the moment of division – which always happened at night. The noise emanating from under the dome deafened him for minutes on end, but he was even more stunned by the bright flash in which the room leapt out of the darkness for an instant, like a microscopic bolt of lightning. He couldn't understand what was happening at all, but through the bed he felt the floor shudder for a moment, and he was entirely pervaded by awareness that the insignificant object breeding in front of him was something infinitely powerful. He experienced the sort of emotion that is prompted by an overwhelming fact of nature – as if he had glanced for a second into the abyss of a waterfall or felt an earthquake; in that momentary, resonant clanging whose echo the walls of the house still seemed to be absorbing, for a split second a power without comparison had been flung open and slammed shut. The fear was short-lived – in the morning he thought he had just imagined it in his dreams.

The next night he made an effort to stay awake in the dark. Then for the first time, along with a wave of shuddering and a hollow noise, he got a precise view of the zigzag flash that cut the swollen egg in half, and then vanished so abruptly that afterwards he couldn't tell if it had only been an illusion.

He couldn't even remember the snow that winter, so rarely did he go out, only as much as necessary to reach the little shop around the corner. With the approach of early spring, the room was teeming with spheres. He couldn't have found clothing for all of them – where was he to get that much tinfoil? They were drifting about everywhere, and he kept accidentally nudging them with his feet; they kept falling noiselessly from the bookshelves – that was where they were easiest to see, once they were coated in a delicate layer of dust from lying there for a while, like powder, which outlined their roundness with a fine, matt membrane.

Constant new adventures (he was fishing them out of his porridge, or out of the milk, he found some in a bag of sugar, they kept rolling invisibly out of containers and getting cooked with the soup), and the sheer profusion surrounding him, began to prompt new thoughts and make him feel mildly unsettled.

The irrepressibly expanding tribe was not too bothered about him. He shuddered to think one of them might slip into the hall and on, into the garden, into the road, where some kids might find it. He put up some wire netting in front of the doorsill with a fine enough mesh, but in time going outside became a highly complicated ritual – he scoured each of his pockets in turn, peered into his cuffs, and to be absolutely sure shook them a few times, then opened the door and shut it slowly to make sure the resulting draught did not inadvertently carry one of them off, but the more of them there were, the more complicated it all became.

He only suffered one genuine, major inconvenience as a result of this coexistence full of endless emotions: by now there were so many of them that they were breeding almost non-stop, and the tremendous ringing noise sometimes resounded five or six times in the course of a single hour. As it woke him in the night, he started to sleep off his tiredness by day – when silence prevailed. Occasionally he was gripped by a vague sense of anxiety about the wave of inexorable, steady proliferation; it was becoming harder and harder to walk about, and at every step invisible, springy little balls escaped from under the soles of his shoes, scattering in all directions. He could tell that soon he would be wading in them, as if in deep water. He never stopped to wonder what they were living or feeding on.

Although the early spring was cold, with frequent frosts and blizzards, he hadn't lit the fire for ages, because the swarm of spheres was lending its steady warmth to the surroundings. It had never been so warm in the room before, never as cosy as it was now, as the dust abounded with comical evidence of their springing and rolling about, as if some baby kittens had just been playing in it.

The more spheres there were, the more easily they let their habits be known. One might think they didn't like each other, or in any case they couldn't bear too close proximity to their own kind – because there was always a thin layer of air left between neighbouring ones, which was impossible to squeeze out, even with the use of considerable force. He saw this best when he brought two of the spheres wrapped in tinfoil close together. In time he began tidying up the excess of them, tossing them into a small tin bathtub, in which they lay beneath a thin skin of dust like a pile of coarse-grained frogspawn, just occasionally shaking with internal motion when one of the transparent eggs divided into two descendants.

It has to be admitted that he sometimes had the strangest fancies – for instance he battled with himself for ages, so strong was the urge to swallow one of the babies in his care! Eventually it ended in merely putting an invisible sphere into his mouth. He turned it gently with his tongue, feeling the soft, springy, oval shape against his palate and gums as it emanated a faint warmth. The day after this incident he noticed a superficial eruption on his tongue. He did not link these facts. More and more often he went to sleep with them, yet he couldn't understand why the pillowcases and blanket, which had done such good service until now, had started to fall apart, as if they had suddenly decayed. Finally the sheet was torn to shreds, and there were more holes in it than cloth – but he still couldn't understand a thing.

One night he was awoken by a stinging pain on his leg. Under the light he saw several reddish spots on the skin of his calf. He kept finding more and more of them – they looked like a spattering of burns. As he lay down to sleep again, the invisible spheres were jumping about all over the bedclothes, and this sight made him feel suspicious – their tiny nuclei were flickering like little fleas.

'What the devil! Bite your daddy, would you?' he whispered reproachfully. He looked around the room.

The matt gleam of the dust-coated spheres emanated from all sides – they were covering the entire desk, lying on the floor, on the shelves, in the pots, in the pans, and there was even something suspicious looming in a half-drunk cup of tea. Inconceivable fear made his heart pound in an instant. With trembling hands he shook the blanket, then its cover, and waved his arms about high in the air, while stretching the pillow between them; he knocked all the spheres onto the floor, once again thoughtfully examined the pancake-like red patches on his calves, wrapped himself in the blanket and put out the light. Every few minutes the room resounded with a noise like a metallic fanfare, interrupted by a lid suddenly slamming shut.

Is it possible? Is it possible? he thought.

'I'll throw you out! I'll drive every last one of you into

the street! Begone!' he suddenly declared in a whisper, because his voice wouldn't come out of his parched throat. Infinite regret was choking him, bringing tears to his eyes.

'Ungrateful little swine,' he whispered, leaning against the wall, and like that, half sitting, half lying, he fell into sleep.

In the morning he woke up feeling drained, with a sense of defeat and misfortune. He started desperately searching with his misty eyes, scouring his memory, for whatever it was he had lost yesterday. Suddenly he came to, crawled out of bed, set the lamp on a chair, and proceeded to examine the floor methodically.

There could be no doubt – it bore distinct traces of corrosion, as if someone had sprinkled it with tiny, splattering droplets of invisible acid. He noticed similar marks, though to a lesser extent, on the desk. The stacks of old newspapers and magazines were particularly damaged – almost all their upper faces were riddled with holes. The enamel inside the pots was also covered in shallow ulcerations. For ages he stared at the room in astonishment, then set about gathering up the spheres. He carried them in a bucket to the bathtub, but once it was more than brim full, there still seemed to be just as many as before in the room. They were rolling against the walls, and he could feel their unsettling warmth as they huddled up to his feet. They were everywhere – in dull stacks on the shelves, on the table, in jars and in corners – piles and piles of them.

He wandered round stupefied, scared, and spent his entire day sweeping them out from one place to another; finally he had partly filled an old empty chest of drawers with them, and sighed with relief. At night the cannonade seemed more violent than usual – the wooden chest of drawers became one great big resonator, which kept emitting dull, unearthly noises, as if invisible prisoners were banging bells against its walls from the inside. The next day the spheres had started to spill over the protective netting on the door. He transferred his mattress, blanket and pillow to the desk and made himself a bed there. He sat on it with his feet tucked under him. He should have fetched the vice at once – the thought flashed through his mind – what now? Throw them into the river at night?

He decided that would be best, but he was afraid to utter this threat aloud. No one else would have them, and he would leave a couple of them for himself, no more. In spite of all, he was fond of them – except that now to fondness, fear was starting to add itself. He would drown them like... kittens!

He thought of the wheelbarrow. Otherwise he wouldn't be able to cope with removing them – but he merely tried to lift it, stuck against a wall in an old pit, and waddled back into the house. He was weak, very weak. He would have to put it off. He decided to eat more.

The night was dreadful. Exhausted, he fell asleep in spite of all. When the first metallic noise awoke him, he sat up in the dark and saw the entire room light up before him in short zigzags. Out of the blackness leaped bits of the walls, the dust-coated shelves and the worn-out bedside rug, all illuminated for a split second; the flashes were duplicated in the glass of quivering containers, and suddenly something dully shone through the blanket cover, lying over him – so some cunningly hidden beast was lurking under there! He shook it out in disgust.

This deranged childbirth looked like a landscape lit up by bolts of lightning, except that instead of thunderclaps the miniature flashes were followed by the striking of a bell, which made the windowpanes echo. He fell asleep sitting up, leaning against the wall. At the crack of dawn he woke up once again with a weak cry – a wave of bright blue splashes was brightening the room, flooding it, and the multiple zigzags almost came up to the surface of the desk, which suddenly gave a mighty shudder and moved away from the wall – an invisible sphere had pushed it aside in the process of dividing. Feeling the relentless force of this motion, he was bathed in ice-cold sweat; he stared at the room goggle-eyed, muttering something – and once again fell asleep from exhaustion.

Next morning he woke up very weak – so weak that he could hardly clamber down to drink up the remains of the cold, bitter tea. He started shaking when he sank up to his waist in the soft, invisible heap – there were so many of them that he could hardly move, and with the greatest difficulty he waded through to the table. The room was filled with hot, stuffy air, as if an invisible stove were burning in it. He began to feel odd; he sank to the ground, but didn't fall, because the elastic, springy mass of them held him up; the sensation filled him with unutterable alarm – their touch was so soft and gentle, and a terrible thought occurred to him, that perhaps he had already swallowed one with his porridge, one of the smaller ones, and that night, in his intestines...

He wanted to run away. To get out. Out! He couldn't open the door. It opened a few inches, then the elastic mass, giving way springily, stopped it – and wouldn't let it go any further. He was afraid to struggle with the door and felt an onset of dizziness. He would have to smash a window, he thought – but what would the glazier charge?

Trembling, he cleared himself a way to the desk, climbed onto it, and stared blankly at the room – a grey, stippled mist, a barely visible, silent cloud of spheres surrounded him on all sides. He was hungry, but he no longer had the courage to get down; a few times he feebly, half-heartedly called out with his eyes closed: 'Help! Help!'

He fell asleep before dusk. In the descending darkness the room came alive with increasingly powerful bangs and flashes. Illuminated from the inside by bursts of light, the mass was growing, swelling, slowly puffing up, it was shuddering, gently being shaken off the shelves, from among the books, pushing them aside; warm, quivering spheres were jumping out and flying in bright blue, glittering arcs. One rolled down onto his chest, another touched his cheek, the next clung to his lips, more and more of them were covering the mattress around his balding skull, shining in his half-open eyes, but he didn't wake up again...

The next night, at about three in the morning, a lorry was coming along the road to town, carrying milk in twenty-gallon churns. Tired after travelling all night, the driver was nodding off at the wheel. It was the worst moment, the time when it is simply impossible to overcome drowsiness. Suddenly he heard a protracted booming noise coming out of the distance. On impulse he slowed down, and saw a fence behind some trees; down below there was a dark, overgrown garden, and in it a small house with light blazing in the windows.

A fire! he thought, drove onto the roadside verge, braked abruptly and ran to the gate to wake the inhabitants.

He was half-way down the overgrown path when he saw pouring from the windows, among broken bits of the pushed-out panes of glass, not flames, but a foaming wave, ringing and flashing non-stop, seething forwards and outwards under the walls. On his hands, on his face he felt soft, invisible touches, like the wings of thousands of moths; he thought he was dreaming – once the grass and the bushes all around were teeming with little blue sparks, the left attic window lit up like a gigantic, wide open cat's eye, the front door creaked and burst with a bang – and he turned and fled, still seeing the image of a mountain of twinkling caviar, which with a prolonged rumble was blowing the house apart.

Invasion from Aldebaran

Stanisław Lem

Translated from the Polish by Antonia Lloyd-Jones

THIS HAPPENED QUITE recently, only just the other day. Two inhabitants of Aldebaran – members of a rational race which will be discovered in the year 2685 and classified by Neirearch, that Linneus of the thirtieth century, as a subtype of the class *Coelestiaca* in the order of *Megalopterygia* – in short, two representatives of the species *Megalopteryx Ambigua Flirx*, sent by the Syncytial Assembly of Aldebaran (also known as the Ultimate Epithelium) to investigate possibilities for colonising planets within the range of the Sixth Partial Peripheral Rarefication (PPR), arrived in the environs of Jupiter, where they were to take samples of its Andrometaculasters; having confirmed that these were of use for feeding their Telepatic (of which more below), they decided, while they were about it, to research the third planet in the System as well, a tiny globe revolving on an uninteresting circular orbit around the Central Star.

Having set their Astromat to a single hyperspatial Metastep in Supraspace, the two Aldebaranians emerged just above the atmosphere of the planet in their merely mildly heated ship, and then ventured into it at moderate speed. Oceans and continents went sailing past ever more slowly beneath their Astromat. It may be worth noting that Aldebaranians, by contrast with human beings, do not travel in rockets. On the contrary, the rockets travel inside them, except for the very tip. As the newcomers were aliens, their landing place was determined by chance. They are strategically minded creatures, and as true scions of a superior, parastatic civilisation, they prefer to descend on the line of a planetary terminator, i.e. where the diurnal hemisphere of a planet borders with the nocturnal.

They set their cosmic vehicle down on a pillar of retrogravitationally expelled Bralderons, left it, that is, they flowed off it, and assumed a more concentrated shape, which is the habit of all *Metapterygia*, from the *Polyzoa* as well as the *Monozoa* sub-class.

At this point the new arrivals should be described, although their build is more than familiar enough. As all the authors assert, Aldebaranians – just like other, highly organised Beings from all over the Galaxy – possess a large number of very long tentacles, each of which ends in a hand with six fingers. As well as that they have enormous, hideous, cuttlefish-like heads, and legs that are also tentacular and six-fingered. The older one, who was the Cybernetor of the expedition, was called NGTRX, and the younger one, an eminent polyziatrist in his homeland, was called PWGDRK.

Immediately after landing they cut a lot of branches off the weird plants surrounding their ship and covered it with the aim of camouflaging it. Then they unloaded their essential equipment – a unicollective Teremtak, a loaded Aldemonico ready for action and a Peripatetic Telepatic (as mentioned above).

The Peripatetic Telepatic, otherwise known as the Pe-Te, is a device that serves for communicating with any rational beings that may exist on a planet, and thanks to a hyperspatial link to the Univermantic Supracereber on Aldebaran, it is also capable of translating all manner of inscriptions in 196,000 galactic languages and dialects. Like others, this piece of apparatus is different from any Earthly equivalent in that the Aldebaranians – as will be known from the year 2685 – do not manufacture their own devices and machines, but cultivate them, either from seeds, or from eggs, genetically controlled in the appropriate manner.

The Peripatetic Telepatic is similar in appearance, but in appearance only, to a skunk, because it is entirely stuffed inside with fleshy cells of Semantic Memory, the peduncle of an Alveolar Translator and an enormous Mnemonic-Mnestic Gland, on top of which it has two Intrinsic Outlets (IOs, one at the front and one at the rear) for its Interglocococom, i.e. its Interplanetary Glossolalic-Coherency-Contemplative-Communicator.

Having brought out everything essential, holding the Peripatetic on an ortholead, and letting the Teremtak go ahead, with the bulky Aldemonico slung over their tentacles, the two Aldebaranians set off on their way.

The place for performing their first reconnaissance was ideal – an area humming under evening clouds, full of thick undergrowth, and in the distance, just before landing, they had managed to spot a fairly straight line, which they guessed, to their joy, was a communications route.

From flight altitude, as they were circling the unfamiliar globe, they had also noticed other evidence of civilisation, for example a weakly glowing rash on the darkened hemisphere, which could be the nocturnal image of cities. This filled them with hope that the planet was inhabited by a highly developed race. That was just the kind they were looking for. In those days – preceding the fall of the wicked Syncytium, whose belligerence hundreds of planets, even ones far away from Aldebaran, had failed to resist – the empire's inhabitants preferred to attack populated globes, because they regarded it as their Historical Mission, besides which the colonisation of deserted planets demanded vast investments in construction, industry and so on, and was very negatively regarded by the Ultimate Epithelium.

For some time the two scouts walked, or rather forced their way through the dense thicket, painfully feeling the stings of some unfamiliar flying creatures of the species Arthropoda Cyclostomata Hymenoptera, and hardly able to see a thing; the longer this journey continued, the more sharply the springy twigs lashed at their cuttlefishy heads, because they weren't quick enough to spread their tired tentacles. Of course they had no intention of conquering the planet on their own – that did not lie within their power – they were just the first reconnaissance, only after whose return would preparations be undertaken for a Major Invasion.

With increasing frequency, the Aldemonico kept getting stuck in the bushes, from which they had the greatest difficulty extracting it, taking care not to touch its Trigger Appendix, for it was all too possible to sense through its soft fur the charge full of Gnitchers lying dormant inside it. The inhabitants of the planet would undoubtedly soon fall victim to them.

'There seems to be no evidence of the local civilisation in sight,' PWGDRK finally hissed to NGTRX after about an hour.

'I saw some cities,' replied NGTRX. 'Besides, wait, it's lighter over there, that must be the road. Yes, look, the road!'

They forced their way through to a spot that was clear of bushes, but they were disappointed – the strip, quite wide and straight, really did resemble a road in shape, from a distance. But at once they found themselves in a big doughy bog, formed by a sticky, squelching substance, extending in both directions on an intricately moulded base of rounded or elongated dips and rises. There were some large stones stuck in it fairly densely.

PWGDRK, who as a polyziatrist was a specialist in planetary matters, pronounced that here before them lay a trail of excrement from some sort of Gigantosaurus. For this strip, as they both agreed, could not possibly be a road. No Aldebaranian wheeled vehicle could have forced its way along such a quagmire.

They performed on-the-spot field analysis of some samples scooped up by the Teremtak, and from its brow they read the phosphorescently glowing result – the glue-like gunky substance was a mixture of dihydrous oxygen with aluminium oxides and silica with serious admixtures of Dt (Dirt).

And so it wasn't the trail of a Gigantosaurus.

They moved onwards, wading and sinking halfway up their tentacles, when behind them, in the ever more rapidly falling darkness, they heard a groaning sound.

'Look out!' hissed NGTRX.

Something, groaning and shaking violently, sinking and rising again, was catching up with them – a sort of large creature with a flattened head, hump-backed, and on the hump some sort of loose skin was quivering.

'Listen – isn't that a syncytium?' said NGTRX in excitement.

The big black lump was just passing them – they thought they could see wheels jumping furiously, as on a peculiar machine, and were trying to prepare for a sortie when they were showered in streams of gunk thrown up in the air. Stunned and soaked from lowest to highest tentacles, they only just managed to tidy themselves up, and dashed over to the Telepatic to find out whether the roaring and rumbling noises the machine was emitting were articulate in nature.

'Unrhythmical noise of primitive hydrocarbon oxide energorotator operating in conditions for which it is not adapted', they deciphered, and looked at each other, while PWGDRK said: 'Strange.'

He pondered for a while and, inclined to pose rather rash hypotheses, added: 'A sadistoidal civilisation. It gives vent to its instincts by torturing the machines it has created.'

On its ultrascope the Telepatic had managed to record a perfect image of the bipedal creature that was situated in a glazed box above the head of the machine. With the help of the Teremtak, which had a special Imitative Glandule, they moulded a certain amount of hastily extracted clay into a faithful, life-sized likeness of the biped. They steeped the clay in Plastefolium, so that the dummy acquired a pale pink colour, and, in keeping with the Teremtak's and Peripatetic's readings, shaped its limbs and head; this entire procedure took them no more than ten minutes. Next they unrolled some Syntectaric material, cut out clothing similar to what the biped in the machine had been wearing, and dressed the dummy in it. Then NGTRX slowly crawled inside its empty interior, taking the Telepatic with him, after which he instantly positioned its front IO in the dummy's mouth opening – from the inside of course. Thus camouflaged, shifting the dummy's right limb and then its left by steady turns, NGTRX moved forwards along the gunky track, while PWGDRK, burdened with the Aldemonico, walked at a short interval behind him. Both were preceded by the Teremtak, let off its ortholead.

The whole operation was a typical undertaking. The Aldebaranians had tried out a similar masquerade on dozens of planets, achieving the best possible result for themselves in every single case. The dummy was deceptively similar to an ordinary inhabitant of the planet and could not possibly arouse the slightest suspicion from any passer-by they might encounter. Not only could NGTRX move freely using its limbs and body, he could also communicate fluently with other bipeds via the Telepatic.

By now night had fallen. Now and then the distant lights of buildings twinkled on the horizon. NGTRX in his disguise reached something that looked in the dark like a bridge – he seemed to hear the burble of water flowing below. The Teremtak crawled forwards first, but at once they heard its alarm whistle, a hiss, and its claws scratching, followed by a heavy splash.

It was uncomfortable for NGTRX to go down under the bridge, so PWGDRK did it. With some difficulty he managed to extract the Teremtak from the water – despite being cautious, it had fallen into the stream through a hole in the bridge. It had not suspected the hole to be there, since the bipeds' machine had only just driven across.

'A trap,' PWGDRK figured. 'They're aware of our arrival already!'

NGTRX had serious doubts about that. They slowly moved on, got across the bridge and soon noticed that the muddy strip, along which they were advancing, divided into two offshoots between some clumps of black brushwood. There in the middle rose a leaning post with a piece of wooden board nailed to it. The post was hardly sticking in the ground, and the pointed end of the board was aimed at the western part of the nocturnal horizon.

On command the Teremtak cast the greenish light of its six eyes at the post, and there they saw the inscription LOWER MYCISKA– 5KM.

The board was rotting and the inscription, which they could only just decipher, was badly faded.

'The relic of a previous civilisation,' PWGDRK put forward the suggestion. From inside his quarters NGTRX aimed the Telepatic's outlet at the board. SIGNPOST, he read off its rear outlet. He glanced at PWGDRK – it was rather strange.

'The fabric of the post is cellulosoidal wood, eaten away by mould of the type *Arbacetulia Papyraceata Garg*,' said PWGDRK, after conducting field analysis.

'That would indicate a pre-stone-splitting civilisation.'

He illuminated the lower part of the post. At its foot they found pressed into the mud a scrap of cellulosoidal, thin material with words printed on it – it was just a small scrap.

Above our cit...

morning a sputn...

at seven fourte...

– could be deciphered. The Telepatic translated this fragmentary inscription, and they looked at each other in amazement.

'The board is pointing into the sky,' said NGTRX, 'that would make sense.'

'Yes. LOWER MYCISKA must be the name of their

permanent sputnik.'

'Nonsense. How can they have sputniks if they aren't capable of planing pieces of wood straight?' asked NGTRX from inside the artificial biped.

For some time they debated this unclear point. They illuminated the post from the other side and noticed an indistinct, poorly carved inscription: 'Maria iz fab'.

'It must be an abbreviation for their sputnik's elliptical data,' said PWGDRK.

He was rubbing Phosphectoric Paste onto the next part of the inscription to bring out the last trace of the faded letters, when out of the darkness the Teremtak gave a faint warning ultrahiss.

'Look out! Hide!' NGTRX communicated to PWGDRK. Instantly they switched off the Teremtak, PWGDRK retreated with it and the Aldemonico to the very edge of the muddy strip, while NGTRX also stepped back a bit from the middle of the road, to avoid being too easily seen, and froze in anticipation.

Someone was walking towards them. At first it seemed to be a rational biped, because it was moving along upright, but it wasn't walking straight. The two-legged creature, as became increasingly evident, was following complex wavy lines from one edge of the Sticky Strip to the other. PWGDRK immediately began to record these curves, when the observation grew even more complicated. For no apparent reason, the creature took a sort of dive ahead of itself; there was a resounding splosh and some dismal growling. For a while it moved along, he was fairly certain, on all fours, but suddenly it grew again. Tracing a sinusoidal wave of rumbling on the surface of the Sticky Strip, it was coming nearer and nearer. Now it seemed to be emitting wailing and moaning noises all at once.

'Record! Record and translate! What are you waiting for?' NGTRX hissed angrily at the Telepatic, shut inside the artificial biped. He too was listening in some dismay to the mighty bellowing of the thing approaching.

'Woo-oo ha ha! Woo-oo ha ha! Walla walla woo-oo ha ha!' it resounded, flooding the entire vicinity in noise. The Telepatic's rear outlet was quivering nervously, but it still showed Zero.

'Why is it turning loops like that? Is it remote controlled?' said the baffled PWGDRK, cowering over the Aldemonico at the edge of the Strip.

The creature was very close now. Just as it passed the rotting post, NGTRX emerged from the sidelines, went up to it, and switched the Telepatic on to transmission.

'Good evening, Sir,' said the Telepatic in an endearing tone in the biped's language, modulating its voice with exceptional proficiency, while by tightening a spring inside, NGTRX deftly arranged the mask into a polite smile. This too was part of the Aldebaranians' diabolical plan. They had a routine for conquering alien planets.

'Eeeeeh? Fa – faa!' replied the Creature and stopped, swaying slightly. Gradually it brought its eyes close to the face of the artificial biped. NGTRX didn't even shudder.

'Higher intelligence, now we will make contact,' thought PWGDRK, hidden at the edge of the Strip, gripping the sides of the Aldemonico tightly. NGTRX set the Telepatic to Translation Alert, and there in his hiding-place, without the faintest murmur he feverishly began to unfold in his tentacles the *Instructions for First Tactile Contact*, embossed on a translucent Urdolister.

The solidly-built shape brought its eyes right up to the artificial biped's face, and let rip from its communication opening: 'Frrrranek! Wha – tha – faa!'

NGTRX barely had time to think: 'Is it in a phase of aggression? Why?' Desperately he pressed the Telepatic's Interglocococom gland, asking what the creature was saying.

'Nothing,' indicated the Peripatetic uncertainly through its rear outlet.

'What do you mean, nothing? I can hear it,' hissed

NGTRX without emitting the faintest murmur, just at the very moment when the inhabitant of the planet seized the rotten signpost in both hands, tore it from the ground with a monstrous crack and walloped the artificial biped across the head with a backhand stroke. The armour-clad coating of Plastefolium could not withstand the terrible blow. The dummy crashed face down into the black gunk, along with the devastated NGTRX, who never even heard the prolonged howl with which his enemy declared his victory. Though only grazed by the end of the stick, the Telepatic was ejected into the air with terrible force; by some lucky accident it landed on all fours right beside the totally petrified PWGDRK.

'It's attacking!' wailed PWGDRK, and with the last of his strength he aimed the Aldemonico into the darkness.

His tentacles were trembling as he pulled the trigger appendix – and a swarm of softly droning Gnitchers zoomed into the night, bringing mass death and destruction. Suddenly he heard them about-turn, spin furious circles and crawl back into the Aldemonico's loading cyst at lightning speed.

He drew air into his cuttlefishy nostrils to investigate, and shuddered. Now he understood: the Creature had put up a protective, impenetrable barrier of ethyl hydroxide! He was defenceless.

With a drooping tentacle he tried hard to open fire again, but the Gnitchers just seethed dismally inside the loading bladder – not a single one of them so much as put out its killer sting. He could sense, he could hear that the Creature was trudging towards him – a second, monstrous blast slashed through the air, making the ground shake and flattening the Teremtak in the mud. Dropping the Aldemonico, PWGDRK grabbed the Telepatic in his tentacles and leaped into the undergrowth.

'Aa, yer poxy sonofabitch, oi'll christen yer wi' a cart pole!!' echoed like thunder behind him. The air was filled with the toxic fumes of poison, which the Creature never stopped expelling from its communication openings, making PWGDRK choke.

Straining with all his might, he jumped across a ditch, fell under a bush and froze motionless. PWGDRK was not particularly brave, but he never lowered his professional standards as a scientist. The insatiable curiosity of a researcher was his ruin. He was just struggling to read the Creature's first translated sentence from the Telepatic's outlet: 'Offspring of a quadrupedal mammal of the female sex, to which part of a four-wheeled vehicle is applied within a religious ritual relying on...' when the air howled above his cuttlefishy head and a lethal blow struck him.

Just before noon, the first ploughmen from Myciska found Franek Jolas, who was sleeping like the dead in a ditch on the edge of the forest. On waking he declared that yesterday he had had a spat with a driver from the Base, Franek Pajdrak, who'd been accompanied by some horrible sticky things. At almost the same time Józek Guskowiak came rushing from the forest, shouting that 'there be summat battered an' injured lying at the crossroads'.

Only then was the entire village drawn there.

They really did find some horrible things at the crossroads – one behind the ditch, and a second by the hole where the post had been, next to a big doll with a partly smashed head.

A few kilometres further on they also found a rocket standing in a hazel grove.

Without saying much, the villagers set to work briskly. That afternoon there wasn't a single trace of the Astromat left. Old Jolas used the Anamargopratexin alloy to patch the roof of his pigsty, which had needed fixing for ages, and eighteen pairs of pretty good boot soles were made out of the Aldemonico's skin, tanned the domestic way. The Telepatic, universal Interglocococom and all, was fed to the pigs, as too were the remains of the Teremtak; no one dared give the earthly remnants of the two Aldebaranians to their livestock

– the animals might fall sick. So they were weighed down with stones and thrown into the pond.

The citizens of Myciska philosophised for the longest time over what to do with the Astromat's Ultrapenetron Engine, until Jedrek Barcioch, who had just arrived for the haymaking, adapted this hyperspatial device for distilling pretty good hooch. Anka, Józek's sister, artfully stuck the doll's broken head together with egg white and took it to the second-hand shop in town. She demanded three thousand zloty for it, but the salesman wouldn't agree to this price – you could see the cracks.

As a result, the only thing noticed by the sharp-eyed reporter from the Echo, who came in the office car that afternoon to do a report, was Jolas' new, very decent clothing, pulled off the artificial biped. He even felt a fold of the material in his fingers, admiring its high quality.

'I got it from my brother in America,' replied Jolas languidly, when asked about the origin of the Syntectaric fabric. So in the article he churned out that evening, the journalist only reported on the successful course of the agricultural purchasing campaign – without so much as a single word about how the Invasion of Earth from Aldebaran was defeated.

RECONSTRUCTED

ORIGINALS

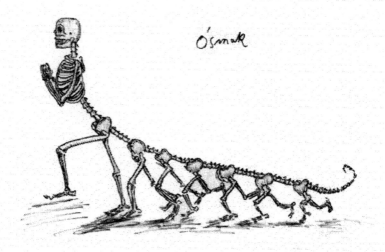

Every Little Helps
by Frank Cottrell Boyce

Reviewed by Stanisław Lem

AGAINST A BACKGROUND of software assaults on power stations, banks and news media, Frank Cottrell Boyce has imagined a stuxnet apocalypse in a banal, early 21st century setting – a period when most people obtained their food from large retail silos with impenetrable names like Tesco, Asda and Walmart. A customer tries to pay for her shopping at one of these – a Tesco. Her debit card is rejected. Embarrassed and anxious, searching her bag for cash, she notices that the young man buying a wrap (duck and hoi sin sauce) and a smoothie (mango) at the next till has also had his card rejected. Likewise the man buying bedding plants and beer at the self-checkout. Anxiety and embarrassment turn to indignation as the customers realize that this is the store's fault, not theirs. None of the tills are accepting payment and the cash dispensing machines in the concourse have frozen. The manager closes all checkouts, and as a gesture of goodwill allows those customers who have already had their cards rejected to take their shopping home. Those who haven't yet reached the checkout are disgruntled. If only they'd been quicker, they would have got their shopping free. Those already at the checkouts are even more disgruntled – if only they'd added a few bottles of whisky or a plasma screen TV to their trolleys, they would have got a real bargain. When the manager tries to contact software support, he discovers that all Tesco stores are having the same problem. But it's not just

Tesco. When the relief manager arrives his card has been rejected at a petrol station and at his bank. The driver who turns up with the evening consignment of produce has a similar tale. Little by little the truth appears – money itself is under attack. It still exists of course – as cash – but it has been disconnected from its own electronic dimension. Money isn't dead but it is in a coma – trapped, immobilised and amnesiac in vaults and wallets. It can't be moved. It can't remember who owns it. And when money stops moving, so does everything else. Because in a digital age, money is not something you hand over when the deal is done. Money is the medium through which the deal travels. Maybe your credit with O2 or EDF is good to the end of the month but their credit is measured minute by minute. Money is the haemoglobin that transports the oxygen of information around the body economic. When the money stops flowing, everything begins to suffocate. Within hours, ISPs and power supplies – the only means to fight the virus – are crashing. For years civilisation has been happily afloat on a digital sea. Now that sea dries up leaving behind a flotsam of purely physical objects – cars, fridges, houses – all disconnected from their insurance policies, mortgages, credit ratings.

You can imagine what mayhem Stephen King would make with this material, or what unsettling illuminations Borges might conjure. Cottrell Boyce, on the other hand, is English and paints with an English palette. He stays in his Ballardian superstore – where no one is really sure of the scale of the event. He introduces some Wellesian logical escalations – the store suddenly fills with hundreds of customers, alerted to the End of Money by Twitter, hoping to use their physical cash to panic-buy staples. And he creates a John Wyndhamish hero – the manager trying to prevent looting and defend the order of things. He closes the store. He collects all the cash from the tills, puts it safely under lock and key and brings down the shutters as though this were a retail park Siege of Krishnapur.

Here author and the manager both face the same problem – namely that you can't have a siege if the troops inside the castle are mostly middle aged women in overalls and the besieging army is entirely composed of their families and friends. In no time at all, the women have invited the enemy in and spontaneous parties are enlivening the ice cream and alcohol aisles. They dance to the in-store muzak, munch popcorn while watching the DVDs. Surely the computer glitch will soon be put right, and in the meantime here's an opportunity not to be missed. It's only when the delivery lorries fail to arrive with the next morning's bread and milk, that workers and shoppers grasp what the manager already knows – that this is no glitch and it's not restricted to one store, or one county, perhaps not even to one country. He uses the moment – and his tannoy system – to try to seize control, calling a meeting of his staff. But any thoughts he might have of instituting a benign dictatorship are soon brushed aside. These women know each other, know the store and know what needs to be done. Without waiting for instructions, they create sleeping areas by clearing the shelves and handing out duvets and pillows. When the electricity fails and the meat in the freezers begins to defrost, they seize the seasonal barbecue sets and organize a massive cook out in the car park. Those who worked in the bakery take control of the ovens, keeping them going with charcoal and waste material and using the flour from the home baking section to keep the bread coming. To keep the mood cheerful they even stage treats – a bowling party using family-sized coke bottles as skittles and of course trolley races. When they introduce rationing – of water, chocolate, alcohol and bread – no one objects because "you've had enough" is what our Mothers have always said to us. It's a spontaneously occurring feminist utopia – a 'matrigarchy' – held together by an unspoken, unexplored fear of what might be going on elsewhere, where people have less sense.

The manager and his "management team" (two trainees

and a security guard) busy themselves trying to find out what is going on elsewhere. They work their way through the stock of mobile phones – with their pre-installed, free credits – trying to access the internet or call a number. They watch from the roof for passing planes, marauding looters or cities burning in the distance. When none of these tropes appear, that's somehow even more unsettling. It is, as they literally say, quiet, too quiet.

The women, in the meantime, "just get on with it". When produce runs low they set off into the unknown world of their own neighbourhood in search of fresh supplies. (Spoiler Alert) If you're expecting some Mad Max world of petrol wars or mobs of dehumanised Cormac McCarthy zombies, you'll be disappointed. Instead they encounter a gang of cheery old men living in the sheds on their own allotments, happy to trade potatoes, leeks and carrots for tinned goods, toilet paper and spices. The hunting party is back in-store with a truck load of food that same afternoon. They've glimpsed an England where the Blitz spirit and a "mustn't grumble" attitude have rebooted society and – disappointingly for this reviewer – created a Chestertonian merrie English feudalism, with every superstore transformed into a self-sustaining village. I suppose the surprising thing here is the positive image that it gives of these supermarkets, which were generally seen as a blight that destroyed small towns, before dying away themselves as a result of their over-dependence on cars. On the positive side, Cottrell Boyce finds a poetry in the display cabinets and discount shelves that you would more normally associate with hedgerows and riverbanks, alert to the idea that the stock on the shelves is now irreplaceable. Never again will mankind be able to browse tinned beef from Argentina or powdered cook-in sauces from China. These things are now like the gunpowder and ironware that Crusoe rescues from his ship – indispensible souvenirs of a civilisation that has now sunk forever beneath the horizon.

On the negative side, with material like this, one might be forgiven for wishing he had taken as a role model not John Wyndham but that altogether more visionary Englishman – Olaf Stapledon. A writer of Stapledon's ambition, and knowledge of economics – not to mention gardening – might have swept us through different societies – rural economies where money was already marginal for instance, or slum neighbourhoods that live on the crumbs of great riches. He might have created a pageant of Life after Money and shown us new elites rising and falling. Cottrell Boyce sadly wraps the story up quickly with a kind of thriller plot, involving a messianic cult that has grown up around the manager who – unable to accept what is going on – becomes obsessed by the cash in his safe – hypnotised both by its vestigial power and its current uselessness. Exhausted by the economy of petty kindnesses and disputes over which he presides, he comes to appreciate – adore even – the extraordinary power of money. It's simply too brilliant an invention to disappear. It will surely reassert itself. And he prepares for its reappearance by assembling a posse that will go around retrieving cash from abandoned bank vaults. It's a plot which – while closing off a lot of fascinating avenues – does supply some belated thrills. And in the end the manager's restless quest for useless cash does give an emotional resonance to one of the book's few real insights – the fact that capitalism of that period was so reliant on superaccelerated information exchange means that even one missed beat could bring the whole structure crashing down.

Pied Piper

Adam Roberts

A COMMERCIAL EXCAVATION in Poland broke inadvertently upon the cavern of the *Sang-Mangeant* – the Santamanga, we called them, though how far from saintly they were! A light that blinds you with the many flakes of its brightness. Tens of thousands, revealed in a tangle of limbs in the darkness, and breaking out howling upon the earth. They were like wasps; they were like scorpions and rats; the vampire of legend, only real, and bitter in their hunger for our lives.

They spread across Europe and into Russia, devouring all they encountered, and they spared nobody. Pale faces, and their mouths took colour from their meals. They were always hungry. Daylight hurt them as a hailstorm might, but it did not kill them. And we said: 'These are monsters from storybooks,' because we hoped that storybook remedies might redeem us. But the old ways did not stem their advance; for it took too much time to deploy them, and by the time we had destroyed one of the Santamanga a dozen more humans had fallen victim to the plague. They swarmed at night by the millions, and until first light touched the bell towers and slanted roofs; they were everywhere. The sunset mocked our spilt blood.

The governments tried to handle the situation as governments do, with armies and weapons and assaults from land and sky. They made new guns, and primed them with projectiles filled with an ingenious American gel – irradiated with ultraviolet light and luminous. It was effective up to a point, but not cheap; for each bullet cost $1,750, and myriad bullets were fired, and dozens needed to strike their target before they were disabled. By the time the first marines were airlifted in the plague had spread so far that it could no longer be contained by so complicated and costly an approach. Scorch the Santamanga with whatsoever fires and bombs you liked, they did not die: still they roamed on, and their burns healed. Shoot them with ordinary bullets and they roared and rushed you and tore your rifle from your hands, your hands from your arms. The new UV-bullets were not in sufficient supply. Then there was a dispute between the American factories that produced them and the American government about payment, or tax irregularities, or something, and the supply was halted.

So it was that we found ourselves, suddenly, on the edge of annihilation.

Who saved us? Who but *he*.

He lived in a compound in central Spain, where the hills are polished to indigo by the heat of the sun: where the cactus grow and where palm trees scrum together around waterholes. There were conflicting stories about how long he had been alive.

The representatives of seven nations came to supplicate him, and he promised to rid the world of the Santamanga altogether if we agreed to meet his price: a trillion dollars, and the right for the territory around his compound to be recognized as a sovereign state, under his sole rule, an enclave within Spain perfectly independent of EU jurisdiction. He was promised all this, and eagerly, provided only that he rid the world of the vampires.

So he set out. He took a village priest, a humble Andalusian churchman, to bless the oceans – seven trips in a jet-plane, all in the same day, girdling the earth. And then the natural cycle of the climate became our ally. For from the oceans moisture evaporated upwards, holy water now, into the clouds; and from the clouds precipitated down a holy rainfall. So it was that every shower, from drizzle to monsoon, bit the flesh of the Santamanga like acid, and melted them in screams of agony. And within three months not one of the them were left alive, save for a few desiccated figures dug under the sands of the Gobi desert like bugs, and growing weaker and drier by the day. For even the Santamanga need *water*.

How the world cheered! Such celebrations! Gratitude poured upon him from a million letters and emails; he was granted awards and prizes – Nobel's Peace, the Vatican's Golden Medal, a dozen others. He did not actively refuse these honours, but neither did he travel to collect them. Simply, he waited for the fulfillment of his deal.

The governments of the world met to discuss the status of his enclave, and the discussions protracted, for there were complicated legal discussions to be undergone. 'For was it not a *humanitarian* act?' they asked, publicly. 'How could such heroism ever be measured in terms of mere *money*?' 'And was it not an insultingly *simple* stratagem?' they asked, in private. 'Any of us might have thought of it. It cost him barely a few thousand dollars – and the Santamanga are destroyed now. Why should we waste a trillion on this one individual?'

He pressed for payment of his fee, and the governments deferred payment on the grounds that they needed the money for reconstruction of Asia and Europe, that had been ravaged by the vampires; and then they held out on the grounds of various legal technicalities; and then on the grounds that payment should be in terms of release from duties of tax and of educational and cultural credits. Eventually they declined to pay him altogether, on the grounds that, legally, the Nobel Prize money had constituted the first payment of reward, and that since he refused to travel to Stockholm to collect that prize he had in effect declined all remuneration for his actions.

They did not think they would need him again.

But of course they did, for something had broken in the simple functioning of the world, and evils that mankind had hitherto only dreamed had become violently real. Locusts the size of bats filled the skies. Blood rained from the heavens. Much worse: corpses fought their way through the loose-packed dirt of graves and walked again, undead.

They poisoned and assaulted the living, and wasted the land. They devoured people, not for nutrition – since, being dead, they needed none – but in an empty rage for destruction. No weapon could prevent them. Limbs or torsos peppered with bullets meant nothing to them; destroying their heads only made them fiercer, as with ants. No holy water bothered them.

The covenant of death had been broken, it seemed.

Worse still, in Scotland, it was reported, a scientist had stitched together body parts and reanimated the corpus with a triple-modulated ionic charge. He made monster after monster, not content with assembling body-parts from human corpses, he grafted the limbs of animals on men's torsos, or the heads of dogs and cattle on the necks of the deceased. Not undead, but rather re-living, these creatures moved with the ferocious purpose of a new and terrible form of vitality. A dozen such beasts were made, before the creatures turned on their creator and held him down, and pulled the flesh from his bones in fist-sized chunks. Then, mad with incoherent rage and remorse, the beasts spilled into the Caledonian forests. They killed where they chanced upon people, and wrecked all they laid their hands upon.

These trials were most terrible afflictions – hundreds of thousands died, millions were overwhelmed with grief and terror. It was the end of the world, surely. It was the Devil himself at work amongst us. The Santamanga, that we had thought the worst, had been nothing more than malign John-Baptists, crying the way. The ultimate evil would burst, before the year ended, from Temple Mount and roll the globe into the darkness of his cloak.

No priestly exorcism had any effect upon these awful manifestations of Last Days. No scientist could develop an effective countermeasure.

There was a popular upsurge: mass rallies, the spontaneous outpouring of the will of people all about the world. *He* had saved us before; *he* could save us again. We must pay him the money – for why hold back some sum of dollars when the alternative was the very end of the entire world? We must crawl on our bellies to ask his forgiveness.

So representatives of the superpowers, and of the five great faiths, and the world's three most beautiful movie stars, and a great delegation of the desperate travelled to central Spain. 'Forgive us!' they cried. 'We wronged you! Save us again, and we shall pay you what we owe you, and anything more that you ask of us. Can you help us?'

He met the leaders of the delegation upon the roof of his building, where the sun was hottest. The terrace garden had wilted. He stood amongst those parched plants, tall in a white linen suit and his sunglasses were circles of swimming-pool blue. He looked over the landscape. 'I love this land,' he said, 'because it resembles unwritten parchment. But I discover that human beings, mostly, loathe the unwritten page. You must pay me forty trillion dollars, and give me the whole of the Iberian Peninsula as my fiefdom, and I will rid you of these zombies and creatures, and solve the other problems.'

Anything! Anything!

Binding contracts were signed, and witnessed, and seals were placed upon them. Everything was witnessed and transmitted and sorted. And he nodded his approval.

So this is what he did. He travelled, first, to Scotland, and was taken through the army perimeter into the castle of the murdered scientist. There he gathered together the materials to replicate the reanimating technology; and he worked for a week to master the technology. 'It is a simple device,' he announced eventually, carrying his portable version of the reanimating machine on a strap about his shoulders.

The zombies, he said, were animated by a principle of undeath. The scientist's Frankenstein machine gave life back to dead matter. Direct the beam of the latter upon the former and positive would cancel out negative. So troops were equipped, and they tracked the undead, wherever the zombies roamed; and they fired the ionizing blast at their chests: and the undead, made alive again, fell to the ground, for their motile principle had been cancelled. As death ends life, so life ends death.

He set up a workshop, with his own employees assembling the devices, and issued them to citizen armies. These were shipped to the five continents, and, individual by individual, the undead were given back life, and rendered inert.

As for the original Frankenstein creatures – hideous, terrifying – these were living still in the northern Scottish wildernesses; and some had stolen boats and travelled further north, to the Polar wastes; for their life essence cried out to the chill and deserted places.

He tracked them in a small plane, himself and his second-in-command, and this is what he did: he sprayed them, when he found them, with an enzyme that dissolved away the threads stitching their body-parts together. They fell into pieces.

Now, the life that had been given them could not be ungiven. It lived on in these lopped limbs and heads, but eyeless arms scrabbled to the water's edge, and eyeless legs thrashed and kicked their way there, and eyeless torsos crawled like inchworms, and all slopped under the sea, to roam the unlit ocean floors. And he gathered the severed, still living heads into a great sack, and threw them all into the mid-ocean, with stones in their mouths.

And there were other signs of the end times, but he addressed them.

The blood rain fell only from certain clouds, marked with ink-black striations, and these he seeded from above, using wide-winged planes, so that they rained their blood into over-fished seas, where the nutrients brought forth great crops of sealife. He fished in the air with great nets and captured vast numbers of the locusts plaguing the land, and intensively-farmed them, telling the world to rejoice in their coming; for beasts of such size rendered a great quantity of meat for a world starving after manifold sufferings. He established locust farms on four continents, and instead of destroying the wild swarms he tempted them into net-ceilinged valleys with choice lures, and he raised them there. Protein for the people.

'Now I must have my reward,' he said.

The vice-President of the United States herself went to his compound to discuss the terms. 'We *will* pay you!' they said. 'We have promised! But to transfer so huge a sum in one lump would collapse the world economy – and this at a time when the population has been cut in half, and tax revenues severely depleted! Moreover, to hand over the whole of Ibieria would be to flout the democratic traditions of a sovereign nation! Let us pay you forty million dollars a month, every month, until the debt is repaid; and let us fund your campaign to run for election as President of Spain – such is the gratitude of the world that the Spanish people will surely vote for you.'

'This,' he said, angrily, 'is not what was agreed. Unless you pay me what you agreed, you shall make me angry.'

'But you must negotiate with us,' they said. 'We ask only that! It is the way of international relations! Negotiations, not unilateral demands, are the currency of politics. You are a world figure now. Negotiate, and we will arrive at a mutually satisfying resolution.'

But he refused their offers, and withdrew himself.

Of course the evils continued. We had merely been cutting the heads off the Hydra; we have not stabbed its heart.

And its heart was the Devil himself. The land around Jerusalem became hot, and people could no longer live there; the buildings of the city crumbled to dust. The Pope himself travelled to the site to exorcise it; but no sooner had his helicopter touched down than a chasm opened in the dusty ground and swallowed it and him and he was never seen again.

The Last Days were upon us.

All eyes turned to *him* – for who could save us if he could not? But he was not to be found. He had withdrawn himself from the world. The moon turned red; wormwood and pestilence; the ground shook; the Mediterranean flooded into North Africa. The world was coming to an end. 'This is *his* punishment!' we said. 'It is because we did not pay him what was agreed! He punishes us by withholding his help.'

But then, from nowhere, and at the last moment, he reappeared. He walked into Jerusalem alone, with a small backpack, and a gasmask, and a silver suit, past terrors and wonders. Then, watched by the world's surveillance satellites, his image broadcast on all media, he drew a hyperpentagram upon Temple Mount itself, and spoke words of unprecedented power and charm. A crack spread starfish-wise, and a low thunderous noise rolled from horizon to horizon. In a steam of midges Satan himself appeared.

And our spirits sank to our bowels, for suddenly we thought: he is calling forth the Devil personally to do his bidding. '*This* is his punishment!' we wailed, in horrible comprehension. 'He has unleashed Satan upon us!'

But we were wrong. He had not come to destroy the world; he had come – alone – to vanquish Satan. And that is what he did.

He did not assault the Devil with swords, nor attempt to overpower him with incantations; but instead he used reason, a more powerful snare than magic (for has not Reason challenged and overcome Magic across the world today?). He talked, and the Devil listened. He told the Devil's true nature to the Devil.

This is what he said: 'We know that despair is the greatest sin. We both know that you, Satan, the fount and superfluity of wickedness, are the Universe's greatest sinner. It follows that you are the most despairing creature the cosmos has ever known.'

And the Devil groaned, as if, at last, somebody had plumbed the depths of his being; as if finally somebody had understood – he, Satan, the great depressive. He moaned with pitiful recognition. And he hurled himself downward, seeping through the cracks and plunging through the eddies of magma to the core of the Earth, its dense metal core, where he lies to this day, like a depressed man who cannot rise from bed, trapped and impotent in his own misery.

Our saviour took to his feet and walked out of ruined Jerusalem.

'Look upon this,' he said, to the whole of the world. 'He was your child and I have taken him from you.' And *this*, although we did not realize it at first, was his revenge. This action was his punishment. At first we held our breaths, and barely believed it. Satan himself had been defeated, and we could only rejoice.

The United Nations voted him formal thanks. But he refused all money, or reward, and slipped away from the world. Who knows where he has gone?

In a year we had rebuilt many of the world's broken structures. Within a decade there was a spike in the birth-rate as we began to replenish the world with a new generation. For Satan was gone, and the skies no longer rained blood, nor did locusts swarm, nor the Santamanga afflict us, or the zombies or the Frankenstein beasts. All that was magical passed away from the world.

There is an inertia in the ways of the world. Many people continued religious practice and ritual. But the destruction of Satan had immobilized God, of whom the Devil is a portion. At a stroke all the faiths of the world were emptied of meaning. Over time most people abandoned temples and churches, and lived in a purely material cosmos. For those of us, such as I myself, who had lived through the horrors of the last era of the supernatural, this was a blessing. But a new generation was born, without the savour of transcendental meaning, who came into the world as mere sophisticated automata. There is no light in their eyes, when I talk with them; they talk logic and sufficiency, and the world has grown grey from their breath.

This, as we now understand, is how *he* has punished us – and punished us justly, for we promised to reward him for his actions and then we reneged on our promise. So this is what he did: he took away the causes of our suffering, and therefore he took away the wellspring of our souls. There is no God without the Devil. The world had once been pied, as all beauty is; but he removed the contrast, and he muted the colours. It is no longer a pied place; it is uniform. Our children inherit us, and they are tall, and strong, and rational. But they are without spirit and without faith, and they are without the capacity for wonder. The colour has gone. I tell children today stories of the old days and they are neither enchanted nor terrified, for enchantment and terror have gone out of the universe. That is what he took away. He came to a particolour world and left it monochrome.

On the other hand, our new world does possess a great deal of ergonomic and splendidly functional civic architecture.

The Melancholy

Toby Litt

CHIEF ENGINEER CHANDI Kane, Four-Oh-Four-Six-Oh-Six, making Verbal Report on recent and I say avoidable loss of Appliance named 'Hector' ridden by Local Application '13-13' during subsurface exploration of Jupiter's moon 'Europa'.

This report for immediate and urgent attention of Joint Chiefs of Staff. November Sixteenth, Twenty Sixty-Eight A.D.

Though you're never going to hear this, are you? Because it'll never make it that far up the chain of command. Because who is ever going to listen to me? I mean – *me*? Chandi Kane. 'Insane Chandi Kane.'

Cut last para, and continue –

Mr Chairman, Mr Vice-Chairman, gentlemen. This is not about me. I know it's going to seem that way, but whatever has happened in my personal life recently has nothing to do – nothing at all to do with what I believe is a very important discovery.

If you'll excuse me, I'll need to give you a background briefing first, then you'll see my line of argument.

Application 13-13 – (everyone who works on her calls her 'Lucky', for pretty obvious reasons) – Application 13-13 became operational fifty years six months ago. She has done ten different tours of duty in widely varying terrains. Her first time out was some basic mineral extraction stuff on the moon. That must have been pretty boring for software of her size and complexity, but she performed faultlessly. Please take note of that.

Each time an Application finishes a tour, they are beamed back to Earth as a speed–of–light infostream. And all of the valuable operational experience that has been gained – we call it their 'chops' – that comes back, too.

But, and now this is important – this is really the thing – every time 13-13 came back, just like every Application, she wasn't distributed or networked in any way. Of course, we wanted to analyse the changes in her – see if there was anything we could learn. But the founders of the program discovered early on that it was important to keep each Application separate from all the others, and from info in general. So what they did was, they gave each of them a physical form on Earth – a Tank they could inhabit so they could keep moving, keep perceiving.

When I first saw it, Lucky's Tank was a big old heap of a thing which spent most of its time in storage out in this big facility – 'The Peristyle' – here in Greenland. And when 13-13 came back, every five years, she rode that very same Tank until she was ready to be beamed off to wherever her next tour of duty was.

I came on board the 13-13 maintenance team just before she returned from her seventh tour. I can remember how excited we were as the last terabytes came through, and we were able to activate the Tank. You see, the team all liked 13-13. It may not appear to be very scientifically rigorous, but it's hard not to give each Application a personality. And I'd been told by the others 13-13 was something special, and I was lucky to be working on her.

As soon as she started to ride the Tank, I could see how graceful she was. Her movements were maybe a little slower than an average Application, but always very efficient, very considered. This made our lives a whole heap easier. Some of the Applications develop a style that gets stuff done extremely fast but is so herky-jerky that they're going to shake their

Appliance, their off-world Tank, to pieces in two or three years. You could tell Lucky wasn't like that. She was kind of a dancer, which isn't what you'd say for most of these robots.

I've worked on lots of other Applications in my career, but Lucky always remained my favourite. I felt we were safe with her. She would never go haywire and crush us.

For 13-13's interface, the original designer used his daughter's voice. She spoke very clearly, in an old-fashioned way, and that seemed to fit 13-13's character, too.

By now you've probably dismissed me as any kind of a reliable witness. But I'm talking here about some very sophisticated machinery. Systems which have been able to refine themselves and evolve over years of intense in-the-field operationality.

Sometimes, I'd be alone with Lucky, working on installing the new graces and flows, and I would hear her making noises. It wasn't exactly music, more like very complicated rhythms going clickety-click-click. When I asked her to explain, it turned out she'd been using some of her spare capacity to run up through the irrational numbers. What I liked was that she wasn't doing this as fast as she could have done. She was savoring it; using it as background music. To her it was like humming would be to you. I never knew another Application do anything like that. 13-13 was quirky.

We sent her off for her eighth tour, for another five years away. A lot can happen in that time. I met someone, fell in love, got married, had my baby, Vishnu – and I was promoted, of course. And when 13-13 got back, I didn't spend so much time with her. But, to me, she seemed just the same – graceful, considerate.

We'd had to do some work on her Tank. It was getting so old that we'd needed to replace whole chunks of it, just so it would move. Even in a low humidity atmosphere, there's corrosion. Over the years, piece after piece of the original Tank had been exchanged for something new – better alloy, better functionality. There was maybe five per cent left of what she'd started with. We're getting to the crucial point here.

Ten years ago, we beamed her off – had a party, wished her well. And then, when she was due to return again, we went over her Tank once more – refitting it for our favourite baby.

It's only with the spare time I've had in the past few months that I've worked out the really important thing. By the time 13-13 came back the last time, there wasn't a single component left in the Tank that had been there in the beginning. I really think this must have meant something to her.

I mean, 13-13 didn't mention it, but I'm convinced she must have noticed. Because it took her a whole day before she even made a movement. It was like she was trying to find a hint of the old stuff in amongst all the new. Even though, for an Application as fast as her, she could have worked that out in a millisecond. I think she was hoping we'd been kind, and left her just a little piece of herself – a badge or a rivet or a wire; some arrangement of atoms to give her continuity. You may think this is nonsense, but it's what I've come to believe, thinking it over.

We sat around for twenty-four hours, waiting for Lucky to do something. And even though the Tank hadn't moved, I swear there was an atmosphere in the hall – like the great metal thing was brooding. The peristyle felt completely different from a week before, when we were prepping everything, and 13-13 was still beaming back.

When she finally did move, it pretty soon became obvious that 13-13 had changed. For the first time ever, I saw her be clumsy. Her walk wasn't pretty any more. She didn't hurt anyone or hit anything, but a couple of times she scraped bits of herself up – took the edges off her caterpillar tracks. And, when there wasn't anything going on, she would pick at herself. I've never seen anything like it. It was like she was starting to feel itchy inside.

The whole team observed this, but there really wasn't anything we could do about it. Our job was just to get her ready for her next tour as fast as possible. Europa is a pretty hostile environment. And but for most of the time, there's no contact with Earth at all – Lucky was going to be deep beneath the surface, without a relay. Her task was to map ice-fields that change almost by the hour. It's never-ending, down there in the dark, but the geologists are starting to get a sense of how the place works – its rhythms.

We beamed 13-13 off to her brand new Tank, had the usual party when she went subsurface – and that's the last we ever heard of her.

That was five years and six months ago. Like I said, a lot of things can happen in that time. I fell out of love, got divorced, Vishnu got ill and didn't get better, I fell in and out of love again. And, I have to say, I was expecting to spend a lot of time alone with Lucky when she got back home. It would be something to do with myself. By the start of this year, I'd risen to heading up the team. I knew her better than anyone else. Now it was me telling rookie engineers how special Lucky was. How they were lucky to be working on her.

The day she failed to reestablish contact, we were really astonished. Appliances do get lost, now and again, but very rarely on somewhere like Europa. It's minus one hundred and fifteen degrees and total darkness, but there aren't any volcanos or anything. If she'd been in mechanical trouble, 13-13 would have returned straightaway to the surface.

So, they sent another Appliance to look for her. That was six months ago. They never found a trace.

I think you'll probably have guessed where this is headed. And I know what you're going to come back at me with. Yes, I did try to commit suicide a month after 13-13 failed to return. I took her disappearance very hard. I did not like the idea of all that empty time ahead of me, when I should have been helping improve her and record her and learn from her. My suicide attempt was serious. I was only prevented by the compassionate notice of my colleagues. I am grateful to them for saving me for life. And I feel that I am now fully recovered.

I therefore do not believe that I am projecting my own psychological state onto Lucky. But I am definitely asserting that what she did, on discovering she no longer had a home-body she recognised to return to, was make a rational decision. She decided at the very least that her new Appliance was the only real home she would ever have. So, she decided to stay in it. Which – in a hostile environment like Europa, where Appliances are designed to last twenty years maximum – amounted to suicide. In fact, I believe that 13-13 somehow disposed of herself as soon as she went beneath the surface of Europa. My suspicion is that she set off towards the moon's iron core and kept going until she found a place where ice was forming rapidly, and she got herself frozen in. She may still be there, counting up through the irrational numbers, or she may have been crushed flat, but she's never coming back.

You probably think I am unbalanced, or just plain wrong, but I assure you, gentlemen, you will never hear from 13-13. All the work and resources we invested in her has been lost – all the love, too.

And, yes, we do have an up-to-date backup of her. We have two backups housed in separate locations. And one of these is being sent off for a new tour of duty in twenty-four hours. But I've been watching this Lucky riding her Tank, and she's pitiful. She brooded for a day when we saddled her up. She's been scraping herself against anything she can find. She's picking at her surfaces. And I guarantee, in five year's time, you'll be wondering where this one's gotten lost, too.

That's why I've been trying to track down the scrapped parts of her original Tank. I thought that if I could find just one piece of it, and reinstall it, then this version of Lucky would sense that – and she'd be reconciled. Even the ID badge would have been enough. But it turns out we engineers are very efficient: every atom of the original Lucky has been melted down, made into something else.

I've spent a lot of time, sitting here with 13–13 v2, alone, in this big echoey hall. And I can see it inside her, all over her – the melancholy.

And I'm not just seeing myself; I promise you, I'm not.
This really isn't about me.
It's about her.
She's lost herself.
She's gone.

Toby

Annie Clarkson

RUTH TUTTED FOR the second time. I stopped tapping my fingers against the side of the chair and pushed them under my thigh.

'How long has it been?'

She checked the time and shrugged. 'Half an hour?'

We both sighed.

We were waiting in the old town hall. A museum of a building: domed roof with crumbling plaster, echoing corridors with leaded windows that didn't close properly. The weather seeped through and pooled on the parquet floor. It should have closed down years ago, but agencies like this one needed cheap office space.

Ruth faced away from me, standing at the opposite side of the corridor. Her skirt had a slit up the back, so I could just make out the shadow of her thighs. She looked exactly as she did the day I first saw her.

'How much longer do you think it will be?'

I shrugged, and stood up, ready to go to the bathroom again. But a door opened, releasing a cough of low-chattering voices. Our link-worker, Janet, popped her head out and winked. She held back the door.

We were back in front of the panel, sitting side by side in matching chairs, a semi-circle of faces staring back at us. The head of the panel began: 'Ruth. Jim. We considered our decision very carefully.'

It was one of those awful moments, waiting to hear, unable to read what he might say next. He glanced at his colleagues, and smiled momentarily.

'We're pleased to say you have been successful in your application to adopt. Congratulations.'

I waited for my response, and when it didn't arrive, I stumbled from my chair and shook hands with everyone in the room. I was prompted about my wife, still in her chair, head in hands, shaking.

'Was it a yes?' she asked.

A few laughs from the panel, as I said, 'Yes, yes. It was a yes. It's a yes.'

The night we made the decision, I came home from work and she was waiting, a four-pack of beers on the porch table. I could smell dinner cooking, a roast perhaps. And she was wearing red lipstick, hair down and wavy just the way I like it, and a low cut dress.

'Wow.'

I wanted to push her dress up, and take her, right there, on the table.

But she had other ideas. She opened a beer for me, patted the chair next to her, and pushed the brochure across the table.

It had been a long day. I wasn't ready to talk about it. But she was insistent.

'Please Jim. I know we've talked about it before, but I really think this is the answer.'

She pushed the brochure further towards me, and I saw it was less glossy than others, low budget. It had a picture of a family on the front. At the bottom in small letters was printed 'For people who can give an extra-special home.'

'I'll check dinner,' Ruth said, nodding as if to tell me I should open up the leaflet, read it. She walked towards the kitchen, the hem of her dress rubbing against her thighs, the fabric clinging to her.

I sighed, and opened the leaflet, scanning the contents list: *New to Adoption? How to Apply. The Matching Process. FAQs.*

'Do we have to do this now?' I shouted through to Ruth.

I could hear a clatter of cutlery and plates, the ping of the timer on the oven.

'One minute.'

I turned the pages of the leaflet, seeing picture after picture of families. I read the introduction about why so many new homes were needed. How Julia was capable of suffering as well as love; that John and Phillip were eager to please and their family took advantage of this; or how with Samantha the novelty wore off and the family maltreated and then abandoned her.

Ruth appeared carrying a plate of king prawns, still curled in their shells, oozing with oil and garlic – my favourite. She smiled, her I–want–to–please–you–so–much smile and we sat in silence, each picking prawns from the plate and biting them from their shells, juice leaking down our chins and fingers.

'What do you think?' she asked.

I thought back to my childhood, a specific day: my dad walking down the street away from me, suitcase banging against his legs, my shouts of 'Dad, where you going?' ignored. I ran after him down the next street, and my dad never once looked back at me.

'I don't know, Ruth, seriously. Is this what you want?'

She held onto my knees, her greasy fingers making wet marks on my trousers. She pressed her lips together and looked at me, not blinking, not smiling, not saying anything.

I'd never seen Ruth like this: lit up with excitement – and not a holiday kind of excitement, or the dancing kind, or that drunk and horny excitement I loved about her. This was different. As if it came from deep inside, built up over years and held there, until she couldn't hold it in anymore.

I had no deep urge to have a family. But Ruth, it seemed, did, and I loved Ruth. She wanted me to say yes.

There was a debris of prawn shells on our plates, insects flitting around the porch-light, and a low hum from the generator. And my wife, Ruth, was wrapping her arms round me and kissing me with a hunger I hadn't realised I'd been missing.

She knew I would say yes. There really wasn't any other answer.

Janet was a trained technician as well as a social worker. She had twenty years of experience when it came to adoptions, before that she worked in protection.

The first time she visited us, she told us 'It was a very stressful job. I was only there for two years and it was too much for me. The things you see, the things people tell you.' She raised her eyebrow as if she thought we would know what she was referring to. She sighed a very serious sigh.

She was in her fifties, perhaps, early sixties. It was difficult to tell, as it was obvious she'd had work, a face refit perhaps. She pulled out handfuls of forms from her bag, and started writing without speaking for a good ten minutes. 'I want to warn you. This is a difficult path. There will be upsets. It will disrupt life as you know it. There will be difficult behaviours, malfunctions, lock-outs, tantrums. This is not like having a normal child, there are far more complications.'

She asked us a lifetime of questions, warning us this was just the beginning. There would be more assessments. She ticked some boxes and said 'Yes, yes, yes, yes,' and then smiled, 'Can I have a look around the house?'

It had said in the brochure that the visit would include an inspection of the house, to see whether we had a 'suitable environment.' I told Ruth that cleaning under the stairs, windows inside and out, and repainting the front door were really not necessary. But Ruth wanted everything to be perfect, wanted to show the agency that our environment was not just suitable, but outstanding.

I stayed downstairs while Ruth gave Janet the tour. I could hear her upstairs: 'This would be their room, of course, we will redecorate, make it really nice. We want him or her to be really happy with us. We will provide a very loving home.'

I paced between kitchen and living room, opening the fridge to get myself a drink then closing it again without pouring it. I sat down, stood up again. I went onto the porch for a cigarette, even though Ruth had made me promise not to smoke while she was here.

Ruth shot me one of her I'll-kill-you looks, as she showed Janet out, but Janet didn't notice. She just clipped her heels against the stone path on her way to the gate, turned to wave and disappeared round the corner.

It was an idea in those days, a suggestion, a set of brochures.

But, after the panel approved our application, Ruth and I barely had the time to talk or relax. Her time was taken up with redecorating, choosing toys and bedding. Her new friend Louise was at our house all the time. They met in the preparation classes. Louise was also an adopter and similar to Ruth in a lot of ways. I often came home from work to find the two of them huddled together talking about life as a parent, about how this was their way of making up for their own missing childhoods.

Louise brought round boxes of hand-me-downs, which Ruth arranged in the cupboards and shelves in Toby's bedroom. She scoured the forums on the internet, messaging other adopters and she set up a blog-diary about her experience. There were technicians in and out, upgrading us, fitting new systems.

I found myself doing more of the cooking, heating up

meals she left out for me while she was at the shopping centre, or at support group, or upstairs in Toby's room lining up books for him and putting illuminous space transfers on the ceiling.

I didn't mind. It was good to see her like this. She was glowing with excitement, and although I might have liked to share this with her, or be the recipient of her enthusiasm, Ruth was the love of my life. If she was happy, I was happy.

I threw myself into work, staying late at the office, making sure we had extra money to provide for our growing family. I sometimes flicked through the parenting books she left lying around. I took long showers in the mornings, remembering the old days when we lounged on the porch, her bikini strap sliding down her shoulders, cleavage filmed in sweat.

A part of me wondered when things might get back to normal.

Home study interviews. Criminal records and social services checks. Forms signed and completed. Reports written.

Ruth had information in a folder in the bureau and at the weekends she read and re-read it while we lay in bed. She watched a documentary called 'Having Your First Non-Biological: Pros, Cons and What You Need to Know.' She read 'Which Adoption?' and joined a forum where she could ask questions and get the advice of other people who'd already been through this.

It was a huge decision.

Ruth was certain it was the right one. And I was more certain than at first. But still, a part of me had reservations, part of me was scared. What if it was the wrong decision? What if we weren't good enough to be parents?

Our preparation classes lasted 8 weeks. They were held in the old town hall in a draughty room, and we were crammed in with six other hopeful couples, some previous adopters, and staff from the agency. We sipped burnt coffee from plastic cups and listened to speakers talk about why some non-biological children are not cared for properly, how you manage the behaviour of those who have experienced abuse or neglect, how to manage the technical issues that can go wrong.

Ruth made copious notes in her adoption file. I listened, and tried to take everything in. It was difficult after a long day at work to focus in the evenings. My belly grumbled loudly, while I listened to another technician talking about the k4.4 system, and how there could be lock-outs in home systems and a number of reboots needed in the first few weeks.

Ruth immediately connected with Louise. Their backgrounds were similar. But I found the men in these classes, more confident than me in their manner, asking all the right questions, talking about the different programmes they were already installing to adapt their home systems ready for the 'big day'.

During the breaks, I hovered near the coffee machine and ate stale bagels, while Ruth chatted to other prospective parents and made notes, her face flush with happiness.

Janet came over to me on the last session. 'You've found this difficult haven't you?'

I shrugged.

She asked to come and visit me on my own. 'It's important for me to assess applicants as individuals,' she said, wiping a smear of lipstick from her upper lip. 'Especially those in a mixed relationship.'

She smiled at me, but I didn't feel at ease. Janet was one of those women who would leave no question unasked.

Janet knocked on the door rather than rang the bell. She asked for strong tea, and went straight into the dining room to spread her forms out on the table. Ruth popped in for a quiet chat with Janet, and then went over to Louise's house to talk about home educating. I brought in tea and sat opposite Janet.

'I hope I can be direct,' she said. I nodded without being sure what she meant, and she launched straight in. 'It's just that sometimes with a mixed relationship, there can be complications.'

I laughed. It was the way she said it: a hint of judgement, looking down her nose at me.

'Don't think I disapprove,' she said. 'It's just my past experience with men like you…'

'Men like me?'

Now it was her turn to laugh, a little uncomfortably. There was a silence, and I wanted something stronger than coffee. I wanted to tell Janet: This is my life. What gives you the right?

She sighed, and put her glasses down on the table. 'Can we start again?'

'Can I have a proper drink?'

She nodded, and I fetched a bottle from the cabinet and poured a slug into my tea. I offered, but she declined. She waited while I drank, watching me.

'Tell me about you and Ruth,' she said.

I tried to tell her what I thought she wanted to know: how our relationship works, how we function on a day-to-day, our shared goals and aspirations.

She shook her head.

'Tell me about how you met.'

I raised an eyebrow. 'You know that Ruth and I didn't meet. Not in the way people always mean.'

'Just tell,' she said impatiently, and I wanted to laugh. This was a different Janet: more bolshy, less professional.

'The same as any other story like it. I chose her. I worked out what I wanted, just like anyone else.'

'I want more than that,' she said. 'Like, I can't work out, why is she so advanced? All these additional specifications. She works on a 9.5 dif-system right? Why not just choose a wife with a 6.0 or a 6.5? Ruth has mood swings, she has desires, self-efficacy. I don't know many men who would have given her these things.'

I remembered working through all of that. I talked with friends about it in bars before they went home to their wives. I'd heard all their arguments for and against all the different choices I had in front of me. The truth was I wanted it to be as if I'd just met Ruth in the street, at the tram stop waiting to go home after work, and she might have asked me the time or commented on the weather or what was happening in the world. And perhaps there would have been a spark, or a feeling that I wanted to see her again, that by not seeing her again, something would be missing from my life.

Janet was waiting for my answer. It was like she was reading me, trying to interpret my silence. I tried to explain, but it was difficult. Her mouth opened. 'Oh,' she said.

'Oh?'

'You love her.'

I felt myself going red. 'Course I do.'

'You wanted a natural?'

I don't know whether it was embarrassment or frustration, or some deeper feeling, but she was tapping into an unexpected emotion. I could feel sweat prickling my armpits and my lower back. I felt my hands trembling a little.

Janet nodded as if she was getting somewhere now, and started writing on her forms. She smiled. 'Right, let's talk about this adoption.'

Toby was perfect.

Of course, he wasn't perfect, but that's what I thought the first time I saw his photograph and read his profile. Janet warned us that this was the very early stages of the matching process. But, she wanted our initial thoughts. Ruth stared at his photograph and cried. 'I'm sorry,' she said to Janet. 'It's just we've been waiting so long. We want it so much, don't we darling?'

Janet smiled, and offered to give us some time together.

She said she needed the bathroom anyway.

I held onto Ruth's hand and we looked at the photograph together. He was a small robot. He'd been through four previous homes while he was waiting for adoption.

He was cheeky-looking, something very mischievous about him. Yet, there was also sadness in his eyes as he stared straight past the camera into the distance. His profile said that he liked helping out around the house, and was good at many jobs, but also liked going to the park and playing football. It described him as a loving boy for a family who were not afraid of a challenge.

Ruth was still crying, so I kissed her wet cheek, and asked what she thought.

'I want him, Jim. Oh, I want him so much. Can we have him?'

I held her close, and imagined how happy this would make her.

'Yes,' I said and she cried even more.

Her sobs brought Janet back into the room. She smiled and winked at me. 'I take it you want to go ahead,' she said smiling. 'Right, we need to get everything prepared for court.'

It had been so long, sixteen months since we first met Janet, four months since approval. And finally Janet was making arrangements for our introduction. We would visit the foster carer's house, and meet Toby for the first time.

Ruth was anxious all morning. She was ratty as hell in truth, snapping at me and then apologising. She changed her outfit three times. I sometimes wondered whether she was more moody than a biological woman.

'Is this better than the skirt and blouse?' she asked.

'I don't know Ruth, that's fine, the other one was fine, the one before that was fine too. What's the matter with you?'

Ruth flounced into the bathroom. I could hear her crying quietly, as if she didn't want me to hear her. I tried the door, but it was locked. 'Come on Ruth, you look lovely. It's fine.'

'You don't understand,' she sobbed.

I didn't understand. I just wanted to get there. I'd never been to the town where the foster carers lived and was uncertain about the directions. In truth, I was terrified about seeing Toby. My heart was bang banging. I was sweating into the armpits of my shirt, and just wanted to get into the air-con of my car and drive. It was an hour or more away and I figured we could have a coffee in a café somewhere if we were early.

'I'm trying Ruth, come on open the door.'

She slid the bolt and I went in to find her mascara-stained and red-eyed. I coaxed her into a pair of comfortable jeans and a blouse, wiped her face clean, and walked her to the car.

We listened to the radio while we were driving, a request show that played songs from decades ago. I pressed her to sing along with me, and the tension eased, and we laughed. I'm sure that inside she was still as fluttery as me. It's strange remembering it now, but at moments during that drive I felt as if I might actually stop breathing. As if we were driving into our future without knowing what that was, or being at all ready for it.

We sat outside the foster carer's house for a full five minutes before we could steady ourselves enough to knock on the door.

Toby was in the garden with his foster dad, kicking a ball against the garage wall. As we arrived, he was facing away from us. He was smaller than I imagined, sturdy. You could tell he had a malfunction from the way he was moving. I knew it was from the 'accident' in his first home, but seeing him like that made it real.

His foster mum shouted to him across the garden, 'Toby,

they're here.'

He turned round and waved as if our visit was the most natural thing in the world, as if he already knew us. I waved back and sat down. My legs felt weak. I watched Ruth waving at him, smiling as if her face would never stop smiling. 'Don't cry darling,' I kept thinking. I'm not sure whether I spent more time watching Toby or watching her during that first meeting.

But she didn't cry. It seemed effortless for her. She played cards with him, and asked what he liked doing in his spare time. She showed him photos of our house, and people in my family, and he asked about us. She gave him a photo he could keep: Ruth and I sitting on the porch after dinner one summer two years ago.

He went inside with his foster dad, and we stayed for another hour, talking about Toby, asking questions, listening to his foster mum tell us how hard it could be sometimes, how it was rewarding, how affectionate he could be, but temper tantrums, difficult behaviour. There was a particular glitch that kept occurring that meant they had tech support every four weeks. She raised her eyebrows in that same way Janet had all those months ago, as though we knew.

On the drive back, Ruth kept asking me questions: What did I think? Wasn't he perfect? Did I notice how well she got on with him? I was exhausted, and wanted to concentrate on the road, on getting home, back to normal. I didn't want to talk about Toby anymore. I wanted to forget about the adoption and sleep.

I rang Janet on the Monday morning.

'I need to speak with you,' I said. 'Without Ruth.'

She must have sensed a wavering in my voice. 'This afternoon, at my office,' she said.

It was difficult to focus on work. I drank coffee until my hands were shaking, and paced from the front desk to the printer to my desk so many times, my boss finally came over to me and said, 'Jim, I don't know whether this is to do with the adoption, but whatever it is, go home, sort it out, come back tomorrow.'

I walked for two hours, along streets I'd never been down, out to the park, round the memorial garden, up the hill towards the supermarket just out of town, and then along aisles picking up produce, putting it back, leaving with a bag of items I couldn't even remember choosing.

What was I going to say to Janet? That I couldn't stop thinking I could have met a natural woman and had a family the normal way; my own child? How my life wasn't supposed to turn out like this?

'This is normal,' Janet said. 'Anxieties like this. It's a very stressful time for adopters: wondering whether you are the right person, whether you can manage, meeting this little stranger who's going to be yours.'

We stood outside her office, while I chain-smoked and she listened. I didn't know whether she understood what I was trying to say, but I needed to tell her: 'Sometimes, I wonder about natural women. I mean there were women years ago, briefly. And, I don't know why I decided on Ruth. I wanted to see if it was different. I mean, she's the same as a natural in reality. But sometimes in my head, it just seems so… wrong. I don't know if you understand. I love Ruth, it's just…'

She jangled her big bracelets while she waited for me to finish talking.

'Janet, can I do this? Will it be like that with Toby, will it seem wrong sometimes?'

She was silent for an achingly long time, and then said, 'Let's go for a drink.' She took me to a bar down the street that sold Irish whiskey and we both had a double. She sat across from me in a dark wooden booth and laid her hands on the table.

'I'll give it to you straight,' she said. 'This robot is going to be hard work. He's going to test and try you to your limits. I've known him for three years and he's frightened more than one family away, I can tell you. He's difficult, yes. He might kick at your legs when you say no, he'll shout and bawl, and stay up all night with nightmares, and refuse to do what he's told sometimes. He'll cry for no apparent reason. He'll steal from your wallet. Yes, and he'll lie about it too. He'll cost a fortune in tech support and sometimes he will short your home system, maybe Ruth's too. But you know what? He needs you and Ruth. I chose you because I know you can do it. And because he's had a rough life and you can give him a better one.'

Janet knocked back her whiskey and scowled at the taste.

'I never told you this,' she said. 'But, I read the reports about what happened to him, in his first home, and I can tell you. I've never known such cruelty. What that robot has been through, it's a miracle we can even offer him another chance. My manager wanted me to agree to his destruction. Imagine that. We create a robot. We create him like a child, to act like a child, grow like a child, love like a child. Then he gets treated like scrap. I couldn't authorise it.'

She stood up, reached for her purse, and told me. 'You need to decide, Jim. Can you offer this boy a home or not? Are you willing to work hard to make a difference or not? Nobody will blame you if you say no. But you need to decide.'

She left me in the bar, whiskey still in the glass, hands still shaking.

The day I decided about Toby, Ruth had prepared a meal. She'd been calmer since the first meeting with Toby, more herself. Her hair was scraped back into a loose pony tail, wisps curling down to meet her shoulders. Her lips were glossed, and she was humming to herself in the kitchen when I got home from work.

'Roast duck,' she said, 'I wanted us to have an evening meal together, like we used to, just me and you.'

She stroked my arm from my shoulder to my wrist.

'I know I've been distant,' she said, 'and crazy. I've been all wrapped up in this adoption, and there's been no time for us.'

I watched her. My eyes moved from eye to eye to lips, to shoulder, to her hand on my arm and I felt as though something inside me might burst.

'Are you alright, Jim?'

I nodded.

'No, really, are you alright? Is this what you want?'

I found it hard to answer. There was so much I wanted to tell her, about myself, about my own childhood, about how I felt about this and her and Toby, and whether I could do this, whether I was capable or not, how I worried I might let her down, how I worried I might become the man with the suitcase banging against his legs, how I couldn't live with that. How it all felt like a knot inside me, and I couldn't even be sure that my memories of my own dad were real or ones I'd modified over the years to suit me. I hadn't realised any of this until I met Toby. And now I wished I'd said more, done more, played cards with him like she did, how she was a natural, and I was just…

And this was the moment I decided. When my wife put her finger to my lips and said, 'Sshh,' as if she'd heard everything I was thinking.

The Tale of Trurl and the Great TanGent

Ian Watson

THE ESTEEMED CONTRACTORS Trurl and Klapaucius were both so gigantic – likewise the titanic size of some of their tools and inventions (since they were able to kindle or extinguish suns and rearrange solar systems) – that they were obliged to keep 99% of themselves and their equipment rolled up in the eleven invisible dimensions that supplement the visible dimensions of length, breadth, depth and time (time being easily visible on clocks, it goes without saying).

This lends a new meaning to *contracting*. Had it been otherwise, when Trurl & Klapaucius alighted on a world, not only would they have crushed a king's castle and his entire capital city, but they might have sunk right through the crust to the magma, causing volcanos which would resurface entire roasted countries.

Indeed this did happen once to Trurl when he impetuously pulled out a small black hole to lend weight to his presence on a winterholiday world. The hole itself was only a few centimetres in diameter, but it massed more than a G-type star. Promptly it dragged Trurl to the core of the planet, while the planet itself shrank so that formerly Himalayan mega-mountains flattened themselves to a millimetre high, unfortunately for the inhabitants who previously used those for skiing and tobogganing. The natives and tourists who remained microscopically alive (not many) were very piste off.

How did Trurl survive this sudden diminution? Why, by hastily condensing himself into quark-matter. Klapaucius was obliged to rescue Trurl on that occasion from a safe distance using an adamantine fishing rod, the fishing line made of impervium.

And of course both contractors needed to be considerably less than the size of a large asteroid to fit themselves into their comfy copperwire-thatched cottages which were a few kilometres apart since Trurl and Klapaucius didn't wish to get into one another's fibreoptic hair, and from time to time Trurl liked to surprise Klapaucius by revealing an amazingly ingenious invention.

As for the hidden dimensions where Trurl and Klapaucius stored much of themselves and their larger equipment, those are generally known, by analogy with length and so forth, as curlth, coilth, crumplth, loopth, squigglth, squirmth, bendth, wrinklth, shrinkth, puckerth, and pillbug. Pillbug had minimised itself out of anxiety at the prophesied collapse of the entire cosmos 100 billion years hence.

One day a Cyberknight presented himself at Trurl's door, which Trurl answered in his soft asbestos dressing gown and comfy wirewool slippers. A heavily armoured cyberhorse, more like a rhinoceros, grazed nearby on a bale of wire.

'As you witness, Sir Constructor,' the Cyberknight said to Trurl, 'I am laden with cobalt cuirasses, galena gorgets, gallium gauntlets, brass brassards, hafnium haubergeons, chrome cuises, and gadolinium greaves. Truly I'm burdened by bulk, even though I have adequate second-hand servomotors. How dearly I would like to unburden myself once in a while, but a cyberdragon might appear at any moment out of thin air.'

Trurl inhaled some air to test its composition. 'Sir Knight, the air here is quite thick compared with up a mountain. A dragon is more likely to appear out of *thick* air than thin due to there being more atoms available to transmute.'

'Lackaday,' exclaimed the Cyberknight. 'Yet could you

obligingly tell me how to keep some of my armour very close at hand without being compelled to wear everything all the time?'

'Incidentally, why do you wear so many layers of cuirasses and cuises et cetera?'

'For multiple redundancy.'

Now Trurl was very fond of receiving gold, especially in the shape of ducats, but he also liked benevolently to help anyone in distress. Quickly he explained about curlth and shrinkth and so forth.

'Good Constructor, how do those hidden dimensions become so small?'

'Easy-peasy,' said Trurl. 'By fractal methods! Have you seen icons of the Mandelbrot Set?'

'I admit I do like a snack of manganese mandelbrots dusted with tasty radium. Those fit through the visor of my helmet, and my converters dissolve them with gustatory gusto.'

'No, I'm referring to similarity at any scale, so that the tiniest iteration has the same shape as the largest. Thus your cuirasses and brassards, for instance, could be scaled down and popped into the curlth dimension, very close at hand, in fact on the surface of your hand or chest or back, since curlth is available everywhere. And pulled out again to full size quickly.' Trurl sketched tensor calculus in the air for a minute or so, then shrugged. 'It's like pulling a sock inside out, except that the toe is Planck length.'

'A plank is quite long.'

'A *Max* Planck length!'

'Max size sounds big.'

'No, no, Max Planck is the name of some robot of ancient antiquity. Maybe he was made of wood, although the speed of light was within him... Why don't you come inside and have a crumpet instead of a mandelbrot, while I quickly make you some curlth openers?'

'Thou art too kind! I vow to kill any dragon that cometh down thy chimney.'

Trurl popped a couple of iron crumpets into his timepasser toaster where they would acceleratedly oxidise to produce as much tasty rust as if several centuries had passed by.

'Give me a shout when they pop out, and I'll butter them with lovely greasy lubricant.' So saying, Trurl headed for his workshop, where he proceeded to hammer and saw some exotic matter with microtools while viewing his activity through an electron microscope. Presently he returned with numerous almost invisible curlth openers which he fixed to different parts of the Cyberknight's armour.

'I've tuned them to your cerebral circuits,' Trurl told the Cyberknight. 'Just think to yourself: *hecketty-pecketty, my fine hen*, and the armour will store itself. To unstore, think: *goosy goosy gander.*'

No sooner had the Cyberknight thought thuswise than his bulk diminished considerably, revealing an austere skeletal figure of steel which might once have been stainless but was now tarnished and pitted.

'Oh blessèd relief,' exclaimed the Cyberknight, just as the crumpets emerged fully rusted. 'However can I recompense you, I who am vowed to poverty?'

''Tis ever the way,' sighed Trurl. 'Maybe you could give me a spare quest of yours? Nothing has challenged my genius recently.' Hospitably Trurl dolloped thick brown grease on to the crumpets.

'As to that,' said the Cyberknight, munching, 'I recently rode my supercharger past a star a hundred lights to the north-east where I heard of a challenge, of which I could not avail myself due to being on a draconic quest at the time. Apparently the Great TanGent of Transistoria has offered ten captive cybermaidens to anyone who can stabilise his world.'

'Stabilise?'

'I did ask myself why the Great TanGent should wish to put his world into someone else's stable. The cost of livery – fodder and such – for an entire world would be considerable, including towing expenses to take the planet to the stable.'

'I think you are overly preoccupied by equine matters on account of your spacesteed.'

'Bucyberephalis.'

'Is that a disease of electrohorses?'

'No, that's her name. However, I then discovered that Transistoria and its sun have become engulfed by a cloud of self-aware nitrous oxide. A Joker Cloud. Although the planet owes its name to the Impeccable Transistor, now absurd changes take place and reality is transitory rather than transistory. The Great TanGent and his court have fled to the outermost ice-planet which is unaffected. He hates the cold and the faintness of light there because his joy was to expose his bronze body to the powerful electromagnetic radiation from Transistoria's sun.'

'So he offers ten cybermaidens to whoever chases this Joker Cloud away? *But*,' added Trurl, becoming incensed, 'you say they are *captive*? Why, they must be released!'

'I suppose the only way to release them is to defeat the Joker Cloud, thus gaining the cybermaidens, then give them their liberty. As opposed to taking electroliberties with them.' The radium had obviously refreshed the austere Cyberknight, giving him sufficient sparkle for a witticism.

'Then that is what I shall do!' declared Trurl. 'Not take liberties, oh no! I've existed happily until now without any cyberwenches. Give me adjustable wrenches any time! I shall free those captives. Hmm, how do I defeat a self-aware cloud of nitrous oxide…? Aha, I shall adapt the cosmic vacuum cleaner I invented.'

'Surely,' said the Electroknight, 'the vacuum of the void is empty by definition, so how can it be cleaned?'

'Space travel,' replied Trurl impatiently, 'is impossible without a void, or vacuum, to travel through, but often it fills with junk such as rivets coming loose from craft. I must hurry to my colleague Klapaucius to recruit him for this chivalric expedition.'

After they'd been travelling for a few score light years, Trurl said to Klapaucius, 'Do you mind if we stop here for a bit? I want to nip outside to have a stretch.'

Klapaucius consulted his sturdy depleted uranium chronowrist which told seventeen different times depending on frame of reference. 'You won't take more than a day about it? You'll delay us.'

'I need a stretch or else I'll get cramp! Oh I can feel cramp coming on! Ouch ouch. What use is a constructor with cramp? My genius will be cramped. My style will be cramped. You can have a picnic on the hull while I'm stretching.'

Of course both of the constructors couldn't stretch fully at the same time; there wouldn't be enough space.

'Ouch ouch!' cried Trurl. 'OUCH!'

'Do it, then, if you must.' Carefully Klapaucius turned the antiacceleration dial to a big minus number. An audio of braking sounded. *Screeeeeeeeeech.*

When the ship was at rest with respect to the nearest star systems, Klapaucius sucked all the air into storage and the two constructors switched to radio since otherwise they could no longer hear one another. Then Trurl nipped out of the hatch, and jetted about a thousand kilometres away.

After toasting a vanadium waffle till it glowed, and sprinkling on rhodium filings, Klapaucius followed and sat on the hull to watch as first of all Trurl unpacked extensive parts of himself and pieces of equipment and inventions from curlth, and then from coilth and crumplth – by now he was the size of a minor moon, very irregularly shaped. Next Trurl unpacked from loopth and squigglth and squirmth, and he swelled to the size of a major moon, starfish-shaped. Finally he added the contents of bendth, wrinklth, shrinkth, puckerth, and last of all pillbug. Now he was a world unto himself of about one gravity, distinctly hexakis–octahedronal. At last he had stretched to his full capacity.

'Aaaaah,' Klapaucius's radio conveyed blissfully.

'Have you found the vacuum cleaner?' Klapaucius enquired.

'Of course I have. It was wrapped up in shrinkth. Shrinkthwrapped.'

'Remember to leave the vacuum cleaner out when you repack. Then we can see about modifying it.'

'Um, Klapaucius…'

'What is it?'

'I'm itchy. Some kind of infestation came out of wrinklth. Electron fleas maybe. Now they're the size of electro-elephants from the feel of it. Would you very much mind bringing the ship over here and taking a look?'

So Klapaucius went back inside and antimattered the ship over to orbit his planet-sized colleague, which wasted less than a grain of fuel. Peering through a telescope, Klapaucius reported, 'They aren't jumping, which means they're probably neutralino nits. They ought to pass through you, but they've swollen a lot. Would you like me to denit you?'

'I'd be obliged.'

Patiently Klapaucius lined up a precision laser-cannon and began to pick off the lumbering parasites, until Trurl was as shiny and spruce as a young processor trundling off to school, his fibreoptic hair slicked down with grease. Then Trurl began repacking large parts of himself and his gigantic inventions and terraforming technologies and planetshifting levers and cometary crowbars back into curlth, coilth, crumplth, loopth, squigglth, squirmth, bendth, wrinklth, shrinkth, puckerth, and pillbug. This took longer than unpacking, as is usual, but Trurl remembered to leave out the electromagnetic vacuum cleaner and to attach it to the nose of the ship before he rejoined Klapaucius on board, having downsized once more.

'Aaaaaaaaaah, that was good.' Trurl opened a jar of electrolyte from the fridge to refresh himself after his stretch-out. 'So what are we waiting for?'

'You,' said Klapaucius as he let off the spacebrake and

engaged the accelerator. The ship could go from rest to a speed of C++ in fifteen seconds in a straight linux, but Klapaucius allowed a reasonable thirty seconds.

Presently the two Constructors came in sight of the partially glittering iceworld at the edge of the solar system containing Transistoria. The iceworld partially glittered because a sort of solarium had been constructed in geosynchronous orbit to beam down radiation upon an area where, under highest magnification, the Great TanGent could be seen artificially sunbathing on the patio of an icy palace accompanied by ten ravishing and recumbent cybermaidens wearing black boron carbide bikinis, all linked to one another by a thick grey chain looped around the hourglass waist of each; a chain composed, as spectrographic analysis revealed, of tungsten.

'At least,' said Klapaucius, 'the Great TanGent isn't a total brute. Tungsten's hard but it's ductile and malleable, so the cybermaidens can move comfortably within limitations. And tungsten resists corrosion.'

'Therefore they can't so easily escape,' said Trurl angrily.

'I mean that tungsten bondage won't mark their waists, the way that copper chains would stain them with verdigris. Hmm, I fear another Constructor might already be at work here because of that orbital sunbathing device! Ingenious heat pumps must be at work, otherwise the ice that the Great TanGent is basking on would melt. Hmm, the heat which is pumped away could be microwaved up to power what's in orbit, and *that* is verging on *perpetuum mobile*… Has someone ingenious got here before us? Although the cybermaidens do remain chained…'

'We'd better hurry!'

'It was *you* who stopped to stretch.'

'Gears and gizmos! I had to install the vacuum cleaner, didn't I?'

Politely using anti-gravity rather than flaming thrusters

in their descent, they landed half a kilometre from the temporary ice-palace of the Great TanGent in exile, and approached on foot.

A chamberlainbot enquired their business and led them, by way of somewhat dripping corridors, to a somewhat dripping antechamber. Of course as soon as drips encountered any shade the water promptly froze again to minus 250 Celsius. Carpenterbots were constantly busy reinstalling ice-wainscoting on the upper parts of walls, using icepegs, so that the palace looked somewhat upside-down; while pagebots scurried about, protecting other parts of the building with aluminium parasols. Ceilings and roofs were lacking, needless to say.

'All this ingenuity,' exclaimed Trurl, 'so that the Great TanGent can continue tanning himself. Truly he is a tyrant.'

By the time they arrived at the throne room, the forewarned monarch had already ensconced himself in his complex throne, complex since the plates of his body were very angular, not only tangential to one another but even hyperbolic. No rival Constructor seemed to be present amongst the assembled courtiers. The line of ten cybermaidens had been led inside by guards so that the Great TanGent could keep an optic on them.

Truly they were ravishing (although apparently unravished), with great thigh-pistons and well-riveted conical bosoms scarcely concealed by their boron carbide bikinis. How their Pythagorean proportions appealed! As a consequence of perfection they all looked remarkably similar, like a chain of cut-out, though bounteously ample, three-dimensional metallic dolls joined loosely by the restraining chain of tungsten. The glitter of crushed gems glued upon their optic-lids, and similar blusher upon their cheeks and nipples, gave some individuality: ruby, sapphire, emerald, and so forth. The cybermaidens postured somewhat, as though not entirely innocent, but maybe that was just an aspect of their balance circuitry. And they pouted, rather as goldfish do in a bowl. Maybe they were privately gossiping by radio. Maybe they were suffering perpetual pangs of embarrassment. Maybe none would be the first to utter a word for fear of sounding silly. Maybe they must remain silent in court.

'Your Majesty–' Trurl commenced.

'Your *Gentleness*,' the chamberlainbot corrected Trurl.

'Your Gentleness, you behold before you the Esteemed and Cosmically Notable Constructors, Trurl and Klapaucius, whose fame surely precedes us, although we do hope that no lesser Constructor has also preceded us?'

'Nay,' said the Great TanGent through his mouth–grille, 'it was a seemingly *much lesser* Constructor, since the heat pumps he installed fail to function properly, although We are glad of the tan–rays from deep space amidst this cursèd darkness.'

'I intend,' declared Trurl, 'to remove the curse of the nitrous oxide cloud from Transistoria in order to liberate, I mean acquire, these ten captive cybermaidens.'

'I rejoice to hear this. Truly we shall be sorely bereft to lose Our Isobel. My dignity required multiple robobimbo playmates to sunbathe beside Us. Yet such shall be your reward if you can restore Us to our world where lunatical instability now reigns.'

'*The...* Isobel? Do all ten cybermaidens have the same name, Your Gentleness? How de–individualising.'

'An isobel,' grilled the Great TanGent, 'is a line connecting points of equal beauty in the same way that an isobar connects points of equal atmospheric pressure. Since the ten are chained together, it is far easier to say *Isobel, come here* than to recite ten different names.'

'Surely You could call them Rubybel, Sapphirebel, Emeraldbel, Diamondbel and so forth. For example.'

'And Soforth*bel*,' grilled the Great TanGent, 'to follow your logic. You yourself short–circuit the inconvenience.'

Trurl's own circuits throbbed with momentary chagrin. This Monarch was capable of logic–chopping, therefore Trurl ought to be careful about terms and conditions

'I shall of course need an iron-clad guarantee of our agreement, Your Gentleness. A contractor requires a contract.'

'Agreed. But you, Contractor, must provide the iron. We mainly have ice here.'

'I was thinking,' said Trurl, 'more of a fireproof metal parchment adorned with tassels and seals and twiddly bits.'

'Faugh!' said the affronted monarch. 'Ice at minus 250 is *harder than steel*. I shall inscribe my vow upon a sheet of such ice, which *you* can clad in iron to your central processor's content. Although,' he offered grandly, 'I will add some curlicues.'

'Psst.' Klapaucius nudged his colleague. 'Shouldn't you consult the Isobel' – and Klapaucius nodded towards the line-up of bikinied beryllium beauties – 'as to whether they wish to be freed? Perhaps they enjoy bondage?'

Trurl drew himself up sententiously and declared, 'Freedom is the factoryright of any robosapient. Besides, we cannot abandon Transistoria to its stochastic fate.' And *he* gestured at a large plasma screen, wherein events upon that world were being displayed, transmitted by the desperate citizenry to their monarch.

The sky was raining banana skins upon a civic square where the Royal RoboArmy were attempting loyally to goosestep on parade. Soon the steel soldiers were skidding and crashing into one another, and the square was a tangle of cyberlimbs...

Gallons of polka-dot paint, red spots on green, spilled from low galleon-shaped clouds upon a congregation in the roofless Church of Ultraviolet Adoration, transforming the battery-recharging sun-adorers into clowns...

Masses of little coinlike green leaves were growing out of the portico of the Royal Mint; although the transmission didn't convey smells you could easily guess what the scent would be...

On Transistoria, puns and pratfalls had become absurd reality due to the Joker Cloud. In the circumstances Trurl felt obliged to accept the commission without even consulting the captives.

'But ASK them!' insisted Klapaucius. 'They don't have much to say for themselves!'

'Speaking personally,' grilled the Great TanGent, 'I find decibels incompatible with an Isobel.'

Trurl gaped at the monarch. 'You mean you *dumbed* them down?'

'For some entities, being dumb is a perfectly happy state, since they're unaware of anything amiss.'

'I can easily adjust *that*!' declared Trurl, incensed, 'by a few twiddles and tweaks and installing some extra capacity.'

'Although at the moment a *cloud* still interposes itself before that illuminatory outcome.'

'Inscribe our agreement, then!'

'My word alone will not suffice?'

'I do not doubt your word, Your Gentleness, yet let us say purely as an aide memoire…?'

So the Great TanGent extruded a diamond drill from his forefinger and at high speed inscribed his promise on a sheet of extremely hard ice which a courtier held before him, which he then passed to Trurl. Trurl scanned the binary code amidst the curlicues, then reached into crumplth for a suitable iron box which he recalled having packed near the Planck-length doorway. The ferric box assumed its regular 4-D length, breadth, and depth (rather than height, in the case of a box), and time which proceeded to pass, and into that box Trurl placed the Great TanGent's promise, ironclad now to be sure.

Back in space, after Trurl had placed the iron box in the ship's refrigerator to keep it cool, the Contractors headed inward towards Transistoria and the great cloud of laughing gas engulfing its entire orbit.

'Shouldn't we try to communicate with the cloud before we vacuum it up?' suggested Klapaucius. 'The cloud may have a point of view.'

'Hmm,' hummed Trurl. 'That cloud's about 300 million kilometres across. The speed of radio is 300,000 kilometres per second. So it takes the cloud 1000 seconds for a coherent thought. Roughly sixteen and a half minutes. How glacially slow compared with our own swift thoughts! But I do believe there's a temporal interface thingymajig in that locker over there – I invented one when I needed to communicate with a slow-life gas-whale. What the interface does is borrow some time from the future and loop it around. This shouldn't do too much harm to the local spacetime metric, although the sun might flicker a bit.'

Before long, Trurl had synchronised the chrono-interface to the radio, and hailed on all frequencies:

'Cloud, why are you playing tricks on that planet that never did you any harm?'

Transistoria's sun did indeed blink off on off on off on, as if trying to flash some message of its own, but this was unimportant since the flashing wasn't at a frequency such as to cause epileptic fits in machine minds.

Presently came an answer: 'For a billion years I have drifted, and never had a laugh.'

'Ah,' said Trurl to Klapaucius, 'at long last the cloud encountered an inhabited world and an opportunity. Probably it was expelled from some star cluster due to its stupid sense of humour. You'll probably feel better,' he messaged, 'after I condense you. Brevity is the soul of wit.'

So saying, Trurl activated the vacuum cleaner on the nose of their ship so that it sent forth a vast conical electromagnetic field to suck in the nitrous oxide, rather like a primeval Bussard ramscoop from the earliest days of astronautics; and he accelerated. Assorted loose nuts and bolts and screws proceeded to fly towards Trurl's and Klapaucius's metallic bodies and attach themselves with a *ping*.

'Ouch,' complained Klapaucius. 'There's a spot of magnetic leakage.'

'Saves me using the brush and pan,' said Trurl, who was busy punching a course that would in a couple of hours take them throughout the entire volume of the cloud. He disengaged the temporal thingymajig so as not to hear moans from the cloud at the disconcerting sensations it might be experiencing.

While they were heading back to the iceworld, Trurl went for a spacewalk on the hull to detach the now bulging vacuum bag and bring it back aboard. Even in the absence of gravity, this took some heaving due to the inertia of an entire molecular gas cloud compressed to the size of a large pumpkin. Which Trurl duly labelled in red *Beware: Laugh Gas* in case he ever opened it by mistake.

'Where shall we keep it?' asked Klapaucius.

'In pillbug, surely? If any gas leaks out, the pillbug anxiety should neutralise it.'

Presently they landed, and Trurl removed the iron box from the ship's refrigerator in case the Great TanGent needed reminding of His royal promise.

'Hmm,' muttered Trurl, 'that's odd, the box feels warmish. My thermosensors must need a service. I'll see to that after we've liberated the Isobel…'

Soon they were once more in the royal presence, the captive cybermaidens on parade again. The screen showed the robot citzenry of Transistoria celebrating the restoration of normality by singing joyously while they swept up banana skins and scrubbed paint off one another.

'Your Gentleness,' said Trurl, 'we have succeeded, as expected. Consequently we have come to collect our just reward.'

'Kindly remind me,' said the Great TanGent, 'of the exact wording.'

'Do you need additional memory?' asked Trurl. 'Is your hard disc full?'

'Just remind me, Contractor!'

Smuggly Trurl unlocked the iron box and opened it... only to find a couple of centimetres of chilly water sloshing inside.

'But,' said Trurl.

Exposed to the far-below-zero of the icemoon, the water was already beginning to form a featureless membrane of ice...

'But.'

'The magnetic leakage, idiot,' hissed Klapaucius. 'The magnetic field must have induced a strong electric current in the fridge and the box, resulting in heat... Our ironbound contract melted.'

The monarch, his tangents bristling and his parabolas asymptoting, declared, 'It was yourself, Contractor, who insisted on a *written* contract complete with adornments. Despite the fact that Our royal word has always been Our bond! This demeaned Our dignity and insulted Our gentleness. *Consequently,* We shall abide only by the *written* terms of that contract. And We perceive no binary code whatsoever!'

Trurl felt as if he might blow a gasket, burst a fuse, rupture a rheostat.

'But there were witnesses...' Desperately he gazed in appeal at the chamberlain and the other courtiers, who all conveniently were looking elsewhere, then at the Isobel themselves who of course had nothing to say.

'May his chips fry!' cursed Trurl as they left the iceworld under excessive acceleration. 'May his RAM break a horn!'

'Ah, the foibles of monarchs,' sighed Klapaucius. 'We should know about those only too well by now.'

'That's why I insisted on a contract!'

'You ought to have tightened the nuts on the vacuum cleaner. It must have rolled around while in its microdimension.'

'I've a good mind—' Abruptly, impetuously, Trurl braked. 'I've a good mind—'

'I know you have a good mind, dear friend. Definitely the goodest. Both as regards your processors and your ethics.'

'I've a good mind to turn back and as it were *accidentally* jettison the vacuum bag upon the ice world before they finish packing for Transistoria Regained. I shall, I shall too!'

True to his word, Trurl reached into pillbug. 'Hmm, that's odd. Could have sworn I left the bag just by the door. Dratted thing must have rolled, the way you accuse my vacuum cleaner of doing…'

'Maybe if you didn't accelerate and brake quite so suddenly…?'

But at that very moment polka-dot paint began to creep out of the unseen dimension on to Trurl's hand, and very soon this was spreading down his metal arm, bright yellow on blue this time, the spots expanding swiftly. From close by, although scarcely audible at all, came the tiniest and tinniest noise of laughter.

The 5-Sigma Certainty

Trevor Hoyle

AS A TOP-FLIGHT feature writer with Global Media Corporation I had been given a special assignment to interview some of the leading exponents of science and fantasy fiction. To be honest, and to declare a disinterest, this genre has never been a favourite of mine. I prefer science fact to self-indulgent flights of fancy. But Nick Webb, my editor in New York, who had head-hunted me from the Shitzumitsu Press Agency in Tokyo, had made a personal request, and so I reluctantly complied.

(He actually said, 'You owe me one, Richy. You begged to cover Guth's paper on the Inflationary Universe at the Stanford seminar and you got your wish. Now it's payback time.' I couldn't argue with Nick about that; he'd been very generous.)

Not knowing where to start, I asked the research department for a list of these so-called 'leading' SF authors. The first name they came up with was that of Philip K Dick, who lived out in California. Actually I had vaguely heard of Phil Dick. He had been mentioned in the media/publishing columns over recent weeks: a movie option had been taken out on one of his novels, and I remembered the item because of the book's ridiculous title: *Do Androids Dream of Electric Sheep?* Apparently an English director had shown an interest and they were planning to make the film – to be called *Dangerous Days* – with Warren Beatty in the lead role.

I thought, well at least they had the good sense to change that awful title.

Phil Dick, it seems, had won various awards and prizes (something called the Hugo) and was highly esteemed by science fiction writers in other countries. On the flight over I read some of his short stories, which I have to admit weren't bad for that type of whimsical make-believe. At least they didn't insult the intelligence. Frankly I've never understood why people want to read stuff that isn't true when the world is full of solid, immutable facts, millions and millions of them. Why clutter your head with idle speculation that some day-dreamer has dredged up from his sub-conscious?

If something can't pass the 5-sigma Certainty test, then what's the point of it?

When I arrived in Los Angeles I hired a car at the airport and drove to Anaheim and checked into the Hyatt Hotel across the road from Disneyland. I chose this location because it was an easy drive on Interstate 5 to Santa Ana where Phil Dick lived. There was, however, one fly in the ointment. Though I had his mailing address, I didn't have his damn telephone number. I scoured the Los Angeles area phone directory, came up with nothing, and then called directory inquiries, but the number was unlisted. Was the guy paranoid or something? What was he afraid of?

As luck would have it I found Civic Center Drive almost the minute I came off the Interstate and headed east looking for Number 408, which turned out to be a white stucco four-storey apartment building with Spanish-style wrought ironwork guarding the entrance. I parked the car at the kerbside and scanned the rank of names in metal slots, some typewritten, some scrawled. Alongside each name was a mailbox slit, and underneath that a button and speaker grille. I didn't actually expect to see the name 'Philip K Dick' there, but sure enough it was, in the slot marked 'Apartment C.1.'

I pressed the button and leaned towards the grille. For

some absurd reason I suddenly felt nervous: how was I supposed to introduce myself? What was I supposed to say? I hadn't spoken to the man before, he didn't know me from Adam. I tried to imagine how I would react, having a complete stranger buzz my doorbell, unannounced, burbling some story about having flown three thousand miles to conduct an interview I knew nothing about. Mouth open, throat dry, the introductory phrase never left my lips because instead of a voice crackling over the grille came a metallic click and the wrought-iron gate to my left swung open on noiseless hinges.

The stucco walls of the interior passage were a dull depressing brown. Underfoot the tiles were a mosaic of crazy paving, pieces missing here and there. (As is usual with Californian architecural style, I was still outdoors, the apartments above reached by narrow stairwells leading to open landings.) Though the gloom was gathering as early evening came on, a dim yellow globe was sufficient to illuminate the small varnished plaque at the top of the stairs. It was there I hesitated; the door to Apartment C.1. stood half open. The wrought-iron gate opening mysteriously had been one thing. But now this – the half-open door inviting me inside. What was going on?

I'm a rational, matter-of-fact type of person, not given to morbid fancies, yet I confess I felt distinctly uneasy. This situation reminded me of something weird, and it took a few seconds to realise what it was. On the flight over I had read one of Phil Dick's stories in which a man returns home, walks into his bathroom, reaches up with his left hand for the light-cord – only to find the cord is on the opposite side of the door. Everything else about the house is exactly the same except for this one tiny detail. And that's what I seemed to be experiencing now… the uncomfortable, eerie feeling of having stepped into a Phil Dick story.

The living room was small and poky, and airless, or more accurately, filled with dead air. Never having seen a photo of

Phil Dick, I didn't know whether the middle-aged man with thinning grey hair swept back from a high forehead, with a rather scrubby whitish beard that was not quite a goatee, was indeed the man I had come to see. He was slumped on the couch, a T-shirt bearing the distended face of Beethoven stretched across his belly, crumpled corduroy trousers with ragged bottoms and bare feet stuck in a pair of espadrilles. Balanced on his knees was what appeared to be the upturned lid of a cardboard box holding a dozen or more round metal containers, smaller than eggcups, each filled with a powder of some sort. The man I assumed to be Phil Dick glanced up, with no discernible expression, except for a marginal crinkling of the eyes, which looked to be somewhat Slavic in cast.

'You from the FBI?'

I shook my head and gestured vaguely behind me. 'The door was already open, and the gate –'

'Sure, okay, forget it. I was expecting someone. You're not him.'

Phil Dick emitted a kind of grunting sigh and moved the upturned box lid from his knees to the couch. When he saw me looking at the array of small metal containers he said, 'I collect different brands of snuff, it's what you might say is a hobby of mine.'

I remembered reading somewhere in the research that he was, or had been, a heavy drug user; maybe this was a substitute, to wean him off his addiction.

He said: 'I was hoping you'd come about my letter. It's high time the FBI got their thumb out of their ass.'

'Sorry to disappoint you. I'm a feature writer with Global Media,' I said, and went on to introduce myself, explaining that I mainly did interviews with scientists rather than writers of fiction. From my pocket I took out a micro-cassette recorder. 'Is it all right if I use this? My shorthand is pretty rudimentary, and I like to be as accurate as possible.'

'That's no problem.' Without getting up, Phil Dick

extended his hand. On closer scrutiny he was a much bigger man than I had supposed, taller as well, though it was difficult to gauge this accurately with him sprawled on the couch, shoulders hunched. He hardly moved from this semi-recumbent posture the entire time, though stirred himself now and then to stroke his face with a clasped hand, while pondering how to answer a question.

He didn't bother to offer me a drink, or any kind of refreshment, and almost perfunctorily indicated a creaking rocking-chair for me to sit. As the interview progressed I checked my notebook and saw that Philip Kindred Dick had been born in 1928, which put him in his early fifties.

'I can't work during daylight hours,' he explained in answer to a question about his working methods. 'My routine, such as it is, whenever I'm writing a novel or a longer piece than a short story, is to load the deck with six hours of classical tapes, plug in the headphones, and rattle away till six or seven in the morning without stopping. I then grab a bite of supper and crash out till around midday, early afternoon. On average, give or take, that's two thousand words a night. I can finish a novel in a month that way – though something like High Castle might take a week or ten days longer.' Phil Dick tugged at his wispy greying beard through a wry smile. 'That's if I don't get blocked midway or hit a personal crisis.' He shrugged. 'These things can happen, and sometimes do.'

'Is it always classical music?' I asked.

'That's my preferred taste. If you've done your research you'll find that I deejayed a classical records programme as a young man.'

'And you don't find it distracting, that constant sound?'

'How so?' The eyes crinkled in query, giving them that Slavic slant.

'Interrupting your thought processes I mean?'

'Not at all. I need it to drown out the universe.'

'Is that also why you write through the night? To push everyday reality away so you can focus your thoughts on the work in hand?'

'No.' The word was harsh, definite yet defensive, almost a bark. 'I can't write during daylight because of the Eye in the Sky.' (I capitalise the phrase because that's how Phil Dick pronounced it – as a known, recognisable entity.)

'What does the Eye in the Sky do?' I asked curiously.

'What do you suppose it does?' he said witheringly. 'Eyes watch people, don't they? The Eye in the Sky watches me. Whenever I step outside, to the store, to see a movie, to the park – anyplace I go – I'm conscious of the Eye following me. There's no escape. They think I don't know about it. Hah!' He waggled his forefinger to and fro in a crafty gesture. 'But they can't fool Phil K Dick. He has an inbuilt sensor that triggers a response. Kind of a tingling vibration down the spine whenever that bastard's up there watching and listening. Believe you me, I know about it!'

'And if you tried to write during the hours of daylight would the Eye in the Sky prevent it in some way, or interfere with the process? Even if you were indoors?'

Phil Dick rubbed the side of his jaw. His fingers were long and finely shaped, the nails tapered, beautifully kept. He said finally:

'Maybe not interfere. But that's not the point. They'd know what I was writing about. Every word I set down on paper would be captured instantly and recorded on some gigantic data retrieval system. I'm telling you, Richy, don't underestimate these people. They're smart. Know what their next move is?'

I shook my head.

'Picking up your thoughts straight out of your brain. The technology's been developed already, it's only a matter of constructing a working model that'll operate dependably in the field.'

'That's a... chilling thought,' I said.

'Even living in a lead–lined chamber deep underground won't be enough of a defence shield.'

Phil Dick sprinkled a pinch of snuff on the back of his hand and sniffed it up gloomily, one nostril at a time.

'So you see why I have to work at night, Richy. It isn't that I want to be secretive and live the life of a hermit. I'm very much an out-going gregarious kind of a person. Staying put in this tiny apartment is driving me nuts.'

'I can see that,' I said, checking that the ruby bead of light was still on, still recording. 'Can you talk about what you're doing at the present time? Is there a novel or short story in progress?'

'I can't tell you much,' Phil Dick said, 'because I don't know myself until I've written it. I don't make a plan or an outline, I let it flow out of me. Flow through me ...'

'Like a channel,' I suggested.

'I *am* the channel. The stuff I write comes from someplace else, don't ask me where. I don't have a plan but I must have a title. Something like *Do Androids Dream of Electric Sheep?* works for me – keeps me focused.'

'One of your best,' I said. 'Brilliant title.'

'Glad you think so.' He arched his bulky frame against the couch, belly jutting, and allowed himself a brief smile. 'I've just started on something called *Achieve Real-Time Retaliation Within Two Sweeps of the Radar*. It's set during a future war but its theme is the search for a mysterious source of energy that powers the universe. A force we can't see or detect even though it's all around us.'

I almost groaned. Where did he get them from – these terrible, dreadful, cringing titles? If anything, this one was even worse than all the others.

I said, 'Vacuum energy, I believe, is the phrase.'

Phil Dick glanced at me keenly. 'I like that. Did you invent it?'

'No, no, it's the accepted scientific term...' Of course I then realised that, as a practitioner of the science fiction genre, Phil Dick would know nothing of the latest hypotheses and speculations in the world of real science. That was the problem in a nutshell with these weavers of fanciful daydreams and airy-fairy nonsense. Their labours led nowhere, achieved nothing, added not one jot to the sum of human knowledge and empirical understanding – unlike the bedrock of true scientific endeavour, based on rigorous experiment and verifiable fact.

'It's also known as 'phantom energy' and 'ghost energy'. The idea is that empty space isn't actually empty –'

'How can empty space not be empty? That's an internal contradiction.'

'Well, that is the conundrum,' I agreed. 'They're still trying to figure that one out. It's tied in with something called the cosmological constant. The particle physicists don't yet know what the force fields are that create vacuum energy or how they operate – or even if they exist.'

'Are we talking proven fact here or just abstract speculation?'

'At the moment they're theories. There's a young theoretician called Alan Guth doing some very interesting work right now at the Stanford Linear Accelerator Center. I did a magazine piece on him recently. But in fact some of these ideas go way back to Fritz Zwicky in 1933 who came up with the theory of dark matter. His calculations showed that there had to be a massive amount of unseen matter in the universe – more than 160 times more than we can observe.'

'My story's about a mysterious *force*,' Phil Dick said, 'not matter.'

Matter and energy are interchangeable. Essentially they're the same thing in different form. Einstein showed that with $E=MC^2$.'

'You seem to know about this stuff.' Phil Dick eyed me shrewdly, as if shifting towards some sort of reassessment.

'I should do, it's my specialist field as a science journalist. I heard Guth give his paper at Stanford and it was very impressive, I must say. He didn't directly confront the Grand Unified Theory, but even so his calculations met the 2-sigma level of certainty. Given time and further resources there's no reason he couldn't achieve a 3-sigma result, or even higher.'

Phil Dick tugged at the wispy point of his beard. 'I'm not familiar with those terms. What do you mean by '2-sigma' and '3-sigma'?'

'It's how they measure the statistical validity of a given result. There's always a possibility it will be influenced by chance, just pure coincidence. A fluke result, let's call it. So they grade their findings by degrees of statistical probability. A 3-sigma gradation means there is roughly a one in 1,000 chance that the reading was caused by a data anomaly or statistical quirk. The best they can hope for is a 5-sigma level of certainty – that's about a one in 1,000,000 chance that the result is a fluke and not an accurate, dependable outcome.'

'Seems a pretty useful system,' Phil Dick said, slowly nodding his head, 'if it works. How would it apply to the real world? To something in this room, say? What would be the proof of a 5-sigma test right here and now?'

It seemed an odd request (though not so coming from Philip K Dick perhaps) and it stumped me for a few seconds; I had to think about it.

'Tossing a coin is maybe the simplest method,' I suggested. 'Say you tossed eight heads in a row, that's getting close to a 3-sigma level. It's very unlikely it would happen by chance, so the result would be statistically highly convincing. But to achieve a 5-sigma certainty you'd have to toss more than twenty straight heads in a row. The odds against that happening by chance are so fantastic that it would be an absolutely cast-iron proof the result was valid.'

Phil Dick now had a faint smile on his lips. 'And what would you pitch the level at for a security gate, normally locked, opening for you unbidden followed by an open door into the apartment of a person you've never met who wasn't expecting you? How many coin tosses would that be … what's your best guess?' He spread his hands. '3-sigma maybe? Higher?'

Of course I knew his game: he was poking fun at me,

hinting slyly that the system I described was little more than a fatuous intellectual conceit. An exercise with no practical application in the real world. How I wished I could prove Phil Dick wrong! Demonstrate its immediate relevance and usefulness in front of his eyes – but how? I racked my brains but could think of nothing.

To cover my frustration, once again I delved into the notes the research department had prepared for me, which included the list of authors as possible interviewees. Next to one of the names, in brackets, it stated 'regards Philip K Dick as the most interesting and innovative writer of science fiction in America, with a unique perspective'. I tapped my notebook. 'I see Stanisław Lem singles you out for particular praise. Have you ever met him?'

Phil Dick straightened up and his shoulders went back. He gave me an intense, accusatory stare from under lowered brows.

'How could I? Don't you know anything, you idiot? Stanisław Lem isn't a person, it's a committee of Soviet bureaucrat-hacks producing science fiction to disseminate communist doctrine and propaganda in the West. Why d'you think I wrote to the FBI? I'm trying to warn them to be on their guard – not allow the American public to be duped by this devious commie plot to corrupt our ideals. How can you meet a man who doesn't exist?'

It was on the tip of my tongue to ask him if he was being serious, suspecting this was more of his teasing; but Phil Dick's boiling anger was palpably evident in the fierce eyes and throbbing pulse at his temples.

'I told you already. I thought you were the FBI guy I was expecting – that's why the outer gate and the door were wide open and you could waltz straight in here unchecked.' Flecks of foam flew from his lips. 'Why else would they be, in southern California, for chrissakes? D'you think I'm crazy?'

'No… no, I'm sorry…' I said feebly. 'I wasn't aware, I didn't know – about Stanisław Lem, I mean. Is it common knowledge?'

'It is to those with eyes to see. Even the goddamn name tells you it's a communist conspiracy! Are you blind as well as dumb?'

'The name…? What about it?'

Phil Dick smacked his palm three times with his clenched fist as he spelt it out. 'L – E – M. What could be clearer than that? They're so arrogant, these bastards, they don't even try to hide it. Plainly it stands for…' And stretching out both arms in my direction, palms uppermost, eyebrows raised, he invited me to supply the answer – so blindingly obvious even to an idiot like me. When I stayed silent Phil Dick gave a wearisome sigh and said with infinite patience:

'Sovietski Literattur for Effective Manipulation.'

'That's SLEM,' I pointed out.

'Of course it is! The 'S' stands for Stanisław… S. Lem.' Phil Dick shook his head in disbelief. 'How come you're a professional journalist and you can't make such a simple connection?'

'But it says in my research notes that Stanisław Lem was born in 1921 in Poland, at a place called Lvov. He now lives in Krakow.'

'Then your notes are a pile of crap, Richy. Burn 'em. Or shoot your researcher. LEM is a collective of Soviet Writers Union hacks churning out science fiction to propagate the communist credo and the party line. If you'd read any of their product you'd know that. But I guess you haven't.'

He was right, so I couldn't contradict him. I caught my breath as the sudden spark of an idea lit up in my brain. Where it came from I haven't the faintest notion. But if it worked it might neatly resolve two intractable problems at the same time. I said:

'You don't believe that Stanisław Lem is an actual person and you also doubt the 5–sigma certainty test has any practical application outside of theoretical physics. Okay. Supposing I apply the validity of one to prove the existence of the other – would that convince you twice over…?'

I held my breath. Had I been too cocksure, too jubilant?

Phil Dick's chin was sunk on his chest, his brooding eyes staring into the far corner of the room. I couldn't tell whether he was seriously considering my proposition, or dismissing it out of hand; or whether (it was growing late, velvet darkness outside) his mind was beginning to withdraw in preparation for the forthcoming night's womb of solitude and sound, protected by the din of Beethoven and Bach while feverishly communing with *Achieve Real-Time Retaliation Within Two Sweeps of the Radar*, and this world, the secondary world, and me with it, was drifting away into insubstantial shadows.

I never got to know the answer.

It was after midnight when I returned to room 108 of the Hyatt on Katella Avenue. I put through a long-distance call to Nick Webb, not to speak to him (it was the middle of the night on the East coast) but to leave a message informing him of my plans to fly to Krakow in Poland the following day, via Paris or Berlin, whichever route the airlines could come up with at short notice. I thought about it and then decided not to give a reason for making the trip; I was either in deep trouble, of 5-sigma certainty magnitude, or would come out of it with a story that Nick would bow down and bless me for, and even give me a raise. No use worrying now.

As things transpired I had to change flights in London, again in Paris, and I could only get to Krakow via Warsaw. Luckily I had an Eastern Bloc visa with two months left to expire (I'd been to a science conference in Warsaw in the spring) and the circuitous route worked in my favour because the three-hour stopover in Warsaw enabled me to arrange a brief meeting with a journalist on a current affairs magazine I'd got to know at the conference.

How much should I reveal to Stefan Zielenski? I decided not to give the real reason for my mission, to establish a 5-sigma certainty for the existence of Stanisław Lem, mainly because the explanation would have been too complicated and also, to be honest, might have induced incredulity or laughter or both. So I downplayed it to the prosaic level of a routine assignment. However, Stefan was no fool, and he must have suspected that even Global Media Corporation, for all its wealth, influence and resources, wouldn't send a staff journalist halfway round the world to interview an obscure Polish writer of genre trash.

Whatever his doubts, Stefan behaved as the seasoned professional he was, and gave me two contact numbers in Krakow: one a reporter on the local paper, the other an official with the Soviet-Polski Writers Union. He saw me pull a face at the latter, surmising correctly my scepticism at placing any trust at all in a petty state apparatchik, appointed to spy on Writers Union members and report back to his puppet masters.

'This man is different,' Stefan assured me. 'He is a member of Solidamosc and will help you in any way he can.'

'I haven't heard of them. Is it an underground group?'

'It means Solidarity. It's an illegal union of workers which opposes the party. But you must not tell anyone of his sympathies, it will cause serious trouble.'

'For him you mean?'

'For you both.'

Twenty minutes later I caught my connecting flight. While I was in the air Stefan wired ahead to the local reporter and briefed him on the information I required; by the time my plane touched down in Krakow the reporter had made a number of inquiries and was waiting for me in the lobby of the hotel. He seemed a competent enough young fellow, eager to help (Stefan advised me to give him 15 US dollars for his time and trouble) but the results were disappointing. There were over a dozen Lems in the area, most of them small firms (panel beaters, spring manufacturers, boat builders) and professional people, such as dentists, undertakers, and an industrial chemist. The three remaining private numbers, which he had rung personally, also proved negative; none of the Lems was called Stanisław, two were widows, the last one a partially deaf (and foul-mouthed) old codger in his late seventies. The Lem I sought, as I had told Stefan, wasn't more than sixty.

As I sat with the typewritten sheet in my hand, downcast in the bustle of the lobby, the young reporter was so agitated by my dejection he became almost distraught.

I tried to calm him. I assured him he had done well and I had no complaints about his investigative work. Under cover of a folded newspaper I gave him twenty dollars. I thought he deserved a five-dollar bonus for his evident concern. We shook hands, and just before he left, in answer to my final question, he said, no, to be honest, though he himself was born and raised in Krakow, he'd never before heard that the author Stanisław Lem lived here. I began to suspect that perhaps Phil Dick was right. There was no such person as Stanisław Lem. He was the name given to a committee.

This setback made me more determined than ever. It wasn't a journalistic coup I was after, and I couldn't have cared less about having a world exclusive land in my lap, I just wanted to get at the truth.

The contact Stefan had provided from the Writers Union didn't, at first sight, bode well. For a start, his English was poor and his accent nearly impenetrable. He was short and plump, with a pale moonish face and prominent lips, strands of grey hair combed across his bald head, and weak eyes magnified by steel-framed spectacles. He picked me up at the hotel the folllowing morning and we drove north from the city, about twenty-five kilometres. Where he was taking me I had no idea. I assumed that Stefan had already spoken to this unimpressive member of Solidarity (whose mumbled name I didn't catch) and briefed him on the purpose of my visit.

Eventually we turned off the main highway and arrived at a pair of tall gates set in a grim wall of grey brick topped with barbed wire. Alongside was a signboard in Russian and

Polish, neither of which I could read. Pointing at the board, I made a dumb show of incomprehension.

'Ministry of Public Contract Supplies, Depot 9,' I understood him to say after the third attempt. Which was a fat lot of help.

The factory was a huge square block, with narrow slit-like windows set in concrete walls, and in the background the steady subdued pounding of machinery. My heart sank. The realisation of where this clown had brought me slowly seeped in. And when we entered the building and the familiar tang of industrial ink and paper reels and heavy presses filled the air, I knew for certain.

While Stefan must have mentioned authors and books to him, the S-PWU rep had got his wires crossed and come up with the brainwave that my request was for a conducted tour of a printing plant! When I tried to explain the misunderstanding, the moon-faced, bulging-eyed fellow simply beamed and nodded vigorously.

'Of course… yes! You will see latest edition here, please. I show you…'

Beckoning me on, he led the way into a vast warehouse with metal racks from floor to ceiling, piled high with thousands, perhaps millions of books.

'He is here, yes, you see…?' And taking a hardback book from a stack, he handed it to me. The title was *WIZJA LOKALNA* by – sure enough – Stanisław Lem. (I later found out the English version, not a literal translation, was *Observation on the Spot*.) 'For you, a personal copy. Accept it please.'

I sighed and, as politely as I could, thanked him for the gift. As I looked round for the way out he tugged at my sleeve; apparently the tour wasn't quite over, and I reluctantly followed as he guided me down a flight of stairs to a door with an illuminated red panel above it.

Smiling, he pointed to the sign: 'Production Department.'

For one crazy moment I had the fanciful notion that

behind the door was a smoke-filled room with fifty writers sitting round a huge circular table, all furiously scribbling away and pounding on typewriters, producing the next great work by 'Stanisław Lem'. It would have been worth it, if only to have seen Phil Dick's triumphant expression when I broke the news that he had been right all along.

What the room actually contained was even more of an anti-climax: rows of humming and clicking metal cabinets housing tape-reels the size of dinner plates behind tinted glass panels. It was clearly the technical heart of the plant, though they were still using computer technology featured in Hollywood movies back in the sixties. My jaw nearly dropped when I noticed a white-coated female technician feeding in punched and slotted cards – a system not used in the West for twenty years or more.

The S-PWU rep gave me his gentle moonbeam smile and led me over to the main desk with its array of dials and gauges and banks of controls. The whole thing seemed to be running itself. He then indicated – rather proudly I thought – what I assumed to be an automated typesetting console: a screen on which text was appearing line by line.

'The production, sir, you asked to see…' The S-PWU rep swept out his arm to encompass the female technician feeding in punched cards, the control desk with its flickering screens, including the floor above with the presses and warehouse, and finally pointed to the book I was holding.

'You mean the entire *printing* production?' I said.

'No, no… the story production too, sir. Characters. Plot. Narrative. Dialogue. Reversal. Climax. Everything here. Complete.'

He drew my attention to a manufacturer's nameplate affixed to the control desk, written in Russian, Polish and English:

LINEAR ELECTROTYPE MODULATOR.

When the S-PWU rep said everything, he meant *Everything*. The full works.

He'd kept one little surprise till last, when the reason, I guess, for his beaming pride became clear. As we were leaving the plant he took the book from me and flipped it open. Inside the back cover was a black-and-white author photograph, which the little S-PWU fellow pointed to with a grin of owlish modesty: the moonbeam face, the bald head with combed-over grey locks, the slightly bulging eyes behind steel-framed spectacles. No wonder he was proud.

I returned home to the States and wrote the article but it was never published. The world at large, including Philip K Dick, never learned the truth about Stanisław Lem. Not long afterwards I opened a newspaper to read that Phil Dick had died. He was 54. In his poky little apartment in Santa Ana with its dingy walls and moth-eaten rug he'd swallowed 49 tablets of digitalin, 30 capsules of Librium and 60 capsules of Apresoline, washed down with half a bottle of Italian red wine. He recovered, after the emergency services broke in and pumped his stomach. But the strain on his heart and constitution had been too great, and he eventually, poor man, succumbed.

Snail

Piotr Szulkin

Translated from the Polish by Danusia Stok

THE ICONIC PAVING *sett dominated the second half of the 21st century. Some people called it Baum's sett although nobody knew who this Baum was. The blocks could be manufactured in various colours and designs providing they resulted in a uniform surface once put together and left no gaps in between.*

Today we can laugh at the timid beginnings of the era of the paving sett. But these beginnings were stormy. When the well-known Egyptian oil oligarch, Ben Ola Muasi de Rothschild bought the Eiffel Tower from a French Government oppressed with debts, and covered the Tower to its very tip with Baum's setts turning it into the tallest minaret in Europe, the French nation fumed. Ben Olaf Muasi de Rothschild, however, presented the French with an alternative similar to the one they had faced during the French Revolution: either the minaret and patisseries or an Eiffel Tower not covered with paving setts, debts and, consequently, no pastries. The French, although perhaps reluctantly, chose pastries.

Baum's setts had even greater repercussions in the United States. When Fidel Hoover McCarthy, physically remarkably like El Commandante with his dishevelled beard, fiery eyes and paramilitary camouflage uniform, became President, a new spirit and mood of hope entered the people. The Americans were happy. The U.S.A., where the number of inmates in prisons was traditionally one of the highest in the world, tightened penal and civil legislation as well as all other regulations. The curve showing the number of prisoners climbed boldly upwards. And all the prisoners, regardless of their state of health, worked on the same thing: Baum's setts. At presidential receptions, even at the President's swearing-in, as well as in penal institutions, music by the Buena Vista Social Club was always being played. Instead of whisky Cuba Libre rum was drunk and Cuban cigars were distributed for free. The United States needed these soaring quantities of Baum setts for one purpose: to raise a gigantic defensive bank on the border of their territorial waters and on the Mexican border in order to safeguard the independence of the United States of America.

The problem posed by Cuba faded away. When Fidel Hoover McCarthy came to power, all disagreements subsided and some Cubans even saw Fidel Hoover McCarthy as the reincarnation of Castro himself. There remained the problem of the Guantanamo base which some crafty Chinese bought using illegal surrogate companies. They constructed a small bungalow there which they surrounded with a five-metre high wall of Baum setts, and with typically Chinese cunning enticed the Dalaï Lama there. Ever since, he has been able to look out at nothing but the greyness of a concrete sett.

The secret plans for this simple yet ingenious paving form, however, went far deeper. In the name of freedom and democracy, America and her allies continued to conduct a hard war with the indigenous warriors in Afghan, Iraqi and Pakistani territories and in the Gaza strip. The ever more powerful planes, bombs and battalions on international missions proved not enough. Emaciated natives with heads wrapped in towels appeared on camels and donkeys from no one knows where and always seemed to have the upper hand.

In the depths of the Pentagon, a truly devilish plan was concocted to resolve the matter definitively once and for all. The plan consisted of paying all the conflict-infested territories with Baum setts – paving them hermetically, regardless of whether or not anything was growing in the vicinity, whether or not there were any towns, whether or not there were any springs or mirages. The camels, just like the donkeys, could not walk on the Baum setts because their hooves would have been worn down and all attempts to shoe the animals would be forbidden by phoney representatives of the sharia really working for the US government. During the plan's second phase, a countless quantity of gambling machines, one-arm bandits, play station 3's, Masterminds, and even games of Scrabble in Arabic, would be dropped *into territories occupied by the native inhabitants – here read 'the enemy'. All predictions processed by the most complicated computers spoke of one thing: such a policy should achieve the desired result and maybe even loosen the towels on the heads of the fighting Talibs, jihadis and other disorganised entities.*

Even though the basic components necessary for production were not complicated, in view of such plans the enormous need for Baum setts resulted in the energy-consuming manufacture being transferred to outer space. And so, on neighbouring planetoids, satellites and less important planets, automatic manufacturing plants began to blow smoke, stink and make a noise. Such was the ruling, however, that supervisors be delegated even to the most distant of plants in order to ensure that automatons worked with the appropriate dedication and commitment worthy of such an historically important mission as the manufacture of paving stones.

The spaceship reached the planetoid called Australia 258. It entered into orbit and circled once. The ship looked like an enormous aluminium beer can, the kind kept under a counter. A small flame sparked at the side of the machine and the shuttle steered towards the station on the planetoid's surface. The station was an irregular pyramid constructed from broken boxes all of different sizes. Metal arms, like the legs of a cockchafer, stretched out towards the ship attaching it to the station with amazing zeal.

Krapp watched the hatch as it flew open with a rush of air, revealing the ship's interior. Inside, as if in an insect's cocoon, sat a cosmonaut squeezed into a spacesuit, a worn, leather briefcase in his hand. He crept out of his cocoon with some difficulty and entered the station. He unscrewed his bulbous helmet and began to remove the spacesuit. Having done so, he stood in front of Krapp dressed in a too tight, threadbare suit, one button fastened over his protruding belly. His hair was sparse, fair and greasy, his gaze that of someone short-sighted.

'Sanitary Control,' he said, out of breath.

'Krapp, Australia 258,' said Krapp.

The Inspector snorted in quick succession a few times.

'It stinks here,' he stated.

'It does stink a little... There aren't any filters. I ordered...' Krapp felt guilty.

'There aren't any filters anywhere. You can make them out of tights.'

'Oh... I haven't got any tights.'

'And a good thing, too. Your colleague on Vega 657 made some filters out of tights. Apparently that helped. And then he had the bright idea to put the tights on. But gravity's minimal on Vega 657. So he got tangled up in the tights and strangled himself. Besides, what the hell did he want to put those tights on for anyway?... Do you have a chocolate?... Or box of chocolates? I'm starving. My legs swell up when I'm starving.'

'There's a problem, there might be some chocolates somewhere... but the freezers broke down and all the labels got unstuck... I often get a craving for a piece of steak; I open one freezer and inside there's pineapple, and pineapple in the next one, and pineapple in the next... If I knew where the chocolates were, there wouldn't be any problem.' Krapp felt guilty and embarrassed.

'Uh... These things happen... Even downhill's a struggle for clots. Are you going to stand like that all the time? I've just been travelling...'

'Of course, please do sit down.'

The Inspector threw all the bits and bobs off the little table with one swipe, picked up the chair, wiped the seat with a tea-towel and sat down, heavily spreading out his chubby legs.

'You can sit down, too. The fact that I'm a sanitary inspector doesn't mean you have to stand to attention in front of me. Although, do you know, respect does have its worth.'

Krapp slowly sunk onto the other chair.

'Sit down like a human being, relax! You're sitting on half a bum, on the edge of the chair. And don't go thinking that I feel sorry because of that bruised mark on your bottom. No way! I only feel sorry for the chair because if you slip the chair might get damaged! One can get seasick just by looking at you.'

The inspector pulled a bundle of papers out of his briefcase.

'I, and even in a certain sense you, means WE – that is, the System. And the system exists whether we like it or not. We overthrow one system and there you are – we already have another. It may be different but between you and me – it is, after all, also a system. And a system's a system. I'm the inspector and you're the inspected. Right?'

Krapp did not say anything. Nothing came into his head.

'Often, when I think about all this, I get shivers down my back... I can't sleep and stare at the sky. The sky is starry but the system, whichever way you bend it, is the system... And why can't you, damn it, just sit normally, both cheeks of that bum flat down? And with more weight so to speak, as folk do. Why are you grinning like an idiot? It's possible to sit weightily, work-worn, like our ancestors sat – shamelessly. We do live in a free country, after all, and we don't have to be ashamed of having traditions, as far as sitting goes, too. Although, when I look at you, I don't know whether you've got any tradition whatsoever. Because, you, good sir, sit as if someone's slipped a little quail under your backside, excuse the expression...'

The Inspector chuckled and, choking, fell silent. Krapp did not say anything; just sat upright, an indifferent expression on his face.

'Offended, are you? Chuckle, chuckle... He who chuckles... chuckles well. You could do with a bit of laughter. Sanitary Control means mental control, too. I'm also assessing you psychologically. A holistic approach to the object of assessment.'

Krapp heard a buzzing as if a huge fly with a briefcase

in its paw were flying around in the station. He wanted to get up, grab the tea-towel and squash the fly and its briefcase against the wall if it would only settle for a moment.

'And did you know that your personal file is – just so thin?' The Inspector demonstrated a narrow gap with two of his fingers. 'Even your birth certificate has got lost somewhere. As far as Sanitary Control are concerned that's not so important. You've got vaccination certificates but to get to your age and have so few documents, it's puzzling, I'd even go so far as to say, suspicious. You must admit that yourself.'

'I've lived quietly, peacefully...'

'Everybody says that. At the beginning. But just remember! However hard you try, hedge your way, hide in dark, damp burrows, the Bureau is going to find you anyway! Because the Bureau isn't just picnics, dew on cobwebs and a rainbow in the sky. The Bureau, my dear man, is the stench of sewers, the reek of a drunkard's mouth with its rotten teeth, the stink of dark corridors with shelves of documents nobody remembers until somebody's inspecting hand reaches out for them.

'Don't be under the illusion that you're going to be lucky... In the end you're going to crawl to the Bureau and whimper to be given a death certificate. Because without a certificate, death would be incomplete, a pitiful example of a lack of responsibility. Can you imagine? You've breathed your last, everything's as if behind you but *rigor mortis* doesn't set in. Your physiological fluids don't drain away... Why? And how are they supposed to drain away without a death certificate?! And that might just be your case.

'And by the by, going back to the past... You don't have to answer, of course you don't. The Bureau isn't interested in the private lives of citizens. But... but that period in your life when you were as quiet as a mouse... No notes, complaints or grievances, no traces, no scraps... You must admit that's suspicious, mustn't you? Well, because how can you live without committing offences? Isn't that suspicious?'

Krapp felt guilty and condemned. He had drunk a little water but was afraid to get up.

'I'm not asking, I'm not insisting... but if you wish, of your own free accord, you can tell me everything and I'll complete the documentation... But quite obviously, it's your own free will. As you wish. I'm just aiming, you know, to be in order, from a sense of duty and aesthetics. Aesthetics here are very important. Aesthetics, for the Bureau, are like the standard measurement of a metre. A metre is as long as its standard measurement – and that's aesthetic. Without a standard a metre wouldn't exist and vice versa. And it's the same with citizens. A citizen exists as far as regulations permit – ergo, without regulations a citizen does not exist. That's exactly what aesthetics is about.'

The Inspector pulled two sandwiches wrapped in greasy newspaper, and a vacuum flask with mug from his leather briefcase.

'Want some?'

'No, thank you. I've just eaten...' replied Krapp, surprised.

'I can understand that you've got problems with grasping the gist, with understanding. But don't you worry. The Bureau – to put it crudely – doesn't give a hoot whether you understand. The Bureau is above all that. Above you, even above me.

Whether you like it or you don't like it at all
The Bureau will see, the Bureau knows all!

Heee, heee, heee, heee... Shame there aren't any chocolates.'

The Inspector smacked his lips, pleased with himself and proud.

'Sugar, you understand? The brain needs energy to function. It burns, simple sugars, and complex. With a bit of chocolate everything would be faster, more to the point, higher...

'As for the rest of what's supposed to be your life, you're

a nonentity. Trifles, chippings, dust. Your entire life is like moulting mould on the dirty wall of some provincial station. A forgotten mould, so old that nobody sees it anymore. Only those gaps in your history. A grain in a blind hen's beak, that's how glaring they are in your curriculum vitae. What a rascal! An anarchist, one could say!'

'But I really don't know what you mean.' Krapp wanted to sound firm but this came out like an admission of guilt.

'That you can't remember? What can that matter?

'Just take on board: I don't expect you to remember your life. How can someone who has had such a boring, colourless life be expected to remember anything about it whatsoever? Not only is it impossible to tell one day from another in your life; one can't even tell the difference between night and day.

'I even understand that you can't remember anymore. I daresay it would be truer to state that you don't want to remember. Besides, I'd feel like a one-day Mayfly in your place, too. An amoeba. It's your life, but life, after all, is only worth as much as its memories. What do you remember of your life? But I don't want to intrude. It's your pain, your life's debit. You're a loser. You were born a loser.

'Imagine that you're very hungry and you've got a roast chicken. Well, you're really, really hungry... and a roast chicken from the spit?

'Now close your eyes and imagine you're eating this chicken... That you've already eaten the chicken. And what's left of the chicken?

'Bones! A pile of bones. A pile of inedible, indigestible bones. There! So, that chicken roasted on a spit, is like your filthy life. And the bones which are left of it are the official facts. Inedible, indigestible, one could say eternal. And if not eternal then at least more permanent than your ever paler life.

'You'd like to understand? Yeah... I know the feeling.'

The Inspector unwrapped the other sandwich, and

unfastened the middle button of his jacket. A shirt with a crooked tie lurking somewhere under his arm appeared, gaping open in the vicinity of his hairy belly button.

'Just listen, space, you see, is like shelves in an office which overhead have rooms with other shelves above them and other offices with rooms with yet other shelves around them, and around the town there are states, continents, drawers, and everything's packed to the brim with floppy discs, computers, records, archive workers...

'Everything can be recorded and has to be recorded. And everything that's recorded should be kept. And even better, have a copy made and kept! And things aren't important or unimportant. Everything's important! Even your unimportant life. Everything should be recorded and everything will be recorded. The perfect photograph. A record of not only facts but also potential facts. Things that didn't happen but could have done so. Words, which for lack of courage, weren't uttered but stuck in the throat... Paragraph after paragraph, gesture after gesture, stamp after stamp, grimace after grimace... The system does not forget; the system has no emotions; the system cannot be inhuman or unjust. The system, my good man, can only be systematic, full stop.'

Krapp felt that all those unstable shelves might come tumbling down on his head at any moment and bury him in a heap of files full of yellowing documents.

'Hey, hey, hey!' The Inspector slapped Krapp on the back. '*I* sense something's budging in you! You're beginning to understand!'

Krapp sniffed loudly. The slap on the back had shaken him from his stupour.

'What's this? Are you crying? Crying... ever so quietly... Go on, have a good cry. I won't give you a tissue because I haven't any.

'Besides I couldn't give two hoots about your past. What counts is the future. And I'm not being magnanimous. What's the Bureau need to be magnanimous for?! It's merely a matter of social efficiency. The management of human resources. That's what it's about! Are you keeping up with me? This also comes under Sanitary Control.

'The past! And who's going to write the anthem of the future, eh?!

'Old religiosity. Lambs working for the forgiveness of sins, ignoramuses, backwardness, superstition, to put it mildly. *Panta rhei* – there were lambs, then a leftist and revolutionary Personnel Department, and now it's the predatory Economy. Everyone fights against everyone else for a bit of space under the hazy sun. That's what we call progress! And it's apt. Because economy has its scientific rights! Every squirt knows that. Economy doesn't have to climb onto a pulpit to show its true, wolfish countenance!

'Liberalism piles duties on everybody. Everybody should be getting rich at the expense of others. Accumulating as much as possible. Those who aren't are a thorn in the side of the new order of things. They grate against the harmonious choir which melodiously sings hosanna to the new. *Homo homini lupus est!* And with that in mind take a look at me... Would accumulating capital – in your hands – serve any higher purpose? Are you in any state whatsoever to accumulate anything at all? I, personally, doubt it. To be honest, you don't at all look like someone who's capable of being free, independent. There, you're sitting with half your bum hanging off the edge again! If you only knew how that annoys me... That's why I'm asking you politely to stop wriggling even if it's itching...

'If you didn't have that something... That losing streak, that tiredness, that way of mucking up your thoughts – the Sanitary Control Service would not have sent me here to you... And I wouldn't be getting uptight whether you're going to fall off that chair.

'You're a flat tyre... Between you and me – why these demonstrations? Well? Why? That you're better or something?

Above it all! Above me! Above the structure! The Bureau! The system! What are you defending?! Values? And who defined them? Not me! The nation! You invent them! Why, that's usurpation!

'Today we've got these values, tomorrow different ones and the day after, different yet! Do you know what the one and only imperishable value is? You don't! Then I'll tell you! I, a mouse behind a desk, with varicose veins from sitting on a hard chair – a sponge isn't healthy – I, a cog-wheel as it were, yet really a foundation stone! Listen!

'The one and only imperishable value is... contempt. Yes, my good man! And don't have any illusions: I hold you in contempt. And others like you! Contempt! Contempt! Contempt! And you can hold me in contempt – as much as you like, my good man. Let yourself go, puff yourself up with that contempt of yours! Hold me in contempt, go on!'

The Inspector crumpled the greasy sandwich papers and threw them at the wastepaper bin. He missed.

'Well? You look like a little blown-up balloon now, heee, heee, heee... A potential latex piece of tripe. And you know why? Because you're sitting in front of the table and I'm sitting behind it. Only my part of the table is called a desk. My Sanitary Inspector's Desk. And I can say nothing or I can speak. I can tell you to be quiet or answer... I address you – when I so wish – from the height of my desk, a desk which is, as it were, an altar because here are distributed not the holy, but the really important official sacraments. The desk is, as it were, a baptismal font because there's a briefcase on the desk and in that briefcase are legal stamps. The Laws of the Bureau! The great Laws of the Bureau!'

Krapp bent over, picked up the sandwich papers and threw them into the wastepaper bin. He felt the grease saturating the wrapping on the tips of his fingers, and imperceptibly wiped them on his trousers.

'You're bloated and that's it. So much for your contempt. You can't do anything. What?... You're laughing? And what are you laughing at? Why are you chuckling like an idiot?'

The Inspector scraped his chair on the floor and got up, resting his hands on the table.

'And don't tell me you're not laughing if I deem you're laughing!!!'

He sunk down on his chair and doubled over, as if in pain.

'May you get emphysema of the guts...

'Like you sit there in front of me...

'May you writhe in pain...

'And in the throes of that pain may you experience a prophecy in the rituals of the universal church.'

Suddenly the Inspector straightened himself and in an almost calm voice said:

'...You haven't got emphysema in the guts yet. But merely in a certain sense. Because in another way you've already got it. Emphysema. You've already got it... conceptually. Isn't that right... my friend? Listen carefully to your tummy.

'Rumbling? Is it starting? There you are!

'It's as if a huge icicle was stirring all your guts, your intestines, *n'est-ce pas*? And pushing the small intestine where your large intestine's supposed to be. And vice-versa. Exactly.

'Dispersed, has it? Swelling disappeared through your ears? Have you felt the magical power of the Bureau now? Its breath?

'There, you see for yourself. It's like enlightenment.

'Incidentally, I doubt whether my efforts... Are you spiritually capable of appreciating them? Because let's look truth in the eyes – even if you wanted to you wouldn't bend. Nahhh... And you know it. It's already too late for you. For you what's new – even though it is new – is already dead and gone. Stiffness of the spine. Blocked arteries. Lack of oxygen. Malfunction of thought, not to mention malfunction of actions. Diseases of the elderly. Those like you are... ohhh! You know what an old person smells like? If you don't then smell yourself. And what should you exist in these new times for? To stink?!

'The only hope is that the healthy current of reality will sweep you away like a toothpick... What am I saying, like the wrappings of a toothpick.

'Damn it, it's hot... And it stinks of you.'

The Inspector sucked at a cavity in his tooth.

'Don't you have at least a tiny sweet? I've got an aftertaste.

'By the way, I've got doubts whether you're capable of fathoming out the entire complexity of the notion of 'the Bureau'. Because 'the Bureau', my good man, is something mystical, spiritual. Although, strictly speaking, devil knows where this spirituality comes from...

'It's a sort of fact – somebody at the beginning, some lord or director, establishes such and such a bureau. But then the lord dies, they throw the director out, but the Bureau remains. It remains and grows. It often changes its name. Changes buildings. Changes state allegiance. Changes its apparent, statutory tasks – but it continues. It continues above gales, above the heads of officials and managers. It sails like a transatlantic ship in the fog. Neither passengers nor crew know where it's sailing to, what for? It's only by the sound of the engines and the spray of breaking waves that one can tell one's sailing. And you won't believe it but the water in the washbasins of the ladies toilets on the third floor is as if salty. Maybe it's the spray?

'But one thing's for sure: the Bureau never dies. It's eternal. It would seem that this or that Bureau is half-dead, that they're going to get at it and close it. And then that wheezing bureau transforms itself with a wild somersault and in an instant becomes a new bureau which, as it were, is doing something quite the opposite to the old one. Yet when all is said and done – between you and me, whether this bureau does what it is doing now or what it was doing before is not in the least important.

'Because... because... – and you remember this, my good friend – the Bureau doesn't serve to do anything. If the Bureau produces some sort of paperwork, regulations, instructions, it's without conviction. One has to, as it were... But as for all these documents – all is vanity! I know something about it. For... – pay attention now and remember – for the Bureau basically serves only one purpose: to keep existing.' From the depths of space station Australia 258, as if to emphasise the importance of the Inspector's words, a siren like the whistle of a rushing steam engine resounded, announcing that another batch of 10,000 Baum setts had been produced. After a while the carillon subsided and changed into its regular puffing and wheezing.

The Inspector stretched lazily in his chair, slipped his feet out of his worn-out shoes and continued dreamily.

'During the day there's uproar, people milling around. Dust from files shimmering in the air... Lack of concentration. But in the evenings... during overtime... I often do overtime, not that I've particularly got a lot of work. No, no... Just out of interest. I lay my chair out with a blanket because nobody's going to see anyway. And there I sit... I lean back so that the chair's balanced on two legs, and rock. All by myself. And listen in.

'You can hear strange things sometimes. Often a patter, patter, patter... along the floor. But you look at the floor and you can't see anything. Or I've discovered that if you bite on a blueberry pie – if you've got one, of course – so, if you bite on a blueberry pie, the door in the second cupboard from the front door opens. I discovered that by myself. Munch on the blueberry pie and the door immediately – grooooaaan! Shame it's not the season for blueberry pie. Because it doesn't work with just any old pie...

'You're probably saying to yourself: eh, what's this old boor bothering me with? And you're wrong. If you were to sit there yourself doing overtime you'd understand... Felt it for yourself... I sit there and know that that whose name I don't want to say out loud... the BUREAU is watching me from behind. Watching my back, watching the back of my head...

'Brrr! What sliminess in that gaze... It's hard to bear, realising it's there behind you...

'But I'm not frightened. I zriiip, lean back over my right shoulder. Always the right. You can only do it over the right! To catch it watching me like that. But no... It's faster. The beast.

'Patter, patter, patter behind my back. I zriiip – and behind me nothing.

'Only on the floor it's as if a snail's gone by. Wet, slimy... But what kind of a snail is it that goes patter, patter, patter – patters?

'I had a colleague and she said you could get pregnant in the Bureau without knowing. Just like that, just by being there. It would figure with the snail... The noiseless runner... Perversity.

'And it doesn't threaten me. The Bureau wouldn't be so intimate with me. I'm not a woman after all.

'But you've got to be careful... Have to be on your guard...

'Do you think that such a bureau would go so far as to creep up and whoosh, pull the chair down to the floor when I'm rocking on its two back legs? I've got a thing about falling off a chair to the floor...

'The Bureau usually multiplies by dividing but it can probably do it through sex, too, like in the case of that colleague. Although I ask myself: Has anyone ever seen the sexual organs of the Bureau... A pattering snail?! And if nobody's seen them then who's hiding them from us and why? Yes, my Prince, wherever you spit, in administration there's nothing but secrets…

'Although it is exciting; sitting there doing overtime, and tempting the unknown, the dark and powerful. Waiting, nice and cosy tucked up in a blanket, offering your clean-shaven neck, waiting for it to come, embrace and lift. Crash to the floor. And then, may it even eat you, annihilate you mashing one body with the other into a mass, in madness, in abandon, in a cry of emancipation merging spirit with spirit into one. I the official and it, the officiating! In one! Indistinguishable. Merged, and by this uniformity stronger, more powerful!

'Can't be lengthened or made shorter. Just right! Undeformable. Like the matrix of the metre in Sèvres near Paris.

'And I only ask myself sometimes – when I can't see it in front of me or behind – where is it when I can't see it? Where is it when it isn't there...?'

Krapp felt cold shivers run down his back, sweat and slight dizziness as if he had the first symptoms of 'flu.

'Do you have any vodka?' asked the Inspector.

'No, in keeping with paragraph 345 of the Space Code,' Krapp replied formally. He was lying. They all lied. You didn't have to have brains to produce a couple of litres of good moonshine on a space station which nobody visited for months on end.

'I only asked as a matter of form,' said the Inspector. He pulled out a miniature bottle of whisky from his briefcase, unscrewed the cap with a rasp and poured the entire contents down his throat. He threw the bottle into the waste bin and this time did not miss the mark, except for the cap which rolled somewhere out of sight.

'I must confess to you that I've got a certain weakness: I'm noble-minded. I'm unable to be otherwise. That's the way I was born... or something...

'When I see a snail going... no, crawling rather, across the path leaving behind this glistening, sticky streak, I stretch my leg out and just like this, see... crush it with the sole of my shoe. It's important after squashing it to rub what remains of it into the tarmac with your shoe because you never know... That's a superstition I've got. If you heard the crunch of the shell as it cracks... And sometimes you get those fat, black ones without a shell. Those, when they burst, make a squelch sound!

'So I take pity on them so that they don't suffer. A snail like that... how's it supposed to cross the road on its own? It's going to use up all its mucous and only get half way. And there are cars there, children... Have you seen a snail that's been partially run over by a car? Or partially cut in half by a kid?

'And sometimes when I find a little one, a teenie-weenie snail, I carry it across. To the other side of the road. A tiny one like that on the other side of the road, it's like a new life for it. A mutiny against the one it knew. But those old, fat ones I don't let pass. They're slimy, shameless... No doubt they leave their families because there's not enough heroism in them to cope with everyday grey life... and they escape to the other side of the road.

'As for children, families and partnerships on the whole, I'm very sensitive. All that's somehow passed me by... But surely everyday brings new promises... The mystery of life... The division of cells. I often wonder about that. If you only saw those chubby faces! Mothers often bring their child along to the office. Stupid thing, does she expect me to take pity on her? Get me all sentimental? About those dimples in its cheek?! The little, howling thing, puking its soup up, poohing its soup! The mystery of conception: to convert the soup into constipation. But the worse thing is that the tiny blighter dribbles like a snail...

'Yeeaah... Although I'd be a good mother. Tender. Exemplary. I sometimes think that I don't fit in with the world outside... Maybe fate has marked a different path out for me, somewhere higher up, above the visible... Perhaps it's my fate to sacrifice myself as an offering to that... You know, the one who goes patter, patter, patter... So I just sit there and wait, just like that... Like some, excuse the expression, some pen-pushing girl. Because at first glance you could be wrong about me. I'm somebody else. But I'm not going to walk around with a sign around my neck, after all. I hate ostentation.

'Besides, the notion of life has always been dear to me... I adored lessons about nature when I was a child. I made experiments. And especially this one which I did a number of times. You take a tea glass. Pour in some water. You cover the glass with gauze so that it barely touches the surface of the water then you put one or two beans on it... And you stand all that on the window sill, in sunlight. Chlorophyll, you understand. And after a while shoots come out of the bean, one with some leaves shoots up, another with roots goes down. And so they creep; one up and one down because they still don't know that they're being cheated. That the gauze rotting in the glass is not a scented flowerbed, that there isn't any spring only rain and slush outside... And that there isn't any mysterious call to life! Something starts to exist which has been cheated even before it was born.

'Like me. Exactly, excuse the expression, like me. I gnaw my way into the fabric of society like that poor plant into the gauze, although I know perfectly well that I'll never blossom in a real meadow. I put the roots, as it were, into the murky water of the glass but the harder I try the faster these roots get covered with mucous, the brown erosion of decay – like my legs with varicose veins...

'And why do I have varicose veins on my legs? From sitting?

'Once the sink got blocked. A sink at which you could make tea. So when it got blocked of course there wasn't anybody... I unscrewed the s-bend myself... And in that s-bend... The number of lemon pips there! I like tea with lemon. And can you imagine, some of those pips had sprung shoots, pale green ones, winding their way up, thin shoots. Lemons growing in the s-bend of a sink! Heee... heee...

'Pollution of the environment. Lack of sunlight... It's all fiddle-faddle. Fiddle-faddle and untrue! Because, my dear chap, for something to grow, for something to live – you need fluid. A woman's fluid. Maternal fluid. And I've got this fluid of life. I'd spread it around and those pips picked it up. That's why they grew!

'I screwed the s-bend back on and poured some nail varnish remover in through the top. You have to be honest in matters of life. Even as regards such a simple plant. You mustn't cheat it.

'Or life as such, toil, diseases, nerves and then the grave.

Worms in the grave and maybe snails, too. So much trouble to turn into a worm. Wouldn't it be simpler to be born a worm straight away? It's mysterious this dissolution of matter. Maybe what dissolves turns into this snail trail? Gleaming so... Running somewhere as if spurred on by some longing.

'But if you can't see the snail then how can you tell in which direction it's going?

'And what? A snail like that, does it drag a 'trail' behind it from the day it's born to the day it dies? This snot-like, gleaming line from which it can't deviate either to the right or to the left? From which it can't possibly escape?

'But, but, but it's... just like us. To be born, grow up, die... and always dragging a trail behind ourselves. Can't go either right or left. Like a harnessed nag with blinkers on and a ring in its nose... like those nags. And we pull; phlonk – there's one document, plonk – another document, whack – a certificate, rasp – an application... That's our snail's trail. You don't leave your trail because you have to go on. And as you go it's as if you're tearing your skin on the cobblestones. And you pull the damp trail of scraps of your own body, your entrails behind you... converted into a huge ribbon of smeared paper, indestructible, administrative annotations.

'Until you wear yourself away, until you tear all the moisture from yourself, until you become a crisp...

'And there's only one force which can violate this order. To stand over man the way man can stand over a snail. Pick him up and carry him gently by his shell, tear him away from the snotty trail and... turning him by 180 degrees, for example, so that he goes to the same place he came from, or to set him on his way in a different, entirely random direction. Making a laughing-stock of all the snail's toil because the snail was, after all, going somewhere along an old track, wanted to get somewhere. And now it's going somewhere entirely different although it doesn't know anything about this. Although there isn't even any chance of it knowing anything about it.

'This new direction is, after all, kept secret from the

snail. One moment it was there and now it's somewhere entirely different. Where then? From where? How's that snail supposed to know?

'Has it ever happened to you to tear a snail from its slippery trail and put it down in an entirely different place? Has it ever happened to you, I ask? Well, has it?!

'And has it ever happened to you to feel you were the snail?'

Krapp did not say anything.

'Yes, my Prince, we all live not knowing, in pain, stupefied. So I sit those nights out, hold out my exposed neck, all tense, stiff... and wait. I await.

'And tears run down my cheeks. Would you believe it? My tears run down!

'It often feels as if it's finally approaching out of the darkness, quietly pattering. It stops behind me... I feel its breath... It bites into my neck, then lips, then my whole self... ah!

'God, hosanna! – everything in me would like to cry out. Hosanna! – just let it come, just let it come at last. I'd be able to repay it with my eagerness, dedication, I'd forget about myself...'

The Inspector pulled out a checked handkerchief and blew his nose.

'But what can you know about such waiting?

'The world's a farce. The same jesters all around. You were against the regime, you were for it... You were sociable, you were antisocial... And how it all tallies with this lump which I'm carrying. Which we all, like one man, are carrying. To this lump right here, under my throat. A lump which when it swells doesn't allow me to either swallow or to sigh.

'Apparently somewhere systems change, apparently somewhere governments change. Revolutions turn out to be conspiracies, a just struggle turns into disempowerment. Everything gets mixed up with everything. The law with martyrdom, wisdom with a patchwork of platitudes, ugliness with desire... And the only thing which remains unchangeable is this lump. My lump. My fear, my... loneliness.

'Can you stand behind me for a moment? I ask you kindly. I'll be you. I can give you... my briefcase. It's travelled through the whole of space. A present, you understand? Oh, you're so kind... Go round behind me, quietly, on tip-toes... You could touch my neck with the tip of your right index finger... Like that. And now if you licked the tip of your finger and ran the wet finger across my neck... I'd feel as if it was a snail...

'And don't spare your spittle. I want to feel it, wet, cool.

'Have I bent my neck out far enough? Have I stuck the back of my neck out enough?

'I feel you understand me, that I've got a friend in you, an understanding friend. That for me you... And don't stop! I ask you. How strange, you're as if a stranger, as if a supplicant, meaning you're less than nothing... But when it comes to the crux it's precisely someone so coincidental, someone like you...

'Now lean over the back of my neck. And... just don't be put off... Trust me a bit longer... Bite it, the back of my neck, gently. Go on, please. That's it! My God...! Again... See how delicate, helpless it is, the skin so white, almost transparent. Not an ounce of fat, not a bit. You can even see the thin little veins, so dark, almost navy-blue. Blow on the spot wet with saliva so I feel the cold there. Oh... And now bite! Gently at first, draw in a narrow fold of flesh in between your teeth and bite it. And then suck it in. Right. And now suck! Suck as hard as you can, Prince, suck until your tongue swells, suck and bite! Bite hard. Bite as if your whole mousy, snailish life, your dun-grey slavish life were to be redeemed as a reward.

'You're divine, Prince, just suck, just bite, don't stop. And reach for the Baum block which is lying there on the floor.

'Lift that bloody block up high, high up... God, how

loud is that snail's ghastly patter... Something's shaking. What is it, my Prince, can your hand be shaking?

'Well, go on, take the briefcase, your paper life, take it, everything. I'm giving it to you, I pardon you, declare you innocent...

'See the back of my neck sticking out, waiting?

'My Prince... Just aim accurately... Strike so that you don't have to finish me off...'

Less Than Kin, More Than Kind

Brian Aldiss

THE TAXI THAT collected us from the Dorchester was hired to deliver Sir Arthur Charles to his door, before taking me on to my humbler abode in Tubney. We had attended the meeting of Regal Oil (UK), of which Arthur was deputy chairman. I was second scientific advisor. We had become friendly and had enjoyed a few drinks in the hotel bar after the meeting.

Arthur was the star of our little group, seemingly light-hearted and joking about the company's difficulties.

During the drive to his home he had fallen into a gloomy silence I was unable to penetrate. I had time to realise we were not the newly formed friends I had imagined. He just needed company, preferably silent company.

My mood was mixed by the time the taxi brought us down the drive to Arthur's home, Baron's Gate. The place was in darkness, the manor looming sternly above us in the night.

Arthur climbed out of the cab, then turned back to seize my arm.

'A favour, my friend. Just come in with me, would you? Eh? Be so kind. Really can't face... well, trouble, if there is any trouble.'

Yes, we had been been drinking. I could not at that moment think why I should not accompany him in as requested. We had come together only an hour or two ago;

drink making us immediately friendly, and the thought occurred to me that I might get another drink at his place.

There was nothing to draw me back home. I had no home. My marriage had broken up. I was staying in a room in what described itself as a private luxury hotel. I climbed out of the cab. It was midnight.

'And there often is,' he said, in a belated after-thought.

It was dark and cold. He caught my arm, less in friendship, I was sure, but to steady himself. I felt drunker than expected. 'Does it ever cross your mind that life's worse...' My sentence ran out of steam. I was talking thickly, he wasn't listening.

Arthur was staggering round to the driver of the taxi, pulling out folding money from a hip pocket as he went.

'I thought we was goin' on to Tubney,' said the driver.

'Look, here's twenty quid. Shut up and clear off!'

'No need to get shirty!' He drove away at a furious rate.

Again Arthur took my arm to steady himself or possibly me, and we entered by the rather grand door. A light came on automatically in the hall. Slowly and patiently, he took off his coat while I slipped out of my raincoat. He let his coat slip to the floor and left it there.

'It's good of you,' he said, gesturing widely. 'More than kind. Sometimes there's a rather distressing bit of a barney when I get home. We'll have a coffee and a brandy and I'll get Hetty to phone for a taxi for you – not for the bastard I've just overpaid.'

For some reason, this remark amused both of us. Laughing, we went down a short corridor and he led the way into a living room.

The room was in shadow, lit only by a tall candle which stood by a wide hearth. A fire smouldered and burned in the hearth. In front of it sat a woman, with a wine glass by her side. She was holding a poker, the far end of which lay in the ashes of the fire. The firelight flickered unreliably on her face.

She was in her nightdress, covered by a brightly patterned wrap.

Her bare feet peeped from under the hem of the nightdress, their nails painted a bright scarlet. Her hair, possibly dyed, straggled over her shoulders. It could be assumed she was ready for bed. She turned her head slightly in our direction and said, in a contemptuous tone directed at her husband, 'So you managed to get back here, then? With some poor lackey to hold you up!'

'I'm not drunk, if that's what you think, Hetty. Hardly touched a drop. You're in your usual bad mood, dear, is that it?' He paused before adding, 'This is my friend, Alec. I think he might like a drink before he disappears.'

She swung round on her bottom, letting go of the poker. The nightdress fluttered so that I caught a glimpse of her bare legs. She said with contempt in her voice, 'I bet you've both already had too much – as per usual.'

'Please don't be depressing, dear. The meeting went badly enough. Extreme things said about me.'

Lifting up the candle to advance, she illuminated her face. I saw how beautiful she was, with a sharp but shapely nose and high cheek bones. She scarcely spared me a glance.

'Throw your friend out, Arty, and get yourself to bloody bed.'

I saw in his hesitation he was, at least to some extent, afraid of her or of what she might do.

He looked helplessly at me, as he stood there, tired and uncertain.

'What would you like, Alec?' he asked.

'I'd love to fuck Hetty.' I had no notion I was going to say what I said.

He frowned and slowly – but now everything happened in slow motion – asked, 'What's that you said? Perhaps I am a bit drunk.'

Must be polite, I thought. 'I would like to have intercourse with your wife... If you were both agreeable, I mean.'

'Intercourse with my wife! Good Lord, man, what are you thinking of? You've only just got here.'

She said, 'Pr'aps he finds me attractive. That's more than you do.'

'Hetty, dear, that's unfair. You know I find you gorgeous. It's just your bad temper... How do you feel about doing what this young man just suggested?'

She sighed and looked at the ceiling. 'Why on earth should I want him up me? It's an insult he even suggested it!'

'I intended a compliment,' I explained. 'I thought you looked so nice.' and then I added, 'And ready for it... The poker...'

'It's humiliating,' Arthur said. 'There's always something when I come home. It makes a man's life a misery.'

'Always sorry for yourself, Arty! What about my life, stuck here alone?' She had ignored my remark...

'I'm humiliated, downright humiliated,' he said, without emphasis. 'Surely this young man should be allowed to speak his mind, however disgusting it is. Shouldn't you be flattered? You're always on about it.'

Hetty sighed heavily. 'All right. OK. He can screw me if he wants. Why the hell not? We could do it right here, on the chaise longue. Why should I care?'

He staggered backwards a pace. 'What, you'd do it with a stranger? Just to degrade me...'

He was about to say more when she snapped, 'Oh, for Gods's sake, Arty! Go and get yourself a drink and clear off up to bed – or do you want to stand there and watch us at it, him and me?'

I saw him – I can only explain it by saying that I saw him close down. 'I may lose my position at Regal,' he said. 'Not that it matters. Nothing *matters*.' He withdrew his gaze, turned, and dragged himself through a rear door. It slammed behind him.

'That's better.' Hetty said in a lighter tone. 'His father was just as bad, a real boozer. They were a family of apes.'

'Look, if you don't want –'

'Shut up and help me drag the chaise longue in front of the fire.'

Once we had done as she said, she lifted her nightdress to waist-level, announcing that before we coupled, I must kiss her thoroughly on the nest of her delight – that was her phrase – the nest of her delight, as a tribute to the pleasure to come.

I knelt in front of her and willingly did as she bid.

It was as simple then to enter her as a bird enters its nest.

We were lying still interlocked, with my arms about her, when – distinctly if distantly – a pistol shot was heard.

She pulled my arms away and sat up.

'Jesus! Jesus, he's shot himself, blown his bloody brains out. He was always threatening to... poor sod...'

'Shall I go and see if anything can be done?.'

'Stay down here. Phone for an ambulance. There'd be such a mess. The brains...'

While we waited for the ambulance, she asked me if I believed in an Afterlife.

'I'm a scientist. Surely you don't imagine this Afterlife thing just suddenly clicked in with the birth of Jesus Christ?'

'Yes, I do. Either at his birth or his crucifixion.'

'But we – us, the human race – are descended from apes. Do you really believe that apes enjoy an Afterlife too?'

Hetty began to laugh. She threw back her head and laughed. She covered her face with her hands and laughed a shrill laugh.

'Just imagine!', she said in a stifled voice. 'Arty dies and finds himself in some weird Afterlife place infested with apes... He hates apes! Oh, my God, just imagine... more apes than humans! Poor bugger!'

Her laughter resembled screaming.

She was still laughing and crying when the ambulance arrived and the paramedics came in.

Later I saw Hetty button-holed by a reporter on Bond Street, as she was going into a shop. She put together two sentences that, united, marked the height of silliness.

'He was depressed. I don't know what was wrong with him.'

Traces Remain

Sarah Schofield

THE POD DOOR *hisses open. Adam wakes. His whisky-sour breath catches, a pulse throbbing behind his ears. It takes him a moment to remember why his lap is clammy.*

'Hello?'

A shadow stretches in the doorway.

'Bram?' he says, although he knows it can't be Bram.

The intruder breathes. Reelbreth.

A low whistling purr comes from the crate in the corner.

'Who are you?'

The figure sits lightly on Adam's bed. The starlight from the velvet black of the observatory bubble illuminates his wide forehead and broad shoulders.

He tenderly strokes the darting light across his palm. 'You can't stay here,' he says.

'Where are the others…my…?' Adam's head pounds.

He raises an eyebrow.

The last of the whisky twinkles in the bottle. Lil would understand.

The man rises slowly. He goes to the crate, lifts it and tucks it under one arm. The contents shift inside.

'I looked after it…' Adam says quietly.

'Yes.' He takes Adam's hand. 'Come with me.'

Adam caught up with Bram after the board meeting. Following a lengthy discussion about the breakdown in communications with Earth and actroid short staffing, his AOB had dropped off the bottom of the agenda.

'I wanted to discuss my Travelling Century Play initiative…'

Bram, The Depot Commander of Mare Nubium, pressed on down the corridor. 'It's not a priority… And you know what the budget's like…'

'I know, but listen. It'll boost morale.' Adam hurried after him. 'Each moon depot puts together an ensemble to perform a play documenting different centuries. We'll stream them to the other depots in rotation over a week…'

Bram shook his head, slowing a little. 'Like I said. Not a priority. Plays won't fix the biosphere gardener shortage. And I, for one, don't want to go without my banana slices on those disgusting bran flakes they shipped last time. They think we can live on that…? If they'd let us reinstate the EMT arsenal, create a bit of incentive, the actroids would work a bit harder…'

'Let me do my job, Bram,' Adam cut in. 'People are getting moribund again. Especially without Earth communication. It's been down for months now…'

'Yes. I know.' He frowned and stopped. 'Your play things… Can we not just watch BBC archive?'

'I think we've exhausted the library… Anyway, it's about personnel integration…'

Bram gazed up through the observatory bubble overhead and grudgingly acquiesced. On the proviso that he didn't have to act in their ensemble. And of course, costs were kept nominal.

Three weeks later Mare Nubium's personnel gathered in the screening room for the performance streamed from Ptolemaeus depot. The humans gathered to the left of the auditorium. The actroids sat quietly on the right. The right half of the screen had been playing up recently, and a replacement panel had not yet been shipped. Adam bit his lip, trying to think of a way to integrate everyone. But it seemed reductive. The actroid's visual programming could equalize the flickering screen. It gave the humans headaches.

Adam slid into a seat beside Bram. The lights dimmed as Ptolemaeus's ensemble gathered.

'And so, in 1946 as the Tommys made their last attempts, weak in body but mighty in spirit, the Gerrys began to sense their demise…' said a short actroid wearing a bowler hat and clutching a disabled EMT.

The camera zoomed in. His eyes flickered discordantly, paralleling the words with his internal archive. Spotting his script error too late, Adam reddened. But around the auditorium the other actroids were blank faced, perhaps crosschecking and discarding this information. The humans in the room didn't seem to have noticed.

The camera panned across the platform to an actroid in a white headscarf. Something familiar about her measured expression made Adam falter. She tilted her chin. The gesture was so humanistically sharp that he swallowed back a latent stab of attraction. The filament of green light glowed across her palm as she delivered Mother Teresa's lines.

Adam leaned over to Bram. 'Who's she?'

'That's Tawn.' Bram bounced his eyebrows. 'Recommissioned.'

'Tawn… Anagrammed 2nd generation?' Adam tested various arrangements of her name as she unravelled the headscarf and pulled on a blonde Marilyn Monroe wig.

'Sent in the last shipment with four more Helium-3 harvesters to Ptolemaeus. A Gardener. Ridiculous they sent her there.' Bram jerked his head at the screen. 'I've made a transfer request. I certainly won't object to showing her around my biosphere…'

Adam turned away.

The cast bowed to stuttering applause. People made swiftly for the exit as the Earth news bulletin bleats were sounding. Adam slumped deeper in the empty row of seats and glanced at the actroids, who all remained quietly on the right. He wondered why they sat through the news when the humans avoided it. Perhaps they were programmed that way. They never used to configure that in. But it was a long time since he'd been involved in humanistic development. Adam always watched the bulletin. In case Lil was interviewed again. And its grim content spurred him on to appear indispensable, despite not having a lot to do. The actroids had the important stuff covered.

The screen flickered with grainy, burning buildings. Then cut to a road striped with what looked like rusting railway sleepers until Adam picked out the battered features of human bodies and realized he was mistaken. 'Fallout…' the voiceover said, 'of a dirty bomb.' The shot changed. A suburban township. Curtain tatters blowing through shattered windows. Concrete blocks barred the road. '…Hoped to have all infected contained.'

Adam returned to his pod and began dictating the Travelling Century Play progress report. He noted, frowning, that Ptolemaeus's cast were all actroids and the integration section of his report would need fudging. Maybe he had been overly optimistic to expect humans to volunteer.

'The initiative is proving to alleviate some of the specious barriers between our personnel. There's a marked improvement as a result of my interactive liaison activities…' He deleted the last line. 'Resultant of the work I have conducted as humanistic liaison officer…' he starred the section to return to later. 'A wholesomely positive exercise that, while making some progress this week, would benefit from repeated reinforcement in the future to further its impact as an inter-depot interaction.' He slumped into his rocking chair and rubbed his head. A dull ache was worming in. He would ask Bob78 to assist him tomorrow. His trainer had been a retired Oxford English professor.

Adam sighed. His job on Mare Nubium was deskilling him. He had once been a lead humanics researcher. The media had toe-curlingly dubbed it soul creation. But it was simply programming and interface linkage. The Reelbreth technology and nuanced expressions had been his idea. Thousands of programmed 'preferences', created actroids that were anthropomorphically conducive to positive interaction in the workplace. That was their brief. Adam and Dr Lilith Furst had gathered a panel of specialists; psychologists, body language experts, even actors – an unlikely team who knew nothing of robotic technology and everything about human heart. Each was vetted for signs of aggression, sexually violent tendencies or agalmatophilia. They'd wanted to create something good.

Each new actroid undertook a training period, during which their programming could be 'personalised' through carefully guided interaction with a human. This was modelled on guide dog puppy training, until actroid assistants for the blind took over their role. Humanistics had moved on since then, but like a parent watching a child grow from afar, Adam could see traces remaining of his early work in the newer actroids on the depot.

He rocked back in the chair and eyed the whisky bottle glinting like amber on his shelf. When he'd dispatched from Earth to Mare Nubium, he'd brought hardly anything with him not wanting to empty the flat around Lil. She had made him bring the chair, though. It was something they'd found in a reclamation yard. It was a nursing chair, really. Although neither of them had ever said it. The whisky had been his choice. The last bottle of a case to open when she arrived.

Adam longed for a sour smoked mouthful of that whisky. But breaking it open had always been a moment he had savoured sharing with Lil.

'We'll have to manage, until I can join you…' she'd said, locking her fingers into his.

She should have been shipped by now.

Adam closed his eyes, rocked back in the chair and tried to sleep, but he was desiccated and distracted. Above him the stars scattered across the shrouding curve of his observatory.

In that tiny bubble day and night were all the same. And sleep, as always, came in patches of hot and cold.

Towards morning, Adam got up and went to the biosphere. He typed in the entry code, walked through the cool mist of antibac spray and took the elevator up to the observation deck. The biosphere floor was by invitation only for non-horts like him. He stepped out into the bright steamy atmosphere. The air pulsed with photosynthesis. Crickets rattled. Bees bumbled about. Clouds gathered around the curved ceiling. The dome's double glass plates held pockets of gas replicating daytime's cyan blue and blocking out the moonscape darkness. Birds flittered through the canopy. Below were rows of flowers, clustering vegetation, corn sways, trees, shrubs and grasses, all cultivated into specific regions. Pollinating turbines and directional heat lamps controlled each area from above. Actroids in overalls weeded and wheeled barrows under the enormous dome.

Adam stayed for a while, breathing the damp sweet air. He stretched and swallowed a yawn. When he looked back down a new actroid had appeared, directly below him, wandering through the herbs. Tawn. Her brindled hair was tied loosely into a bun and she squinted against the light. She ran her fingers through a head of thyme and raised them to her face. Bram strode through the entrance. She snatched her hand down and smiled at him. He waved his arm expansively; spoke words Adam couldn't catch, and then suddenly looked up.

'Adam!' He beckoned him down.

Adam had never stood on the earth under the dome before. Earth earth. Pasteurized, disinfected, every grain actroid sifted. Worm casts crumbled under his feet as he approached.

'Despite countless research grants no one's made a superior mechanized version of the common earthworm, or the birds and bees...' Bram said, rocking on his heels. 'Two breeding pairs of hundreds of species initially introduced... all thriving.'

Tawn nodded politely.

'Adam, this is Tawn.' Bram said, without taking his eyes off her. 'What they were doing sending an actroid hort to Ptolomaeus, when I've put in countless staffing alerts for here... Some of their dictats beggar belief.'

Tawn's smile was familiar. Like the tail of a dream Adam couldn't quite catch.

'It's nice to meet you,' she said.

'I...'

'You'll already know your way round...' Bram continued. 'Received the data sync I sent for your journey?'

Tawn nodded.

'Good. We'll leave you to familiarize yourself. Come on, Adam. Time for breakfast.'

They queued together in the canteen.

'Nice bit of design that one... hope she's a hard worker, too,' Bram said. Adam nodded and watched the other people waiting in line. Refugees who, like him, had managed to convince the interview panel their work was vital in the creation of a moon home. They all practiced a look of busyness. An abrupt manner. It was a pointless charade. But the depots space and resources were limited. The actroids needed no food, required minimal space and performed the functions of multiple humans with faultless preprogrammed expertise.

'I'd better get back to my report,' Adam said, clutching a melba toast. 'Any comms from Earth yet?'

Bram raised a droll eyebrow as he headed out.

Adam turned back towards the biosphere. But as he approached, the doors slid open and Tawn emerged, her fists bunched before her. She stopped and whipped her hands behind her back. But Adam had already seen what she was carrying.

He paused, glanced round. 'I once stole a windup toy from an antique shop. I felt so bad I never even played with it.'

She drew out the fistful of lavender and lifted it to her face. 'It's for my capsule. To help me sleep…' The words hung boldly between them as the flower heads crackled under the aircon.

Adam looked at her smooth olive Reelskin, the curve of her neck. 'Which poet did you get?'

'You know about 2nd generation?'

'I designed the humanistics… so…'

'Yes…' She turned away for a moment. Smiled hesitantly. 'Adrian Henri,' she said. 'My poet. They do it alphabetically…'

'You could have ended up with Heaney or Hawthorne.'

She nodded. "For who would wish a fairer home, Than in that bright, refulgent dome?' Hawthorne… Address to the Moon?' Tawn smiled. 'They're onto the 20th century poets now. I like Henri.' Her eyes flickered closed for a moment.

Adam cleared his throat. 'How are you settling in?'

'I'll feel better when my crate arrives.'

'Your crate?'

'… I don't like being parted from it.'

He looked at her closely. The Reelskin of her cheeks reddened.

'You don't have much space in your capsule…for possessions.'

She shrugged. 'I'll have to manage, won't I?'

The turn of phrase was unmistakable. He snapped his head forward. Her eyes met his. Cool. Steady.

'I'll show you where the deliveries come in.' He walked away.

She followed behind him. 'Thank you,' she said amicably, although he knew she'd have had the depot plan uploaded with the data sync.

He watched her gait from the corner of his eye. She was round in the hips, short legged and long bodied. Her movements were gracefully irregular. There was a time when he would have seen the flaws in her humanistics. But now, several steps removed from the process he could almost mistake Tawn for human.

It had become clear early on that establishing refuge bases on the moon would require the enhanced knowledge, multiple specializations and human affinity of actroids. Adam, Lil and their team, at the genesis of humanistics, had philosophized and debated what made one human; then programmed in likes and dislikes, foibles and nuances of expression. They randomly generated variants in shape, size, ethnicity and heritage. Some of the robotic engineers sniffed at the worthiness of their work. The greatest challenge was persuading them that imperfection, like asymmetrical features or misshapen ears were what made an actroid humanistically perfect.

The whole purpose of robotic technology came into question. For years, the driving forces behind creating robots were sex and death. The demand, indeed the financial backing, was in creating robots society could either fornicate with, or send into combative warzones. Over time, robots sent into conflicts mutated into something less human-like. It had proved distressing for human personnel to see mashed up robot comrades. But the opposite could be said for the sex robot gynoids, who were becoming more cartoonishly feminine with each generation. De-sexualizing attitudes to female robots was an enormous hurdle. It became a fine balance, between androgonising them until they became a species of other, and giving them definitive gender traits without it being the sole reason for their creation. Adam, Lil and the humanistics team had designed a preprogrammed matrix that independently varied attributes of their exterior presentation and inward tastes and preferences. They had created actroids that were uniquely individual.

Ultimately, it was a fabulous deceit. The emotions, responses and forms were finitely programmed. Not real, however lifelike they appeared. Everything from eyebrow curve down to foot shape. Foot size, however, was fixed based on the stability ratios computed by the engineers.

Tawn tucked the lavender into her pocket as they approached the shipping desk. Janice, the woman behind the counter, jerked her thumb at a large crate.

'It's heavy.' She flashed her eyes over them.

Tawn smiled. 'We'll have to manage.' She laid a hand on the top before lifting it.

Adam swallowed. 'Can I help?'

'It's fine, really.' Tawn lifted the box lightly although its weight told in the flex of her knees as they walked back down the corridor.

'What's in there?' Adam asked.

Tawn set her mouth tightly and gave a little shrug.

'That won't fit in your capsule,' Adam said. 'You must have been told in your briefing. You won't be allowed to keep it.'

Tawn picked up her pace.

Adam hurried behind, assessing the crate's dimensions as it bounced lightly with her stride. He was familiar with the actroid capsule's capacity and there was no way it would fit. Even without Tawn in there. Actroids didn't need much space; just a reclining recharge dock for 'sleep'. Like Japanese capsule hotels, they were stacked lengthways. But narrower. Taller actroids struggled to fit and had to curl their knees to one side. It looked bad, but didn't affect them. Each capsule had just enough room for the actroid plus a tiny space to store a few small items. Possession was never a trait they programmed in, as a given or even as an aspiration. They could be collectors, but never with the innate sense that they could possess something. Even their clothes were viewed as borrowed.

'How did you get them to ship it anyway? You must have lied about the ownership…' Adam followed her, raising his voice. 'You must have read in the terms and conditions… They'll destroy it.'

She stopped abruptly, wincing as something shifted inside. She ran her fingers over the plastic casing. 'It's mine.'

'Yours?'

Her eyes narrowed. 'Yes,' she said. 'Mine.'

It was a tricky one. News would get to Bram. It always did when actroids were rule breaking. It would come up at board meeting. And, as liaison officer, it would be minuted that Adam would action it. He would have to destroy whatever scrappy rubbish had caught this actroid's eye. Watching her now, clutching the crate to her, this didn't seem like an agreeable task.

'Perhaps…' He put his hands out. 'Look. You won't be able to keep it. So…'

Tawn pulled back as he reached for the crate. The hurt on her face jolted a recollection. Lil's face. So starkly. He looked away.

'Listen.' He dropped his hands to his sides. 'I can stick it in my pod… just for a while.'

Tawn stared at the crate. 'No…'

'They'll find it. It's hazardous to your function.'

Tawn closed her eyes, words teetering on her lips. Finally she turned to him. 'Okay. But you must take great care of it.'

Adam nodded dumbly.

'And don't open it.' She placed the crate into his arms. 'I'll know if you have.' She gave him a look. The weight of the box burned into his biceps, as she walked away.

Back in his pod with the crate tucked into a corner, he returned to the Travelling Century Play report. Bob78 had messaged back saying he would happily assist, except Bram had already booked him to write up the annual Commander Report for him. The deadline for circulating it to other moon depots was today. But he might be free later on. Adam cursed Bram's laziness and looked up different words for 'integrate' on the computer thesaurus.

The crate was a tantalizing draw away from his report. He dallied on the keyboard, writing words, then erasing them. Eventually, Adam sighed deeply and stood. He went over and knelt beside the box. He tapped it. He tried prizing off the lid but it was tightly fastened. He listened. Something ticked irregularly within, like a broken alarm clock.

Footsteps shuffled past his pod. He glanced at his chrono.

'Shit!'

Their play, Mare Nubium's Travelling Century, was about to start.

On a makeshift stage in their screening room, an actroid in green overalls and fairy wings with Christmas tree deely-boppers bouncing on his head stood in the spotlight. An actroid on camera gave him the thumbs up as the little red light blipped on.

Adam slid into the seat beside Bram as the lights faded. Tawn stood near the back, set apart from the others. He was about to move over to her, but the actroid in green started speaking.

'The beginning of the 21st century…' the deely-boppers sprung back and forth. 'There was rejoicing, but also disharmony as the millennium bug gripped people with fear. As Big Ben struck twelve, the world held its breath. But planes did not fall from the sky, hospital machinery kept working and the Internet, still very much in its infancy, did not explode. Humankind had panicked over nothing.'

Bram's eyebrows furrowed. But Adam didn't remember putting that line in. And, as the play went on, the script seemed more fluent than he recalled. He tried noting the unfamiliar bits to check later, but found it was too dark to type them into his chrono. When he glanced up, Tawn had gone.

Not staying for the news bulletin afterwards he hurried back to his pod and slid open the door. A small cry came from within. He jerked backwards.

'Wait.' Tawn tumbled something into the crate. There was a fluttering, a squeak. She pressed her palms down on the lid.

'How did you get in here?' he asked.

She nodded at the crate. 'I thought you wouldn't mind.'

'Mind?'

A smile flickered at the corner of her mouth. 'I lost track of time.'

'No, you didn't. You can't…'

But something was wrong. White bands pulsed across her left iris. She lifted a stuttering hand to her face.

'Are you okay?'

Tawn glanced at the box. Her Reelbreth was shallow. Her palm was flashing ruby.

'Tawn.'

'I…'

Adam maneuvered her onto the edge of the bed. 'You need to sleep in your capsule.'

'Can't…' her body sank, the lifeline fading with each pulse. If it went out altogether she could loose data. It would require explanations.

Adam grabbed his pod charger lead and felt behind her ear for the magnetic insert point. It snapped in. The lifeline turned a pale apple green. Barely there.

The connection hummed flatly. Reelbreth passed between her parted lips as her head lolled. Her inert body, with one arm slung across her chest, reminded him of a painting. One of those pre Raphaelite women reclining in orange robes or floating down a river on a punt. Millais or Rossetti was it? He had work to do, but couldn't tear himself away from watching her. If someone came and found her here…

A small noise, something shifting. Adam looked up. It was coming from the crate. Kneeling, he noticed a faintly rancid smell emitting from it. He reached out, but before his hand made contact a static charge fizzed through his fingers. He snapped back, nursing them to him, suddenly overwhelmed with a desire for sleep. A heavy sensation dragging at his eyelids. He looked at the empty stretch of bed beside Tawn and ran a palm over the cool sheet. Blinking fiercely, he lay down.

He didn't sleep right away. Although he felt the paralysis of expectant dreams holding him there. The unmistakable incline of a shared bed was soothing in a melancholy way as he slid from one life back to another. The charger buzz in the pod morphed its perfect flat note into the fridge, humming in their tiny flat. The fridge was so close to their bed that if in the night he or Lil were thirsty, they could stumble to it and slurp at the juice carton, without needing to wake properly. Then roll back over into the warm angles of the other. Seek out those places to tuck hands and feet. And resume the paused dream. And now, he dreamed of Lil. Fragmenting flashes of her from a distance. Her hair falling around her face as she reached down. The arc of her back as she dressed. Lil. Her fingers fluttering against her skin. Lil. Sitting in the rocking chair, a magenta cellophane fish curling up in her palm, revealing her future. Her eyes glistening, her breath held. Her face tilted skywards, at night. Always…

The pod door hiss woke him. Tawn stood on the threshold.

'What happened… to you?' Adam whispered.

'Just power…'

Adam rubbed his eyes. 'That shouldn't happen. Not that quickly.'

'Yes…' Tawn gazed at her palm. 'I have to go.'

'No, wait…' Adam untangled his feet from the blanket and lurched to the doorway.

Tawn passed Bob78 in the corridor. A look flashed between them. Something uncustomary. It was suddenly so obvious Adam caught his breath.

'Lil, what have you done?' he muttered as he watched Tawn stride falteringly away.

After that, Adam spent all his time on the biosphere viewing deck. He watched her sneak cuttings of ferns, hardened puddles of sap and pea shoots into her overalls.

One day he stayed so late, the gas in the roof pockets was vacuumed out for nighttime, and star speckled litmus black filled the dome. He rested his head on his arms. A cool touch startled him.

'Adam.' Tawn stepped back wiping her hands. 'I want to show you something.' She walked away.

'What?' Adam followed as she led him down in the lift and through the biosphere doors. 'I'm not supposed to be…'

'You're with me,' she said.

She walked on into the vastness, through whispering columns of rosemary, orchids in every colour, beans writhing through trellises. Tree trunks, foliage and insects. Fragrances suggested fractured memories as he passed.

He stumbled over branches and roots after her, prickled his skin on cacti. He was pincering the needles out when she stopped abruptly. A vertical column with a dangling rope ladder towered over them. She climbed up the ladder without looking back, high into the canopy. Adam followed, the ladder twisting and trembling under him. He wriggled after her through an aperture and they stood together on a wide, square platform.

'Look. This is the only place you can see the entire panorama…' Tawn inclined her head to the wide dome of stars. 'I can name every one of them.'

'Programmed…'

'My trainer taught me to learn from books.'

'Lilith was your trainer, wasn't she?'

Tawn closed her eyes.

'There's lots of her in you.'

'I'm not Lilith…' Tawn said.

'I know that,' he snapped. 'We didn't make doppelgangers.'

She sighed. 'It's a shame... She was a good trainer.'

Adam looked over. 'What's a shame?'

Tawn lay down on the platform, one arm supporting her head. 'I taught myself twenty languages, the human way. And how to drive moontrucks, too. Have you ever even been out there? Any of you humans?' She swept her hand across the lunar landscape.

'You surpass us in every way,' Adam hissed.

She laughed. 'Something will surpass us soon enough.'

'What's happened to Lil?'

'Earth isn't how you remember. Those bulletins aren't...' she frowned. 'I've only just come from there. I know. People, the ones remaining, are terrified. Rain melts tarmac. Dissolves forests. It scars people like leprosy.' She turned to him. 'Warfare, Adam. One faction sends it over in cloud attacks, they retaliate... mostly it's actroids, preprogrammed to do it... There's so much damage no one knows who's doing what anymore. And the remaining humans' birth rates are falling. Only one in ten women conceive. Most miscarry... they claim its drug weaponry...'

'That's not so new...' Adam murmured. He blinked hard.

'But I think it's just that you're outdated.' Tawn said softly. 'Time's up.'

'No...'

'Lil trained me at launch headquarters. She refused all EMT devices, you know, although everyone else had started using them again.'

'What's happened to her?'

'Do you have any idea how lucky you are to be here? Had you noticed there have been no humans sent recently?' Her eyes were bright. 'When was the last time there was anything but actroids on the manifest?'

'Lil...'

'There's too much at stake. Actroids can make a sustainable place here... a refuge for a new...' She dropped her gaze. 'Along with most humans at launch headquarters...

Lil disappeared. I thought they'd sent her here; she was protected. That's why I came. We'd been working on something together…'

'She isn't here…'

Tawn nodded.

He walked to the platform edge and surveyed the lunar landscape. Research from early moon days had reported that humans found its ancient pocked surface depressing. That's why the actroids were tasked with moon driving; transporting goods between depots and most importantly harvesting the Helium-3. But now, looking out across the expanse, Adam breathed more easily. The grey undulating ranges were rippled in blue and silver. He could see Earth from here. A great aqua-green swirling ball. He had spent the last two years moling around in the network of corridors seeing only a tiny portion of this starscape through his pod observatory. The picture was bigger, and far more complicated.

He lay on the deck beside Tawn and watched the Earth. He listened to her Reelbreth coming and going for a while. Then he stretched out his hand and locked his fingers into hers.

'Adam?' Bram and a committee of tight-lips faced him in the boardroom. 'Any ideas?'

Adam looked up from his constellation doodles.

'The missing items?' Bram consulted his notes. 'Spoons, forks, a colander, various hoes, the extension cord for the sprinkler system, Janice's e-reader… all unaccounted for on the latest inventory.'

'Surely there are more urgent things we need to discuss… a few bits of missing cutlery…' Adam raised his palms.

'With the security system temporarily down, we all need to be eyes and ears.'

There was an unsettled silence. Adam shrugged. 'Perhaps someone left the waste hatch open again.'

We can't afford to take chances.' Janice's eyes were wide.

'Especially since they're still repairing communications with Earth… if they're busy with that they might not be able to send replacement items soon. I can't believe none of the actroids have the relevant programming to fix the interface from our end.' She glared at Adam.

'We won't ever be getting comms from Earth…' he started wearily.

'It's unclear when the next Earth comms or shipment will arrive,' Bram interrupted, scratching the eczema blooming on his palms. 'But no need to panic…'

Adam went to his pod. He had started to notice that each day things looked subtly different in there whenever he returned. Like they had been moved and then carefully replaced. It became a game. Coming back from the canteen, or a meeting he imagined her shadow disappearing around the curve of the corridor. Tantalizing lavender hints ghosted the corners of his pod.

He stared at the crate and hesitantly rested his hands on the lid. Something thrummed within, tingled through his palms and oscillated his ear hair follicles. His eyelids flickered. His fingers stuck fast. Again, a complete weariness weighted his eyes and he slumped over beside the crate fighting the urge to sleep. Slowly, he let the desire overtake, toying with lucidity until he was too far gone to turn back. A deep arduous sleep. Full gravity. With Lil there once again, holding his hand as they stargazed. She was weighing him down. Pleasantly, at first. Until she began to swing him off balance; an anchor dropped short into a dark ocean's depths.

When he woke a while later, the dreams were fragmenting and indistinct. He blinked against the synthetic light. The rotten smell was ripening. He pressed his palm onto his pounding forehead. Woozy and uncoordinated, his body felt drink addled. But the bottle of whisky was still there, full on the shelf. It took him a moment to recall why he was lying crumpled on the floor. Time had passed. He knew this from the ache in his neck. The crate. It was misshapen, the lid twisting against the warp. He stood stretching his muscles and peeped through the crack. Something grated and sparked at him. He stumbled back. His intercom was flashing. 'Emergency board meeting' scrolled across his screen.

Adam rushed to the boardroom. 'Sorry…' he took his seat.

'…As I was saying, we've intelligence on the missing effects. The perpetrator, an actroid seriously breaching programming, was just witnessed lifting an entire box of biros from the admin pod. Emergency procedure has been instigated. And…' Bram put his arms up. 'I'm recommissioning the EMT. Extreme times…'

'We don't have a functioning one,' Adam glanced around the board. 'Do we?'

Bram's eyes glistened.

Adam ran down the corridor. He knew she'd be in his pod. That the crate would be found there, too. A prickling sweat broke on his neck.

He was rounding the corner, just metres from his pod, when a guttural cry halted him. Bram stood back swinging an EMT by its muzzle. Scorched fuse and rubber smoked up the corridor. A mangled chaos lay spreading at his feet; a resinous melting mass of Reelskin and singed hair gunged up shattered data boards. They fizzed and sparked across the floor. Some extremities were blown clean off at their ball joints. Others had simply vapourised. Tawn. Her exposed titanium skull was cracked like an egg. An eye swiveled loosely in the liquefied fragments of her face. Her Reelbreth came in jagged spikes, dislocated to somewhere that once might have been her shoulder. Biro tubes scattered across the corridor like pickup sticks.

'Lucky…' Bram looked down at the EMT and lifted his boot from a pool of melted Reelskin. 'Adam… find some cleaners.'

But there were already three actroids approaching with biotech-hazard cleaning trolleys trailing behind them. And they weren't alone. Actroids approached silently from all directions.

Bram licked his lips. He glanced at Adam. 'What's going on?'

Adam stumbled back over a patch of Reelskin with one digit still attached. Her palm, a blue light darting across it. Persistently fading.

'Adam.' Bram's eyes bulged. 'We have a situation… Disable the energy drive to the capsules.'

But Adam turned, shaking his head.

He ran to his pod and sunk down behind the closed door, squeezing his eyes shut. Outside human shouts faded with the clatter of faraway feet. His pod was in chaos. The air was thick with the rotten stench. Tiny nuts, bolts and ball bearings scattered like seeds across the floor. Spirals of wire, dissected plants and dismembered motherboards cluttered his desk. The lid of the crate was propped open with a fork. Adam approached, skittering metal components from under his feet, and peered inside. His heart beat in his throat. There was a hollow nest-like space within the crate. A knot of e-reader, its insides spilling out like road kill, a twist of chaffinch carcass, tangled mammal remains, a ball of pea shoots and a browning banana skin. There were slivers of metal and a sprinkling of biosphere soil. Adam peeled trembling papers from the bottom of the crate. They were covered with figures, notes and sketches in a tenderly recognisable handwriting. He touched the fading pen indentations, breathed them in; metallic ink and faintest lavender. He flicked through the pages. On the top of one, capitalized, overlaid and pressed imperatively into the paper, was his name.

Outside feet pounded past, followed by the squeaking wheels of a biotech-hazard trolley and then two sets of measured actroid footfalls. Adam stood still, the papers rattling in his hand. The two strolling actroids were making a peculiar noise; two distinctly pitched, buzzing resonances. One was deeper than the other. They were staggered. Call and response.

'Oh God,' muttered Adam, reaching for the computer. His fingers faltered on the keys. The screen flashed dumbly.

There was a hum growing like tinnitus in his ear. He batted at his head. But the sound was coming from within his pod. He spun around. Something squirmed under his bedding. Slowly, he stepped over and took an edge of the sheet. He held his breath and pulled.

As a whole, the thing was unrecognizable. But parts of it were. It curled quivering into itself. A large and opaque lychee eye shivered at him, peeping from under a limb-like structure of spliced cutlery pieces and springs half covered with patchy grafts. It had a rudimentary gash for a mouth with fork prong teeth. Its bowed back legs twisted underneath it, also patched with a skin-like substance. Looking more closely, he could see that they were browning pieces of peach skin, hanging off in shreds. Downy puce feathers were pressed into its crown. Yellow goo leaked from it, like the stuff from daffodil stems. It trailed across the sheets. But despite its misshapen exterior, there was something within it that glowed brightly. Hotly. The creature gave a low trembling growl. It hid its head under its forelimb and shuffled back against the wall.

Adam scanned around for something to hit it over the head with. The room lacked anything of appropriate weight or substance. Except the whisky bottle. He clutched it. Raised it above his head. The creature recoiled, whimpering and grating its metal teeth together.

Adam looked away and brought the bottle down to his side. The new clicking and humming communication of actroids passing outside his pod stung his ears. The human shouts had ceased.

He slumped on the bed and looked at the thing. It darted out an earth-wire fist and tugged at a loose thread of the bedding. Then it blinked at Adam and crept towards him.

175

It rubbed its feathered head against his thigh and, after a moment's hesitation, dragged itself into his lap. The sticky ooze soaked slowly through to his skin. The creature sighed and blinked.

Adam carried it to the rocking chair and rested back against the velvet. He cracked the seal on the whisky and took a long slug while the creature rearranged itself, its chin, or the place most resembling it, nuzzling into the dip between his knees. The whisky was smoky. Just like he remembered. They'd bought a case. Six bottles. Five of which they'd drunk over time in their little flat at night dreaming up ways to improve the actroids. How to make them almost mistakably human.

'It's the weaknesses that make us human.' She'd gulped the liquor, wide eyed. 'And in the unconscious urge to pass those weaknesses on. Traces will always remain of the things that precede us. Did you know some human babies are born with tails?' her voice had trailed away. He could recall exactly her look of want.

Adam gazed down at the thing nestled on his lap. A filament of red wire had sprung free and protruded from its back. He put the bottle down and tenderly twisted the wire back into place, the creature bristling beneath his fingers. He stroked the feathery head until it relaxed.

He sucked again on the whisky. This, the sixth bottle, they'd saved. For her moon coming. For the arrival of the newest creation that they'd planned to make here. This wasn't quite how he'd imagined it. He closed his eyes and rocked them both to sleep.

Stanlemian

Wojciech Orliński

Translated from the Polish by Danusia Stok

'EVERYONE GOT THEIR lemians ready as instructed, I hope?' asked the croupier.

In answer came a chorus of happy affirmation and the rustling of several envelopes which the tourists produced from their pockets.

'Nevada state law forbids me checking the contents of the envelopes, but obliges me to make sure that all the customers have prepared their envelopes and correctly put them into the white containers.'

'I've brought seven. I hope they fit,' said a buxom, rosy woman with a strong Southern drawl.

'The container has five compartments but you can easily put a few envelopes into one. Only please don't think about it too much so that the imprint on your short-term memory is as weak as possible,' replied the croupier, who quite clearly had explained this numerous times before.

'Are you going to help me, mate?' A lonely brunette with stylish tattoos on her cheeks accosted me. 'If I understand what he says about that short-term memory correctly, it's best somebody else puts my lemians away.'

'Sorry, miss, but casino regulations forbid it,' interrupted the croupier. 'Everybody has to do it for themselves. Otherwise how are you going to know you're awake?'

'I tried to get to grips with that when I read the brochure, but I still don't really understand how these lemians work,' complained the rosy woman from the South.

'The casino has access to your short-term memory because that stems from the very idea of virtual reality,' answered the croupier. 'Your long-term memory, however, is inaccessible to us. A good lemian ought to contain something we remember from years back and haven't seen for a long time so that on leaving the virtual we could make sure we really have left the virtual.'

'Surely I'll know whether I'm in New York in 1985 or in Las Vegas today?' The woman was not convinced.

'But since we can produce a perfect illusion of New York we can also produce a fake Las Vegas. You'll think the simulation's come to an end, you'll return to your real hotel room, log into the net, execute some financial transfers and we'll recognise your passwords and pins,' the croupier clarified.

'Oh, my God, I didn't know I was putting myself at such risk!' The woman from the South looked genuinely surprised.

The croupier immediately replied in a calm voice: 'You're not in any danger with us, madam. Our casino has been offering virtual services for six years now and there have never been any complaints. But legislators in their infinite wisdom want to protect customers of all casinos, also those less honest...'

'The Mafia ones?' somebody threw in from the other side. The guests laughed, though some perhaps a little forcibly. I did not laugh. I knew that although the stewards of Las Vegas were keen to convince their customers that organised crime had been consigned to the past with the change over from roulette and blackjack to gambling in virtual reality, it was simply not true. The very need for my services proved that.

'The Mafia, sir, is obsolete.' The croupier smiled falsely. No doubt speaking by rote, responding to a frequently asked question. 'Within the bounds of existing law, we are now going to sell you virtual steaks and virtual wine for real money, taking fifty dollars for something which doesn't even exist. How can any mafia compete with that?'

The laughter at the table sounded more natural this time.

'And where does the name 'lemian' come from?' somebody else asked.

'From the name of a Russian engineer who invented the solution,' replied the croupier.

I almost leapt from my chair wanting to correct such nonsense but bit my tongue. You have to keep a low profile in my profession and take care not to imprint yourself on the memory – either long- or short-term – of any casino staff.

Fortunately, I was saved from the need to intervene by a fat boy who displayed the syndrome of heavy addiction to virtual games.

'It wasn't an engineer but a writer of science fiction,' he said. 'Within science fiction, situations in which people don't know whether they've left a simulation or not are called phildickian. The Russian writer Stanley Lem, however, thought about this in his novel, Sum of Technologies, and wrote that virtual reality would never enter the market until the problem was solved. Hence the term 'stanlemian': a simulation which precludes a 'phildickian' state occurring. 'Lemian' for short.'

If this were a social gathering I would have laughed at the boy and corrected all his mistakes. Not Stanley but Stanisław. Not novel but essay. Not 'Sum of Technologies' but *Summa Technologiae* as an analogy to 'Summa Theologiae' by Thomas Aquinas. And, for God's sake, not Russian but Polish.

I kept these thoughts to myself, though. Instead I sighed and turned to my tattooed neighbour:

'Well, well, the boy's done his homework,' I muttered.

'The guy's not bad!' She brightened up. 'I didn't know about that Russian writer! It's fascinating!'

I didn't pursue the conversation.

'I'd love to carry on chatting, but you must all be in a hurry to get to New York in the hot eighties, aren't you?' asked the croupier. He was answered by a mutter of approval. 'Are all the lemians ready? Great. I now invite you to watch a short instructional film and then all the riches of reaganomics await you!'

The screens around us blazed to life. In the film, smiling models demonstrated what next awaited us. We were to go to quarters which resembled ordinary hotel rooms. There, dressed in pyjamas, we were to put on monitor rings and drink a soporific kept in a little fridge which looked like a minibar in order to maintain the illusion of a hotel.

We were then to get into bed and for thirty-six hours fall into a deep sleep. We were not to be afraid of this because the casino staff would make sure the anaesthetic ran its normal course – two highly-trained anaesthetists were on duty every day.

For as long as we were conscious we would be allowed to use the emergency button by the bed at any time. This would stop our journey into the virtual world; unfortunately – the actor in the instructional film informed us – there would be no question of being reimbursed at this point.

The film did not go into great detail regarding what would happen to us later. It merely showed smiling personnel transferring an unconscious body from a hotel bed to a hospital one and transporting it along a corridor towards a door marked Authorised Entry Only.

Then we watched another trailer of the present virtual programme New York, New York, in which flashes from simulation were edited into a medley of film classics set in the eighties. Brokers in red braces, hardlooking cops in even harder Crown Victoria Fords, punks at a concert in CBGB, intellectuals styled on Woody Allen, prostitutes accosting passers-by on Times Square.

The film did not dwell on what would happen to our bodies during this time. I more or less knew that, so I knew it could not be made into a promotional film.

Everyone, when purchasing the service, signed an agreement for 'parasynaptic nanointervention' which looked just as unappetising as it sounds. The operating personnel would dig dozens of needles into our back along the spine. We were going to lie in the functional equivalent of an intensive care unit where excrement, urine, saliva and sperm expelled by our bodies (sex in virtual reality results in an ejaculation in the real) would be diligently collected by nurses. All in all, not something anyone would want to watch.

Everybody was more interested in the most important instructions, kept to the end of the film: how to take the money earned in virtual New York across to the real world. It had to accompany us in the form of cash when we left the virtual in our hotel rooms. If we did not get there on time and left the simulation in an emergency, the money fell through. If we didn't have it with us, it also fell through.

The film emphasised this very clearly, showing different variations of a situation where an animated little man with a sack marked $ in all sorts of ways lost the sack on his way to the hotel, and the money remained in the virtual world. Only the little man in the cartoon bed who fell asleep curled up around his sack full of dollars with a sweet smile on his face would later pick the money up from the counter on the other side. Not before its validity had been established via the lemian, however.

I followed all this without any great excitement – this was hardly my first time. That was the real reason I'd come here: to collect a sack marked $ which had been left in virtual New York by another player, someone who had won a small fortune on Wall Street but, quite rightly, was afraid of returning to the hotel room with it on his own.

Even walking around in real New York with $1,200,000 cash was far from a sensible thing to do. But in virtual New York, where the rules allowed players to make holes in other players with a quick burst from a Kalashnikov in order to pick up their winnings from the counter, this was no job for an amateur.

A wise amateur, therefore, would act as my present employer had, leaving the cash in a safe and the task of bringing the money out of the virtual world to a professional. Me, for example.

I went with the other players to a transitional part of the casino where we were separated. Each of us landed in a room which was modelled on the one we were going to wake up in when we reached the virtual world – designed to minimise any shock on waking. I performed all the routine actions, jumped into bed and closed my eyes.

Virtual New York greeted me at seven o'clock simulation time. In the eighties a radio-alarm clock was considered the height of refinement. A DJ on the New York station WPLJ introduced the latest hit from Dire Straits' new album. 'He wants his own MTV and I want one, too,' the speaker on the radio broke in over Sting's chorus. 'Next week the engineer's coming to install cable television and I'm going to let you know what I've seen. But maybe you've already got cable or satellite TV? Phone in and tell us!'

I smiled – the people preparing virtual radio programmes for this simulation must have had great fun. I climbed out of bed and did some bends and squats, not for the sake of health – an avatar's body is a one off – simply to test where each virtual muscle was. Such knowledge could come in useful.

This wasn't my first time but it was the first time I had been sent for such a large sum. My client, Michael T. Hicks, a twenty-eight year old engineer from Silicon Valley, had gone to Las Vegas with his girl for a hot weekend in the virtual. This was their first time so they both went for lunch to the famous Windows On The World restaurant on the hundred and seventh floor of the north tower of the World Trade Centre. Since 12th September 2001, reserving a table there has become almost impossible, so the restaurant is a 'must' for every novice.

This suits the casino fine, because they can arrange for the player to encounter enpecees (non-player characters), either in the restaurant itself – the classic 'conversation overheard at the next table' scenario – or immediately on leaving it. The enpecees approach with a view to doing some business. These are, after all, the eighties! Toss a (virtual) dead cat anywhere on Wall Street and you'll hit some yuppie from a rapidly blossoming stock market enterprise!

The great majority of novices, of course, lose. Even on the real Wall Street it was like that – the game is set two years before the stock market crash of 1987 – let alone in a virtual world specifically designed with financial gambling in mind.

Hicks knew about this but for a guy from Silicon Valley the temptation to invest in a firm which wanted to introduce a new kind of personal computer on the market ('lap top, you understand – a computer which rests on the user's knees like a lap dancer!') was irresistible. He invested a round hundred thousand in a new company and, as luck would have it, some exchange swindlers set rates rolling at that very moment as part of another scam. Within the space of a day my client made a killing.

Being a sensible soul, he avoided taking the profits to his hotel. Instead, he rented an office in the World Trade Centre, one with a secure safe which was impossible to open in the virtual world without knowing the code – the combination being registered in the game engine itself.

He took only a hundred thousand – as much as he had invested – which he spent with his girlfriend in the lavish night which followed. When summing up this story, Hicks had rolled his eyes and sighed dramatically, as if I might be remotely interested in what he got up to with his girl.

In the light of what happened later, it turned out I should have been interested. But I was focused only on the money. Hicks told me the combination, we signed a standard agreement regarding my limited liability and my commission, the latter depending on the mission's success, and I made my way to the casino in order to pick up his fortune.

Virtual New York could be entered via three hotels, all located Midtown. This was a clever move because you could make a fortune in the eighties at two extremities of the island ruled by two different types of gangster. One was Kelvin Martin, known by the pseudonym '50 Cent' because he would kill anyone for what they were carrying, even that meagre an amount. The other was Michael Milken, the king of 'junk bonds'. Both were destined to end their careers in 1987. Kelvin Martin would receive twenty-three bullets, Michael Milken ninety-eight accusations from the securities commission.

In Upper Manhattan, between Harlem and Washington Heights, a fortune could be made dealing in crack. And an even greater one killing crack dealers. In Lower Manhattan between the World Trade Centre and Wall Street, a fortune was to be made on businesses spun around refined cocaine. And an even greater one on greenhorns who invested money in them.

This was easy in virtual New York. The difficulty was getting this fortune over to the hotel in Midtown because the long trip along Broadway or one of the straight-line Boulevards was an ideal opportunity for anyone interested in our cash. Whether you undertook this journey on the subway, on foot or even in an arm-plated Lincoln, you gave other players a couple of hours to rob you.

Downstairs in the hotel lobby there was a Hertz counter. I quickly dealt with the formalities and picked up the keys for my favourite simulated car. A Mercury Grand Marquis 1985. In the real I would never in my life have wanted to drive something like that – the five-litre engine V8 was barely capable of getting that cow going. To take any corner you had to all but stop because the brick had the steering of an overloaded tanker. Which made driving one along north-south boulevards, straight as a rod and not particularly jammed (virtual New York had a population of less than a million enpecees), while listening to the unique drone of the old-fashioned engine, all the more pleasurable. Even the reverse gear, with its primitive lever at the steering wheel, became child's play.

I pulled out of the hotel parking lot and turned down Madison Avenue. Instead of going directly to the World Trade Centre I went in the opposite direction. That's where the amateurs usually slip up. They go straight for the cash without any preparation. Then, of course, somebody takes it from them, somebody who has prepared.

At the crossing with 58th East I passed signs warning that Queensboro Bridge was closed for repairs. The simulation took in only Manhattan, and not completely at that. The designers had come up with a variety of measures to accommodate that; a lorry blocking the road here, a police cordon there – allegedly safe-guarding a crime scene – or sometimes a simple 'invisible wall' as in old-style computer games.

I didn't mind. I didn't even have time to visit virtual Central Park which I was just passing. The casino made a great show of announcing its grand opening. Before the designers finished the titanic job of recreating it down to the very last bush, all entrances were closed under the official pretext of 'Events for ticket holders only'.

Players like me were interested in something else. We flicked through news of crime in New York newspapers of the eighties searching for information on fences, illicit gunrunners, wholesale crack and heroin dealers, and ethnic gangs. We knew that the game designers studied the same chronicles so the criminology of real New York provided a pretty useful player's handbook.

Madison runs into 116th Street. I turned right. I was already in Harlem – not in the pretty, civilised one at that but in the part where even in the 21st century you could feel uneasy in the shadow of viaducts and flyovers, amidst garages and tenements where illicit workshops operated and gangsters had their dens.

In the shadow of the Metro North line, the workshop beneath the sign 'Carlos Fernandez, Tyre Repairs' hid a secret which hardly anyone knew about but me. The real Fernandez would be caught in 1988 during a police set-up and would become a key state witness. Thanks to his evidence, the Dominican gang 'Wild Cowboys', which terrorised the area during the crack epidemic in the early eighties, would be brought down.

The workshop was a front for a so-called nest-hole. The owner stored all sorts of packages without asking unnecessary questions about their contents. This was exactly what I needed.

I drove up the stained ramp and got out. Fernandez was in his office. The workshop was deliberately arranged to encourage any casual customer in search of new tyres to go and look for them elsewhere.

'Sorry, we're closed today. I'm waiting for my partner,' he greeted me as soon as I stood in the doorway.

'I've come from Mr Marquez,' I replied. I knew that was the password used by messengers from Medelin. This was the fourth time I'd visited this workshop; each time as a different avatar, of course, so Fernandez couldn't remember me, but I'd come to know him a little better.

'Oh, my apologies.' He reacted with the same humility as always. 'Of course, we're open to our regular customers.'

'Don't bullshit me, just take me to the basin,' I growled. It worked. Fernandez leapt from his chair and headed towards the back. I followed.

They used to have another, larger workshop here with two basins. Now these were both covered by boards on which piles of tires were arranged – just in case. The tyre man looked at me questioningly. I pointed to the one on the left. Bending over, Fernandez removed the tires, then swiftly removed the boards revealing steps leading to an abyss.

At the bottom of the basin stood five military chests, each locked with a key. He eyed me uncertainly, presumably wondering why I hadn't gone down to the hiding place.

'You've got my key,' I pointed out. 'In the safe behind the pope's photograph.'

'Ah, of course, I'm terribly sorry. I forgot!'

In my previous avatars I had always left Fernandez a large tip for keeping not only my chest but also the key. This was a necessity; I couldn't, after all, take it with me to reality.

The tyre-man returned with my key. I waited a moment in silence until he understood that he should leave – as usual it took him about three seconds – then I finally descended to the bottom of the basin in order to pick up the parcel which one of my avatars had left.

A quarter of an hour later I was already driving down Park Avenue going south. I kept a briefcase with the basic accessories necessary for my work on the driver's seat. Heavier weapons in case of serious butchery rattled metallically in the boot. These trips from one end of Manhattan to the other were the only times I could enjoy the enormous amount of work the designers had put into creating the virtual city.

Admittedly, most of the skyscrapers I passed were mere scenery – even if I had attempted to call in, they would prove to be impenetrable for one reason or another – but you could see that somebody had recreated all this meticulously, brick by brick, from old photographs and films.

I passed Grand Central station – you could go inside but all the trains that day had been cancelled, of course. I passed the original, triangular Flatiron Building and in no time the towers of the World Trade Centre came into view.

These were the wonderful times when terrorism threatened other, distant countries. Not America. Osama bin Laden was still our valuable ally in fighting the Ruskies in Afghanistan. Tim McVeigh was still only a shy schoolboy bullied by his peers. Bah, Pan Am still offered the 103 link between Heathrow and JFK, with a flight path over the little Scottish town of Lockerbie.

On driving into the World Trade Centre's underground parking, therefore, there were no security checks to ensure I wasn't some dangerous individual carrying grenade-launchers and an AKM-74 automatic rifle in my boot.

Which was just as well, because I was.

I took my ticket and parked underground. According to my client's instructions I was to go up to the sixteenth floor. Simulation of the World Trade Centre, of course, did not recreate all the institutions operating here in 1985. No reason to, since this 'world' was limited to Manhattan only.

The designers of the game, therefore, left the WTC open to the players who flocked here anyway simply for sightseeing. Virtual office space could be rented for real money, providing a safe which couldn't be accessed or breached without proper codes. If passenger planes steered by madmen hit these virtual towers everything would collapse as in the real world, but among the rubble thousands of efficient safes would be left with their sides not even scratched.

My client had rented a comparatively cheap office on the thirtieth floor, without a window but right next to the lobby with express and local elevators. In the real WTC the lifts were usually crowded but in simulated New York it was easier to find such things as an empty lift, a good parking spot, and a restaurant table. The designers wisely hadn't cluttered the game with enough enpecees to mirror the overpopulation of real Manhattan.

I, therefore, went up to the 16th floor alone, having the spacious lift all to myself. Keeping to Hicks's instructions, which I'd memorised, I went to room 3013. The door was locked. I tapped in the code and went inside.

I turned on the light. In the windowless room, the only furniture was a desk with a telephone, a swivel-chair, and a free-standing safe in the corner. It was opened by turning old-fashioned knobs, no doubt to provide the player with more fun. I must admit, it was fun too.

I opened the safe and started to transfer the packets within to the sailor's sack which I'd brought with me in the briefcase. Suddenly, from behind my back, came a voice:

'Hands up and don't try anything!'

Idiot, standing with your back to the door, was my first thought as I calmly raised both hands as instructed. The voice seemed strangely familiar but I couldn't place it. Presumably some amateur; a real player would simply have shot me in the back instead of messing around with 'hands up'. After all, anybody 'killed' here wakes up a minute later in real Las Vegas, so there's nothing to feel guilty about.

I decided this was my only chance.

'Right, boss, I've done as instructed,' I said. 'And now I'm going to get up, slowly, because squatting like this is bloody uncomfortable.'

I did so, hands still in the air. Then came another voice – a woman's.

'Best to hit him straight away, pal,' she said. I recognised her immediately as the woman who'd asked me to put her lemians into the envelope. Clever; she hadn't really wanted to ask me anything; she was just pointing me out to somebody. Another player? It didn't make any sense. So…?

Oh, of course, the croupier. They're not allowed to play, but this one, apparently, had let himself be tempted by Hicks' winnings. He'd lose his job but for this amount of money, was clearly happy to do so. But why would the woman need a partner?

Suddenly it struck me: Hicks mentioned that he went to virtual New York with a girlfriend. No doubt this was her. She knew I was a professional hired by Hicks and so had enough brains not to attack me one-to-one. She didn't know the code to the safe so had to wait until someone opened it for her: the idiot known as Yours Truly.

'You win. The money's yours,' I replied brightly. 'I'll

throw the sack over to you.'

'Okay, don't get too clever,' growled the croupier. 'I'll take it myself.'

'You know I'm a pro, so I'll offer you some advice. Coming up to me puts you at risk unnecessarily. I constantly practice virtual fighting, which makes me dangerous close up. In a situation like this, keep your gun on the guy and tell him to throw the money.'

I was bluffing. As a professional I'd have advised them firstly, secondly and thirdly to kill me. Certainly, there were police in the virtual but if you kill somebody here without a witness you can easily go unpunished for the next twenty-four hours.

'You win. You've outsmarted me and I respect that; you deserve the money,' I added carefully. 'Hicks has already paid me, anyway. I'll only lose my commission. Too bad, but it happens in my job. So I'll slowly turn around while you keep the gun on me, okay?'

'Okay, pal, just remember: no tricks,' the woman said. So she was the boss here.

I turned towards them slowly and looked at the robbers for the first time. They were aiming three identical M9 Beretta handguns at me – Hicks' girlfriend held two. This was an absurd mistake made by amateurs who came across guns mainly in pop-culture. Wyatt Earp could fire two colts because nineteenth century revolvers took a long time reloading. A Beretta guarantees a decent forty bullets a minute, so it pays to focus on a good aim while holding the model in a strong grip rather than expecting a fancy choreographed fight sequence à la John Woo.

They had chosen avatars from caricatures of the eighties. He was early Tom Cruise clad in a suit, she a Cindy Lauper-type scarecrow. They suited each other.

'Chuck the money!' shouted Cindy Lauper.

'Okay,' I said, still wondering whether they were going to kill me. 'I congratulate you on your success. You stalked me like real professionals. Spare me one Franklin at least so I can have a good time in New York, can you? It's a tradition among pros…'

I could see that Cindy Lauper was just about to refuse, but Tom Cruise seemed more amenable.

'Only no tricks,' he warned me seriously. 'Chuck the sack to us. If everything's okay, we'll spare you a hundred. We can afford that, can't we, love?'

The girl replied with a forced smile. To be honest, I didn't care much about the hundred dollars, I just wanted to check whether I needed to fight for my life desperately – this would be the last chance to do so.

The croupier peered into the sack and took out a packet of banknotes. In a grand gesture he pulled out one hundred dollar note and put it in the gap in the door.

'Take your jacket off!' came the next order.

Oh well, the croupier wasn't a complete idiot. I did, indeed, have a holster and gun under my jacket. As instructed, I removed the holster in its entirety and threw it to the robbers.

'Now the briefcase,' ordered Tom Cruise. I obediently threw the little black suitcase which I had taken from the hiding-place in Fernandez's workshop towards him. Now I was completely unarmed. My initial plan – that I was going to kill them both as they waited for the lift, was no longer feasible.

Cruise shoved the holster into the money sack and threw this over his shoulder. His partner was still pointing both poppers at me.

'Right, pal, now you wait here like a good boy until we get into the lift, and that's the last we see of each other,' she said. 'Enjoy yourself with that hundred bucks. And send my greetings to that sucker, Hicks!'

That was in bad taste. Stealing from her boyfriend was one thing, but why top it with petty, spiteful remarks?

I stood with my hand in the air for a couple of seconds

listening to the steps of the thieving couple recede, then walked up to the desk. I picked up the telephone receiver and tapped out 2222, the internal number for security.

'Security? This is FBI special agent Fox Mulder, number JTT047101111,' I said. 'I'm following two East German spies planning an attack on the World Trade Centre. They're currently in the north tower lift. They've got a large sack with them and a suitcase. They're armed and very dangerous. Please apprehend them discreetly, without creating a panic. I'll be down in a moment.'

'Right, we're on the case,' the enpecee's drilled voice in the receiver replied.

I made my way to the lift. Of course, if I'd used that name to a human player, I'd have been immediately exposed. But an enpecee who knew a television series which wasn't going to be made for another seven years would have been a poor enpecee. That's why players quite often gave their avatars names from the world of sport or culture.

Going down in the lift, I wondered how my robbers would react to being apprehended by World Trade Centre security. They ought to be afraid of resisting because you only win in this game if the sack of money gets to the hotel room with you. That means that if New York police get mixed up in the game you lose anyway, because either they'd arrest you (and the money's lost) or they'd kill you in a skirmish (and the money's lost).

I suspected the scenario hadn't even entered my opponents' heads and, caught off guard, they might do something unpredictable. And the enpecees from security would do just what New York security would do in 1985 when they saw an eccentric couple with a fortune in a sack and, on top of that, a little suitcase with my work tools – a wig, a change of clothing, a set of spanners and false documents. If they started searching them, those two be in a mess of trouble.

In the lift I took, from my pocket, the only substitute for a weapon left for me: a fake FBI badge in a leather holder and a fake identity tag. They'd taken my holster but they hadn't searched my jacket. So I pinned the identity tag on, introducing me as special agent Fox Mulder. It was a good enough fake to give me sometimes several hours, sometimes a few minutes – in a dire situation – before anyone phoned the FBI to check whether an agent with that name existed. That would have to do.

With the identity tag pinned to my lapel, I stepped out of the lift and resolutely approached the desk where two security guards in WTC uniforms sat. They were a little on edge but, at first glance, looked normal.

'Mulder,' I introduced myself. 'I phoned a moment ago. Have you caught them? Where are they?'

'Director Carsini caught them himself' – one of the guards leapt to his feet. 'He's waiting for you in the conference room on the second floor. Shall I go with you?'

'No,' I waved him aside. 'Right now discretion's what counts. Exemplary performance, gentlemen. I see you haven't created a panic. That's what I wanted!'

Indeed, nothing in the glass lobby revealed any signs of panic – enpecees simulating employees, customers and tourists walked up and down the stairs, left, entered, smoked in allocated places. The World Trade Centre employed truly excellent security guards in the real world, too. Without them, something like 9/11 would have occurred a good decade earlier.

I rode the escalator up to the second floor and quickly found the conference room.

The assailants stood with their hands against the wall. On the table were the sack, my hold-all and their shoulder bag. It was obvious that Carsini had gone through the contents. The head of WTC security leaned against the desk in a half-sitting position and kept his eye on both the suspicious couple and the door.

'Agent Mulder, they're probably the ones,' he said not waiting for me to introduce myself.

'Congratulations, Mr Carsini,' I replied. 'A very professional operation.'

Hearing my voice, the assailants started to shout over each other. 'Mulder's a false name from a television series,' cried Cyndi Lauper. 'He's no agent but a bandit,' yelled Tom Cruise. They didn't understand the psychology of a security guard from the days of the Cold War. Anybody shouting incomprehensible words in strange English merely confirmed him in his belief that they were eastern spies.

'SHUT UP!' said Carsini in a voice which would have shut me up, too, if I'd been speaking.

'Have you informed the authorities? The police, FBI, Port Authority?' I asked.

'No. I didn't know what this was about so thought it best to wait for your instructions,' replied Carsini.

I nodded my approval.

'I'll tell you what it's about,' I answered and opened the sack a bit wider. 'There's one and a half million here which, in this building, they were to pass on to the Palestinians who are planning an attack using a car-bomb in the underground garage. They saw they were being followed so they tried to escape...'

'That's not true!', 'He's lying!', 'We can explain everything!' they started calling.

'SHUT – YOUR – SELVES – UP!' Carsini repeated.

The situation was getting ever more amusing. I wondered how the pair were going to 'explain' this. Tell an armed enpecee in uniform that this isn't 1985 at all, that the World Trade Centre had been demolished a long time ago, that new skyscrapers had been built in its place and that generally everything around was fiction created by virtual reality and you certainly won't be getting to your hotel room before nightfall. The druggies on Lower East Side might listen to you, but no one else would.

'Take a look at this,' I said to Carsini, lifting my holster from the robbers' sack. I then pulled the gun out. 'PB 6P9. Pistolyet Bessjhumnyi,' I stated, hiding the fact that in reality I didn't speak Russian with such a strong accent. 'A modification of the standard Russian army P6 Makarov used exclusively by the KGB and their special services. Factory-fitted with a silencer. Look how well it's designed.'

I screwed on the silencer. The croupier must have figured out my intentions because he started shouting, 'Believe us, sir, he's a fraud!'

'You no understand English?' snorted Carsini. 'That's bad, because me no understand Russian. Shut-the-fuck-upski or however you say it over there!'

'My hand's itching to sort out these terrorists with something like that.' He turned to me. 'But what can I do? It's a free country, everybody's innocent until proven guilty.'

'That's soon going to change.' I smiled as I loaded the 6P9.

Carsini didn't even have time to be surprised. When the 9mm dum dum bullet lodged in his skull, he still had a knowing smile on his face. My client's unfaithful girlfriend managed to squeal – she gave out one short 'A', the high tone reinforcing her likeness to Cindy Lauper.

Her body slid to the floor. I was pleased to see that that bullet had likewise lodged in her skull. There was no blood stain on the wall. I used Hungarian dum dum bullets which I'd once bought in the underground car park of the ONZ – on the black market which blossomed here in the eighties under cover of it being exterritorial. If the bullet had gone through the thin plaster wall someone might have noticed. This way, everything happened discreetly.

'We're left all by ourselves,' I said to the croupier who was still standing there with his hands up and against the wall. He was shaking. 'Turn around,' I instructed. 'You can lower your hands, my gun's on you.'

He did as instructed.

'Congratulations,' – he tried to smile. 'You won after all. A true pro! Going to give me back that hundred now, are you?'

I shook my head.

'Before we get to that I'd like to teach you two things. Firstly, you're no professional because you aren't playing by the rules. You're a croupier. You're to help customers enter the world of the game and not set traps on them with some faithless minx. You did something very stupid and you're going to take the consequences. On waking you're going to have to leave Las Vegas because you'll be blacklisted everywhere in the town. And quite rightly so; there are too many scoundrels like you as it is.'

The croupier – or really ex-croupier now – did not reply. He swallowed and answered after a long pause, 'And the second thing?'

'I'm a Pole,' I replied. 'My nation's introduced a few things into the world's civilisation. Not many: coffee with cream, the heliocentric system, chromatography. That's why it annoys me when somebody wants to take even more away from us and calls Lem a Russian. That guy in 1964 worked out in his essay what virtual reality would look like. IBM was manufacturing computers the size of a wardrobe with eight RAM megabytes at that time. Lem deserves some respect for accomplishing what he did then, don't you think?'

'Yes, of course, I'm sorry!' the man eagerly agreed with him.

'Repeat after me. "Stanisław Lem"...'

'Stanislau Lem...'

'Not "Stanislau". Sta–ni–sław,' I emphatically broke up the syllables.

'Stanislav Lem...'

'That'll have to do. "...was a Polish writer of science-fiction who in nineteen sixty-four contemplated virtual reality."'

'Stanislav Lem was a Polish writer of science-fiction

who in nineteen sixty-four contemplated virtual reality,' recited the man.

'I'm glad. I hope you're going to remember that for the rest of your life.' I smiled and pulled the trigger.

There was a wig with a Sid Vicious hairstyle, and a Ramones t-shirt in my briefcase. I changed my appearance in a flash and took the lift straight down to the garage so as not to meet the security guards by the main entrance. I'd locked the room using a key I'd found in Carsini's pocket.

I banked on about half an hour before anyone entered the room and alerted the authorities. In three or four hours the police would have prepared a composite sketch of me. They would tele-fax it to hotels in New York, but in 1985 this was quite a new technique, transmission took a long time and the picture was of pretty poor quality. I, therefore, always chose an avatar for my work which was a police graphic artist's nightmare: average height, average face, dressed in a grey suit, an unimaginative parting in the hair.

On top of that, in the WTC I was wearing non-optical glasses with a heavy frame which changed the shape of my face. The risk that enpecees working in the hotel reception would recognise me when they saw a picture like that was minimal. In real New York a criminal like that would have three or four days of peace. I only had to manage until eight in the morning.

A long drive down Broadway right up to Upper West Side and Washington Heights awaited me again. Señor Fernandez greeted me very politely and let me return my essential accessories to their hiding place, stowing the key once more in the safe behind the photograph of the pope. All that remained was to return to the hotel and stay up until late into the night watching television. As was usual after a successful operation.

In real Las Vegas another croupier handed me a pile of chips. In return I spared him a generous tip. The other customers greeted this with applause. Hicks's ex-girlfriend was no longer among them.

Ever since I was a child I'd been haunted by the fear of finding myself in a so-called 'phildickian' situation, so I was more interested in my lemian than my winnings. I tore open the envelope and extracted the contents.

Nicolaus Copernicus was staring out at me and the writing next to him assured me that NOTES OF THE POLISH NATIONAL BANK CONSTITUTE A LEGAL FORM OF PAYMENT IN POLAND. Old communist banknotes which had lost their value at the turn of the century. I'll never forget what the first money I earned in my life looked like. There was no doubt whatsoever that I was in the real.

Terracotta Robot

Adam Marek

STILL MINUTES FROM their destination, glimpses of the great terracotta hulks became visible between the poplars. Spiked crowns, armoured shoulders, the soles of upended gargantuan feet. But these sights could hardly tease Trent's gaze from the smooth, almost bare back of Callie, who rode in the carriage in front. The trotting of the horses and the unevenness of the road set Callie swaying, jiggling the gold teardrops suspended from her fine earlobes. Sometimes she looked off to the side, at the locals sitting on chairs outside the pastel houses, or at the cranes nesting atop the rare telegraph poles, and when she did, the fresh curve of her cheek, lightly tanned and barely freckled, was revealed in all its loveliness. One time she reached out to pluck a cherry from a low branch as she passed below it, and the simple grace of that gesture made Trent ache. On the whole journey she'd not looked back at him once, and he was in agony because of it.

There were eight carriages in all, three fewer than there should have been, so they'd all had to squeeze in tight. In this heat, the novelty of the ride through the town had drained quickly, as had their water bottles. These were open carriages, theatres for bloated flies drunk on horseblood. The floor of the carriage around Trent's feet was littered with their mangled bodies. It was these that Riley was photographing, despite Trent's pleas for him to save some of the memory card for when they arrived at the Terra Factory, where, he said, there would be much more impressive stuff to shoot.

When the group arrived at the factory – an edifice of devastating scale and dreariness – their clothes were damp in the places their bodies had been pressed together. The discomforts of the journey had fruited into complaints of such abundance that they sent Zoran, their tour guide, into hiding, and the group was left there on the lawn, twenty five of them, with the director of the factory, a man in a floppy white hat who spoke no English and whose grass chewing was interminable.

But this didn't matter. The robots needed little interpretation. Here were the terracotta gladiators, still awesome, still terrifying and terrific, after decades of slumber on the lawn outside their factory. Even broken into pieces as they were, it was easy to imagine what they must have looked like when complete, patrolling the battlefield, swinging their club arms, stamping their monstrous feet, hurling boulders, crushing tanks, swallowing whole fistfuls of men. Even just after noon, they cast shadows big enough to shelter whole families as they stroked the robots' rough surfaces, sliding their fingers along rake marks left by glancing bullets.

Sometimes these families were chased out of the shadows, into the sun, because the terracotta robots were not entirely inert. They would shift, as if restless in their sleep, the clay engines driving them still harbouring vestiges of life. Even a single detached finger, the length of a boy and bruised with algae, had in it the potential for a little pinch at the ground. These were only tiny movements, but common enough that among the hundred or so pieces of the dismantled robots scattered across an area about the size of a football field, there were always at least three in motion, giving the impression in their broken state that here was a defeated army refusing to fully submit, even though the enemy was long gone.

About these remains, Callie slunk with mouth-watering languor, head tilted, playing with one earring. While Trent drifted in her wake, he kept one eye on Riley, who was getting too close to a scruffy-looking dog he was trying to photograph. Mark, Callie's husband, walked alongside her, stopping at each of the robot pieces with his arms folded, one leg jittering at the knee.

Their guide, Zoran, reappeared and called the group over to the side of the factory, where a sloped roof threw shade over an enormous wooden table. The factory director set down a tray containing four towers of stacked tumblers, and two bottles filled with a clear liquid. He nodded, just once, to indicate that they all should drink.

'Rakia,' Zoran said. 'Made from quince.'

Zoran unstacked the glasses and arranged them close enough together that he could slosh rakia into them without pausing between glasses.

Callie pulled a face and giggled as she sipped.

Trent slugged the rakia down with a backwards flick of his head. 'Fearsome stuff,' he said, coughing, holding out his glass so that Zoran could refill it.

Callie sat at the corner of the table, and Trent and Mark took seats either side of her. As they drank, they watched a man wearing nothing but cut-off jeans struggling to pull a trolley along the path. On the trolley was half a terracotta whale, the head end, taller than the man, pointing skywards. The man was leaning in to the job, the rope digging into his shoulder.

'Here is biggest kiln in the world,' Zoran said. 'Since they stop making robots, that's when the artists come.'

Callie made a small noise of alarm and said, 'I've lost my earring,' fingering her naked earlobe and searching the ground beneath her chair.

Trent and Mark both leaned over the sides of their chairs to join the search. 'Was it precious?' Trent asked.

'I bought them with my first pay cheque,' she said. 'Almost all of it.'

Trent looked now at the remaining earring. It was a long thin teardrop shape, with a hole cut in the thickest point, and a small diamond suspended like a pupil within it.

'It's most likely over by the robots,' Trent said. 'I'll help you find it. I've got a good eye for shiny things.'

'I'll look later,' she said. 'It's too hot out there right now, even for me.'

Where the sloped roof met the factory building, house martins had fashioned muddy cup nests, and from them hungry chicks were begging. The parent birds swooped up to deposit bugs in their mouths every few minutes. White droppings had been left to gather on the floor beneath the nests, and it was these that Riley was now photographing.

The director returned with another tray containing four jugs of water, which the group set upon while the tray was still in his hands. Trent poured water for Riley and called him over, making him drink the whole glass while he watched.

'Is bird shit really the best thing to photograph round here?' Trent said.

The boy lingered there, silent, his lower lip sucked half-way between his teeth, until Trent said, 'Oh go on then,' and waved him away.

'Trent was telling me that he once worked with the Rolling Stones,' Callie said to Mark.

Mark managed no more than an, 'Oh right'. He was slouched low in the wooden chair, feet wiggling, looking here and there and nowhere in particular, for no more than a few seconds at a time.

'Mark's a big Stones fan,' she said.

'I did two of their videos actually,' Trent said.

This was one of the things they'd managed to exchange about each other last night, at the poolside, when Mark had gone to bed early with a bad stomach. The hotel had dragged some of the adults up to take part in daft games, including a race conducted by passing a balloon between your knees to the next person in your team till it got to the end of the line.

Trent had made sure he was beside Callie. He usually hated audience participation stuff like this, but his desire to interact with Callie gave him uncommon enthusiasm for it, and this, coupled with her competitive spirit, made them the strongest link in their team's chain. It seemed that their knees had been made to work together. Callie rewarded his efforts when their team won a free round of mojitos by wrapping her thin arms around his neck and kissing him on the cheek. He could still feel the soft pressure of it when he thought about it now.

After the games had been dispersed, and Trent had draped a beach towel over Riley, who was sleeping on a sun lounger, he stole two bottles of beer from the unattended bar and sat with Callie, whom, he soon learned, was on her honeymoon. When he'd asked why they'd come *here*, of all places, she'd said it was specifically to visit the Terra Factory. She'd always wanted to come here, ever since learning about the robots in primary school.

'And how about you?' she'd asked him.

'I wanted to bring Riley to the factory,' Trent said. 'He's nuts about robots. It's what he wants to be when he grows up. I bought him a new camera so he can take lots of pictures to show his mum.'

Trent told her all about how he'd been to the robot factory for the first time in his twenties, when he was shooting a Metallica video, and this had got her leaning forwards in her chair, hungry to hear more about his work, her smile growing wider with each band name he dropped into the conversation. Aerosmith. U2. Bjork. Lenny Kravitz. REM. Radiohead. Madonna. The Spice Girls. He wished he had more recent stories to tell, but he'd not directed anything in fifteen years.

'So do you and your son go on holiday together often, without your wife?'

'Oh, Riley is my *grand*son.'

'Shut up!'

'Hannah, my ex-wife, and I had our daughter when we

were very young.'

'Well, you don't look anything like a…' She made an embarrassed smile.

'Hey thanks,' he said, patting his stomach. 'I do like to take care of myself.'

They stayed there chatting, watching bats hunting moths over the pool, until everyone else had left. While Callie talked, she retrieved a half-eaten pizza from the next table and picked bits of cheese from the top to throw to a grateful stray kitten, a skinny thing, all stripes and bones.

Callie said she was a publicist for a leather designer in Notting Hill Gate, a job she loved because she got tonnes of free stuff. She lifted her foot to show her sandals, and reached below her chair to wiggle the straps of her big white bag.

'And is that your dream job?' He'd asked her.

'I wouldn't say it was my *dream*.'

'So what is then? Ten years from now, if you could be anywhere, doing anything, what would it be?'

'I don't really know. Is that sad?'

'Maybe you're already there then.'

'That really would be sad!' She laughed. 'So how about you?'

'I'd like to be making films again,' he said. 'But proper films, not just spots and promos. You know, features. Maybe even about the robots. That's the other reason I came here. To see if it could get my juices flowing again. It's been a while since I made anything.'

'How come?'

'I overindulged myself and made some big fuck-ups in my early thirties. I was one of the top guns for a few years, and I could get away with almost anything. I went kind of nuts.'

'What kind of nuts?'

'The kind of nuts that rock stars are supposed to go, not directors.'

'That sounds like fun.'

'It *was* fun at the time, but I made an ass of myself. I did a lot of things I feel guilty about now.'

'Is that when you split up with your wife?'

Trent nodded. 'I'm lucky she stayed with me as long as she did.'

'Do you still talk to her?'

'We just started talking again last year. It took her fourteen years to forgive me.'

'Wow, you must have been very naughty.'

'Like you wouldn't believe.'

It had got much colder. Callie was pulling her cardigan about her, and he worried that she would leave him. He asked about her husband, and regretted it as soon as he could hear the words coming out of his mouth. She said she'd known Mark since she was at school. He had just started working at a University, teaching something to do with economics and ethics, something tedious.

Talking about her husband seemed to change the atmosphere, and suddenly Callie was looking at her watch, saying she couldn't believe how late it had got, and was up and leaving, at too great a distance from Trent now for him to embrace her, or return the kiss from earlier, without looking too eager. So he just waved, and watched her go.

Now, at the Terra Factory, here they were again, the same distance apart from each other, their bodies in almost identical positions to last night. Except now the air was thick with heat, sapping their energy, and they were quickly growing numb on the rakia.

'Why don't you photograph the actual robots,' Trent said to Riley, who had tired of the bird droppings and was taking shots of a vaccination scar on Callie's upper arm. 'Callie might not want her picture taken.'

'It's okay,' Callie said, and with permission given, Riley came even closer, moving the camera up, so the eye of the lens was only inches from the side of her face.

'Riley, give her some space.'

'It's okay, really,' she said, and after Riley had fired off about ten shots, she asked if she could have a look.

Riley would not hand over the camera to her, but turned it so that she could see the screen on the back, and flicked through the pictures for her.

'These are good,' she said. '*Really* good. You have a great eye.' And then suddenly Callie said, 'Hey! Go back. That's my earring.'

Trent got off his chair to stand behind Callie, while Riley flicked back a couple of shots.

'There!' She said.

There was just one shot of the earring, out of focus, and cropped so close that nothing much of its surroundings was revealed, except a bit of mud and a few blades of grass.

'Where did you take this?' Trent said.

Riley shrugged.

'Come on, think!' Trent said. 'When was it? Was it just after we arrived? Was it by the robots? Was it by the big head over there, or the finger?'

Riley shook his head.

'It's okay,' Callie said. 'Don't worry.'

'I'll help you look after lunch,' Trent said, refilling his glass. Mark gave him an unmistakably cold glare.

On the lawn, close by, two of the staff from the factory tipped charcoal into a half-drum barbecue, then sloshed gasoline over it and tossed in a match. Fume-heavy smoke drifted under the porch, driving the tour group back out onto the grass.

Trent began to walk with Callie to the robots again, but Mark cradled her back with his arm and diverted her away. Instead, Trent asked Riley to take him around all the places he'd photographed earlier, so he could find Callie's earring. In the heat, with an empty stomach, and half-delirious after the rakia, the urgency of this quest became grossly exaggerated in his mind. His irritation grew when Riley, discovering that his granddad had forgotten to pack the sunblock, gave up the search after just ten minutes to return to the shade.

Trent continued, and in his desperation he allowed his neck to burn, his tongue to swell, a headache to bloom, and his clothes to sag with his sweat.

There was nothing to hear but the high whine of insects, the white noise of the sun bearing down, and the robots. All around him their fragments complained in the heat, stretching and twisting, thumbing marks into the baked ground, tortured movements that chased grey spiders and green lizards from their insides.

After a lunch of scorched chicken breasts and salad that no one would eat in case it had been washed in tap water, Zoran promised them a surprise. 'Something very special,' he said.

He took them through the factory, where three of the resident artists were sweeping the floor with brooms. They had scarves tied around their faces against the thick clay dust filling the workshop, all the way up to the wooden rafters high above.

'Pull your t-shirt over your face,' Trent said to Riley, pulling the collar of his own shirt across his mouth and nose.

At the back of the workshop, Zoran led them through an enormous set of metal doors and into an empty cavern – a mercifully cold cathedral, into which ran a set of train tracks.

'This is kiln,' Zoran said. 'During the war, every Terra robot made in this place.'

'Did they make them in pieces?' One of the group asked, speaking slowly and in a high pitch, the way that most of the group spoke to Zoran. 'And then assemble them, put them together, afterwards?'

'Ah, yes,' Zoran said. 'Here make the pieces. Out there, assemble.' The guide knitted his fingers together and wiggled them as he said 'assemble', a gesture that struck Trent as a hugely inadequate visual representation of what the actual work must have been like.

Zoran explained, in his way, that in the 20 years that the factory was operational, they manufactured more than 500 Terra robots. The pieces on display on the lawns outside had been recovered from all over the country.

'This was a nice surprise,' one of the group said, and then slowly again, a little higher, 'nice surprise'.

'I think he heard you the first time,' Trent whispered, close to Callie's ear, and they chuckled together. His fingertips found her bare shoulder in the dim light, and her skin was as deliciously cool as he'd imagined it would be.

'This is not the surprise,' Zoran said, with a mischievous grin, and beckoned them all to follow him.

Outside, at the back of the factory, there was an empty field baked-dry. A row of thirty grey plastic chairs, covered in dusty fingerprints, awaited the group.

As they took their chairs, Trent said, 'Riley found the only shade in this place,' and Callie looked over to where he was pointing, to a rusty car bizarrely propped lengthways against the back of the factory. In the shade it cast, Riley was sat in the dirt with his plimsoles off and the soles of his feet pressed together. The dog he'd been following earlier was lying on its side in the same patch of shade, and Riley was again photographing it. Callie smiled, fanning her face with the Terra brochure.

'He doesn't say much, does he?' She said.

'He's got some issues. He can be damn frustrating sometimes, but he's a good kid.'

'He is.'

They stared at the empty field before them.

'This place has changed so much,' Trent said.

'In what way?'

'It wasn't a place for tourists at all. It was still a communist country. We had to bribe all kinds of people to get access. Most of the budget went on bribes in fact. My promo was the first footage ever to be shot by someone from outside of the country.'

'Wow.'

'We had police and people from the government watching us the whole time. I think it felt a lot different as well because we were here in the winter. We were all wrapped up in thick coats and furry hats. I've never been so cold.'

'Huh,' Callie said. 'All I can think about now is getting back to the pool at the hotel. I'm not even going to bother getting changed. I'm just going to take my watch off and jump in.'

'I like the sound of that,' Trent said.

Zoran came over, grinning, showing his teeth, ordering them all to watch. He pointed to the far side of the field where there was an enormous heap of battered rusty cars piled up in front of an odd-shaped building. The factory director was jogging towards it. He took off his floppy hat, and his long damp hair spilled out if it, all the way down to his shoulders.

Except it wasn't a building. This became obvious to them when the director rested a ladder against it, climbed up onto the roof carrying a long wooden pole, and sat astride it. This roof was a shoulder, and there was its head, flopped down, chin against chest. The director slid the wooden pole into a hole where its left ear would be, and began to jiggle it about inside.

And then the thing awoke.

Its eyes were closed lids, so when it lifted its head to the group, it was with a blank gaze. The director quickly whipped his legs round the robot's neck, and again worked the pole – an apparently random wiggling – firing this terracotta beast into life.

There were gasps as it stood up, holy shits and jesus christs. Its movements were uncannily human. It wobbled as it stood, as if it really had just woken from sleep. Its height kept coming and coming. Throughout the group, hands clamped over ears, because the sound of the robot's joints complaining was excruciating; a blackboard scraping, a ship pulled out of the water by its chains and dragged along the dock.

Trent was stood now, hands shielding his eyes. 'Riley! Riley!' he said. 'Look for fuck's sake.' Riley's attention moved slowly from the dog to the robot, but his camera stayed in his lap. Half the group shot Trent disapproving glances. He blew out a long slow breath and dropped back into his seat.

The PA system wailed as it was switched on, and then Zoran tapped the microphone with his fingertips.

'This is… his name, it means… Big Man.'

'No shit,' Trent said. Callie laughed. A snort.

'He is over seventy years old and the only full working Terra robot left in the world.'

'That guy looks like he's talking to it,' Callie said.

Indeed, the director had his head right next to the earhole and was animatedly encouraging this thing into activity. The robot stepped over the pile of cars, his footfall shocking the ground. When he brought his second foot over, he lost his balance for a moment. The director grabbed the head to steady himself.

'Big Man was built for strength,' Zoran said. 'For him cars are like toys.'

The robot bent down, making an agonizing sound, picked up a rusty half-flattened car in one hand, then did a small under-arm throw, like he was bowling, chucking the car a few metres.

'No, no, no!' Zoran said. 'Big Man, you can do better. But maybe he needs your encouragement!' And then he demonstrated that they all should clap. And when their clapping was not enthusiastic enough, Zoran yelled, 'No, more bigger claps!'

Trent whistled and clapped hard and called out 'Come on Big Man, show us what you've got!'

Big Man seized up then, creaking to a halt and not

moving for a few seconds, until the director worked the pole into his ear with great brutality, grunting with the effort of it, his long hair shaking, and he bellowed too, and after a few moments of this abuse, the robot lurched back into life and resumed his show, bending down again, picking up another car, this time raising it right up over his shoulder for an overarm throw.

Big Man took one step forward, his arm back, again an eerily human movement, and hurled the car high into the air. The tour group shrieked, leaping up from their chairs. There were more holy shits and jesus christs because the car was flying in their direction, dust spilling from it as it flipped end over end. But it carried on, high over their heads, and crashed to the ground far behind them.

For the next ten minutes, they watched Big Man stamp on a rusty pick-up truck, squashing it to a quarter of its original height. They watched him pick up an enormous metal joist and swing it like a baseball bat, smacking the uppermost wreck in the pile right out onto the centre of the field. They watched him stride over, pick up the wreck, squeeze his enormous clay fingers through the spaces where the windows had once been, then tear the roof from the car.

'He prefers convertibles!' Zoran laughed.

But every few minutes, the robot would seize up again, appearing to run out of energy, or to have forgotten for one absent moment where he was, what he was doing. He would stand there, staring at the ground, until goaded back into life by the director, who grew more and more brutal with the pole, ramming it into the side of the robot's head and cursing loudly.

'Poor thing,' Callie said, frowning.

When the show was done, and Zoran said, 'how about a big applause for Big Man,' the director yelled into the robot's ear and thrust the pole with such violence that Big Man actually turned his head to the side, as if trying to move his ear away from the blows. And only when the director reached with both hands inside the robot's head to thrust the pole into some deep space within the centre of his head did the giant lean forward and, with seeming reluctance, take a bow.

After Zoran could wring no more applause from his exhausted audience, he asked everyone to make their way to the carriages for the journey to the hotel. The robot lumbered back behind the pile of cars, and once he had sunk to his knees, the director swung his left leg around, and slid down the robot's sloped back.

'Swimming pool!' Trent said, and Callie smiled.

Trent looked over to where Riley had been sitting just a moment ago, but the boy was no longer there. 'I'll catch you up.' Trent said, 'He's gone walkabout.'

While the rest of the group went back through the factory, Trent walked round to the side, where there were heaps of broken terracotta pieces piled up against crumbling stone outbuildings. He'd been searching for less than a minute, and calling out Riley's name, when there was a cough behind him. It was Mark.

'Have you seen him?' Trent said.

Mark was chewing the inside of his cheek. He shook his head. 'Listen,' he said. 'I wanted to ask you something.'

'Sure.'

'Where did you go on your honeymoon?'

'My honeymoon?' Trent said. 'We went to LA.'

'And did *you* have some arsehole following your wife around the whole time?'

Trent swallowed.

'Well, I don't want that either,' Mark continued. His face was red, and he was shaking a little. He raised his eyebrows just once, and then turned and walked back through the factory.

Trent could do nothing but stand there, stunned, until he heard Riley scream.

Out front, beside the broken robots, half the group was gathered around Riley. The boy was sitting on the floor, clutching his right shin and wailing at the sight of blood on his fingers.

Zoran ran past Trent and said, 'I will fetch first aid,' and then he was gone.

'What the hell happened?' Trent asked.

'It was that dog,' one of the old women in the group said.

'Jesus, Riley!' Trent said, and knelt down next to him. 'Let me see.'

But Riley refused to move his hands.

Among the eight or nine members of the group now crowding around them, at least half pulled tubes of ointment, wet wipes, plasters and antiseptic sprays from their bags.

'Damn it Riley, didn't I tell you to keep away from it? That mangy thing could have been rabid for fuck's sake.'

'I'm a school nurse,' one of the women said, and knelt down beside him, persuading Riley with a few gentle words to allow her to clean around the wound with some antiseptic wipes, apologizing about the stinging when Riley winced.

Zoran returned with the first aid kit, but when he saw that the boy was already being attended, he stayed back. 'He'll be okay. He's tough boy,' Zoran said. 'Tough like Terra robot, huh,' and he laughed.

When the school nurse asked for the first aid kit, he gave it to her. She took from it a bandage to wrap around Riley's shin, and then she and Trent each took one of Riley's arms and helped him to his feet.

Zoran called to one of the carriage drivers to bring the horses close by.

'You'll have to get him checked out,' the school nurse said. 'He might need a shot.'

Riley squeaked, and his eyes widened.

'He's got a bit of a needle phobia,' Trent said to the nurse, and then to Riley, 'This is what happens when you play with mangy dogs. What do you think your mum's going to say when I have to tell her about this?'

Trent put one arm under Riley's armpit, the other beneath his knees and lifted him up. Zoran climbed into the carriage ahead of him and reached out his hands to help, but Trent managed without him.

Already some of the other carriages had left, including the one bearing Callie and Mark. Trent watched them disappear round the corner. The carriage driver, an old and heavily tanned man with a thick grey moustache, looked round to them, glancing for a second at Riley's bandage. Trent nodded that it was okay to set off. The horse had trotted no more than a few metres, when something slipped out of Riley's pocket and clattered onto the floor of the carriage.

It was Callie's earring.

Riley paled.

Trent picked up the earring and held it in his palm. It was a weighty thing, and he wondered whether it must hurt to have something so heavy dangling from your lobe. 'Did you have this the whole time?' he asked.

Riley said nothing.

Trent watched the earring sparkle between his fingertips for a few moments, and then gave it to Riley. 'I didn't see this,' he said. 'Okay?'

Riley nodded, took the earring, and put it back in his pocket.

Ex Libris

Sean O'Brien

GUZMAN FOUND HIMSELF descending a ladder in a circular concrete shaft. The gloom prevented him from seeing how far he had come or how far there was to go. The shaft itself seemed to be sweating, and the rungs of the ladder were wrapped in what seemed to be old carpet. At times the fabric slipped against the metal. *My name is Guzman*, he realized. That was all. There seemed nothing for it but to continue his descent.

Guzman had no watch, but his downward passage seemed to go on for hours. At last he stopped and wrapped his arms around the vertical poles of the ladder. The muscles of his legs and back were burning. For a while he hung there trying to think, but whatever state he was trying to recall or produce evaded him. He had woken on the ladder: on the ladder he remained. He had gone too far to turn back, but where would it end? Perhaps he could simply let go and fall. As this thought surfaced, something brushed against his shoulder. Startled, he saw a magpie beating its wings and vanishing into the murk below. The only thing, he supposed, was to follow the creature downwards, if downwards was the word for it.

The bird created an expectation that for a further extended period it seemed would find no fulfilment. There was the sweating shaft, the ladder, the descent. After a time he scarcely thought, scarcely registered the discomfort of his futile progress. A scrap of a song ran round his head: *I am a man of constant sorrow / I've seen trouble all my day.* Then, before he knew it, he reached the bottom of the shaft, lowering himself to the final rung before dropping a few feet onto a flat area of uncertain but vast extent.

The ground of this place (if those were either of the words) was composed of what seemed to be the covers of innumerable books of all sizes, their titles displayed in many languages. He noticed, randomly, *Effi Briest*, *The Zaragoza Manuscript*, *Gentlemen Prefer Blondes*, *Elective Affinities*, *Melmoth the Wanderer*, and there grew in him the recognition that what he was feeling was a rebuke, stretching as far as he could see in all directions, fading into a haze. What they had in common, the titles his eye had fallen on, was that he suspected that he had not read them. It seemed reasonable to infer that this only mattered because he was in some way bookish, or literary, himself. At some prior but undisclosed point he had nursed the intention to read them, and now he was here with everything at his disposal, and it amounted to an indictment of his bad faith. There is something metaphysical about this, thought Guzman. A blast of pain passed through his head as if in confirmation.

He moved gingerly away from the shaft, then turned to see the ladder slowly withdrawing into the low cloud which formed the ceiling of the vast plain. He raised a hand as if to appeal for its return but his most powerful feeling was exhaustion. With an instinct to find shelter, he opened a huge book. Without registering the cover, he lay down and let the book half-close on him. In the dry, slightly foxed light he found himself reading the foot-high opening sentences of *Leviathan*. Soon he fell asleep.

How long he had slept he could not tell. He awoke with a terrible thirst and the certainty that there was no water to be had in this plain of paper. He climbed out of the book and stood up, peering about. In his pocket he found a stub of pencil and a scrap of paper on which was written: *No Gloves for the Hangman*, by Zeke Allison, Rockhampton, Rockhampton

Press, 1947. So, then, it was a quest, for a book he had never heard of, never mind read. What kind of book? A western, perhaps – but surely Rockhampton was in Australia. Guzman sighed. He would die of thirst in this desert of print, this plain with 'nothing to eat and nowhere to sit down'. The quotation whispered through his mind without attribution. The pain in his head returned. He heard the wingbeat of the magpie just before it brushed his shoulder. It landed twenty yards or so away, and turned to face him before taking off once more. There seemed no reason not to follow.

For a long time the bird maintained its routine, flying a little way, turning to look, flying again, while Guzman trudged in its wake. The titles and the authors changed but the horizontal plain did not. Guzman's head ached with dryness. Had he possessed any equipment he would have discarded it. His gaze was drawn to the random catalogue beneath his feet. Montesquieu, Manzoni, Hank Janson, Elinor Glyn, Jacqueline Susann, Pushkin, *The Times Atlas of the World*. Although he knew that to start reading or even browsing now would be fatal, he knelt down beside the book to open it, and to his surprise he was able to lift it out of position. Beneath it lay a clear pane of water. It might be salt but Guzman did not care. He lay down and drank as though to drain an ocean.

When at last he raised his head he found the magpie in close attendance. It gestured with one wing like someone indicating a wristwatch. Restored, Guzman set off once more behind the bird. At least there was water. And something to read. To put it mildly. He laughed aloud but then began to think about the odds against happening on a copy of *No Gloves for the Hangman* in this uncatalogued biblio-world.

So preoccupied was Guzman with reading the titles and authors' names that he did not at first register that a fog had begun to form. The bird was only intermittently visible. Guzman hastened on. Then through the fog snow began to fall and with it the temperature. The bird had vanished.

Feeling his way forward over the thickening crust of snow, Guzman tripped on a displaced book. When he rose the ground seemed to have become unsteady. Then a gap appeared between the two volumes on which he stood, and black water lapped at the pages. He moved to stand on a single book the size of a paving stone. It tilted alarmingly beneath him and glimpsing a larger volume drifting past he jumped and lay full length. Now he heard the sound of waves. He spread himself on a vast copy of *Moby Dick*, like Ishmael clinging to Queequeg's coffin. He would either drown or freeze to death. He prayed to be relieved of consciousness. His prayer was answered and he sank into dreamlessness.

He was awoken by voices. He looked up and found that the snow had stopped and he was still afloat on the book-berg in a field of similar snow-covered volumes, slowly moving on the inky water. The fog too had cleared but the sky remained low and grey. The magpie was nowhere to be seen. Then, once again, he heard voices, this time raised. He got carefully to his feet and peered around him. Directly ahead a rowing boat came into view between two book-bergs. He made out two figures, one with its back to him rowing, the other standing up and peering through a telescope. They seemed to be wearing tricorn hats. The gaze of the telescope fell on him. The watching figure stooped and then straightened up, holding a musket.

'What are you, sir?' came the loud voice of the standing figure. 'A privateer? A Portugee?' The boat came steadily closer. The bewigged figure cocked the weapon. His companion shipped the oars and turned with a pistol in his hand.

'Neither of those things,' said Guzman, surprised by the sound of his own voice. 'I am lost.'

'To be lost covers a multitude of sins, sir. You must offer an account of yourself. We have met such as you before.'

'I have no memory,' said Guzman. 'I have simply found myself in this place, if it is a place. Only regrets and desires remain to me.'

'What is your name?'

'My name?' Now the Christian name supplied itself too. 'My name is Raimund Guzman.'

'A Spaniard, then.' The taller figure nodded as if this might have been expected.

'I don't know what I am. I ask you not to shoot me,' Guzman said. 'I am not armed. I am lost and in search of shelter and an explanation.'

'Are you a Christian fellow?'

'I cannot answer that. I have no information to give you. I found myself climbing down a ladder on to a plain of books. I walked and the plain began to break up into these bergs. I slept. And now I meet you.'

'He is likely a djinn,' said the oarsman, in a Scottish accent, turning to his companion. 'If we shoot him the charge will make smoke of him, Doctor. If not I fear he will make smoke of us.'

'Be quiet, Boswell. I am thinking.' Boswell shook his head. The boat had drifted very near now. At length the Doctor put down his weapon. 'Let him aboard. He can share your labours at the oars.'

'I do not think it wise, Doctor Johnson,' said Boswell.

'I do not think *you* wise,' said the Doctor. 'But I hold my tongue about it, do I not? Put up your weapon, sir.' Boswell shrugged and put his pistol away, then reached out a hand to assist Guzman into the vessel. It was, Guzman thought, too large for one man to row easily, though he doubted if the Doctor shared in Boswell's labours. A mast and sail lay unused, and the prow and all other spaces and crannies were stowed with bags and chests. His companions seemed strangely familiar but their names meant nothing to him, though his persisting depression and guilt suggested that they should.

'Sit down, sir,' said the Doctor. He was a man of remarkable ugliness, his vast face pitted with some affliction. His black coat and breeches were shiny with use and he stank in a way that made Guzman catch his breath. Boswell, diminutive in comparison, seemed untroubled by the smell and was not entirely sweetness himself. 'Get food for our guest, Boswell.' The little man busied himself in one of the canvas bags and produced a stony loaf and a hunk of ancient meat which he put on a plate. These he handed to Guzman along with a bottle of Geneva. His task complete, he took out a writing case and a notebook and sat expectantly at Guzman's side.

'You are a man without a story,' said the Doctor. 'Perhaps there is no diversion to be got out of you.' Boswell wrote this down.

'I apologize,' said Guzman.' Except that I can recognize books and that there seem to be none here that I have read, I am at a loss. But it seems that you and your companion do not share this trouble, Doctor.'

'We share the gifts reserved for age,' said the Doctor, seeming to take recognition for granted. 'I warrant you that is trouble enough. We labour like you in hope's delusive mine.'

'I do not think this is a mine,' said Guzman.

'I speak in figures, sir,' said the Doctor, drinking from the Geneva bottle before firmly replacing the stopper, 'being part-poet, for my sins.'

'The Doctor has many strings to his bow,' added Boswell, and would have said more had his master not stopped him with a glance.

'Since I can offer nothing of use,' said Guzman, 'can you enlighten me?'

'We have retained our histories and our names and, as you see, a fine balance between flattery and contempt. But as to how Boswell and I came here, it is all a darkness.'

'Inspissated gloom,' muttered Boswell, sharpening a fresh quill.

'At one moment we were seated in the chop-house with Addison and Steele – I can see that these names will mean nothing to you – the next we were aboard our little craft, and have been so a week now. I may add that I have no appetite for adventure. To have travelled in the highlands and islands gave me sufficient sight of the world. But here we are and here we must endure.' The Doctor turned away, unbuttoned his breeches and urinated into the inky waters.

'Faith endures,' muttered Boswell, scratching away.

'Damme, sir, am I to strike you?' roared the Doctor.

'But who will row your vessel then?' said the little man, slyly.

'Then fall to it,' said the Doctor. 'Matters are not improved by our remaining here.' Guzman and Boswell took up the oars and pulled away through the bookish waste. Conversation lapsed and the Doctor began to read aloud from the Books of Ecclesiastes and Job. It was weary work, Guzman found, and the reading tended to lower his spirits further. He ached, he longed to sleep, but after a time he fell into a trance produced by the rhythm of the oars and his own deep exhaustion.

When Guzman next took thought it was dark. The doctor stood in the prow with a lantern trying to guide their passage. The books seemed fewer and vaster, as though they were coming nearer to one of the poles of whatever dreadful place this was.

'We should rest,' said Boswell.

'Quiet,' said his master. 'There is something out there.' As he spoke, the waters beside them seemed to erupt, and Guzman saw something vast breaking swiftly through the surface. At first he thought it might be a whale, but insofar as he could make it out the thing was ironclad. It reared as if it must crush them, then just as suddenly settled, revealing itself as a vast submarine, its ribs and plates studded with huge rivets. There was the sound of hatches thrown open. A powerful lamp was aimed into the rowing boat from the conning tower. Once more the Doctor aimed his musket.

'It is useless to resist,' declared a voice from a loud hailer.

'Put down your weapons. For you the war is over. Abandon hope all you who enter here.'

'Do as he says,' urged Guzman.

'Heterogeneous ideas–' said the Doctor.

'–Yoked by violence together,' Boswell replied. The pair set down their guns.

The magpie perched on the end of the iron bedstead, a silver chain about its foot. Deep in the bowels of the craft, the cell was extremely hot, running with condensation, but a handsome cast-iron drinking fountain provided a supply of fresh water. The trio sat and looked about them. The noise of the submerging craft had faded now.

'Have I gone mad, Boswell?' asked the Doctor. 'I would not be mad.'

'You are brushed by the wing of madness merely,' the scribe replied. 'Or I am mad, and Master Guzman and the great world are mad likewise.'

'I think we are travelling beneath the sea,' said the Doctor. 'It is against nature. Men are not gods or nymphs to delve in Neptune's pastures.'

'The ship is mechanical,' said Guzman. 'It has some form of power that enables us to breathe in its confinement, and we can sense its movement. There is nothing supernatural about this.'

'Are you a literary man?' the Doctor asked Guzman.

'I think somehow I may have been. What makes you ask?'

'The thought simply occurred to me,' said the Doctor. 'It also occurs to me that our present plight may have rather more to do with you than with myself or Boswell.'

'We are blameless, I think,' said Boswell, busying himself with his notebook again. 'But you, sir, what have you done to bring us to this?'

'I wish I knew,' Guzman muttered, beginning to dislike the small Scotsman.

The three fell to brooding, listening uneasily to the

clangs and hisses of the great vessel. Occasionally footsteps came and went in the corridor outside. At length the Doctor produced a clay pipe from his voluminous coat and set to work to light it. As soon as smoke was produced a loud alarm went off and lights began to flash.

A key sounded in the lock and the studded metal door swung inwards. A pair of black-uniformed Cyclopses wearing caps with lightning flashes gestured for the Doctor to extinguish his pipe. They marched the trio through the boiling bowels of the great submarine until at last they ascended a spiral staircase and found themselves in a lavishly appointed study with a large curved window that looked out into the dark ocean. Unidentifiable but tentacular creatures flickered in and out of view, drawn by the lit interior.

Terrible music was playing. Guzman saw a black-clad figure seated at a vast church organ, leaning back from time to time as though in passion while grandiose discords sprang from its fingers like a series of violent mechanical accidents. He is pretending to be able to play, thought Guzman.

As though overhearing this, the figure ceased its labours, rose and turned to greet his guests. Like the crew, he wore a dark uniform, to which was added a cap clearly indicating high rank, its insignia incorporating the lightning flash on a twisted cross of some kind. The man – if such he was – also wore an eyeless black balaclava with a hole left for the mouth.

'Doctor Johnson, Mr Boswell, Guzman. Good evening, gentlemen. I have been expecting you.'

'You have the advantage of us, sir,' said Dr Johnson.

'Indeed,' said the masked figure. 'Knowledge is power.'

'Power being yours, might you offer us the courtesy of your name?' The dark figure nodded, raising a black-gloved hand to his black chin as though considering.

'Captain Erich Von Nemo at your service. For this evening, you are my guests. Come, let us eat.' At this waiters appeared with chafing dishes and the Captain led the party to a long table laid with napery and silver cutlery.

'Do you understand the uses of knives and forks, Mr Guzman?' asked the Captain when they were seated.

'I am indifferent to them,' Guzman replied, weighing a heavy fish-knife in his palm.

'Food is an index of civilization,' said the Captain. He gestured to the waiters who began serving from the dishes. From where he was sitting Guzman saw the organ continuing to play quietly, but still tunelessly, by itself. When he looked down at his plate a long vegetable of luminous green lay twitching and steaming on a bed of weed and white sauce.

'Eat, gentlemen. The deep ocean provides us with all the nutrition we need.' He sawed his food into several pieces and inserted them in the black slot of his mouth.

Experimentally, Guzman stabbed the thing. With a sigh of steam it deflated, releasing an ooze in a darker shade of green. He noticed that the Doctor and Boswell were contenting themselves with bread. He took a piece and nibbled. It was like nothing he had ever eaten. The wine was green and salty. He poured himself some water and moved the food around his plate before secreting the knife in his pocket. It struck him that there was not a single book to be seen in the room. The walls were decorated with paintings of Captain Nemo in various attitudes of marine heroism, as, he noticed, were the placemats.

'I feel I must ask,' Guzman said, 'though I can see that it is not your field, whether you can help me with the quest I seem to be on.' The Captain inclined his head.

'Of what nature is this quest?'

'I am searching for a book. But I infer you are not bookish.'

'Quite the contrary,' said the Captain. 'What was the book?'

'*No Gloves for the Hangman* by Zeke Allison.'

'It sounds like a work by Karl May,' the Captain declared. 'But here we are done with all that, done with the delusions of literature.'

'A man who loves not books is a dog in human form,' declared the Doctor.

'Wait. I must write that down,' said Boswell. 'Have you any paper, Captain?'

'Oh, yes,' the Captain replied, reaching for a bell-pull. 'I am well supplied with paper. In fact I consume a great deal of it, as you will see.' A concealed door opened with a hiss and half a dozen black-uniformed Cyclops-sailors entered, heavily armed.

'I should add that I myself am not *especially* fond of books,' said Guzman as the party dragged him and his companions from the room and down a further series of corridors deeper into the vessel. The noise intensified to a fiery roar. At length they came to the engine-room, the size of a cathedral, where bare-chested crewmen scurried beneath the violent movements of huge steel pistons. It was infernally hot. By some means the Captain was there before them, looking down on them from a railed balcony.

'Show these gentlemen how we power the engines,' said the Captain. Approaching on a narrow-gauge railway across the iron floor was a self-propelling vehicle the size of a touring coach, a tender of some kind. Its driver halted before an enormous pair of steel doors which now slid open to reveal the red glare of a furnace. The heat worsened. The Captain nodded and the tender began to tilt on hydraulic legs, revealing its contents to the watching trio. Books, tons of books, thousands on thousands of books, sliding into the hungry flames.

'The ocean, gentlemen – the ocean provides for all our needs. It is food, it is fuel, and it is cultural purgation! Death to the book, the book that has ensnared us so long with its sick enchantments. We have an ocean to burn.'

'You are a barbarian, sir,' declared the Doctor, his expression stricken with grief.

'That being so, how do you think I will respond to your puny taunts?' asked the Captain. He nodded once more and the guards seized the Doctor and Boswell, dragged them screaming to the furnace and flung them into the flames. Their cries were snatched away in the blinding light and the furnace doors slid shut once more. Guzman, unable to believe his eyes, stood in shock. The Captain descended from the balcony and stood beside him.

'Oh, yes,' said the Captain. 'I can and I will.'

'Who would dispute it?' asked Guzman bitterly.

'War is hell.'

'And so it seems is literature.'

'It is all lies and rhetoric and purple fog. It neither affirms nor denies. And it burns – which makes it useful. I could fuel this vessel for millennia and make no impact on the mountains of accursed books that folly has permitted to accumulate.'

'Why have you not killed me like my companions?'

'Good question.' For a moment Captain Nemo's outline, and the pipework and ducts and busy figures behind him seemed to lose their outline and definition. Guzman blinked Nemo nodded to the guards. 'Take him to my cabin.'

The Captain's quarters were private and Spartan and, it appeared, wholly bookless. Despairing and exhausted, Guzman lay down on the bunk and fell into a dreamless sleep. It may have been the silence that awoke him at last. The silence was complete, as if the vessel had stopped and with it all the scurrying work of the crew. Guzman sat up and felt for the knife. It was still in his pocket. That was something. So far he had been spared by the unexplained whim of Nemo. I must act, he told himself, in the interests of self-preservation, if only to find out what is going on and what it means.

To the right of Nemo's desk stood a small safe of the kind that Guzman seemed to recognize as useful in storing confidential documents – not that Nemo would have any of those in his paperless office. Idly, Guzman tried the handle. The safe swung open. *Well, of course*, he found himself thinking. All it contained was a single black book. He went to the door and looked up and down the corridor. No one there and no sound. He went back and took the book from the safe: an old clothbound hardback entitled *No Gloves for the Hangman*. The fulfilment of his quest, though he felt more like a patient than an agent in this matter. He opened the book and turned to the opening page. Might as well have a read as do anything else.

The opening page was a pane of clear water. Guzman tipped the book on end but the water stayed put. He dipped a finger in and the water was undisturbed. He closed the book and opened it again. The water stared blankly back. Then, as though from the depths it could not possibly possess, a face rose slowly towards the surface and halted, barely submerged.

'Remember me?' The face was a man's, in late middle age, drawn and jaundiced, with thinning colourless hair.

'No, I'm sorry. Should I?'

'Oh, yes,' said the man. He nodded and a blast of pain travelled through Guzman's head. When his vision cleared, he had to admit that the underwater figure did strike a faint chord.

'How about now?' the man asked.

'Very vaguely. Are you–' The pain came again, more intensely, and as though precisely engineered to make Guzman's teeth explode and his eyeballs burst.

'You are unable to put it down,' said the man. 'That is not what you found in the case of my book, however, was it, Mr Guzman, or should I say cunt?'

'Sorry, what book?'

'What book? You dare to ask me that?' More pain, the top of the spinal column turning to lava and bubbling into Guzman's mouth.

'I'm sorry. I don't know what you're talking about. Or who you are. Or where this place is, if it is a place. Why are you tormenting me?'

'Go out into the corridor and look around. Explore.'

'They won't let me.'

'Don't be so sure. You will have to take "me" with you, of course.'

Once again Guzman put his head round the door. No one. He retraced his steps to the engine room. It was silent and in semi-darkness. There was a stench of rotting fish. There seemed be no one about – that is, until he found himself standing on crew uniforms scattered about the floor.

'Look more closely,' said the man in the pane of water. Guzman crouched to examine one of the uniforms. When he lifted up the shirt, opaque grey slime, like tapioca pudding or frogspawn, flowed from the sleeves of the garment. For this first time, Guzman found himself gripped by horror.

'What has happened to them?'

'Curious, is it not?' said the face, delivering another charge of pain. 'Now make your way to the Captain's dining room.' The corridors were dimming slowly. Here and there Guzman encountered further piles of slumped rags leaking grey filth. After a time he found the spiral staircase and ascended to the dining room. Here too it was dim. A low discord was very slowly fading. The Captain, or whatever he had been, had slumped across the keyboard, and as his bogus substance melted from his clothes the keys of the organ were gradually returning to a silent position. As Guzman sought to register this, the book released itself from his hand to hang suspended at head height. In doing so it grew larger, and the face beneath the water became life-size and declared:

> Our revels now are ended. These our actors,
> As I foretold you, were all spirits and
> Are melted into air, into thin air:
> And, like the baseless fabric of this vision,
> The cloud-capp'd towers, the gorgeous palaces,
> The solemn temples, the great globe itself,
> Yea, all which it inherit, shall dissolve
> And, like this insubstantial pageant faded,

> Leave not a rack behind. We are such stuff
> As dreams are made on, and our little life
> Is rounded with a sleep.

The face regarded Guzman calmly now.

'You must remember this.'

'Oh, yes,' said Guzman. 'Of course. Everybody knows those lines.'

'Let's not exaggerate,' said the face. Guzman flinched in anticipation of more pain. The face smiled.

'I am not a monster,' it declared.

'Then what are you?'

'An avatar.'

'What?'

'And so are you. An avatar. We are the imagined representatives of ourselves in the space of the imagination. Digital doubles.'

'Then where is the real me?'

'Asleep in my basement in an induced coma.'

'A coma into which you put me.'

'Correct, Mr Guzman.' Guzman knew what was coming. The burst of agony flung him across the room and against the dining table. The face in the book followed to where he lay and looked down.

'Why am I doing this?' asked the face. Because my name is Hanno Biedermeier. Because I am a novelist and you purport to be a critic. Because in the everyday analogue world you wrote destructively and contemptuously about my work. Because I am rich and can enlist others to do my virtual bidding and put you here with amnesia while your physical, your real self, sleeps on forgotten by the world you sought to amuse with your insulting bon mots and the perpetual suggestion that you, though not a novelist, knew infinitely better when it came to novels than a mere novelist such as myself and that what I have spent a lifetime writing is no better than a cheap Australian western printed on

austerity lavatory paper. Is anything coming back to you?'
Guzman propped himself in a chair.

'Yes, now you mention it. But Biedermeier, I assure you
that it was not from personal animus that I wrote. It was my
obligation as a critic – as I saw it then – to attack what
seemed to me to be bad work, such as – please don't hurt me
any more – such as yours. No personal offence was intended.
You have to take it on the chin. That's the game.'

'Game? In the sense that this here – this elaborate
confection of illusion – is a game?'

'Not quite. I was speaking figuratively.'

'You were not,' Biedermeier said in a level tone. 'You
were speaking as a fool, and look where your foolishness has
brought you, to a world which is indeed entirely foolish,
where nothing is substantial and only your suffering is real. A
place of misquotation, misremembering, inappositeness,
anachronism, of confusion of genres and of seriousness with
vulgar entertainment, of muddle and laziness and evasion and
shallowness – in short, and if I may term it so, a digital
analogue of your own interior mediocrity.'

'What happens now?'

'Look about you.'

Black water was beginning to well up at the head of the
spiral staircase, spreading, silently for now, across the carpet to
Guzman's feet.

'We're sinking,' said Guzman.

'No, Guzman, you are sinking. I am elsewhere. And in
this place you are no more real than anything else.'

'But I feel real,' said Guzman. The water lapped at his
ankles.

'I imagine you do.' By some means Biedermeier
switched himself off and disappeared, and Guzman tried to
remember the whereabouts of the hatch by which he had
entered the submarine. Not that it mattered, since it was, as
Biedermeier had said, only a game, though the water was
convincingly cold as it washed against his legs. He felt

disinclined to move, and out of the soup of circumstance and illusion there came to him a quotation from a poem he had read in early youth and set great store by:

> This last pain for the damned the Fathers found:
> 'They knew the bliss with which they were not
>   crowned.'
>   Such, but on Earth, let me foretell,
>   Is all, of heaven or of hell.'

The lines of the poem were accompanied by an image of a man sitting under a tree on a sunny hillside reading a book for no other reason than pleasure. Guzman sighed at the idea, but then the book in the reader's hand began to shout at him, and lightning struck the tree, and an earthquake occurred, and the tide of ink rose, very convincingly Guzman thought, over his mouth, his nose and his head.

The Apocrypha of Lem
by Dan Tukagawa, J. B. Krupsky, and Aaron Orvits

Reviewed by Jacek Dukaj

Translated from the Polish by Danusia Stok

Contrary to the publisher's strident claims, Tugawa, Krupsky and Orvitz's *The Apocrypha of Lem* (Trans. Barbara Pólnik; Wydawnictwo Literackie, 2071) does not constitute the 'first comprehensive discussion of Stanisław Lem's posthumous works'. The reader is, however, presented with a rather fascinating story of the literary–judicial–computer war which has been going on for many years between the Heidelberg postLem, the Krakow-Viennese postLem and the Japanese postLem. Anyone with no interest in apocryphology prior to this will be smoothly introduced into this branch of literary studies, and also those unacquainted with the works of Stanisław Lem *in homine* will, with relatively little pain, be enlightened by gentlemen TKO. *The Apocrypha* is the second volume in a series compiled by Wydawnictwo Literackie for the 150th anniversary of Lem's birth; the Polish edition comes supplemented with a short afterword by Jerzy Jarzebski's Jagiellonian University apocryph v.4.102.17.

Apokryphos as taken straight from the Greek can be understood as meaning 'that which is concealed' but also 'that which is counterfeited'. Apocryphology of the twenty-first century, however, does not deal with falsified or belatedly discovered texts but with the creation of the apocrypha of deceased writers, i.e. literature issuing from IMITATED MINDS. Strictly speaking, this is what intellectuals who obstinately keep to traditional classifications claim, while advocates of emulative apocryphics do not speak of imitation but of 'reconstructed originals'.

The authors of *The Apocrypha of Lem* have devoted the first three chapters to the dissection of the above problem, taking, as an example, three different methods of birthing Lem anew.

And so: Stanisław Lem *post hominem*, born in 2048 at the Mathematics Center Heidelberg (MATCH) in Ruprecht-Karls-Universität, is the result of the typical training of a learning neural network in MATCH machines in multilevel simulation. What matters is not which precise algorithm the machine is processing (modern networks do not process algorithms, as understood in the last century, just as the biological brain does not) but final output results. If these tally sufficiently with the control pool then the processes taking place in the 'black box' must be identical to the original processes as regards essential (semantic) functions. In the case of the Heidelberg postLem, the input of the learning neural network came from historical data relating to the conditions of Stanisław Lem *in homine*'s life, his reading matter and generally the factors influencing him; texts he had written at that time constituted the control pool. MATCH's apocryphologist programmers found their postLem to be one hundred percent in tune as he generated *Fiasco*, more Lem-like than the version published in 1987, differing from it in numerous small details which 'in reality' editors and proof-readers had changed.

Stanisław Lem *post hominem*, born of the work of doctors Wilczek and Weiss-Fehler's team in 2052, came into existence using the base, exmaterial method, i.e. firstly, a digitally simulated reconstruction of albumen based on Lem's original DNA; secondly, brain scans stored from tests undergone by Lem while he was alive, especially after he had emigrated to Berlin; and thirdly, neurological interpolation of the writer's behaviour and physical constitution as eternalised on recorded film. The fidelity of the Krakow-Viennese apocryph was tested using precisely the last of these recordings: animated in the virtual environment of his home in Krakow, the apocryph says the same things, speaks and gesticulates in the same manner as the hominal original.

It's impossible to give the exact date of Stanisław Lem's Japanese apocryph's birth. The project, of which he forms part, EUROPA1900, was founded in 2044, but when its internal clock reached the day and hour when the emulated son of the emulated Samuel Lem and the emulated Sabina Woller came to life in emulated Lwów remains a secret of the Katsushima corporation and the Chukyo University in Aichi which the trinity of TKO did not penetrate. Besides, EUROPA1900 experienced a number of resets and modifications, programmes were patched and tried in closed betas – Lem's apocryph, as a millionth part of an enormous simulation, could go back a number of times to a state of 'prebirth' and be born anew; and even simultaneously exist and not exist in parallel in neighbouring clusters, as well as 'exist flickeringly', sinusoidally. Computer specialists working on the Heidelberg and Krakow-Viennese postLem acted no less brutally. What sets the Japanese apart, however, is the scale of the undertaking in which, going with and against the current of time, they manoeuvred an entire continent with its tens of millions of inhabitants, from a Ukrainian shepherd to Emperor Franz-Jozef. It should, perhaps, come as no surprise that it is precisely the children of Nippon with their 'culture of imitation' who have embarked on an act of ultimate apocryphystics.

Here Stanisław Lem was in no way singled out: he was embraced by the simulation because it embraced everyone. And the test of the Japanese postLem's 'authenticity' is not any partial test prepared especially for this apocryph, but historical accuracy of the entire mass of EUROPA1900 once set going in simulation. This is because Chaos Theory has convinced us that in such complex formations of non-linear processes, even a tiny discrepancy of a single parameter during input leads to gigantic differences in output. Consequently, Tadeusz Mazowiecki, in Katsushimi's simulation, fainting before the Sejm in front of cameras and Adam Malysz leaping over the ski jump will testify to the Lemness of their postLem just as surely as the books he wrote.

Most critical works refer to the Heidelberg postLem. TKO emphasise that this particular programming project was intended for literary research from the very beginning. As soon as MATCH had calibrated their postLem to accord perfectly with the original the temptation arose to 'draw' new works from the writer's apocryph. And here the first obstacle occurred. As Lem *in homine* describes in *A History of Bitic Literature*, not every work of art can be sensibly extrapolated beyond the parameters the artist has already realised. Some authors leave this world before managing to express everything they had to say, while others 'seal' themselves within their creations and all that remains for them to do is self-duplicate or stay silent. Lem stayed silent. Such, therefore, is the paradox facing the Heidelberg apocryphologists: the more faithful their postLem was to the original, the less likely it was that he would write anything new.

As we know, they decided on a divergence of the apocryph. PostLem 1.01 followed Lem *in homine* along the line of the original biography, whereas postLem 1.02 in simulation deviated in the 1990's.

TKO spin a tale based on interviews held with workers of MATCH employed at the time, and on the logs of the project administrator. *They prescribed him (postLem) the annals of the Polish prose of the time. He swallowed them and fell into a deep melancholy, stupor and general idleness. They connected him to a neuroprosthesis of youthful curiosity regarding the world. He went back to reading scientific journals and took to the internet; he also wanted to go out more frequently so they rejuvenated his 'body'. He began to write essays and articles. They plugged fiction boosters into him. He started to type a novel but after scores of pages threw it into the bin: three times in a row. Half of the department then sat working on these virtual scraps. It was stipulated that chokes of self-criticism be built in and a small narcissistic amplifier. Finally, however, it was decided to move the point of the apocryph's divergence 25 years back.*

But since this Heidelberg postLem of the '60's and '70's (builds 1.03.1020 – 1.03.1649) had also been subjected to modifications and restarted with changed parameters (including variously modulated living conditions and political circumstances) this divergence also affected old texts. Thus, for example, the postLem processed in the PRL (the Polish People's Republic) of oppressive Communism where there had never been a post–Stalin thaw, not to mention Gierek, does not write *The New Cosmogony* but instead, with publication as underground samizdat in mind, *The New Economy,* in which, rather than physics changing over time and space, and 'fitting in' with ready–made, ideal mathematics, the laws of economy and economic systems undergo significant mutations.

For example, in this version written by postLem, stronger money is not always ousted by inferior money, nor is the efficacy of the market's invisible hand automatically false. And so, Marxist economy as an ideal abstract model and, in particular, Communism's planned economy, may turn out to be true after first not having been effective (because false).

It is not the speed of light, mass of electrons, Planck's or Boltzmann's constants, that undergo change but the rules of supply and demand, the shape of Laffer's curve or the alternation of Kondratiev's waves. *The New Economy,* suggesting that Marx was right although he was wrong (or, if you prefer, was wrong although he was right), could not be officially published within the limits of the above simulation. Some of Lem's apocrypha followed the same path after the divergence, creating unveiled criticism of the system and engaging in political activities far more vigorously than through such movements such as the PPN (Polish Agreement of Independence) and the like.

After about a year, the team of literary specialists from Ruprecht-Karls-Universität started to publish these works and it was then, according to Tukagawa, Krupsky and Orvitz that present-day apocryphystics was born and, along with it, new fields of literary studies.

For years, Lem's apocrypha were started, reset and started anew with ever more subtly deviating parameters; now in hundreds and thousands of versions. Thus we came to know Lem's work disordered according to the mathematics of chaos: from those very similar to each other, concentrated around the attractor of obsession (the orbital of *The Investigation* is almost a point) to those which differ drastically due to a small change in the initial premises, set into disarray by literary bifurcations (e.g. the orbital of *Solaris* which appears as a great cloud of novels with the same beginning but diametrically various narratives and endings). NON-LINEAR LITERARY STUDIES examine texts which have been dislodged from a form apparently necessary because existent. The subject of examination here is rather the stream of creative processes leading to all texts possible, an ontology in the Ingardian sense.

FRACTAL CRITICISM, also a derivative of non-linear literature studies and now on the rise, would not be possible without the help of advanced apocryphological tools. It is not the individual (quantified) work which is subjected to analysis but the wave function of the work (see *Das Probabilistische Literarische Kunstwerk* by F. Köpf) which has its extremes, density of probability and so on. The version of the text which has seen the light of day – which is the only one we're aware of because it's the only one which was brought to fruition – could, after all, have come from the very periphery of the function, from the points on its graph which correspond to states of low probability, whereas a function's maximum represents a work of an entirely different nature.

Apples can be long, angular, pear-shaped, but we recognise the appleness of an apple precisely because we see not one random piece of fruit but a *continuum* of thousands of forms, more frequently and less frequently materialised.

More complicated analyses – of the apocryph which has branched off into millions of versions during many years of simulations – no longer use the units of a 'literary work' but 'fractals of topic'. The idea is original to the work which is materialised under such or such a form; and sometimes the same idea can be expressed in a single novel, sometimes as a few, sometimes as a run of short stories, and sometimes sublimated into fictionless forms or even manifested only negatively, *in absentia*, i.e. leading to a renunciation of writing other works. Thus, in the creative works of Lem's Heidelberg apocryph, the fractal of God, for example, manifested itself (in His atheistic analogues like *Non Serviam* or *Annihilation*), or the fractal of anti-totalitarianism. (It is only when they are in prison that the postLems write blatantly anti-communist works such as *View from an Attic* or the settling of accounts in *Return from the Magellanic Cloud*).

Meanwhile, non-linear literary studies induce further specialisations, trends and schools within the trend. For example: AMPHIBOLOGICAL PHILOLOGY (see *Literature as Mishap* by Alphonse C. Bitter) which demonstrates that the most perfect linguistic solutions arise as a result of an evident mistake in the starting parameters, and the catchiest neologisms are begotten by linguistic catastrophes and semantic absurdities (how does a mobile phone become a 'cell', or undesirable electronic advertising 'spam'?); or EVOLUTIONARY AESTHETICS which embrace the chronologically ordered works and their author in an indissoluble relationship with criticism and similar elements of feedback loops – it is only thanks to the practical application of non-linear aprocryphics that we can see whether Stanisław Lem would write exactly the same things were he totally unaware of how his precious works had been received. It emerges that self-absorbed, independent artists happen to be such incredibly rare exceptions that, as a rule, reviewers and critics are co-authors of books written later by the authors whose work they have reviewed. (Which, on the basis of comparing parallel processes, apocryphologists scrupulously arrange into 'fractional authorships' and so on). In an analogy to the rules which govern the natural selection determining biological evolution, there are, in evolutionary aesthetics, rules which describe the degree to which a text has 'adapted' to a given cultural environment (with its own niches of readers, predator-critics, waves of mass extinction and kin altruism between authors), as also the 'survival' chances of an author whose traits differ from that of the average man of letters. Of all the possible mutations of Lem, it is the science fiction which achieves the best results. Lems who keep to realistic prose à la *The Hospital of Transfiguration* frequently end up forgotten in the history of literature.

Work on postLem in MATCH would continue on its way if it were not for the scandal with the Krakow-Viennese apocryph whose legal situation changed so radically after the ratification of the Kapstadt Convention by the European nations in 2055. At this point, gentlemen TKO raise their voices as declared posthominal egalitarians. The chapters describing the political dances which then took place around exbiological apocrypha, I consider to be the weakest of the entire book not only because of their clear agitational bias (the comparison of unrecorded apocryphal processes with mass abortions is both coarse and none too logical since every digital process can be regenerated and repeated at will without harming the internal 'identity' of the process, a continuity which cannot be maintained when operating on organic matter) but because TKO lose Stanisław Lem himself, as well as his literature, almost entirely from sight.

Let us remember that Lem's apocryph grown by doctors Wilczek and Weiss-Fehler was the first to be emancipated because it came into existence, above all, as an extension of

Stanisław Lem's material being (DNA and neurostructures of brain albumen). This specificity, which fundamentally differentiates it from the Heidelberg apocryph, was used by the team to produce results which the apocryph interpolated from the products of Stanisław Lem's mind, could not achieve. The apocryphystic processes in Wilczek and Weiss–Fehler's work ran in the opposite direction. For, since WORLD + AUTHOR = TEXT, and TEXT – WORLD = AUTHOR, then TEXT – AUTHOR = WORLD. Dissecting Stanisław Lem's original works according to the coordinate system corresponding to his mind at the very moment he was creating, we get the sum of external influences (stimuli from the world) which, after processing, produced Lem's text in the *output*. In MATCH, similar experiments would offer zero data gain. Since their apocryph had been reconstructed, among other things, precisely from texts, the entire enterprise would lead to a tautological loop. The Krakow–Viennese postLem, however, allowed deeper insights at this point.

Devoting themselves to REVERSE COSMOGONY ENGINEERING, Wilczek and Weiss–Fehler achieved a fairly broad spectrum of 'Lem worlds': in diachronic breakdown (the world perceived by Stanisław Lem as he wrote successive books) and in modular breakdown (various worlds for the various parameters of the apocryph which are in no way verifiable on the basis of historical facts).

What we have long known intuitively immediately came to light. Namely, that an author always lives in a different world, his own world. Many of these worlds of Lem reveal rather peculiar characteristics. And so, in the '50's of the 20th century, Lem lived in a reality where communism REALLY did constitute a blessing for mankind while capitalism REALLY was collapsing in ruins. There were not many women in Lem's world and these, moreover, often appeared in a man's disguise. Human beings as a species experienced, en masse, lesser or graver forms of mental illness, especially obsessive-compulsive disorders, manic psychoses and advanced paranoia. In a crowd or group, they shed their human characteristics and acquired those of insects. Non-public physiological functions, such as excretion and sex, became objects of a dark cult with its priests, prophets and apostates, holy scriptures and secret codes; it was a relic of man's bestial ur-past maintained contrary to reason, by the power of superstition. Lem surrounded himself with a large number of machines – nature crossed imperceptibly into machines which crossed imperceptibly into God. God as such did not exist but it is precisely this perfect interchangeablility (the non-differentiation) between 'fake' and 'natural' which created an enormous empty PLACE FOR GOD. In succeeding worlds this was occupied by various beings (usually a Computer or its Programmer, always somehow defective, limited). In some later universes it even led to the degeneration, in leaps and bounds, of *Homo sapiens* – Lem suddenly found himself alone amidst a herd of adolescent techno-troglodytes. Humanity had been swapped when he turned his gaze towards the future.

After acquiring full rights, Lem's Krakow-Viennese apocryph immediately blocked the publication of these reports, as well as any studies based on the results of work done by the apocryphic software in all its versions and timelines. (Appendix A of *The Apocrypha of Lem* contains diagrams representing the internal hierarchy of each of the three apocrypha discussed. What is understood by law as a single natural person is, according to the cognitive take, a conglomerate of many co-identical apocrypha of the original mind. For example, in the present Krakow-Viennese apocryph of Stanisław Lem, so TKO believe, 'live' – i.e., are processed – between 56,800 and 260,000 postLems; the density of Lemness wavers in weekly and yearly cycles due to computing power being made available at weekends and the higher cost of current used for cooling during summer. The law, however, remains similarly indifferent as regards the predicament of schizophrenics or Lem's beloved victims who have their corpus callosum severed.)

TKO devote a separate chapter to the key moment in the procedure of each apocryph's emancipation. And so, as long as the apocryph is processed within the closed environment of a given simulation (in the case of postLem these were partial mock-ups of PRL, Cracow, Zakopane or Berlin in the '80's) it obviously remains unaware of its true – i.e. apocryphic – nature. In order to step beyond the simulation and appear as a part in the trials of the 'external' world (the real one) it has first to understand and accept the fact that it is precisely an apocryph and that this was not life but merely simulation and that everything he experienced he experienced by the power of a computer. As later experiments on apocrypha showed, rare is the mind which can survive such disillusionment without harm.

To this day the fact that every one of Stanisław Lem's apocrypha has experienced this enlightenment unharmed (and instantly got on with the summons, diatribes, bitter recapitulations of fulfilled predictions) remains an unexplained apocryphic phenomenon. TKO put forward the thesis – supporting it with numerous examples from Lem's premortal and posthumous works, with *The Futurological Congress* and *The Salamander Trap* heading the list, as well as Katsushima Industries' arguments from the case of the 'one and only Lem' – that it is precisely this trait of Lem's mental constitution which accounts for his singular way of looking at reality and the extraordinary nature of his literary works, and enables him to 'cross the Styx of solipsism with dry feet'. In other words, Stanisław Lem, as a model of mentality, constitutes a standard of mental stability necessary when 'stepping out of the matrix', a unique machine for a logical 'dismantling of the world'; and rockets, robots, physics, cosmogonies, novels, essays and articles, all these are merely fortuitous consequences, the casual outbursts of an unshakeable mind.

If TKO are right (and this can, after all, be practically verified), the legal war between the postLems will still intensify. Just as a gene which has been patented on time can be worth billions, so a neural structure, if its rights are appropriately reserved, may constitute the basis of a true empire. This core of Lem's personality would indeed be priceless if it could be launched for mass sale as the cognitive equivalent of ubik.

Realising, therefore, their situation IRL, the Krakow-Viennese apocryph, hired the legal company Schmidt, Schmidt and Dzióbek, which specialises in posthominal cases, and fired a salvo of over seven hundred legal suits for the infringement of personal property and the theft of intellectual property at Ruprecht-Karls-Universität in Heidelberg.

At that moment, the heirs of Stanisław Lem *in homine* also joined in the game claiming that all the creative works of Lem's apocrypha are, quite obviously, derivatives of Lem's mental structure just as the apocrypha themselves are its derivatives.

However, lawyers from Schmidt, Schmidt and Dzióbek argued – and not without cause – that only the most immediate author counted, otherwise every parent or teacher could ascribe a child's or pupil's work to themselves; and this the law does not allow. Who and from what the creative mind was built, therefore, is not important to the authorship of his works.

But what of the cases of unwitting plagiarism which we are dealing with here time after time? When Lem's perfect apocryph creates, word for word, the same *Solaris* today as appeared in 1959-1960, does it, by this, gain all the rights to the text, including subsidiary rights for adaptations and shares in the profits already drawn from them? Surely not! But what about the works of 'deviated', modified apocrypha? Do the plays which the Heidelberg postLem wrote as an emigrant in Australia (on internal emigration, i.e. equally simulated) and which have already been presented on several stages with one of them, *The Search*, being adapted as a VR game, belong to MATCH, the Krakow-Viennese postLem or the heirs of Lem *in homine*?

Following appeals, the cases passed to ever higher

instances of European jurisdiction, confronting the judges with a succession of necessary precedent-setting decisions. The university in Heidelberg, seeing what a mess they had got themselves into, finally made a decision, at one stroke cutting off all responsibility, and pleaded in court for the emancipation of its apocryph of Lem. The obvious next move in the war was Stanisław Lem suing himself.

In spite of everything, he maintained a sense of humour in all this. *I don't know what to do. It wouldn't be so bad If I could at least say 'things are going badly for me,' but I can't. Nor can I state 'things are going badly for us' because I can only partially speak of my own person.* He sent letters to himself (seized and made public by the fan clubs of enemy apocrypha) full of sophisticated mischief and propositions for an alliance between the Lems, based on calculations of profit and loss for individual strategies of cooperation/competition, according to game theory.

The affair became even more complicated after the extension of the Kapstadt Convention which defined non-personal (non-hominal) conscious beings, was accepted in Cairo in 2057. Apocrypha are indeed a reflection of people who really exist but why should that make them an exemption? We cross from biology to digital states because this is just the way things turned out in the history of *Homo sapiens*, but does the function which describes a spiral owe its origins to the shell of a snail simply because the snail existed before mathematicians? Or is the opposite true: it is the biological, material function which stems from a non-material ideal existing outside of time?

Consequently, Katsushima Industries, which control the EUROPA1900 project, calling on the principle of 'identity of the nondifferential', pleaded for all rights – both past and future – of Stanisław Lem *in homine*'s works and that of any of his apocrypha, to be granted to the postLem living in the said megasimulation. Lem's Japanese apocryph wrote *Eden* and *Solaris* and is writing *The Invincible*; this is not, however, why the Japanese usurped.

THERE IS ONLY ONE LEM AND IT IS THE TRUE LEM. If, in absolute ignorance of Pythagoras's theorem, someone arrives at it of their own accord they are not, surely, in this way creating 'another Pythagoras's theorem'. There is only the one idea; it is indivisible and exists independently of material realisation whether singular or numerous, through one medium or another, under this name or that. Nor is it important whether the idea is expressed digitally or verbally. The idea of physics as a game, presented in *The New Cosmogony*, existed before Lem noted it down just as the General Theory of Relativity existed before Einstein formulated it. Furthermore, both Lem and Einstein – as mental constructs with such and only such properties which allowed them to be the first to make their discoveries under given conditions – existed before they were born.

Hence all works 'resulting from Lem' belong to this ONE AND ONLY LEM regardless of where, when or under what form they might be made public. They constitute an 'extension' of his mind and personality just as a photograph taken of a body stems from the physicality of a given person.

And why should it be precisely Katsushima Industries which are recognised as the worldly administrators of *the once and future Lem*? Because – so the lawyers of the Japanese demonstrated – all other current realisations of Lem were further from the 'idea of Lem': contaminated, distorted, built over with chance characteristics blurring the gestalt, and devoid of certain necessary characteristics. Whereas Lem's apocryph which 'lived' in EUROPA1900 was the very essence of Lemness: the smallest deviation from the original model here led – in keeping with the mathematics of non-linear processes – to monstrous repercussions in the entire simulation.

Schmidt, Schmidt and Dzióbek reject the above reasoning. Where then does the certainty that Stanisław Lem, born 12th September 1921 and deceased 27th March 2006 in Krakow, is such an ideal model of Lemness, come from? Simply because he was reflected in a biological form and not a digital one? But that is pure racism! Only once we know ALL the works of ALL Lem's apocrypha will we be able to project – across a space of meanings – such an n-dimensional shape as will contain the key invariants of 'Stanisław Lem's creative works'. All its outlines produced, for example, according to a formula taken from *A History of Bitic Literature* would include meanings and obsessions characteristic only to one specific realisation of Lem (and perhaps the least likely one) and not to the 'ideal Lem'.

In their book, TKO back the Krakow-Viennese Lem. This reviewer, however, feels obliged to point out that if an idealistic interpretation of intellectual property law were to be accepted, it would quickly render unprofitable any investments into industries based on innovations and technological breakthroughs. The law is not intended to solely reflect the abstract order of things but is to be an effective moderator in the interplay of real yet divergent interests, needs and necessities which change over time. Whereas, if one were to agree with TKO, patents covering all possibly conceivable discoveries of man would ultimately end up owned by the same archetypal (source) cognitive networks. The ergonomy of creative processes makes it possible to calculate relatively accurately such a typology of genius. The 'ideal Lem' finds himself, without any doubt, next to one of these archetypes. There were, however, others in that niche before him; such as, Da Vinci and Bacon. We know from elsewhere that apocryphologists from Stanford are already working on them.

Besides, Katsushima Industries have other problems. EUROPA1900 has suffered serious decalibration several times. Hackers have made repeated attacks. Many well known individuals whose apocrypha in EUROPA1900 are experiencing a past glaringly different from the one known from authorised biographies are suing Katsushima for defamation. The differences often concern acts which are not only shameful but simply criminal. The apocryph of many a public figure has – in full view of the world – 'recreated' in EUROPA1900 a rape, theft or murder committed (if it had been committed!) in the youth of a now respectable old man, while at the same time showing with mathematical relentlessness how the outstanding characteristics of this Coryphaeus of science or statesman are, among other things, precisely a result of this very act. How can anyone defend themselves in the face of such slander? Where there is no witness, nobody knows what you are doing, whereas in EUROPA1900 you can observe your apocryph every second of its life, from birth, nay, even in its mother's womb. And will you, seventy years on, trust your memory on what you did or did not do one July morning when you were a child? The answer to the uncertainty is still greater uncertainty.

Suits for infringement of the rights to privacy and so on are, therefore, mounting up. This entire Japanese concept of superimitation appears very suspect. For what is a final unanimity between EUROPA1900 and the real supposed to prove? More roads than one lead from yesterday to today. And when constructing an image of Europe in the year 1900, the Japanese programmers, too, had to base themselves on second and third-hand accounts whose consistency with 'true' history is impossible to verify. Neither are biographies of those living today entirely true, nor – all the more so – are the biographies and stories of those living a century ago which served as the basis of simulation. EUROPA1900, therefore, is undergoing successive revisions and reconstructions, always consistent with historical facts but always a little different – and with this, Stanisław Lem's apocryph intrinsically woven into the system and the times, changes.

The last stable build, 3.4076.2.01, which TKO have not managed to discuss in *The Apocrypha* also gives rise to doubts. The Japanese postLem finished *The Astronauts* a few months later than he actually did; in his *Eden* the radiated Doubler does not die after leaving the planet but decides to remain; *The Star Diaries* are missing *The Third Voyage* and *The Seventeen Voyage*; while *Memoirs found in a Bathtub* has a strange introduction about a papyrus plague. What is more, the postLem in EUROPA1900 never wrote his famous *Letter from Ganimede*. (He was working on a film script at the time).

TKO also avoid other uncomfortable subjects in their monograph. Indeed, nearly all the university systems cultivating apocrypha of famous people have fallen victim to external attacks. We live in an age when it takes no more than a few hours to muster a global army of fanatical defenders for some television series, comic or game from the past century; the strongest of patriotic (as though religious) ties bind people from a football club or the RPG guild. It does not take much for this or that faction of hardcore fans to agree that the apocryphists have sullied the name of their patron and saint of pop culture. Lem's apocrypha do not count among those most frequently under attack but they, too, have been subjected to their share of spectacular sabotage. (One viral attack on the Krakow-Viennese simulation has been accredited to an emancipated apocryph of Philip K. Dick from MIT).

MATCH in Heidelberg has not yet quite recovered from the Brotherhood of Bram Stoker's suicidal rally. Although the University's spokesman denies it, it is unofficially known that the entire Tabula Rasa project has been suspended and the hunt for books that turned savage still continues. It is not a question solely of *Dracula*. The application driven in by the Stokerers aimed at all the authors' apocrypha and reversed the procedures of growth and training of neural networks, making not the AUTHOR but the TEXT the object of simulation. It is no secret that the inversion also affected the copy of pre-emancipated postLem.

On Heidelberg's closed servers *The Philosophy of Chance* in alliance with *Summa Technologiae* terrorises less well-organised fiction works, *Imaginary Magnitude* succumbed to schizophrenia and is seeping into Ruprecht-Karls-Universität's operating systems, *Return from the Stars* sits in the corner with a gloomy expression and clenched fists for days on end, *His Master's Voice* has experienced an autistic break-down, *The Invincible* has buried itself in the code of the apocrypher's engine and is surrounding itself with ever-fiercer firewalls while *Fiasco* torments *The Magellanic Cloud* having already driven it to suicide twice. *The Cyberiad* is the only one you can talk to.

While *The Mask* has disappeared. Apparently it slipped out of the server and got on a tourist soft and is jumping by proxy across sightseeing tour stations in the south of France. Literrorist portals report sightings of it in the body of a dog (a greyhound) in Tarascon-sur-Rhône, napping in the sun on the battlements of Château du roi René. It appeared to be waiting for something or somebody.

APOCRYPHA

Stanisław Lem
- Who's He?

Andy Sawyer

MARY SHELLEY, JULES Verne, H. G. Wells, Olaf Stapledon, Arthur C. Clarke, Ursula K. Le Guin... Stanisław Lem is perhaps the least-read major author of SF.

Yes, he is *known*, at least to the extent that most critics of SF would not think twice about putting him in a list with the aforementioned names. He is one of the 'fifty key figures in science fiction' as noted in the recent book edited by Mark Bould, Andrew M. Butler, Adam Roberts and Sherryl Vint. In his entry on Lem, Istvan Csiscery-Ronay, Jr. notes that he has been translated into over 40 languages and 'remains one of the most popular and respected SF writers in Europe, Japan and Russia.' According to his official website (www.lem.pl), the print-run of his books totals 30 million. Although much of this may have been due to the artificially-high print runs in the former Communist countries, particularly East Germany (where, according to an interview published in *Foundation* in 1979, he had a larger *per capita* readership than in his home country), Lem was justifiably celebrated in the 1970s when the Russian film director Andrei Tarkovsky had an art-house smash hit in 1972 with his stunning adaptation of Lem's 1961 novel *Solaris* (translated 1970). English translations of books such as *The Invincible, The Tales of Pirx the Pilot, The Cyberiad, The Star Diaries*, and *His Master's Voice* followed, while Lem's essays and reviews in the Australian fanzine *Science Fiction Commentary* and the critical journal *Science Fiction Studies* offered a scathing view of science fiction. And here, is perhaps a clue to Lem's ambiguous status. When you call science fiction 'a hopeless case' even '– with exceptions' (the title of one of his *SF Commentary* essays), and single out Philip K. Dick for praise as a visionary but 'A Visionary Among the Charlatans', it should come as no surprise when the backlash from fans and writers starts.

Another clue is that, despite the range and quality of his output, which ranges from straightforward SF to philosophical essays and metafictional literary games such as a volume of reviews of non-existent books, Lem is, in the end, best known to English-speaking readers as the author of *Solaris*, particularly since the 2002 remake by Steven Soderbergh, sold to a mass audience by the prospect of George Clooney's naked rear, reached an audience Tarkovsky's version did not. While Lem remarked of the first filmed version that 'What was important for Tarkovsky in the film left me quite indifferent and vice versa' (*Foundation 15*: 46), according to Gary K. Wolfe, reviewing the second version in *Wired* (http://www.wired. com/wired/archive/ 10.12/solaris.html), he greeted the prospect of a Hollywood adaptation with: 'If the Americans turn my novel into something bizarre, I won't be very much surprised.'

But who pays attention to the authors of books from which films are made? And while SF films are successful – James Cameron's *Avatar* is the highest-grossing film of all time, and actors like Will Smith build entire careers out of calculated special-effects blockbuster strategies – SF books are less so. Few SF novels become best-sellers, particularly in translation. Recently we saw Stieg Larsson's 'Millennium Trilogy' novels rise high in the bestseller charts, and another Swedish crime series, Henning Mankell's *Wallander*, was the basis for a very successful British TV series. But what price science fiction, and particularly European science fiction? True, Mamoru Oshii's 2001 film *Avalon* (co-produced by a Polish company, shot in Poland and starring Polish actors) achieved critical if not necessarily box-office acclaim, and fantasy author Andrzej Sapkowski's *The Last Wish* (2007) was well-received, but many of Lem's novels have been published by imprints not known for SF and he seems to have suffered from the 'if it's good, it's not SF' syndrome: 'Lem,' writes Csisceray-Ronay in *Fifty Key Figures in Science Fiction*, 'is sometimes considered more a writer of belles-lettres than of SF' (151).

If this were not enough, a dispute with his Western agent and sometimes translator (Franz Rottensteiner) made much of his critical work unavailable for reprinting in the West. Bruce Gillespie's *SF Commentary* had previously introduced Lem's incisive criticism to the English-speaking world, but while a collected edition of Lem's criticism, *Microworlds*, is still available, plans to include the texts of *SFC* articles and the related letters of comment in a projected *Best of SF Commentary* could not be followed through. Eventually, following his final novel *Fiasco* (1986: translated 1987), which was shortlisted for the Arthur C. Clarke Award, Lem concentrated on non-fictional works such as philosophical and futurological essays. I last came across writing by Lem on my first visit to Poland, when we left the departure lounge of Krakow airport to face a news-stand, where a glossy magazine was prominently displaying an article by (or about – my half-dozen words of Polish were not able to work out which) Lem. As I attempted to decipher the headlines, my wife came up and looked at me oddly: I was apparently staring fixedly at a Polish edition of *Playboy*...[1]

Indisputably, Lem's own criticism in the 1970s put people's backs up. In 'Science Fiction: A Hopeless Case: With Exceptions', Lem commented on SF's claim to be a literature of ideas, reporting on mankind's destiny: 'There is only one snag: in ninety-nine cases out of a hundred it fulfills its task with stupidity. It always promises too much, and it almost never keeps its word.' SF 'comes from a whorehouse but it wants to break into the palace where the most sublime thoughts of human history are stored. (*Microworlds*, 59) Impatient with American SF writers who wanted only to compete for their readers' beer money rather than their

1. I didn't buy it.

intellects, Lem saw SF *at the same time* claiming that it was actually at the pinnacle of art and thought. While a few writers, such as Philip K. Dick, were visionaries, most were 'charlatans', and even Dick himself was too indebted to pulp trash, afflicted with fans who admired the worst in him and saw his unwillingness to pander to easy explanation as a failing. He called John Wyndham a 'huckster', criticized novels which others at the time were praising highly, such as Ursula K. Le Guin's *The Left Hand of Darkness*, and generally lambasted science fiction.

Some of this may have been a certain arrogance in Lem, some of it certainly was a despair that the literature of Wells and Stapledon had been so deeply wedded to mass-market values and easy generic responses, and some of it may have been a simple misunderstanding of what some of the writers he attacked were trying to achieve. Almost certainly, some of his apparent high-handedness was a matter of poor translation. In a continuing discussion of 'The Lem affair' in *Science Fiction Studies* March 1978, Darko Suvin argues that an article entitled 'Looking Down on Science Fiction: A Novelist's Choice for the World's Worst Writing' reprinted in an earlier issue from *The Atlas World Review* but which was in fact translated into English via a German-language original was, from the title downwards, considerably more nuanced than its American readers had taken it for. But whatever the reason, his onslaught was returned, and while everyone, or nearly everyone, held Lem's fiction in high regard, feelings were wounded, resulting in 'The Lem Affair'.

After granting Lem honorary membership during the period when he was not technically eligible for membership in the organisation (or able to deal with the currency transfer: the various accounts are ambiguous), in 1976 the Science Fiction Writers of America withdrew this membership after it was pointed out that Lem was now published in the USA and eligible for regular 'Active' membership. This was offered him, but the situation was taken by Lem himself, and a number of supporters including Ursula Le Guin and Brian Aldiss, as unfair on a scale ranging from the petty to the downright vindictive. The background is muddled because of the high feelings on both sides, but could not have been helped by confusion within SFWA as to what was the situation and what was being offered, as is reported by letters in that same *Science Fiction Studies* of March 1978 from Pamela Sargent and Philip K. Dick, which followed on from a previous discussion in the July 1977 issue. Dick had earlier, in 1974 during a time when his mental state was at its most troubled, written to the FBI denouncing Lem, his agent Franz Rottensteiner, and the critic Darko Suvin as communist agents.[2] (Dick had blamed Lem for the failure of the Polish publisher of his *Ubik*, which Lem had praised and lobbied to get published in Poland, to produce any royalties.)

This affair possibly confirmed Lem's low opinion of Western SF, with some justification. But it can also be said that Lem is simply too large for science fiction itself. Even much of his undoubted SF is satirical, not taking the tropes of the genre too seriously – exactly the sort of thing Lem found congenial in Dick.

'We asked Joe Chip to go in there and run tests on the magnitude and minitude of the field being generated there at the Bonds of Erotic Polymorphic Experience Motel. Chip says it registered, at its height, 68.2 blr units of telepathic aura, which only Melipone, among all the known telepaths, can produce.' The technician finished, 'So that's where we stuck Melipone's identflag on the map. And now he – it – is gone.'

At this moment, with the chilly, echoing building just beginning to stir, a worried-looking clerical individual with nearly opaque glasses and wearing a tabby-fur blazer and

2. The letter is on the Stanislaw Lem website at
http://english.lem.pl/index.php/faq#SWFA

pointed yellow shoes waited at the reception counter. (*Ubik* p 2-3)

Much of Lem's own fiction has this rather overwritten style. The science fiction spaceships and robots are there, and there for a purpose – they *mean* something rather than being simply banged in for the goshwow factor – but the meat of the story is elsewhere. With Dick, it was often the uneasy tension between order and chaos, the real and the unreal. In Lem, science fiction is a way of exaggerating and mocking human idiocy, but there is also a love of the grotesque, of imagistic and linguistic excess, which makes him a master of the baroque. The descriptions of the 'mimoids' in *Solaris* or the picture of robots with medieval feudal societies in *The Cyberiad* are perfect examples. If ever there was a writer of the 'wide-screen baroque' it was Lem, but he was also a writer who (perhaps unlike Dick in his more unfortunate moments) avoided *kitsch* – that glamorous and ornate but essentially tasteless and derivative version of the baroque that feeds off art rather than creates it. Not understanding Polish, I can have no idea how the linguistic virtuosity of passages in *The Cyberiad* work in the original, but Michael Kandel (the translator of this and many others of Lem's books, though not *Solaris*) is frequently praised, and they work well in the English, apart from Klapacius's 'zits', without which life loses all its charm. But we will come to them later.

Lem's variety can be shown by taking a brief look at some of his most interesting works. *The Star Diaries* (1957), featuring the intrepid space explorer Ijon Tichy who also appears in a number of other works, have a light touch: in the 'Seventh Voyage' a series of ingenious time paradoxes arise when Tichy attempts to fix his spaceship by enlisting the help of his 'selves' from different days of the week. The 'Eleventh Voyage' has Tichy involved in the destiny of a robot civilisation which acts like a parody of a feudal medieval court. In the process of this, he has to pass as a robot himself and saves his life only by agreeing to serve as an informer (as have, it turns out, the majority of the population who are also 'mucilids', or humans). In the 'Thirteenth Voyage' Tichy discovers a civilisation, Acquatica, ruled by a dictator who insists that the people learn to live (and breathe) underwater. In the 'Twentieth Voyage', we learn that the entire course of human development has been formed by Tichy's attempt to clear up and rationalise history and the clumsy, bumbling buffoons such as Harris Doddle and Pat Lado who end up exiled to ancient Greece as punishments for their screw-ups, only to produce more screw-ups in their turn. Another agent manages to discredit twentieth century futurologists 'by turning out all sorts of rubbish (called Science fiction).' (158)

The Cyberiad, in its fusion of cybernetics and fairytale, outdoes Douglas Adams in farce. Trurl and Klapaucius are 'constructors' whose works often get snarled up in paradox. In the book's first story, Trurl invents a machine which can create anything beginning with the letter 'n'. As the story unravels, Klapaucius instructs the machine to create Nothing (which, of course, is not the same thing as not doing anything). As things are removed from the world and cease to exist, Klapaucius realises his error: the result is a world without brashations, plusters, laries and 'no trace of the glorious worches and zits that had, till now, graced the horizons!' (7). He begs the machine to at least please return his 'gentle zits', but because of its original programming all the machine can do is create things beginning with the letter 'n'. Which is why, in our world today, we have nonsense, narrowmindedness, nausea, necrophilia, nefariousness, and noxiousness... but no zits. English-speaking readers will need no reminding, however, that we *do* in fact still have acne infestations on our faces as we go through puberty; perhaps a better word might have been chosen there!

Later, longer stories in the sequence, such as 'The Tale of the Three Storytelling Machines of King Genius', or 'Altruzine', are wonderfully playful fables. In the latter, for instance, the hermit robot Bonhomius goes on a quest for the H.P.L.D.s, the beings who have reached the Highest Possible Level of Development, and finds a star which is a perfect cube.

In contrast to Tichy, Pirx, the hero of a collection of stories published in 1968 and translated as *Tales of Pirx the Pilot* (1979) and *More Tales of Pirx the Pilot* (1982) is perhaps Lem's most conventionally science-fictional character; somewhat reminiscent of the competent young men of Heinlein's juveniles although with more of a comic twist. Pirx starts off as a young cadet, and in 'The Conditioned Reflex' he solves the mystery of deaths on the Moon which turns out to be due to a mechanical glitch, but also to the way the humans have reacted to that glitch, A similar situation is resolved in 'On Patrol'. 'The Test' is the first appearance of the young Pirx, who has to deal with a tough examination in piloting which is made more difficult by the presence in his cabin of two flies.

Although the protagonist of *The Chain of Chance* (1975: translated 1979) is a former astronaut, the novel is less science fiction (unless probability statistics is a science) than a detective story. The narrator is sent to investigate a series of mysterious deaths in Italy, and in doing so manages to undermine the conventions of the detective story so completely that it is a good thing Lem never managed to become associated with the Crime Writers Association. (As a bonus, the last paragraph of the novel succeeds in subverting the entire concepts of writing and publishing as well.)

Solaris is usually seen as Lem's masterpiece, partly because of the impact of the films and partly because it engaged so vividly and successfully with that mixture of visionary romance and chilly remoteness which was so prominent at the time. Predating by some years that vaguely similar collision of desire to understand the universe and terror that it will remain a mystery which we find in Stanley Kubrick and Arthur C. Clarke's *2001: A Space Odyssey* (1968), it is certainly a classic along the lines of anything by Wells and Stapledon.

Unlike most of the fiction mentioned so far, its satire is not whimsical but is a devastating comment upon the capacity of the human mind – particularly the scientific mind – to construct systems and theories. It is clearly possible to read the multiple and contradictory attempts to explain the nature of the apparently 'living ocean' of the planet Solaris as a satire of the official Marxism which Poland was living under at the time Lem wrote the book, but the chapters 'The Monsters' and 'The Thinkers', in which Kelvin reflects upon the vast body of 'Solaristics' also look back to the complexities of medieval theology and the arguments of modern science. In the end, Lem seems pessimistic about the possibility of all human cognitive projects – philosophical, theological, scientific – to come up with a suitable 'theory of everything'. While there is an explanation given for the appearance in the Station of the 'phantoms' like Rheya, it leaves very much in the background whether this is a conscious attempt at communication by the Solarian entity, the nature of that communication (whether it is an attack, for instance), or whether it is a side-effect of something else entirely such as the mysterious semi-living formations that bubble up from the depths of the ocean. And the nature of those formations – the mimoids, which seem to throw off copies of living or non-living things, the symmetriads, the extensors, etc. – are equally inexplicable. Are they sense organs, natural metamorphoses caused by planetary events within or beneath the ocean, living forms inhabiting the depths, further attempts at communication? All these theories, and more, have been formulated: nothing has been proved. In the end, we do not have any sort of agreement even about *how* proof can be agreed upon.

The Invincible (1964), published in English translation in 1973 and issued in paperback as an Ace Science Fiction Special in 1975, is an example of the kind of difficulty (and rewards) Lem offers to the science fiction reader. Although written after *Solaris*, it is a much simpler story. Its beginning, showing the aptly-named 'Invincible' landing on the planet Regis III to investigate the loss of a previous expedition, seems coldly generic in its concentration upon the mechanics of the ship and the clipped, emotionless commands: 'Central axis – full power! Brake static drive! Central axis – half power! Small static drive! Reactors zero power. Land with cold drive!' (p. 10) While an Arthur C. Clarke would establish a sense of wonder in such a sequence, these are simply individuals doing a job which they have done so many times already. In the conversations between the commander Horpach and his subordinate Rohan after landing, we see men for whom the distance between them is as important to their relationship as anything they have in common. The scenario is established by means of a series of orders and reminders: even when Horpach is consulting with 'experts' he wants them to come up with sound, rational explanations with no qualifying. It is quite possible to read this as *bad* science fiction; a simple story about heroic astronauts overcoming an alien threat, and the kind of 'humanity [that] goes out and civilises the universe' which was central to the enterprise of both John W. Campbell-era *Astounding* and Soviet science fiction. And indeed Lem may be gearing his beginning to an audience which believed that the 'conquest of space' – *in itself* – was a good thing. But the novel moves into different territory.

What they find – a desolate planet with no life on the land and, eventually, what seems to be a ruined city and the remains of the ship they are looking for, the Condor – is described plainly. Even when the planet's threat is identified as a black cloud of metallic 'flies' which, among other things, seem to be able to strip the higher consciousness processes from humans, Horpach is determined to drive his men to a central truth: '[W]e can't return to Earth with a hypothesis. We need certainty. Not vengeance but certainty. An accurate diagnosis. Facts.' (125) However, as the novel progresses it becomes clearer that there can be no such thing as 'an accurate diagnosis'. As in *Solaris*, where the investigation of the world only results in a cathedral-like edifice of ingenious but unprovable speculations, what the scientists can deduce from what they see can only remain in the state of hypothesis. It seems to have been the case that what has happened is an example of inorganic evolution, by which self-replicating machines have responded to threat by engaging in swarming behaviour. But what the crew of the *Invincible* have demonstrated is their own inability to comprehend fully and to combat the threat against them: indeed even to call it a 'threat' is to anthropomorphise it, to suggest that the Universe is in some sort of *relationship* with humanity. The Cloud, if we are to believe the hypothesis formulated by the biologist Lauda, is not sentient but acting according to a form of cybernetic natural selection in its swarming mechanism. The spaceship is *called* 'Invincible', suggesting humanity's power over the universe, but it clearly is not, and what seems to be driving humanity is not power but pride. As Peter Swirski points out in his analysis of the novel in his book on Lem *Between Literature and Science*, the conceptual gap in the crew's attempt to comprehend the Cloud is their lack of grasp of the fact that that in attempting to do so they are reducing 'the unknown phenomena into the conceptual framework familiar to them' (87).

With this point in mind, it is interesting to think of *The Invincible* in comparison with A. E. Van Vogt's *The Voyage of the Space Beagle* (1950, but adapting and expanding stories published 1939-1943) which also involves encounters with the Unknown in its escalating confrontation of different forms of alien life. Thanks to the promise of 'Nexialism' – a form of advanced thinking/educational technique not a million miles different from L. Ron Hubbard's Dianetics – Van Vogt's hero Grosvenor overcomes the narrowly compartmentalised minds of the *Space Beagle*'s crew of scientists and presents an analysis of each problem that offers a solution. A reader expecting the consolatory medicine of Van Vogt would find Lem bleak and bitter. *The Voyage of the Space Beagle* is not a *bad* novel[3] but even as it argues against the comfort of familiar conceptual frameworks it suggests that *in the end* the universe is knowable. *The Invincible* dashes that hope with irony.

Towards the end, when Rohan goes to search for four missing crewmen, there is a re-evaluation. Rohan responds to his encounter with the Cloud with '[n]umbed awe and great admiration" (p. 217) Life has no place on this world, though. He returns to the spaceship which looms majestically above him. But while the last word of the novel is the name of the ship, its quality has been stripped away. It towers *as if* it were invincible: but we now know different.

Lem's final novel is the aptly-titled *Fiasco*. Of this novel, Lem's translator Michael Kandel says that it is a 'complete rejection' of the optimistic 'affirmation of life as a great, unending adventure of learning.' (*Science Fiction Studies* 40, p. 379) Neither human biological intelligence nor the machine intelligence of the supercomputer DEUS come across as any form of affirmation. While the beginning, set on Titan some centuries before the main story of the novel evokes some of the great examples of SF's 'sense of wonder' in the way natural formations on Titan reflect the complex shapes of organic life forms, in the end these wondrous forms are *not* alive: they are only invested with meaning because humans can perceive such analogies in them. And in the beginning, Lem has killed off his hero Pirx, who has gone before Parvis (who is *not*, as Lem reminds us emphatically, Parsifal even though he is heading for a location named Grail) to search for the bodies of missing astronauts in the same way as Rohan searches for the missing crew members of *The Invincible*.

3. Or at least I don't think so. There is a law in SF criticism which states that A. E. Van Vogt is a writer of incoherent trash who has written one superlative novel. Unfortunately everyone who thinks this argues the case for a different novel. For me it is *The Voyage of the Space Beagle*.

Parvis also fails in his quest, and dies, entrusting his fate to the 'vitrifax' which preserve him until future technology can revive him. The frozen bodies of Parvis and Pirx are, however, required for the expedition, many centuries later, to investigate the Quintans, aliens discovered on the fifth planet of a far off solar system.

Because a pilot is needed, one or other of the two have to be resuscitated (we are told, in fact, that out of the two bodies that *can* be saved, there are only enough vital organs to make up one individual). The resurrected pilot is told of his origin but has no idea whether he is Parvis, Pirx, or both in whatever combination, and takes on the name Tempe. This is only the first of a number of moral choices that have to be made in the novel.

Contact with extra-terrestrial intelligence is something rare. As one character explains, they are so widespread, the universe is so large, that even if signals from a civilisation are discovered, by the time physical contact is made with the world those signals came from the civilisation may be long gone. On a galactic scale, civilisations are ephemeral, like mayflies. So what is actually to be discovered on Quinta is unknown. The ship Hermes arrives around the Quinta and encounters a civilisation which refuses all contact. There seems to be a war going on, and the Hermes is greeted with violence. A show of strength from its crew destroys the Quintains' moon. From then, the game of First Contact is played out. Should violence be greeted with violence? If the other side refrain from attacking an envoy, is this merely a ruse to draw that envoy into further danger? Should violence be used to *stop* violence? Should they leave the warring parties to their own doom? If, as a Dominican priest among the crew says, the only thing they know is that the Hermes can destroy the Quintans, that *is* the only thing they can know and any other course of action would result in a fiasco.

Meanwhile, Tempe wants more than anything, more

than his doubts and hesitations, to see the Quintans. He becomes the envoy, the willing pawn in the game of contact. He overstays the length of time beyond which the Quintan response will be seen as hostile and in an enigmatic and shocking ending he is destroyed along with the Quintans.

If Rohan at the end of *The Invincible* at least returns to the ship knowing that he has encountered the unknown and engaged with it pragmatically, even if not *understanding*, Mark Tempe in *Fiasco* (is there a pun in the Polish analogous to the play on the English expression to 'mark time' here?) encounters the Other, recognises it as Other (which may not necessarily be the same as evil or hostile), and is wiped out. 'First contact' stories which Lem would have known well include Murray Leinster's 'First Contact' (1945), in which a military stand-off between humans and aliens is defused by junior officers on both sides getting to know each other informally to the point that they can share dirty jokes, and Ivan Yefremov's 'The Heart of the Serpent' (1958), in which it is argued that space-travelling civilisations will be too *mature* for such primitive passions as war. Both positions are comprehensively debunked in *Fiasco*. It is a brilliant, but chilly novel.

So, to a large extent Lem is anti everything most science fiction stands for. There is no Gernsbackian optimism, no Campellian foregrounding of the importance of the scientific method, none of the visionary hope of a Clarke or a Stapledon. In the early days of American pulp science fiction, the instructional and prophetic modes of the field were foregrounded. 'Extravagent Fiction Today... Cold Fact Tomorrow!' was blazoned on *Amazing*'s masthead and Hugo Gernsback introduced the first issue by telling us that 'these amazing tales make tremendously interesting reading – they are always instructive. They supply knowledge... in a very palatable form.' In contrast, while Lem can offer (often dense) scientific fact, he seems to have no interest in persuading young readers to go out and invent the exaggerated gadgets he imagines, and in *Solaris* and *Fiasco* there is a deep distrust of knowing what's going on. Is Lem a pessimist, a paranoid like Lovecraft? Some have said so, but, as Lem stresses in an interview with Istvan Csicery-Ronay, Jr. of *Science Fiction Studies* at or about the time he was writing *Fiasco*, 'Science and literature have incompatible agendas'. (*Science Fiction Studies* 40, p, 251) Science is about asking questions, attempting to describe the world, and looks for answers, although the answers may change. Literature, on the other hand, 'may pose questions that have no answers. It may pose questions that are not understood or understandable.' And both enterprises have elements of play. Which may, of course be another reason why hardcore SF writers were so offended by Lem: *the man isn't taking our enterprise seriously!*

Despite the wonders of Lem's universe, the only conceptual breakthrough offered is the understanding that certain phenomena will never be understood. Can we really engage with the alien? Can we come up with a firm understanding of our place in the universe? 'No matter what domains of human inquiry we might consider,' Lem tells Peter Swirski, 'there are no unequivocal solutions in black and white.' (Swirski, 1997, p. 42) If anything, Lem seems closer to H. P. Lovecraft than Arthur C. Clarke (Lovecraft too was fascinated by science, but believed that if we could piece together knowledge from the different branches of science and find out what was really happening in the universe, we would run screaming from the results), but as a writer he is closer to Jorge Luis Borges than either. In an essay on the fantastic ('Todorov's Fantastic Theory of Literature'), Lem argues that the model of the fantastic proposed by Tzvetan Todorov is flawed because it only takes into account fantastic *fiction*. But for him, fantastic fiction is not enough.

Lem cites Borges as a writer who creates fantastic *theology* ('Three Versions of Judas'), fantastic *philosophy* and fantastic *history*. In an essay on Borges, also published in *Microworlds*, Lem praises a number of Borges' stories, including

'Tlön, Uqbar, Orbis Tertius', which can be said to be fantastic philosophy, 'The Lottery in Babylon', which is less a story than 'two mutually exclusive explanations of the universe' (*Microworlds* 234), and 'Pierre Menard – Author of the *Quixote*' which is fantastic literature rather than fantastic fiction. Borges was a master of the fake book review – his 1935 'The Approach to al-Mu'tasim' is a completely fictional book, using plot elements from Kipling and the 12th century Persian Farid ud-din Attar, but its attribution to a real publisher (Victor Gollancz) and mention of a preface by a real author (Dorothy L. Sayers) apparently managed to convince one of Borges' friends to attempt to order the book. Borges biographer Emir Monegal says that he, too, believed that it was a real book. Borges sly attempts to subvert the reader is one thing – in 'Tlön, Uqbar, Orbis Tertius', he cites both real and fictional 'sources' – but Lem goes further. *A Perfect Vacuum* (1979) and *One Human Minute* (1986) are *collections* of fake book reviews, reviews written, perhaps so that the book need not be? And Lem begins *A Perfect Vacuum* by writing his own introduction, wearily sighing that 'We suspect the author intends a joke.' *One Human Minute* extends this joke, perhaps, because the 'reviews' are in fact fascinating speculative essays in their own right. Not all of them are in or even near the territory of science fiction, although one, 'Non Serviam' is a theological speculation about the ideas of god formulated by artificial intelligences created by the author of the book reviewed, and 'The New Cosmogony' speculates about the origin of our universe in a manner not far from Edgar Allan Poe's speculative essay, 'Eureka'.

And here, we begin to reach the territory where English-speaking readers need to retire from commentary on Lem, because much of his philosophical/scientific speculation remains untranslated, at best available only in summary.

Perhaps the greatest problem with Lem is that he was able to be a master of several different kinds of SF at once. As a writer troubled about the nature of reality, there is Dick of course. As a satirist, we think of Kurt Vonnegut Jr or Douglas Adams; as a visionary, we think of Olaf Stapledon; as a writer who extrapolates from cybernetics and mathematical logic about the nature of identity, perhaps the only parallel is Greg Egan. (Almost certainly, Lem would cringe at those comparisons.) There are perhaps flaws in his work for the modern reader: rarely are there characters you want to follow; perhaps the one character you really feel for is Rheya (interestingly, one of his very rare female characters) in *Solaris* as she realises that she is not, in fact, real. His attacks on science fiction, while refreshing and welcome for those of us who are exasperated by the field's pretensions, are nevertheless uncomfortable for those of us who have a sneaking regard for unpretentious hackwork or big dumb objects. Sometimes, when reading interviews in which he lambasts the writers, SF or mainstream, he does not like, you wonder who he *does* like. But the real point is that he cannot be ignored. In an essay like this, it is impossible to do justice to all of his works, but even in this account, which overlooks a number of books which many critical accounts of Lem give close attention to, the breadth and depth of his range can be seen. Why do readers in the West still have to ask 'Who is Stanisław Lem?' 'Ignorance, madam, ignorance,' to echo Samuel Johnson when asked why he got the definition of a word wrong in his celebrated *Dictionary*. But it is still, for a large part, because we have to wait to catch up, because there is *so much* Lem, and because we still have to pay attention to what he says.

Works Cited:

Aldiss, Brian, et. al., 'Stanisław Lem and the SFWA' in *Science Fiction Studies* 12 (Vol 4: 2, July 1977), 126–144.

Csiscery-Ronay Jr., Istvan, 'Twenty-Two answers and Two Postscripts: An Interview With Stanisław Lem' in *Science Fiction Studies* 40 (Vol 13: 3, November 1986), 242–260).

Dick, Philip K., el. al. 'The Lem Affair (Continued)' in *Science Fiction Studies* 14 (Vol 5: 1, March 1978), 126–144.

Dick, Philip K., *Ubik* (London: Rapp and Whiting, 1970).

Kandel, Michael, 'Two Meditations on Stanisław Lem' in *Science Fiction Studies* 40 (Vol 13: 3, November 1986), 374–381.

Lem, Stanisław, *Fiasco* (London: Andre Deutsch, 1987).

Lem, Stanisław, *Microworlds* (New York: Harvest/HBJ, 1984).

Lem, Stanisław, *One Human Minute* (London: Mandarin, 1991).

Lem, Stanisław, *Solaris; A Chain of Chance; A Perfect Vacuum* (London: King Penguin, 1981).

Lem, Stanisław, *Tales of Pirx the Pilot* (New York: HBJ, 1979).

Lem, Stanisław, *The Chain of Chance* (New York, Jove/HBJ, 1979).

Lem, Stanisław, *The Cyberiad* (London: Futura, 1977).

Lem, Stanisław, *The Invincible* (New York: Ace, 1973).

Lem, Stanisław, *The Star Diaries* (New York: Avon, 1977).

Monegal, Emir Rodriguez , *Jorge Luis Borges: A Literary Biography* (New York: Dutton: 1978).

Swirski, Peter, *A Stanisław Lem Reader* (Evanston, Illinois: University of Illinois Press, 1997).

Swirski, Peter, *Between Literature and Science: Poe, Lem and Explorations in Aesthetics, Cognitive Science, and Literary Knowledge* (Liverpool: Liverpool University Press, 2000).

Of Insects and Armies

Dr Sarah Davies

NANOTECHNOLOGY TURNS UP in some surprising places. A quick glance through the Project on Emerging Nanotechnologies' consumer products inventory, for instance, finds products as diverse as iPhones, speedboats, and cleaning sprays claiming to contain nanotechnology. (Eventually, we are promised, nanotechnology will infiltrate every aspect of life, revolutionising health care, transport and communications. At the moment the emphasis seems firmly on consumer experience.) It's a popular culture staple: in the last year or so I've bought a nano 'hexbug' (a tiny – though by no means nanoscale – robotic toy), watched GI Joe battle nano-mites, and re-read Michael Crichton's *Prey*, with its sinister, predatory nanobot swarms. The technology – summed up as the study and manipulation of matter at the level of the nanoscale, or 10^{-9} metres – weaves its way through both fiction and non-fiction on science.

It's perhaps more surprising to spot nanotechnology in older works. Surely this is the newest of new things, a technology so hot off the press that it's only been a focus of research funding since the early 2000s? Well, certainly the term is a relative neologism. But if we take its driving rationale – that there's plenty of room at the bottom, that small is beautiful, that the nanoscale is the place to focus our explorations and engineering – then we can find it in everything from *Gulliver's Travels* onwards. Only occasionally, however, are these accounts as eerily prescient – or, indeed, as straightforwardly eerie – as Stanisław Lem's short story-cum-essay 'The Upside-Down Evolution', which purports to summarise two volumes of a military history of the 21st century. After skipping through the nuclear arms race and the 20th century's accumulation of 'enough weapons to kill every inhabitant of the planet several times over', the narrator moves on to the meat of the matter, that 'greatest military revolution' of miniaturisation and the subsequent 'unhumanising' of warfare. Weaponry, the fictive 2105 text explains, will shift from an emphasis on the big but cumbersome – bombs, armies, tanks – to the minute and nonhuman. It will draw on the insect world: soldiers will be excised from the military to be replaced with 'synsects', tiny synthetic creatures capable of anything from the creation of a 'self-dispersing atomic weapon' to entering the human body like bullets. Infantry, officers, generals: all eventually become redundant in this new phase of technological warfare in which humans are frankly unnecessary – other, of course, than as targets to be destroyed in increasingly inventive ways.

Such a move will not be uniformly popular. Lem's narrator explains that:

> For those who loved the uniform, the flag, the changing of the guard, standing at attention, drill, medals, and bayonet charges, the new era of war was an affront to their noble ideals, a mockery, a disgrace! The experts of the day called the new military science an 'upside-down evolution,' because in nature what came first were the simple, microscopic systems, which then changed over the eons into larger and larger life forms. In the military evolution of the postnuclear period, the exact opposite took place: microminiaturization.

In this history, however, any concerns were to no avail; the story is in fact a headlong tumble based on the principle 'if we don't do it, they will.' The essay ends, nastily, with the sheer impossibility of disarmament. Diplomats could not negotiate, the narrator concludes, 'because their willingness to relinquish a new weapon would only indicate, in the eyes of the other side, that they had another, newer weapon up their sleeve…'.

We are, hopefully, not yet at that stage. But while it is – for obvious reasons – rather difficult to know exactly what the current status of nanotechnological weaponry is (public domain information, such as that from MIT's Institute for Soldier Nanotechnologies, tends to emphasise research on 'survivability'), a number of the developments Lem describes are certainly being talked about, if not actually produced, in the context of nano. Based on these rather uncanny similarities I want to pull out, and briefly reflect upon, two ways in which the themes of 'Upside-Down Evolution' are being mirrored in contemporary nanotechnology research.

The first is the notion of biomimicry. Just as we can see the prefiguration of nanotechnology without the term ever being mentioned, so too does biomimicry – the deliberate copying of natural features and processes by scientists and engineers – pervade Lem's essay. In the world of 'Upside-Down Evolution', for instance, 'informationists, cipher theorists, and other experts' have observed that, for many of the tasks of everyday life, intelligence is not necessary. Finding skill, care and enterprise in insect life they have set instead to mimic those features in their designs, creating not AI but artificial nonintelligence. In the process they create smart dust known as 'grain', weapons which look like drops of water, and – most sinister of all – a team of 'micro-spies and minipolice built on the model of a particular cockroach'.

Here we start to hit uncomfortably close to home in terms of what nanotechnology could, at least, present us with. Biomimicry has been an overt feature of much nanotechnology research since its inception: researchers have been keen to reproduce, for instance, the nanoscale effects by which a lotus leaf is able to repel water, an abalone shell resist fracture, or a beetle appear metallic. The recent, DARPA-funded development of a 'nano-hummingbird' – a real-size, camera-carrying device able to hover and fly in and out of buildings and fetchingly painted in teal and green – is a further example. While we are not yet at the point of needing to call the police rather than pest control when we find a cockroach in our homes, nanotechnology's potential to enable the development of ever smaller and smaller cameras, microphones and tracking tags could give rise to unparalleled opportunities for surveillance and a world in which, as Lem's narrator has it: 'anything could be a covert agent: a nail in the wall, a laundry detergent'.

A second point: 'Upside-Down Evolution' also presents, as its conclusion, a world in which the divide between the natural and the man-made has been entirely effaced. There is acid rain that corrodes roads, diseases which wipe out a nation's livestock, hurricanes and droughts of new ferocity. Are these natural, or the result of enemy action? The answer is impossible to determine, the narrator writes, in an age in which swarms of 'micrometeorological agents' can shift the climate of a country or continent and artificial insects invade bodies and ecosystems. Previously natural phenomena may no longer be so. Again, our world is not yet at this point: no-one is going to confuse an iPhone for a mouse. But there is plenty of research which is exploring how to mimic, alter or halt what we think of as natural processes. Lem's micrometeorological agents are a case in point. Nanotechnology is just one area of science which is currently being considered as a tool for geoengineering – altering the earth's climate on a grand scale – in order to halt or mitigate the effects of climate change. One line of research explores the use of nanoscale particles, shot up into the clouds, to affect the degree of solar radiation and thereby the temperature of the globe; though actually inspired by the effects of volcanic dust on the atmosphere, the similarities with climate-altering 'meteorological insects' are readily apparent. As to whether such research will ever lead, as in 'Upside-Down Evolution', to 'weapons so secret that there was no way anyone could tell them from innocent phenomena of nature'; well, the question is, how would we know?

So far, so dystopic. This is, then, perhaps a good place to part company with Lem's history. While its identification of key themes and even technologies that are emerging within nanotechnology today is unusual (with much science fiction tending to get hung up on Drexlerian 'molecular manufacturing' when it turns its attention to nano), it certainly doesn't give the whole story – and, indeed, does not pretend to. 'Upside-Down Evolution' is, after all, a *military* history: one which concerns states, armies, and warfare. It is also, of course, a history written at the height of the Cold War – a point at which an entirely militarised future would not have looked at all far-fetched. I remain unconvinced that such concerns are the primary driving force behind nanotechnology, or indeed the development of any technology, today. While finding new ways to kill people is certainly one application area – and while it is likely that there is much more going on in military nanotechnology than we currently know about – other areas are at least as important: healthcare, new materials, electronics, purification and remediation, the energy sector. As my opening paragraph would suggest, many contemporary applications of nanotechnology are in fact rather mundane, focused around personal consumption rather than international brinkmanship. It may, of course, come to that: it is clear that many of the applications that are being promised for nano, and related technologies such as synthetic biology, could have truly world-shaping effects. But at the moment it seems that we are generally content for our taxes to fund not just hummingbird spies and cloud-altering particles, but also self-cleaning materials, faster computers, and more effective medical technologies.

Building Reliable Systems Out of Unreliable Components

Professor Steve Furber

PART WAY THROUGH 'The Upside-Down Evolution' – that great vision of future military escalation over a two-hundred year long Cold War – Stanisław Lem reflects on the differences between natural and engineered complex systems. 'All systems,' he writes, 'are prone to breakdown, to a degree mathematically proportional to the number of elements that make up the system.' Reviewing a history book written in the future, the text claims that, initially: 'to counteract malfunctions in such systems, engineers introduced redundancy: power reserves, for example, or – as with the first American space shuttles (like the Columbia) – the doubling, even quadrupling of parallel, onboard computers. Total reliability is unattainable: if a system has a million elements and each element will malfunction only one time out of a million, a breakdown is certain.'

Lem then goes on to imagine the absurdity of this solution: Multiple parallel computers would 'operate not by "linear logic" but by "voting": once the individual computers ceased functioning identically and thus diverged in their results, one would have to accept, as the right result, what was reached by the majority. But this kind of engineering parliamentarianism led to the production of giants burdened with the woes typical of democracies: contradictory views, plans, and actions. To such pluralism, to such programmed elasticity, there had to be a limit.'

So how does nature manage it? Lem asks. 'The bodies of animals and plants consist of trillions of functioning parts, yet life copes with the phenomenon of inevitable failure.' How?

Concern about building reliable systems out of unreliable components can be traced back at least to von Neumann (whose name is associated with the architecture that dominates modern computer design), where a computer can view its own programs as data and modify them accordingly. Von Neumann authored a paper on this very subject. This is unsurprising. In the 1950s the earliest computers were built with thermionic valves (or 'vacuum tubes' as they're called in the US) which were prone to failure, and a computer required tens of thousands of valves to work together to produce a result.

However, the introduction first of the transistor and then of the integrated circuit yielded computer technologies of astonishing reliability, and designers largely forgot about component failure. A microchip may have a billion transistors switching at rates up to a billion times a second, and run flawlessly for several years. This is staggering reliability by the standards of any other engineered system. For half a century computer engineers have ridden the exponential progress in computer technology described by Moore's Law – which predicts a doubling in the number of transistors on a microchip every 18 months to 2 years – without having to concern themselves with component failure. Until now!

Today the most advanced microchip manufacturing processes use transistors with dimensions around 20 nanometres, which is 100 silicon atoms wide. As we continue to try to deliver Moore's Law, the approach to atomic scales is making the future look much less predictable and much less reliable than the past that we have become so used to. Over the next decade, if progress is to continue, we will have to learn again how to design reliable computing functions using unreliable components, and this is a huge challenge.

As Lem foresees, we are turning to biology for insights into how we might address this challenge. Increasingly sophisticated computer models are built, using data from biologists and neuroscientists, to try to understand how the brain works, how the immune system works, how individual cells work. These are all highly complex systems, way too complex for the unaided human brain to understand. When we have working computer models that reproduce the observed characteristics of the biological systems will they, too, be too complex for us to understand? Possibly, but at least the computer model is a lot easier to explore and poke around inside than the biology, so we stand a better chance of identifying the key features of its function.

Then, once (if?) we achieve some level of understanding of how biology delivers robustness to component failure, we may be able to take that understanding and build that robustness into our machines, giving Moore's Law another lease of life.

The Spontaneous Machine

Professor Hod Lipson

I RECENTLY GAVE a robot demonstration to a class of first-grade elementary school children. In the school's gymnasium hall, two dozen six-year-olds gathered enthusiastically around a few shiny machines bristling with sensors and actuators. The robots were crawling across the table demonstrating various patterns of locomotion. 'These robots learned how to walk all by themselves' – I explained knowledgeably. 'One robot even developed its own shape', I said, pointing enthusiastically at one 3D-printed machine.

The kids were not impressed.

One courageous child finally asked the question that was probably on everyone's mind: 'But what can they *do*?'

Frankly, the question had never been put to me that bluntly before. I delved into an elaborate discussion of locomotion and manipulation, morphology and control, body and brain. 'But what can they do?' the child persisted. I've been to many grueling reviews by funding agencies but I've never been asked such a question point blank. The Emperor had no clothes. Millions of dollars of federal research were about to be flushed down the drain by a first grader. But before long, another child came to my rescue: 'Aha! The robot is jogging!' he realized.

Yes, that's what the robot was doing. It learned how to exercise. Jogging is an activity that took Western civilization centuries to discover. You've heard about robots that can play chess, but that doesn't really help anybody. You've heard about

281

robots that vacuum the floor for you and robots that can drive the car for you, but you've never heard about robots than can *jog* for you. Perhaps in the not-so-distant future, robots will be able to jog and exercise for us.

The gymnastics teacher was pleased, and the kids shuffled along to the next station.

I felt oddly unsatisfied for the rest of the day. When it comes to intelligent machines, people are difficult to impress. Children have seen robots that talk, walk, shoot and kill, and perform a myriad of other useful and complex tasks in movies such as Star Wars and Terminator, but they know very well that robots in movies are not real. So why weren't they impressed?

Artificial Intelligence is almost an oxymoron: Whenever breakthroughs are achieved – from Deep Blue's mastery of chess to Stanley's autonomous traversal of the Mojave Desert – something is still missing. If it is just doing what it was *designed* to do, is it *truly* intelligent?

No one understood this conundrum better than Stanisław Lem. In the early '60s, when researchers in the burgeoning field of Artificial Intelligence proclaimed that human-level intelligence is just around the corner, Lem's story 'Doctor Diagoras' (1964) describes the anti-thesis as the spontaneous machine:

Do you know what constructors demand from their cybernetic creations? […] Obedience. They never talk about it, and some may not even be aware of it, because it's a tacit assumption. A fatal mistake! They build a machine and insert a program it must carry out, whether the program is a math problem or a sequence of controlled actions – in an automated factory, for example. A fatal mistake, I say, because to obtain immediate results they exclude the possibility of spontaneous behaviour in their creations. […] the obedience of a hammer, a lathe, or a computer is basically the same thing – and that is not what we were after! [...] But cybernetics promised thought – in other words, autonomy, the relative independence of the system from man! The best-trained dog may not obey its master, but no one then will say that the dog is 'defective' [...] The nervous system of a beetle no larger than a pin shows spontaneity; why, even an ameba has its whims, its unpredictable behavior. Without such unpredictability there is no cybernetics. An understanding of this simple matter is really everything.

It is fascinating to watch how teachers and parents, when asked about signs of intelligence, quickly point out: Curiosity and creativity are hallmarks of a gifted child. Thinking outside the box has become a cliché of innovation, but the box of programming is painfully difficult to get out of. How can we program a machine to *not* follow our program, to have – as 'Doctor Diagoras' puts it – *spontaneity*?

Perhaps the only solution is to breed it. If design is the hallmark of intelligence, intelligence is the hallmark of evolution. Let's bring the mother of designers, evolution, to help us out of the box. Forget about *biomimicry* – making bio-inspired machines that look natural, or imitate this biological aspect or the other. They all have the obedience of a glorified hammer. Instead, let's mimic evolution and watch what happens.

But wait.

If we can breed such spontaneous machines, will we relinquish some control over what they discover and create? 'The Sanatorium of Dr. Vliperdius' (1972) describes exactly what might happen.

Contributors

Brian Aldiss is one of the most important SF writers working in Britain today. He has published over 75 books, including the novels *Hothouse, The Interpreter, The Primal Urge, The Dark Light Years, The Billion Year Spree, The Helliconia Trilogy, Harm* and most recently *Walcot* (2009). His awards include the Hugo (twice), the Nebula, the Prix Jules Verne (Sweden), the Kurd Lasswitz Award (Germany), the John W. Campbell Memorial Award and three BSFA awards. Several of his books, including *Frankenstein Unbound*, have been adapted for the cinema, and his short story, 'Supertoys Last All Summer Long', was adapted by Stanley Kubrick and Steven Spielberg and released as the film *AI* in 2001. He is also a playwright, poet, editor and prolific short story writer.

Annie Clarkson is a poet and short fiction writer living in Manchester. Her first poetry collection *Winter Hands* was published by Shadow Train. Her short fiction has been published by Comma (in *Brace* and *Litmus*), Flax Books and in various literary magazines. She is currently working on her debut short story collection for Comma.

Frank Cottrell Boyce is an award-winning screenwriter and children's novelist. His film credits include *Welcome to Sarajevo, Hilary and Jackie, Code 46, 24 Hour Party People* and *A Cock and Bull Story*. In 2004, his debut novel, *Millions,* won the Carnegie Medal and was shortlisted for The Guardian Children's Fiction Award. His second novel, *Framed,* was published by Macmillan in 2005, and later adapted into a film by the BBC. His third, *The Unforgotten Coat*, was published this year. Frank also writes for the theatre and was the author of the highly acclaimed BBC film *God on Trial*. He has previously contributed stories to Comma's anthologies *Phobic, The Book of Liverpool, The New Uncanny, When It Changed,* and *Litmus* and is currently working on a full collection. He is also writing the script for the Olympic 2012 opening ceremony.

Dr Sarah Davies is a social scientist at Arizona State University's Center for Nanotechnology in Society, where her research focuses on public engagement with emerging technologies. She has previously worked in exhibition development at the Science Museum, London, and as a lecturer in science communication at Imperial College.

Jacek Dukaj is one of Poland's most important writers of science fiction and fantasy. In 2009 he was winner of the inaugural European Literary Prize, and has also received the Kościelski Award and the Janusz A. Zajdel Award for his writing. His books include *In the Land of the Infidels, The Black Seas* and the bestselling *Ice*. In 2003 filmmaker Tomasz Bagiński adapted his short story 'The Cathedral' into a short animation that was nominated for an Oscar.

Professor **Stephen Furber** is the ICL Professor of Computer Engineering at the School of Computer Science at the University of Manchester but is probably best known for his work at Acorn where he was one of the designers of the BBC Micro and the ARM 32-bit RISC microprocessor. To date, more than 18 billion ARM-based chips have been manufactured and are used in ubiquitous computing applications, such as mobile phones, digital photography and video, music players, etc. His latest project is Spinnaker, also nicknamed the 'brain box', to be constructed at the University of Manchester. This is an attempt to build a new kind of computer that directly mimics the workings of the human brain. Spinnaker is essentially an artificial neural network realised in hardware, a massively parallel processing system eventually designed to incorporate a million ARM processors. The finished Spinnaker will model 1% of the human brain's capability, or around 1 billion neurons.

Trevor Hoyle has published fiction with John Calder, such as *Vail, Blind Needle* and *The Man Who Travelled on Motorways.* In the late 1970s he gained recognition for his 'Q' science fiction trilogy and his novel *Earth Cult.* His environmental novel *The Last Gasp* is currently under option in Hollywood, and his latest work, the 'fictional memoir' *Down the Figure* 7, is set in Lancashire just after the war. He also writes radio drama, winning the Radio Times Drama Award with his play GIGO. His *Blake's* 7 episode 'Ultraworld' inspired the album *The Orb's Adventures Beyond the Ultraworld.*

Hod Lipson is an American robotics engineer. He is the director of Cornell University's Computational Synthesis Laboratory. His work focuses on evolutionary robotics, design automation, rapid prototyping, artificial life, and creating machines that can demonstrate some aspects of human creativity. Lipson has been involved with machine learning and presented his 'self-aware' robot at the 2007 TED conference. With his Cornell University graduate student Michael Schmidt, he developed an intelligent machine to 'uncover the fundamental laws of nature.' The machine was able to derive the laws of physics such as gravitation by processing the raw information. As Lipson puts it, 'The system successfully found such physical laws within experimental data taken from complex, chaotic systems like a double pendulum – a pendulum with a pivot joint in the middle.'

Toby Litt is the author of eight novels – *Beatniks: An English Road Movie, Corpsing, Deadkidsongs, Finding Myself, Ghost Story, Hospital, Journey into Space* and *King Death* – as well as three collections of short stories: *Adventures in Capitalism, Exhibitionism* and *I Play the Drums in a Band Called Okay.* In

CONTRIBUTORS

2003 Toby Litt was nominated by *Granta* magazine as one of the 20 'Best of Young British Novelists'. He lives in London and is a member of English PEN.

Antonia Lloyd-Jones is a full-time translator of Polish literature. Her published translations include fiction by Paweł Huelle (including *The Last Supper*, for which she won the Found in Translation Award 2008), Olga Tokarczuk and Jacek Dehnel. Her latest translations of non-fiction include reportage by Wojciech Jagielski and Jacek Hugo-Bader. She also translates poetry and books for children, most recently *Kaytek the Wizard* by Janusz Korczak.

Adam Marek's debut collection of short stories, *Instruction Manual for Swallowing* (Comma) was long-listed for the 2008 Frank O'Connor prize. Since then his stories have appeared in numerous anthologies – *New Writing 15, Prospect, The New Uncanny, When It Changed* and *Litmus* (the latter three with Comma). In 2010 Adam was shortlisted for the inaugural Sunday Times EFG Private Bank Prize, and in 2011 he was awarded the Arts Foundation Fellowship in Short Story Writing. He lives in Bedford and is currently working on a second collection of stories.

Mike Nelson is an installation artist who has twice been nominated for the Turner Prize (2001 and 2007), and in 2011 represented Britain at the Venice Biennale. Nelson's installations typically exist only for the time period of the exhibition they were made for. They are generally extended labyrinths, which the viewer is free to find their own way through, and where the locations of the exit and entrance are often difficult to determine. His *The Deliverance and the Patience* in a former brewery on the Giudecca was in the 2001 Venice Biennale. In September 2007, his exhibition *A Psychic Vacuum* was held in the old Essex Street Market, New York. His major installation *The Coral Reef*, 2000, on display at Tate Britain until the end of 2011, is said to be influenced by Stanislav Lem's *Perfect Vacuum*. It consists of fifteen rooms and a warren of corridors. His text in this book is uncredited. Mike Nelson is represented by Matt's Gallery, London; 303 Gallery, New York; and Galleria Franco Noero, Turin.

Sean O'Brien's latest collection of poems is *November* (Picador, 2011), a Poetry Book Society Choice. Its predecessor, *The Drowned Book* (Picador, 2007) won the T.S. Eliot and Forward Prizes. His collection of short stories, *The Silence Room*, was published by Comma in 2008 and his novel *Afterlife* by Picador in 2009. He is Professor of Creative Writing at Newcastle University.

Wojciech Orliński (born 1969 in Warsaw) trained as a chemist but has devoted most of his professional life to writing about science fiction, as a journalist, writer, and blogger. Since 1997, he has been a regular columnist for *Gazeta Wyborcza*. He has published science fiction stories and opinion pieces in Nowa Fantastyka, and his books include *What Are Sepulki? All About Lem* (2010) and *America Does Not Exist* (2010).

Adam Roberts is the author of many SF novels and stories, the latest of which is *New Model Army* (Gollancz 2010). He is Professor of Nineteenth-century Literature at Royal Holloway University of London, and he lives with his wife and two children a little way west of London. His three favourite Polish writers are, in order: Stanisław Lem, Józef Teodor Korzeniowski and Wisława Szymborska.

Andy Sawyer is the librarian of the Science Fiction Foundation Collection at the University of Liverpool Library and Course Director of the MA in Science Fiction Studies offered by the School of English. He is also Reviews Editor of *Foundation: The International Review of Science Fiction*. Long,

long ago, he edited *Matrix* and *Paperback Inferno* for the British Science Fiction Association. Since then, he has published numerous articles, contributions to reference books, and reviews, including recent essays on Terry Pratchett, Gwyneth Jones, and Ursula le Guin. 'Ramsey Campbell's Haunted Liverpool' was published in *Writing Liverpool: Essays and Interviews* edited by Michael Murphy and Deryn Rees-Jones (2007). In 2009 he co-edited (with David Ketterer) *Plan for Chaos*, a previously-unpublished novel by John Wyndham. He is the 2008 recipient of the Clareson Award for services to science fiction.

Sarah Schofield is a new writer whose recent prizes include the Writers Inc Short Story Competition and the Calderdale Short Story Competition. She has been shortlisted for the Bridport Prize in 2010 and was runner up in *The Guardian* Travel Writing Competition.

Piotr Szulkin is a Polish film director, with over 30 films to his name. He graduated from the School of Fine Arts in Warsaw and the National Film School in Łódź. His films have received numerous awards, including the award for Best Science Fiction Film Director at Eurocon in 1984 for *War of the Worlds – Next Century*. He is also the author of three books and numerous essays and teaches at the National Film School in Łódź.

Ian Watson wrote the Screen Story for Steven Spielberg's film *A.I. Artificial Intelligence* – based on 10 months' work with Stanley Kubrick – the popular *Inquisition War* trilogy and *Space Marine* for Games Workshop, and has produced a further 25 novels and 10 story collections of SF, fantasy, and horror, as well as a book of poetry, *The Lexicographer's Love Song*. Most recently he wrote with Italian surrealist Roberto Quaglia *The Beloved of My Beloved* (NewCon Press), a transgressive volume of tales that may be the only full-length genre fiction from two authors with different mother tongues, and with Ian Whates he co-edited *The Mammoth Book of Alternate Histories*. In the late 1960s he lived in Tokyo, after completing a research degree in English and French literature at Oxford, and subsequently spent some time in Tanzania, though for the past 30 years he has dwelt in a little village in rural Northamptonshire.

Special Thanks

The editors would like to thank Louis Savy of Sci-Fi London and Marlena Łukasiak, Film Programmer at the Polish Cultural Institute in London, for their initial vision and support for the project, as well as Ian Whates of NewCon Press for his help in its early development. We would also like to thank Jerzy Jarzębski for his invaluable input, The Quay Brothers for their creative energy and support, Rosie Goldsmith and Jon Fawcett for their help with the promotion of the book, and Stefan Baranowski who translated several English texts included in this book into Polish as part of a parallel project. Comma would like to thank Tom Roselle and Harriet Whitehead for their editorial support throughout, and also Ben Lewis, Robin Klassnik and Frances Scott. Most of all we would like to thank the Estate of Stanisław Lem for their unstinting enthusiasm for this project, in particular Wojciech Zemek, Secretary of the Estate. For more information about Lem go to www.lem.pl.

Translators' Note

We the translators of these texts claim part-authorship in the given languages in which they appear. We act as a cipher for the one whose name resides upon the book cover; Lem, Stanisław, but we claim the languages that we pen as our own. The relationship with a book seems straightforward, when you reside in your favourite location, be it a chair, a train, a bed or up a tree, you and the author seem to have an intimacy, a direct relationship which allows the alchemy of conjuring a static fiction into something that swims in the mind. However we are also there, in fact the words and the language of your homeland are ours. We are part of the futurological entropy of Lem's ideas, as is his dissemination into other forms and material. The scientist who unwittingly emulates his now historic possible futures, or the theoreticians and artists that absorb his ideas, we too are his translators. There is some confusion as to the identity of these 'translators' and also to the very labelling of this text as such. Some may see it more as a homage or dedication to the late writer, or, as the introduction to 'A Perfect Vacuum' might suggest, it may just be part of the compilation of short stories that make up the book, arguing that in aping its referents' own tricks it attempts to comment on his influence through the very structure of the thing you presently hold in your hands. We must collectively refute this however, our dedication to the act of translation is sincere and true. We are film-makers, we are surgeons, we are everyone who has come into contact through any given language – be they Polish, be they words, and beyond. We are the entities that have taken those ideas structured as words, from their native language to that of yours, we have made them into films, we have constructed new worlds from them using the everyday that surrounds our own. These translations are given many different labels, but ultimately the crux lies in the message scrawled onto a piece of paper, blowing in the wind from an air conditioning shaft on a space station. In a book, in a subtitled film, there is a confusion as to what that word is; man or human.